PRAISE FOR *THE WATER RAT OF WANCHAI*

## WINNER OF THE ARTHUR ELLIS AWARD FOR BEST FIRST NOVEL

"Ian Hamilton's *The Water Rat of Wanchai* is a smart, action-packed thriller of the first order, and Ava Lee, a gay Asian-Canadian forensics accountant with a razor-sharp mind and highly developed martial arts skills, is a protagonist to be reckoned with. We were impressed by Hamilton's tight plotting; his well-rendered settings, from the glitz of Bangkok to the grit of Guyana; and his ability to portray a wide range of sharply individualized characters in clean but sophisticated prose."
— Judges' Citation, Arthur Ellis Award for Best First Novel

"Ava Lee is tough, fearless, quirky, and resourceful, and she has more — well, you know — than a dozen male detectives I can think of…Hamilton has created a true original in Ava Lee."
— Linwood Barclay, author of *No Time for Goodbye*

"If the other novels [in the series] are half as good as this debut by Ian Hamilton, then readers are going to celebrate. Hamilton has created a marvellous character in Ava Lee…This is a terrific story that's certain to be on the Arthur Ellis Best First Novel list."
— *Globe and Mail*

"[Ava Lee's] lethal knowledge…torques up her sex appeal to the approximate level of a female lead in a Quentin Tarantino film."
— *National Post*

"Formidable . . . Ava is unbeatable at just about everything. Just wait for her to roll out her bak mei against the bad guys. She's perfect. She's fast"
— *Toronto Star*

"Imagine a book about a forensic accountant that has tension, suspense, and action…When the central character looks like Lucy Liu, kicks like Jackie Chan, and has a travel budget like Donald Trump,

the story is anything but boring. *The Water Rat of Wanchai* is such a beast...I look forward to the next one, *The Disciple of Las Vegas*."
— *Montreal Gazette*

"[A] tomb-raiding Dragon Lady Lisbeth." — *Winnipeg Free Press*

"Readers will discern in Ava undertones of Lisbeth Salander, the ferocious protagonist of the late Stieg Larsson's crime novels...she, too, is essentially a loner, and small, and physically brutal...There are suggestions in *The Water Rat of Wanchai* of deeper complexities waiting to be more fully revealed. Plus there's pleasure, both for Ava and readers, in the puzzle itself: in figuring out where money has gone, how to get it back, and which humans, helpful or malevolent, are to be dealt with where, and in what ways, in the process...Irresistible."
— Joan Barfoot, *London Free Press*

"*The Water Rat of Wanchai* delivers on all fronts...feels like the beginning of a crime-fighting saga...great story told with colour, energy, and unexpected punch." — *Hamilton Spectator*

"The best series fiction leaves readers immersed in a world that is both familiar and fresh. Seeds planted early bear fruit later on, creating a rich forest that blooms across a number of books...[Hamilton] creates a terrific atmosphere of suspense..." — *Quill & Quire*

"The book is an absolute page-turner...Hamilton's knack for writing snappy dialogue is evident...I recommend getting in on the ground floor with this character, because for Ava Lee, the sky's the limit." — *Inside Halton*

"A fascinating story of a hunt for stolen millions. And the hunter, Ava Lee, is a compelling heroine: tough, smart, and resourceful."
— Meg Gardiner, author of *The Nightmare Thief*

will find great amusement in Ava's unconventional ways and will certainly enjoy accompanying her on her travels."

— Literaturkurier

## PRAISE FOR *THE DISCIPLE OF LAS VEGAS*
### FINALIST, BARRY AWARD FOR BEST ORIGINAL TRADE PAPERBACK

"I started to read *The Disciple of Las Vegas* at around ten at night. And I did something I have only done with two other books (Cormac McCarthy's *The Road* and Douglas Coupland's *Player One*): I read the novel in one sitting. Ava Lee is too cool. She wonderfully straddles two worlds and two identities. She does some dastardly things and still remains our hero thanks to the charm Ian Hamilton has given her on the printed page. It would take a female George Clooney to portray her in a film. The action and plot move quickly and with power. Wow. A punch to the ear, indeed."

— J. J. Lee, author of The Measure of a Man

"I loved *The Water Rat of Wanchai*, the first novel featuring Ava Lee. Now, Ava and Uncle make a return that's even better…Simply irresistible."

— Margaret Cannon, Globe and Mail

"This is slick, fast-moving escapism reminiscent of Ian Fleming, with more to come in what shapes up as a high-energy, high-concept series."

— Booklist

"Fast paced…Enough personal depth to lift this thriller above solely action-oriented fare."

— Publishers Weekly

"Lee is a hugely original creation, and Hamilton packs his adventure with interesting facts and plenty of action."

— Irish Independent

"Hamilton makes each page crackle with the kind of energy that could easily jump to the movie screen…This riveting read will keep you up late at night."

— Penthouse

"Hamilton gives his reader plenty to think about...Entertaining."

— *Kitchener-Waterloo Record*

## PRAISE FOR *THE WILD BEASTS OF WUHAN*
### LAMBDA LITERARY AWARD FINALIST: LESBIAN MYSTERY

"Smart and savvy Ava Lee returns in this slick mystery set in the rarefied world of high art...[A] great caper tale. Hamilton has great fun chasing villains and tossing clues about. *The Wild Beasts of Wuhan* is the best Ava Lee novel yet, and promises more and better to come."

— Margaret Cannon, *Globe and Mail*

"One of my favourite new mystery series, perfect escapism."

— *National Post*

"You haven't seen cold and calculating until you've double-crossed this number cruncher. Another strong entry from Arthur Ellis Award–winner Hamilton."

— *Booklist*

"An intelligent kick-ass heroine anchors Canadian author Hamilton's excellent third novel featuring forensic accountant Ava Lee... Clearly conversant with the art world, Hamilton makes the intricacies of forgery as interesting as a Ponzi scheme."

— *Publishers Weekly*, STARRED review

"A lively series about Ava Lee, a sexy forensic financial investigator."

— *Tampa Bay Times*

"This book is miles from the ordinary. The main character, Ava Lee, is 'the whole package.'"

— *Minneapolis Star Tribune*

"A strong heroine is challenged to discover the details of an intercontinental art scheme. Although Hamilton's star Ava Lee is technically a forensic accountant, she's more badass private investigator than desk jockey."  — *Kirkus Reviews*

"As a mystery lover, I'm devouring each book as it comes out… What I love in the novels: the constant travel, the high-stakes negotiation, and Ava's willingness to go into battle against formidable opponents, using only her martial arts skills to defend herself…If you want a great read and an education in high-level business dealings, Ian Hamilton is an author to watch."  — *Toronto Star*

"Fast-paced and very entertaining."  — *Montreal Gazette*

"Ava Lee is definitely a winner."  — *Saskatoon Star Phoenix*

"*The Wild Beasts of Wuhan* is an entertaining dip into potentially fatal worlds of artistic skulduggery."  — *Sudbury Star*

"Hamilton uses Ava's investigations as comprehensive and intriguing mechanisms for plot and character development."  — *Quill & Quire*

## PRAISE FOR *THE RED POLE OF MACAU*

"Ava Lee returns as one of crime fiction's most intriguing characters. *The Red Pole of Macau* is the best page-turner of the season from the hottest writer in the business!"
— John Lawrence Reynolds, author of *Beach Strip*

"Ava Lee, that wily, wonderful hunter of nasty business brutes, is back in her best adventure ever…If you haven't yet discovered Ava Lee, start here."  — *Globe and Mail*

"The best in the series so far."  — *London Free Press*

"Ava [Lee] is a character we all could use at one time or another.

Failing that, we follow her in her best adventure yet."

— Hamilton Spectator

"A romp of a story with a terrific heroine."

— Saskatoon Star Phoenix

"Fast-paced...The action unfolds like a well-oiled action flick."

— Kitchener-Waterloo Record

"A change of pace for our girl [Ava Lee]...Suspenseful."

— Toronto Star

"Hamilton packs tremendous potential in his heroine...A refreshingly relevant series. This reader will happily pay House of Anansi for the fifth instalment."

— Canadian Literature

## PRAISE FOR *THE SCOTTISH BANKER OF SURABAYA*

"Hamilton deepens Ava's character, and imbues her with greater mettle and emotional fire, to the extent that book five is his best, most memorable, to date."

— National Post

"In today's crowded mystery market, it's no easy feat coming up with a protagonist who stands out from the pack. But Ian Hamilton has made a great job of it with his Ava Lee books. Young, stylish, Chinese-Canadian, lesbian, and a brilliant forensic accountant, Ava is as complex a character as you could want...[A] highly addictive series...Hamilton knows how to keep the pages turning. He eases us into the seemingly tame world of white-collar crime, then raises the stakes, bringing the action to its peak with an intensity and violence that's stomach-churning. His Ava Lee is a winner and a welcome addition to the world of strong female avengers."

— NOW Magazine

"Most of [the series'] success rests in Hamilton's tight plotting, attention to detail, and complex powerhouse of a heroine: strong but vulnerable, capable but not impervious...With their tight plotting and crackerjack heroine, Hamilton's novels are the sort of crowd-pleasing, narrative-focused fiction we find all too rarely in this country."  — *Quill & Quire*

"Ava is such a cool character, intelligent, Chinese-Canadian, unconventional, and original...Irresistible."  — *Owen Sound Sun Times*

## PRAISE FOR *THE TWO SISTERS OF BORNEO*
### CANADIAN BESTSELLER

"There are plenty of surprises waiting for Ava, and for the reader, all uncovered with great satisfaction."  — *National Post*

"Ian Hamilton's great new Ava Lee mystery has the same wow factor as its five predecessors. The plot is complex and fast-paced, the writing tight, and its protagonist is one of the most interesting female avengers to come along in a while."  — *NOW Magazine* (NNNN)

"Ava may be the most chic figure in crime fiction . . . The appeal of the Ava Lee series owes much to her brand name lifestyle; it stirs pleasantly giddy emotions to encounter such a devotedly elegant heroine. But, better still, the detailing of financial shenanigans is done in such clear language that even readers who have trouble balancing their bank books can appreciate the way conmen set out to fleece unsuspecting victims."  — *Toronto Star*

"Hamilton has a unique gift for concocting sizzling thrillers out of financial misdoing."  — *Edmonton Journal*

# THE
# KING
# OF
# SHANGHAI

## AN AVA LEE NOVEL
## THE TRIAD YEARS

## IAN HAMILTON

**SPIDERLINE**

This edition published in 2014 by
House of Anansi Press Inc.
110 Spadina Avenue, Suite 801
Toronto, ON, M5V 2K4
Tel. 416-363-4343
Fax 416-363-1017
www.houseofanansi.com

Distributed in Canada by
HarperCollins Canada Ltd.
1995 Markham Road
Scarborough, ON, M1B 5M8
Toll free tel. 1-800-387-0117

House of Anansi Press is committed to protecting our natural environment.
As part of our efforts, the interior of this book is printed on paper that
contains 100% post-consumer recycled fibres, is acid-free, and is processed
chlorine-free.

18  17  16  15  14   1  2  3  4  5

Library and Archives Canada Cataloguing in Publication

Hamilton, Ian, 1946–, author
The King of Shanghai : the triad years / Ian Hamilton.

(An Ava Lee novel)
Issued in print and electronic formats.
ISBN 978-1-77089-246-0 (pbk.). — ISBN 978-1-77089-247-7 (html)

I. Title.  II. Series: Hamilton, Ian, 1946– . Ava Lee novel.

PS8615.A4423K55 2015          C813'.6          C2014-902736-2
                                               C2014-902737-0

Book design: Alysia Shewchuk

*We acknowledge for their financial support of our publishing program
the Canada Council for the Arts, the Ontario Arts Council, and the
Government of Canada through the Canada Book Fund.*

Printed and bound in Canada

MIX
Paper from
responsible sources
FSC® C004071

For Robin Spano and Karen Walton,
two good friends and two exceptional people.

( 1 )

**AVA LEE'S PLAN WAS TO GO BACK TO WORK AFTER** four months. She thought that would be enough time to get over the death of Chow Tung, the man she called Uncle. For ten years he had been her business partner, mentor, friend, and the most important man in her life. Then cancer took him. Ava was in her mid-thirties now, wealthy, had friends and family who loved her, and was a partner in a venture capital company called Three Sisters. But she was emotionally adrift, still mourning the passing of Uncle.

She had left her downtown Toronto condo only once during the first month back from Hong Kong. She went to the neighbourhood bank where she had a safety deposit box that contained Moleskine notebooks detailing every job that she and Uncle had undertaken together. They had been debt collectors. Their clients were desperate people who had exhausted all legal and conventional means of recovering the money that had been stolen from them. It was a business fraught with peril — it was one thing to find the money, but it was entirely another to convince the thieves to return it. Over the years Ava had been shot, knifed, kicked, hit with a tire iron and a baseball bat, kidnapped and held for ransom, and survived assassination attempts. Without Uncle, she would never have survived. Now she was determined to relive every single case, every adventure.

She put away her computer and new iPhone, closed the condo curtains, and spent her days sitting at the kitchen table, reading the notebooks and filling her head with memories. But she didn't disconnect her land line or cut herself off completely from the outside world. Her mother, Jennie, called and visited several times. Her girlfriend, Maria Gonzalez, came by with food.

Maria wanted to stay but Ava wouldn't let her, and she refused to have sex. "I'm not ready," she said. Maria was forlorn. It was only after two more rejections that she stopped asking and came to accept that Ava had to find herself again.

It is Chinese tradition to wear white for ten days after the death of a loved one. Ava wore white every day for the entire month. There was no plan; it just felt like the right thing to do, until one morning it wasn't. She had finished reading the last notebook the night before, and when she woke and went to her closet, she found herself reaching for an orange T-shirt. That afternoon she went for a long run.

The next day, she ran again. When she got back to the condo, she phoned Maria. "I'd like to go out for dinner, and then maybe you can come back here and spend the night with me," she said.

Connecting with Maria was her first step back. A few days later she drove to Richmond Hill, a suburb north of Toronto, and had dim sum with her mother. Then she called her best friend, Mimi, and arranged to visit her and the baby. After a week of running, when her energy level felt close to normal, she walked to the house of Grandmaster Tang. She hadn't seen her instructor in more than two months, but he welcomed her as if they'd been together just the day before. For two hours they practised bak mei, the martial art that he had been teaching her one-on-one — as was the custom — since she was a teenager. Her body ached when she got back to the apartment, and it did so for the next week after her daily visits. When the aching stopped, another piece of her well-being had fallen into place.

In the middle of the second month, Ava began to chat with May Ling Wong and Amanda Yee, her friends and partners in the new business. Three Sisters had already taken ownership positions in a furniture manufacturing business in Borneo and a warehouse and distribution company based in Shanghai, managed by Suki Chan, a long-time associate of May Ling. Ava knew that her partners were actively seeking other investments, but when she called May Ling and Amanda, she made it clear that she wanted to be the one to initiate contact with them, that she had no interest in discussing business matters just yet.

Shortly thereafter she received her first phone call from Shanghai, from the man she knew as Xu. When she saw the Chinese country code, she assumed it was May Ling. She answered at once, thinking something terrible must have happened if May Ling was calling against her wishes. Instead she heard the soft, confident voice of Xu. He spoke to her in Mandarin, and she had never heard anyone speak it better, each word carefully pronounced as if it had a value that set it apart from the others.

"I hope you are well and I apologize if I am inconveniencing you. I think often of Uncle, and whenever I do, you come to mind. No two people could have had a better mentor."

"I am well enough," was all Ava could say, flustered by the unexpected call and by the way he was linking them through Uncle.

She hadn't known that Xu existed until the day before Uncle died, and she had met him exactly once — at Uncle's funeral. Any doubts she had about the depth of the relationship between the two men had been put to rest when she went through Uncle's papers. The men had indeed been close. What alarmed her was that most of their correspondence concerned Xu's management of his Triad gang in Shanghai.

During the course of their first conversation, Xu focused solely on his memories of Uncle, and Ava found herself sharing some of hers. It was cathartic for her, and when he asked if he could call again, she said yes. He phoned her regularly. Xu was well-read, and they shared an interest in Chinese films and good food. And then, of course, there was Uncle: every call involved at least one story about him.

One time Xu veered off into a discussion about his business and Ava had to pull him back. "I don't want to talk about how you make your living," she said.

He retreated, but not without saying, "My business is in a constant state of flux. What it is today could turn into something entirely different tomorrow. When things are settled in your life, I would like you and Madam Wong to visit me in Shanghai. We may have some areas of shared interest, *mei mei*."

At Uncle's funeral he had made the same request, but Ava had put it down to politeness. Now it had more import, but not enough that she wanted to pursue it.

"Tell me more about that young female film director from Yantai you mentioned last week," she said, changing the subject.

In her third month at home, Ava felt the urge to travel. Maria took a week off from her job as assistant trade commissioner at the Colombian consulate in Toronto and they flew to Aruba. Four days into the trip, Ava felt the first touch of guilt about being idle. By the end of the week she'd had enough of beaches and dining out and was ready to go back to work.

She called May Ling as soon as she got back to Toronto. "I want to step into the business," she said.

"This is sooner than you thought," May said.

"I think I've worked through enough of the pain."

"Are you sure? We can wait."

"There will always be a hole in my heart where Uncle was, but I can't let it paralyze me. He wouldn't want that either."

"Well, in that case, how about meeting Amanda and me in Shanghai in a few days?"

"Shanghai?"

"It's year-end for Suki Chan. I'll be going over her numbers and looking at her plans for the coming year. She tells me she has some ideas she wants us to consider. I could use your input."

"How about Amanda?"

"She has her own project there, some mysterious investment proposal that she tells me has to be seen."

"Seen?"

"I've asked for the business plan. She says she'll give it to me when we're in Shanghai."

"That isn't like Amanda."

"I know, but she's quite giddy about it, and I was going there anyway. She'll be even giddier knowing that you're coming."

"Yes," Ava said softly.

"Ava, is something wrong?"

"Why do you ask?"

"You don't sound particularly enthusiastic."

"It's Xu," Ava said.

"What about him?"

"He's been calling me."

"What does he want?"

"We share memories of Uncle. It's helped me get past some things."

"And he lives in Shanghai," May said. "Is that the problem?"

"Yes. He asked me at the funeral, and again over the phone, if you and I could meet with him there."

"Both of us?"

"He hints that he has some business interests that could be mutually beneficial."

"Why on earth would we ever do business with a Triad gang leader? I know he's sophisticated and doesn't look like your typical gangster, but he didn't get to be as successful as he is without a very sharp cutting edge."

"I'm not suggesting we do business with him, May," Ava said. "I just don't think I can go to Shanghai and not meet with him. If you're uncomfortable with the idea, then I'll go alone."

"Is this about both of you being tied to Uncle?"

"It's partially that, of course, but I also can't forget that I owe Xu my life. We both know I would have been killed in

Borneo without him," Ava said. The memory of being kidnapped and held for ransom by a local Triad gang was still fresh. Uncle had been in Shanghai with Xu when it happened and had prevailed upon him to send men to rescue her. Ava was saved, but ten men died as Xu exacted revenge for reasons that had nothing to do with her.

"He did what he did for Uncle. I'm not sure you owe him anything."

"That could be true, but I can't deny that a connection runs between us, and that an obligation — if not a debt — must be recognized. Meeting with Xu, especially socially over dinner or lunch, would be a trivial thing for us, and it's the only thing he's ever asked of me. So I can't go to Shanghai without telling him, and I can't be there and refuse to see him."

"All right, I'll go along," said May with a sigh. "I'll ask Amanda to build a meeting with him into our schedule. Which do you prefer, dinner or lunch?"

"I think dinner shows more respect."

"Dinner it is."

"When Amanda forwards me the complete schedule, I'll call Xu and make sure the time works for him."

"From what you're telling me, I'll be surprised if he doesn't make any time work," May said.

"Perhaps, but regardless of when we end up meeting with him, I don't want Amanda there. He was quite specific about its being me and you. Do you think she will be offended by that?"

"She isn't that sensitive. In any event, I'll tell her it's strictly a social thing."

"Okay."

"Ava, do you have any idea what he wants with us?"

"No."

"Really?"

"I don't have a clue."

## 2

AFTER AVA ENDED HER CALL WITH MAY, SHE FELT AN
incredible surge of energy. It was as if she had pulled
down the last brick in the wall she had built around herself after Uncle's death. In rapid succession she phoned
her mother, Maria, and Mimi to let them know she was
going back to work. Then she put on her running gear
and headed outdoors.

The weather was still vacillating between winter and
spring, but there was warmth in the air, buoying her spirits
even further. Over the past couple of weeks she had worked
her way up to ten kilometres a day. Today she ran sixteen,
and would have gone farther if her route hadn't taken her
back to the front door of the condo.

She showered, dressed, and went to the computer. An
email from Amanda had already arrived.

I'm so excited that you're coming to Shanghai. This
is what I propose as a schedule, it read. Both May and I
arrive early Thursday morning. I checked the flights and it
looks like the earliest you can get there is Thursday afternoon. May intends to spend the day with Suki. I'm going

to be tied up all day and into the evening with the young couple whose business proposal I've been looking at, so I'll meet you at the hotel on Friday morning and the three of us can go to their office to hear their pitch. May says you want to have dinner with Xu. Friday night will work, or any night after that, depending on how long you want to stay. So looking forward to seeing you. Love, Amanda.

The sign-off *Love* wasn't uncommon among the three partners, and Amanda was more than just a partner. She was married to Ava's half-brother Michael, and Ava had been a bridesmaid at their wedding. Michael was the eldest son of Ava's father, Marcus, and his first wife, Elizabeth. Ava's mother was Marcus's second wife, and a third wife lived in Australia. Marcus still lived with Elizabeth and his other marriages weren't legal in the formal sense, but it wasn't unusual for wealthy Hong Kong men to have more than one wife. Ava had been raised in keeping with the multi-family tradition.

She checked her watch. It was one in the morning in Hong Kong. Ava imagined Amanda sitting at her desk in the living room, looking out at the harbour view. Amanda and Michael's apartment was in the Mid-levels of Hong Kong. Their suite was not so far up Victoria Peak as to cost millions of dollars, but it was high enough that at night they had a sliver of a view of Victoria Harbour. She dialled their number, and Amanda answered on the first ring.

"I just got your email. Why aren't you in bed?" Ava asked.

"Michael is travelling with Simon To. They're in Guangzhou, looking at some possible sites. I'm waiting for him to get home."

Simon To was Michael's partner in a chain of noodle

restaurants. Ava had helped them out of a difficult situation in Macau more than a year ago, saving their business — and Simon's life.

"Their business is still good?" she asked.

"It must be. They've been using Sonny almost constantly to run them here and there."

Sonny Kwok had been Uncle's bodyguard and chauffeur, and it had fallen to Ava to keep him employed and out of trouble. She couldn't use him in Toronto, so she had made him available to her father, Michael, and Amanda. It was understood — and by no one more than Sonny — that he was, ultimately and always, Ava's man.

"I got your schedule," Ava said. "It looks fine, except I think I'd like to have dinner with Xu the day I arrive. I don't really have to see Suki unless May thinks there's a need."

"That works just as well. I assume you'll contact Xu directly?"

"Yes. Let's leave it to May to figure out Suki. You must have enough on your plate with that proposal you're looking at."

"It has been hectic," Amanda said. "Ava, I'm so happy you're ready to come back to work. We can get things moving in full gear now that we've got Borneo sorted out and Chi-Tze is working with me in Hong Kong."

"She doesn't miss Borneo?"

"She couldn't wait to get out of there. Ah-Pei isn't involved in the business anymore but she didn't leave Kota Kinabalu, and Chi-Tze kept running into her. Every time she did, she couldn't sleep for days. May agreed that Chi-Tze should join me here. The Chiks are running the business now. Chi-Tze keeps in touch with them and is available whenever they need her, but that dependency should ease up over time.

I hope so, because I need her full focus. Now that people know we have money to invest, proposals are arriving every other day, and to go through them properly takes quite a bit of time. Chi-Tze is a superb analyst. When we were at business school together, she always had the better marks."

Chi-Tze Song and her sister, Ah-Pei, had owned a Borneo furniture business that Three Sisters invested in. Their involvement in the firm had not resulted in a smooth transition.

"I'm so happy she's in a better place, both physically and emotionally," Ava said.

"It sounds like you are as well."

"Well, I am ready to work again."

"Are you really over Uncle's death?"

"He was in his eighties. He lived a long and productive life, and he was ready to go."

"But how are you feeling?"

"I miss him every day. Every time the phone rings, some part of me thinks it's him. I don't know when I'll stop reacting like that."

"He was a marvellous man."

"He would have died for me."

"And you for him."

"I like to think that I would."

"Ava, I know we'll never be able to replace what you and Uncle had, but hopefully this business of ours will give you as much satisfaction as working with him did."

"I keep telling myself that it will be nice to invest in something long-term, something that we can grow. Every job Uncle and I did was one of a kind and had a short lifespan. It was get in, get the money, and get out, then sit around and wait for the next job. Whenever I had to describe what I did for a living, I said it involved months of boredom interspersed with days of stress and excitement, and sometimes punctuated with minutes — or even hours — filled with terror."

"I can handle boredom, or at least predictability," Amanda said.

"I'm not so sure about either of those," Ava said, laughing. "Now go to bed. I'll see you in Shanghai."

After hanging up, Ava sat quietly by the phone for a few minutes. Amanda and May Ling were loyal friends, and Ava felt as tightly bound to them as she had been to Uncle. It would be good to reconnect in person, and to be in Shanghai. That thought reminded her of Xu. She opened the contact list on her computer and found his email address.

Something has come up and I have to be in Shanghai at the end of this week. I arrive Thursday. If you want to meet, May Ling and I will be available that evening for drinks or dinner. We're staying at the Peninsula Hotel. If you can't reach me beforehand, leave a message there. Regards, Ava.

She went to the kitchen to make a cup of Starbucks instant coffee. When she got back, there was already a reply. Dinner it will be. I will make the reservation and contact you at the hotel with details. Thank you, Xu.

It was an hour later in Shanghai than in Hong Kong, past two o'clock in the morning. *Doesn't anyone over there sleep?* she thought.

## 3

**AVA BOOKED THE ONLY DIRECT FLIGHT FROM TORONTO** to Shanghai. It departed from Pearson International at one in the afternoon and would land her at three in the afternoon, fourteen hours and an International Date Line crossing later, in Shanghai.

Air Canada didn't have a first-class section, but the business-class pods gave her ample privacy. She drank a glass of champagne before takeoff, turned on the in-flight entertainment system, and searched for the latest Chinese films. She chose *The Red Cliff*. She had seen the edited version, which was just over two hours long, in Cantonese with English subtitles. This was the original cut, which ran more than four hours and had no subtitles. She ordered a glass of Pinot Grigio as soon as they reached cruising altitude, and nestled into her pod to watch Tony Leung, Takeshi Kaneshiro, and Zhang Fengyi put an end to the second-century Han Dynasty and introduce the era of the Three Kingdoms. The film was a spectacle, the highest-budget movie ever made in Hong Kong or China, with a cast of thousands doing battle on land and on the sea. She adored Tony Leung. Some actors, such as Andy Lau, were fine in contemporary roles but looked absurd in battledress. Leung was a chameleon, flitting from moody romantic roles to Hong Kong gangster films and period pieces such as *The Red Cliff*, always embodying his character fully in time and place.

Ava drank three more glasses of wine and passed on dinner. By the time the film concluded, she was ready to sleep. She reclined her seat into a bed, put in earplugs, slipped on an eye mask, and within minutes was gone.

She dreamed she was in a small one-room apartment, lying in bed with her feet towards the front door. She heard a noise and opened her eyes. Only then did she notice that the apartment walls went only three-quarters of the way to the ceiling, and that the door went only three-quarters of the way to the lintel. A man peered over the wall. "Go away!" she yelled. He disappeared for a few seconds and then popped up again, closer to the door. She watched as he swung a leg over the top of the door and began to squeeze through the gap. She tried to get up, but her legs were frozen in place and she could barely lift her head. "Get out of here!" she screamed.

She sat upright, panic flooding over her. The dimmed cabin lights cast shadows. She drank some water and then settled back into the bed and closed her eyes. Within minutes she was out again. She didn't dream this time, and when she woke, it was to the gentle voice of a flight attendant saying, "Ms. Lee, we will be landing soon. Would you like some breakfast?"

Ava ate an omelette with sausages, drank two cups of coffee, and went to the bathroom to freshen up. Back in her seat, she opened her Chanel bag and took out the information May Ling had sent her on Suki Chan's warehouse and distribution business. Then she reached deeper into the bag and took out a Moleskine notebook. She might not be collecting bad debts anymore but she still found that the simple act of putting pen to paper helped her organize her thoughts. She wrote *Suki Chan* across the top of the first page and then copied the numbers and impressions she wanted to remember in case she was called upon to participate in a meeting.

About forty-five minutes from Shanghai, the plane began its descent. Ava looked out the window. Through light cloud cover she saw the East China Sea sparkling below. She had been to Shanghai once before, on a collection job. She had taken a flight from Dalian, a city in the north of China, near Manchuria, and had landed at Hongqiao Airport, on Shanghai's west side. Her visit back then had lasted only a day and a half, and she hadn't left the city's western perimeter, so downtown Shanghai was unknown to her. Still, it almost felt like coming home.

Ava's mother was Shanghainese, and Ava had heard tales about the storied city for as long as she could remember. So she knew that in the 1920s and '30s the city was considered the most cosmopolitan in Asia, if not the world, before being gutted and occupied by Japanese invaders and then Communist insurgents. In recent years it had come roaring back to claim its place as the number one economic and cultural power in China. According to Jennie Lee, it was as sophisticated as Paris, New York, or London.

Air Canada's destination was Shanghai Pudong International Airport, on the east side. The airport was only about ten years old and had been built to move large volumes of people. Within half an hour of landing Ava had cleared Customs and Immigration and walked into the arrivals hall, to see a uniformed man holding a Peninsula Hotel sign with her name on it. She waved at him and he hurried towards her to get her bags.

She had packed just as she would have for any business trip for her and Uncle's collection agency. Her Shanghai Tang Double Happiness black leather bag held most of her clothes: two black pencil skirts; two pairs of linen slacks; four Brooks Brothers shirts in various colours, all with French cuffs and modified Italian collars; Cole Haan pumps; a pair of crocodile stilettos; various items of underwear; a small makeup bag containing her hairbrush, black mascara, red lipstick, and a vial of Annick Goutal perfume; and a light blue kidskin pouch that contained her Cartier Tank Française watch, ivory chignon pin, and two sets of cufflinks, one green jade and the other blue enamel with gold Chinese lettering. She had put on a black Giordano T-shirt and her Adidas track pants, jacket, and running shoes for the flight. Rolled into a ball and packed into the corner of her bag were three more T-shirts, socks, a sports bra, and running shorts. Her Chanel bag contained her laptop, the Moleskine notebook, and work documents.

She gave the driver the Double Happiness bag and followed him from the terminal to the car. The sun was pale in the sky overhead, and a brisk wind buffeted her. Ava shivered. The weather was much as it had been in Toronto, the last days of winter reluctantly giving way to spring. The man who had greeted her was two steps ahead, walking down a line of limousines. When he stopped at a green

Rolls-Royce, Ava gaped. It was a Phantom. She had never seen a car quite so big. A driver stood by the back door, and he swung it open for her. She climbed in and was enveloped in the smell of freshly cleaned leather.

As the Rolls pulled away from the curb, she realized she hadn't tipped the man who had met her in the arrivals hall. When she mentioned it to the driver, he turned his head, smiled, and said in English, "Not to worry, miss. Now let me welcome you to Shanghai and the Peninsula Hotel."

"Thank you. I don't know much about the city, but from what I've heard, it's marvellous. What is your name?"

"I'm Zhang."

"You speak English very well."

"Thank you. I graduated from the University of Shanghai with a degree in English and I worked as an interpreter for a few years. But driving for the Peninsula pays better," he said. He spoke with his eyes locked on the highway ahead. It was so quiet inside the car that she could have heard him if he whispered. Not even the noise from the construction sites that lined the road on both sides could penetrate its silence.

"How far to the hotel?" she asked.

"We'll drive about forty-five kilometres through Pudong and then we'll cross the Huangpu River and enter Shanghai."

She leaned back and looked out the window. For the first fifteen or twenty minutes they drove past apartment towers, shopping centres, and what looked like industrial estates. Ava noticed that they seemed to be covered in the same dust she'd seen in many Chinese cities that were in the grip of building booms. "Everything looks so new," she said.

"Pudong is a special economic zone. Twenty years ago it

was nothing but farmland. Now there are more than five million residents. The area's economy is as big as that of some European countries," he said. He smiled at Ava in the rear-view mirror. "They're even building a Disneyland."

Ava noticed that the dust had now given way to a pale yellow fog. "Is this smog we're driving through?" she asked.

"Yes, Pudong and Shanghai share the Yangtze Delta with Jiangsu and Zhejiang."

"What does that mean?"

"They're major industrial provinces, with many heavy industries and lots of coal consumption. The discharge blows our way, and when you add the pollution from the Pudong factories and our traffic, you end up with this. It actually isn't that bad today. Last week we had three days of yellow haze alerts."

Ava thought of the foul air she'd survived in cities such as Dalian and Shenzhen, another special economic zone, but they were rough-and-tumble places that concentrated on economic growth. She hadn't expected anything like this in Shanghai. She was about to mention it to Zhang when her attention was captured by several massive buildings that had loomed into view on the hazy skyline. "What are they?" she asked.

"The tower is the Oriental Pearl TV tower. The taller building next to it is the Shanghai World Financial Centre. They're both more than four hundred and fifty metres high."

As they drew near, the Oriental Pearl Tower became more distinct. Ava tried to remember how high Toronto's CN Tower was. She thought it was more than five hundred metres tall, but it lacked the grace of the Oriental Pearl, which had a huge coloured pod near its base that echoed another pod three-quarters of the way up. The pods looked like two giant pearls connected by a golden strand.

"And that's the Huangpu River," Zhang said, pointing to a slow-moving body of water. "We're going to cross it on the Nanpu Bridge. On the other side is Shanghai."

The bridge was almost a kilometre long and soared at least a hundred metres above the river. Ava looked down and saw a large collection of barges, tankers, and container ships, their brightly coloured hulls in stark contrast to the sluggish grey-black water they churned through. Like every urban river she'd ever seen in China, the only flashes of colour were from floating debris and the green and blue iridescence of oil slicks.

The car crawled across the bridge and entered Shanghai on the Inner Ring Elevated Road. They had travelled only a short distance when Zhang said, "This is Zhongshan East First Road, and straight ahead is the Bund."

Ava knew about the Bund from her mother, who spoke of it often, but she wasn't prepared for just how beautiful it was. The Bund had been the centre of the International Settlement, the section of the city where, from in the middle of the nineteenth century, the Chinese government had permitted foreigners to live and work. The community that resulted was striking in many ways, and no part of it more so than the Bund, with its kilometre of European-inspired architecture — all of it restored and preserved — situated in the middle of China's largest city.

In the 1920s the owners of this stretch of banks, embassies, newspaper offices, and company headquarters had hired European architects to reflect their Western roots in Shanghai. Few of the buildings were more than five or six storeys high, but they were expansive and represented a range of styles from art deco to beaux arts to Renaissance revival and Romanesque. Fifty-two buildings were officially listed as original, and they were double-numbered. Each had its official Zhongshan Road address and then, befitting the uniqueness of the Bund, it was assigned a number that cemented its place as one of the fifty-two. The first building in a line going from south to north was the Asia Building — 1 Zhongshan Road and also No. 1, The Bund. The Shanghai Club was 2 Zhongshan Road and No. 2, The Bund.

Zhang drove slowly, naming each building as they went past. Directly across from the buildings, a paved esplanade ran alongside the river. It was almost as broad as the road itself, and a mass of people was moving along it in both directions.

The Peninsula Hotel was at the north end of the Bund and stood on land that had once housed the British Consulate. "We are home," Zhang said. He turned into the Peninsula's circular driveway.

The hotel's design was art deco, all clean lines of glass and concrete, with touches of gold trim. As Ava stepped into the lobby, she marvelled at the marble floors flecked with black and gold, the marble front desk inlaid with gold curlicues, and a marble fireplace at least two and a half metres high that was burning real logs. Above the fireplace was a mirror that stretched six metres to the ceiling. An enormous white porcelain bowl sat on the mantel in front of the mirror, along with metre-high red vases filled with fresh-cut flowers. The fireplace was flanked by two rows of red velvet chairs. Overhead, an enormous chandelier flooded the lobby with sparkle and light.

In her Adidas pants and jacket, her hair tied back with a red rubber band, Ava felt decidedly underdressed. The young woman behind the desk didn't seem to notice. She smiled and welcomed her so effusively that Ava almost turned to see if someone was standing behind her.

"Madam Wong reserved a deluxe garden suite for you on the same floor as her and Ms. Yee," the woman said. "Please give me your passport and fill out the registration form."

"Of course." Ava handed her passport to the desk clerk and took the registration form. She glanced at the room rate. The suite cost 10,500 renminbi a night, just over US$1,500.

When the woman returned, she slid the passport across the desk with one hand while sliding the form towards her with the other. "Two notes have been left for you," she said.

Ava put them in her jacket pocket and turned to look for the elevators. A bellman was standing a few feet away with her bag in hand. "If you would follow me," he said.

They walked towards a majestic staircase made of black marble and gold. It was covered in rich red carpeting and looked as if it could accommodate twenty people on a single step. Before they reached it, the bellman turned left and led her to a bank of elevators.

Ava had a corner suite on the fifth floor. The living room was furnished with grey and taupe thickly cushioned sofas and chairs that were covered in throw pillows. She walked into the bedroom and was bathed in a sea of white.

She went to the window and looked out onto a garden and a bridge that spanned a small body of water. "That's not the Huangpu River," she said.

"No, it's Suzhou Creek. It feeds into the river," the bellman said.

"And the garden belongs to the hotel?"

"No, it's a public garden. It used to belong to the British Consulate."

"Very nice view."

"Many of our guests prefer rooms in this part of the hotel to those that look out onto the Bund and the river."

"I can see why," Ava said as she gave him a tip.

When the bellman left, she took the notes from her pocket. The first was from May: *Hope you had a nice flight. We're meeting Xu at seven for dinner. The restaurant is within easy walking distance from the hotel. I'll be with Suki until five thirty and back at the hotel around six. If you're up to it, meet me in the Compass Bar downstairs. Amanda may join us if she's back from the factory in Pudong.*

The next was from Xu: *I spoke with May Ling and she has the dinner details. Looking forward to seeing you.*

Ava looked at her watch. It was four thirty. Her body felt stiff from the flight, and her head was muddled from jet lag. Ideally she would have loved to go for a run, but then she remembered the air quality and discarded the idea. Instead she went into the bedroom and unpacked her bags.

When that was done, she went back to the living room and stood by the window. She closed her eyes, breathed in deeply, and began to fill her mind with images of bak mei, slowly allowing her body to respond to them. The martial art was designed to cause damage, with kicks that never went above the waist and short, pile-driving hand thrusts that attacked the opponent's most vulnerable body parts: eyes, nose, ears, and areas with sensitive nerve endings. The phoenix-eye fist was bak mei's most famous move; it concentrated all the muscle power from the shoulder, back, and abdomen into the first knuckle of the right hand. Strength and speed were generated by the legs and hips so that the knuckle became a lethal weapon. For half an hour she followed a routine that hadn't varied since she'd begun to learn the art. Bit by bit her body loosened and then came back together in a different form — fighting form. She went through her exercises: the *kata* for the tiger, for the dragon. *Bam!* Her right fist shot forward, almost too fast for the human eye to track. *Bam, bam, bam!* She stopped, closed her eyes again, and resumed deep breathing. When the tension had left her body and her mind could focus on where she was, she was done.

Ava stripped and went into the bathroom. She adjusted the shower nozzle to its most powerful setting, set the water temperature to as hot as she could bear, and stepped into the stall. She let the water batter her for at least five minutes before reaching for the shower gel and then the shampoo. She dried herself with a thick, fluffy towel, slipped on a Peninsula terry cloth robe, and dried her hair.

Back in the living room, she sat at the desk and opened her laptop. There were three emails from Maria, full of love and longing and already bemoaning her absence. For the first time in her life Ava was in a relationship that she felt was going to last. She wasn't ready to share a house, and she certainly wasn't ready to get married, but she loved Maria and wanted to hang on to her. Where it went, only time would decide. I miss you too, and I'll be careful, and I'll be good, she wrote back.

The room phone rang.

"Yes," Ava said.

"It's May."

"You're early."

"Just a bit. How was the trip?"

"Not bad. How was your day?"

"So-so."

"What happened?"

"Nothing too dramatic, just Suki pushing us to help her expand faster than we planned. We can talk about it when we meet."

"That's fine with me."

"You ready for a drink?"

"I need to get dressed."

"That usually takes you about five minutes."

"I just stepped out of the shower."

"Seven minutes, then."

## 4

**THE COMPASS BAR WAS OFF THE HOTEL LOBBY, AND** May Ling was already there when Ava arrived. Ava was wearing a black skirt, a pink shirt with the cuffs fastened by green jade links, and her black Cole Haan pumps. Her hair was pulled back, fastened by her ivory chignon pin, and she wore a light touch of red lipstick and black mascara. In the right light, she looked as though she was in her mid-twenties.

May Ling sat at the bar turned sideways, her legs crossed. She was wearing a sleeveless black linen dress that fell to just above the knee, its square neckline exposing just the top of her generous bust — one of the things that Ava and May had in common. Ava was five foot three and weighed 115 pounds; May was the same height and maybe five pounds lighter. Ava's bak mei and running regimes had toned her muscles over the years. May lifted nothing heavier than a glass of wine but had a lithe, feminine figure. She was fine-boned — like a Chinese Audrey Hepburn, Ava had always thought. Her hair was cut in a short bob. She was in her mid-forties but looked as if she was in her early thirties.

When May saw Ava, she slid from the stool and stepped towards her. The two women hugged each other tightly, heads pressed into shoulders.

"I'm so happy to see you," May said.

"Me too," Ava said, feeling an unexpected surge of emotion. "I've missed you."

Theirs was a friendship that had begun with lies, mistrust, and betrayal. Ava and Uncle had been hired by May Ling and her husband, Changxing, to find out who had sold them fraudulent art. When Ava found the perpetrators, May Ling sent killers to slake her husband's need for revenge. Ava had reacted with fury, threatening to destroy the more than sixty million dollars she had recovered. Less than a month later, she had found herself in the middle of a crisis that threatened her entire family's financial health, as well the life of her half-brother's partner. May came to her aid, and a relationship was forged.

May was Taoist, as Uncle had been. The first time she met Ava, she had felt *qi*, the Taoist life force, pass between them. They were two kindred souls, she said, bound in ways they could never understand. Ava may not have bought into the *qi* part, but she had to admire May for what she had accomplished. And she listened to Uncle, who told her that friends with *guanxi* were friends to be treasured.

Now when Ava thought of May, her *guanxi* was irrelevant. She was simply a good friend, and someone she trusted as much as she had trusted Uncle. She had never said this to May. But then she had never said it to Uncle either; it had always been understood that there was nothing they wouldn't do for each other. She sensed that whatever flowed between her and May was just as pure.

Ava looked around the bar. The carpeting was purple with a black line running through it. One wall was purple, along with the leather bar stools. She would never have imagined the colour as a design choice for any Peninsula Hotel, but somehow they had managed to pull it off.

"I'd call this stylishly garish," she said.

"I know you love the Mandarin Oriental, but I have to tell you, the Peninsula is not day-old noodles," May said.

There was a half-empty glass on the bar. "Martini?" Ava asked.

"Of course."

Ava climbed up onto the stool next to May's. The bartender was in front of her in a flash.

"Prosecco," she said.

"And another martini," May said.

"Will Amanda be joining us?" Ava asked.

"No, she can't get away from Pudong. She said they're putting the final touches on the pitch they'll make to us tomorrow. I have to say, it's all quite mysterious."

"It has certainly piqued my curiosity."

"Me too."

"And your day with Suki was just so-so?"

"It was mainly positive. The money we invested in Suki's business is already reaping dividends. Our timing was good, I think. She's very aggressive. She's opened a couple of new warehouses and she's added to the truck fleet. She tells me that we now have the largest privately owned storage and distribution business in Shanghai. Not that she's satisfied with that."

"What do you mean?"

"She wants to get bigger and better. A cold-storage facility is the next thing on her horizon. They aren't cheap to build, but there's a shortage. We'd fill it to capacity the day we opened."

"How much more money would we have to put up?"

"For the cold storage, or for everything else she wants to do on top of that?" May said wryly. "I'm afraid we've unleashed a bit of a tiger in Suki. For years she was strapped for cash, and her husband's lack of ambition didn't help. Since he died and we gave her the money, she's seen what she's capable of."

The waiter placed two drinks in front of them. May finished her first martini and picked up the fresh one. "*Gan bei*," she said.

"Cheers."

"The thing about the cold-storage warehouse," May said after they had each taken a sip of their drinks, "is that we can pay for it by reinvesting our profits. We don't have to put up any new money."

"I like your idea."

"Me too, and it isn't mine — it's Suki's. She's quite driven, that woman, very intense, and she keeps right up to date. She's installed every new system she can find to make the business more efficient," May said.

"So you're obviously comfortable with her cold-storage proposal."

"Yes, but that isn't her only idea."

"So you said. What else does she have in mind?"

"She wants to expand the Shanghai business and extend her reach to Beijing," May said.

"The cold storage isn't enough?"

"No. She says we have to keep growing to keep pace with

the economy. Pudong is booming, and Shanghai has come roaring back. There are more than twenty million people living in this immediate area. The need for logistics — for trucking and warehousing and distribution networks — has never been greater. The manufacturing sector keeps expanding, and the more products that are made, the more need to be warehoused and shipped. Changxing and I experienced the same phenomenon in Wuhan and Hubei, but it was a more manageable growth. Here it's crazy, and the costs are greater."

"From what I've read, she already has the largest operation in Shanghai."

"I know, but she wants to get bigger yet. And she's not wrong. If you stand still you'll get run over by the competition."

"Let her continue to invest our profits."

"Our profit margins are healthy, and they'll get even stronger if we can throw up the cold storage quickly, but she still wants more money."

Ava finished her Prosecco and passed the glass to the bartender. "I'll have another."

The bartender looked at May.

"No, we're going out to dinner and I want to be able to walk to the restaurant."

"What's this about Beijing?" Ava said when the bartender left.

"There's a warehouse and distribution company on the outskirts of the city that a friend of hers owns. He's ready to retire and he wants to sell the business to someone he knows, someone who values the effort he's put into it."

"How much money would that entail?" Ava asked.

"Three hundred million renminbi."

"Fifty million dollars?"

"More or less."

"We don't have that kind of cash," Ava said.

"Suki thinks she can find a bank that might give it to us if we pledged the Shanghai assets."

"We agreed when we set up our business that we would avoid highly leveraged situations. None of us likes debt, right?"

"I agree. Expanding in Shanghai and also adding a Beijing location would amount to close to a hundred million dollars. We have thirty million available, and the girls are looking at some other investments that are attractive. I don't want to put too much into one basket."

"Then we won't."

"Fine. I wanted to discuss it with you before telling Suki she'll have to make do with the cold storage."

"Will she be upset?"

"No, she knows she's pushing the envelope. She just can't help it. She sees the potential and wants to grab it."

May's cellphone rang. The noise sounded especially shrill in the quiet bar. "*Wei*," May said, then smiled and passed the phone to Ava.

"How was your flight?" Amanda asked.

"Just fine."

"Sorry I couldn't make it back for a drink. I'm still at my meeting, and it doesn't look like I'm getting back to the hotel anytime soon."

"Is there a problem?"

"No, just some details that have to be worked out. Let's meet for breakfast in the morning."

Ava turned to May. "Amanda won't be back till late. She wants to meet for breakfast."

"Tell her eight o'clock."

"I heard that, and eight is fine," Amanda said. "Now I have to get back to the people here. See you tomorrow."

Ava handed the phone back to May. "She sounds excited."

"I've had enough excited conversation for one day," May said. "Let's hope that dinner with Xu is calmer."

The phone rang again. May looked concerned as she answered, and Ava wondered if Changxing was on the line. Instead, May once again passed the phone to Ava.

"Ava, welcome to Shanghai," Xu said.

"You could have told me that when we meet."

"That's why I'm calling. Something has come up that needs my urgent attention. Can we possibly do dinner tomorrow night? I'm sorry to ask at the last minute, but I have a crisis of sorts."

Ava covered the microphone with her hand. "He wants to postpone dinner until tomorrow night. Are you okay with that?"

May nodded.

"Yes, that's fine. And truthfully it will probably be better for me to have a good night's sleep behind me," Ava said to Xu.

"It will be the same place and the same time."

"I'll tell May."

"Thank you for being understanding. I'm anxious to speak with the two of you."

## 5

**IT TURNED INTO A SHORT EVENING FOR AVA. AFTER** her second glass of Prosecco, jet lag began to take its effect. Her mind was clouded, and despite the bak mei workout her limbs felt heavy. May wanted her to come to the Yi Long Court restaurant across the hallway for dinner, but Ava had started to yawn and knew there was no way she could last. She excused herself just after seven o'clock and headed upstairs to her room.

She began to take her clothes off the second she had closed the door behind her, and slid into bed in only her underwear. Sleep took her instantly. She woke twice, the first time to pee and drink a glass of water. It took her a while to get back to sleep, her body clock insisting that it was mid-afternoon.

When she finally nodded off, she found herself immersed in a recurring dream. She and her father were in a hotel trying to check out and get to the airport to catch a plane. As always, hotel rooms disappeared, bags were nowhere to be found, and transportation to the airport proved to be unreliable. They reached the airport with only minutes to spare. She left her father at the curb as she rushed inside to the check-in counter. When she looked back, he was gone. She was at the back of a long, snaking check-in line. Her frustration at its slow movement was compounded by the anxiety of having lost sight of her father. Then she heard her name and the dream took a twist. Uncle was standing at the front of the line, dressed as always in a black suit and white shirt buttoned to the neck. He waved at her. "Join me," he said. She hesitated, worried that her father might not find her.

As she was weighing her options, she woke. The room was entirely dark except for the light thrown by the bedside clock. It wasn't quite six o'clock. She lay quietly, the dream still with her. Had it been one dream, or had Uncle's presence signalled the start of a second dream?

She pulled herself out of bed and went to the window. The first morning light was creeping across the gardens below, the larger plants' leaves moist and glistening in the sun. She turned back to the room, turned on the coffee machine, found her running gear, laid it on the bed, and then went to the bathroom to brush her teeth and hair. Fifteen minutes and two coffees later, she walked into the lobby of the Peninsula.

"I would like to go for a run on the Bund. How is the air quality this morning?" she asked the concierge.

"As good as it has been in weeks," he said. "I don't think you need to worry." Ava thought about pressing for details but let it pass.

Even at that time of the morning the promenade was busy. There were stretches where she had to reduce her pace or swerve to avoid collisions, but the run was magnificent all the same. The air was fresh, with a slight saltwater snap to it, and there was no visible trace of yellow fog. The river seemed to be flowing with more vigour, although it still reflected shades of green, blue, and black from the oil slicks. The historic buildings were coming to life. A steady stream of workers walked across the plazas that fronted the buildings along the Bund, and lines of cars were sliding into underground parking garages.

She ran six kilometres, three times up and then back along the Bund. When she got back to her room, the *International Herald Tribune* and *Shanghai Daily* were at her door. She made another coffee and spread the *Tribune* over the massive desk. The Middle East was in turmoil, the European Union seemed to be in danger of falling apart, and another American investment guru had been caught running a Ponzi scheme. She turned to the *Daily*. The front page almost exclusively covered economic news: the forecast for next year's growth in GDP had been reduced from nine to eight percent, and new housing starts were projected to grow by only fifteen percent. These numbers were a cause for concern in the new China — numbers that would have caused glee anywhere else.

At five minutes to eight she took the elevator to the breakfast room in the lobby. Amanda and May were already there, sitting side by side, a sheaf of papers in front of Amanda. This was the first time Ava had seen them together like this, and it jolted her. She was in a new business and they were her partners — it wasn't just theory anymore.

They both stood as Ava neared the table. Amanda was the smallest at just a little over five feet and weighing perhaps a hundred pounds. Her shoulder-length hair hung loose, framing her fine features. When Ava first met her, Amanda had been into heavy makeup; now it was just mascara and lipstick. She was wearing designer jeans and a black silk blouse. Ava stared into Amanda's face, searching for any lingering effects of the attack in Borneo, and found none.

"Excuse all this paper," May said. "I wanted Amanda to see Suki's final numbers."

Amanda took a few quick steps forward and threw her arms around Ava's neck. "It's so good to see you," she said. They hugged fiercely, each of them understanding the pain the other had suffered. Over Amanda's shoulder, Ava saw May wipe a tear from the corner of one eye.

"And it's wonderful to see you."

"Amanda was waiting for you to get here before she gave a briefing on what we can expect today when we see her mysterious investment proposal," May said.

"You certainly have our interest," Ava said.

Amanda smiled. "Then let's start."

Ava sat across from them and poured herself a coffee from the carafe. A platter of muffins and croissants was pushed off to one side of the table. They appeared not to have been touched. "No one's eating?" she said

"I'm still stuffed from last night," May said.

"And I'm too excited," Amanda said.

"Is the deal you're looking at that thrilling?" Ava asked.

"Well, it has that potential," Amanda said.

"I don't like the word *thrilling* when it's attached to a business," May said.

"I'm joking, or at least partly joking," Amanda said. "In about an hour you're going to be meeting Clark and Gillian Po. They're siblings. He's a fashion designer."

"I've never heard of him," May said quickly.

"That's because he's never designed under his own name."

"I see."

"He's spent the past ten years designing clothes for other people's labels, mainly retailers in Europe and North America. It's a business their father started with their uncle about thirty years ago. The company was originally based in Hong Kong, but when it became too expensive to operate there they set up shop here.

"The brothers were very sharp businessmen. They leased a factory in Pudong, but it's only about two thousand square metres. It's what's called a sample factory. They have about a hundred workers involved in designing clothes and making samples for the salesmen and agents. If they get an order, they outsource production to a real garment factory somewhere else in China or Asia."

"So they don't actually make anything themselves?" Ava asked.

"Just the samples. The production is jobbed out."

"So no big overheads."

"No, but that's getting us off the point. I have no interest in that business," Amanda said. "I just want you to understand Clark and Gillian's background. The two brothers were named David and Thomas. David was their father. Thomas had no children, so Clark and Gillian were encouraged to join the business. She's a friend of a girl I went to Brandeis with, and she has an MBA from an Australian university. Clark went to a prestigious institute of fashion design in the U.K."

"So you're saying that the two children went into the business," Ava said.

"Yes, they did, and they've made quite a success of it."

"And now they want out?" May asked. "They're prepared to walk away from the family company?"

"This is where it gets complicated. The two brothers were equal partners, and in their original agreement they had the right to buy each other's shares if one of them left the business for any reason, including death. David Po died two years ago. Thomas bought his shares at a price that was set out in their agreement, but the agreement hadn't been updated in ages and he paid a fraction of their real worth. Now, both Clark and Gillian are quite clear that this did not change the operating arrangements, and they were happy enough to continue working with their uncle. They thought — naively, maybe — that he would eventually retire and pass along the business to them," Amanda said, and then paused. "Instead, he sold it a year ago to one of their biggest customers."

"Lovely," May said.

Amanda nodded. "As you can imagine, this did not go down well with the siblings. But they weren't independently wealthy and didn't have the money to set up their own business, so they stayed on as employees."

"And now they want to leave and they want us to finance — what, exactly?" May said.

"The Po fashion line. They want to launch their own label."

May shook her head. "Amanda, one of the founding principles of Three Sisters is that we won't invest in start-ups until we have built a solid and self-sustaining base in existing businesses."

"I know, and I told my Brandeis friend who approached

me exactly that. But she was very insistent that I meet Clark and Gillian, and eventually I gave in. After spending many days with them, and hours on the phone doing due diligence with customers, I formed the opinion that Gillian is highly organized, efficient, and a tremendous manager. Clark . . . well, Clark is a genius."

"*Genius*, I've learned, is used far too often to describe someone who has talent. There is a wide gap between genius and talent," Ava said.

"That isn't my word," Amanda said. "It's what I've heard over and over again from the sample factory's customers. I called them as part of the due diligence — I pretended I was a buyer for a Hong Kong retail chain — and they were surprisingly open with me. Most of them told me that Clark is the best designer they have ever worked with, and that it's a shame — a crime, even — that he's never had a chance to design his own line."

"Why didn't they give him the chance?" May asked.

"Those customers don't want originality. They want to copy the best new clothes from well-known designers, dumb them down, and stick their own label on them. They don't have time for anything else. They're on a private-label treadmill, one buying season just rolling into the next."

"So we're the chosen ones?"

"May, I wouldn't have asked you and Ava to meet with them if I didn't think there was an opportunity for us to do something very special from a business standpoint. We're going to leave here in a few minutes and go to the factory. If you don't want to take the jump after their presentation, then we'll move on."

"How old are they?" May asked.

"I think Gillian is in her mid-thirties. Clark is younger."

"And how much money do they want?"

"There's a considerable amount of flexibility, but I don't think we could start the business with anything less than ten million dollars."

"U.S.?"

"Yes."

"And you said *start*?"

"I won't soft-sell this. If we want to do it properly, the amount we'd eventually have to invest could be ten times that. The operative word, though, is *eventually*. I think we can ease our way into it. The first and most important thing is for you two to meet them and understand what they want to do. I haven't made any other commitments."

"And what do we get for our ten million?" May asked.

"Forty-nine percent of the business."

"You know we don't like to be in that kind of position."

"I know, May, but I've told them we would need to have sign-off authority on every budget and that a cheque larger than ten thousand dollars couldn't be issued without our approval. With rigorous financial controls in place, we can leave them with fifty-one percent and still maintain control. The point is — and you've said this to me many times already — if we have control of the money, we have control of the business."

"And they're okay with that?"

"I wasn't that blunt with them. The fifty-one percent is almost symbolic."

"And you mentioned that we would absolutely insist that they couldn't sell any of their shares without our approval?"

"I did, and they were okay with that as well."

"So, structurally, the deal does make some sense."

"It does."

"And if nothing else, it will be a change from discussing trucks and warehouses and logistical challenges with Suki Chan," May said. She turned to Ava. "Are you up for this?"

"I'm game for anything," Ava said.

## 6

AMANDA HAD BOOKED A CAR TO TAKE THEM TO THE factory in Pudong. They chatted while they drove, Amanda bringing Ava up to date on the noodle shop and convenience store business that Michael owned with Simon To.

"I'm glad Sonny is driving for him," Ava said.

"No more glad than Michael. He says he gets treated more seriously with Sonny around. Sonny has an edge that can't be ignored."

The talk then turned, almost hesitantly, to Borneo. The furniture business was running smoothly again, and they had found new customers in Europe and the United States. May had sent Peter and Grace Chik — a young man and woman who weren't related — from Wuhan to run it, and the plan was to keep them in Borneo on a permanent basis.

"I hope Chi-Tze never has to go back there," Amanda said as the car slowed in front of a red-brick building surrounded by a wire fence. A guard peered at them through a gate made from steel tubing. Amanda waved and the gate swung open.

They parked in front of the double wooden doors of a one-storey building with small, dust-encrusted windows.

Ava glanced around. There was no sign on the door, or anywhere, for that matter.

"This hardly looks inspiring," May said.

"As I told you, this is a sample factory. It's functional and that's about it," Amanda said. "But everything the Pos need for their presentation is here. So, we thought, why not use it?"

They left the car and started towards the door. It opened before they reached it and a young woman stepped into the yard. "Welcome," she said.

"This is Gillian," Amanda said.

Ava stopped in her tracks, her mouth partially open. She was looking up at one of the tallest women she'd ever seen. Gillian Po had to be six foot two, her height magnified by her slim, almost gaunt frame. She was wearing jeans and a plain blue cotton tank top that exposed her sharp, angular collarbones. Her hair was cut short and shaved along the sides, and she was heavily made up.

"This is Ava and May," Amanda said, motioning to her partners.

"Welcome. Please come in," Gillian said.

"Where's Clark?"

"He's waiting for us in the boardroom."

They shook hands at the doorway, Ava and May both making a point of looking up at Gillian. When they walked past her, they were immediately in the factory. There was a row of sewing machines and two rows of tables where women were cutting fabric and stitching it by hand. On one side was a blackboard with a dress pattern on it and several large corkboards with drawings pinned to them.

"Our offices are this way," Gillian said, making a left turn down a hall.

Curious eyes tracked their progress past glass-walled offices. At the far end of the corridor a man was sitting in a room at a round table that looked just big enough to accommodate them.

Clark Po stood as they approached. He was dressed in a plain white silk shirt and white painter's pants. He was as skinny as Gillian but three or four inches shorter, and Ava doubted that he weighed more than 140 pounds. But it was his face that really caught her attention. It was long and pointed, and his big brown eyes were rimmed with heavy black liner. His hair was gelled, swept to one side, and tossed over his shoulder. It was tied with a red ribbon.

Ava entered the boardroom first. "You must be Clark," she said. "I'm Ava. Pleased to meet you."

"The same," he said. Ava noticed that his voice was very deep.

May and Amanda followed her into the room, greeting Clark with nods and smiles.

"I apologize for the size of our meeting place," Gillian said. "Things are quite barebones here. It will be more comfortable if we all just sit."

Gillian sat down in front of a stack of binders. "I will give each of you one of these binders when we finish our presentation," she said, tapping them. "I went through the numbers with Amanda last night, and then I got up early this morning and refined them. But the first thing I want to do is thank you for being kind enough to come here today."

"We are curious, not kind," May said.

"Can I assume that Amanda gave you a rough description of what we want to do?"

"She did."

"Madam Wong —"

"My name is May, or May Ling, whichever you prefer," she interrupted.

"Of course, May Ling, and can I also assume that Amanda explained the history of our business?"

"She did, and she said you're now working for a European owner. What she didn't say was how well that owner is treating you."

"Well enough," Gillian said with a shrug. "But working for someone else wasn't what we envisioned when we got into this business."

Ava glanced at Clark. He sat completely still, his hands folded in front of him, his eyes locked on his sister.

"Not everyone is meant to have their own business. Why are you?"

"May Ling, my brother is an incredibly talented designer."

"The world is full of them, no? What makes Clark particularly special?"

Clark moved quite suddenly, as if the mention of his name had given him a jolt. He stretched a hand across the table towards May. She looked at it uncomfortably.

"Give me your hand," he said.

May hesitated and then placed her hand on the table. He took it and held it gently. "My father despaired for me," he said, staring at May. "When I was a boy, it was obvious that I was different, and after he realized he couldn't pretend that I wasn't, he spent years trying to protect me. He thought that if he sent me to the best schools, got me the best education he could buy, it would prepare me for the world, that I could come into this business and run it. What he never understood was that I liked being different, and that I had no interest in his schools or mathematics or science or any of what he called the 'building blocks' a man needed to be successful. I flunked out of every school, and for a while we were estranged. It was Gillian who knew what had to be done, and she did it."

"I went to our father," Gillian said. "I told him that Clark should be brought into the business, but not to run it. I told him I was more than capable of doing that, if he was agreeable. I said Clark loved clothes — women's clothes — and he wanted to design them. We needed to ensure that he was properly trained to do it."

"He let me work here in the sample factory," Clark continued, still holding May's hand. "Most of our designers — though you couldn't really call them that — are women. They may not know how to design but they know how to copy, how to cut and sew, and I spent three years learning the basics of the trade from them. Our customer base was mainly American and low-end, so there wasn't much demand for originality. Mainly they wanted cheap. We tried to give them cheap and good."

"Clark didn't work just here. He went to the factories where we jobbed out our production and made sure that what was coming off the line was what we had intended," Gillian said.

"There isn't any point in a design if it can't be manufactured in an efficient way," he said.

Ava had to smile as she followed their conversation. They were like professional Ping-Pong players as they lobbed back and forth to one another.

"The point I'm trying to make is that Clark did his apprenticeship, learning the business from the ground up. After three years he could sew and cut with the best of our women and he was doing his own designing. As our customer base slowly moved upscale and expanded into Europe, he had a chance to work with other designers and a wider range of fabrics. If I didn't know it before, I saw it then — that he was tremendously creative and could more than hold his own with professional designers. That was when I went to our father and said it was time to send Clark to a fashion design college."

"He didn't want to do it," Clark said, a tinge of bitterness in his voice.

"He said it would come to more than fifty thousand U.S. dollars a year, with all the costs figured in. But I didn't believe him. I think he was afraid that once Clark left the family business, he'd never come back."

"But you went," May said.

"Yes, he did," Gillian replied. "We forced the issue and our mother took our side, so he gave in. Clark went to Central Saint Martins in London. It's part of the University of the Arts."

"I'm sorry, I've never heard of it. Is it supposed to be good?" May asked.

"It's one of the very best — if not the best — fashion design schools in the world. Alexander McQueen, John Galliano, Stella McCartney — they're all graduates," Gillian said.

"I took the fashion design womenswear program. It was a wonderful three years . . . and then I came back to the family business and total boredom."

"Pardon me, but you had some very good customers. They weren't all middle-of-the-road," Amanda said.

"No, but they all copy, and that's all they wanted me to

do. Take some Stella McCartney or Jil Sander design and adapt it. That's what they call it — 'adapting.' I call it stealing. Not to their faces, of course."

"Then even that part of the business was sold out from under us," Gillian said, "and we found ourselves employees in what used to be our family business — our heritage. I told Clark we had to find our way out of this."

"All right, I understand your disappointment and your dream, but you need to tell us why we should support it," May said.

"To begin with, the profit margins can be fantastic," Gillian said quickly. "We can make eighty percent, maybe even more. Then, if the label attracts a following, there are so many licensing opportunities we can attach to the name."

"You have a label in mind?" Ava asked.

"PÖ."

"Just Po?"

Clark smiled. "No, actually capital P, capital O, with an umlaut over the O."

"What's an umlaut?" said May.

"Two dots."

"That isn't Chinese."

"No, it's German."

"Why do you want to do that?"

"I like the way it looks, and it represents the melding of East and West that I'm aiming for in my clothes," Clark said.

"Going back to the numbers, I've prepared an analysis of the profit margins that can accrue to designer labels," Gillian said.

"No, just a minute. I'm not interested in looking at those right now," May said.

Ava glanced at Amanda and saw her lower lip tremble. Clark closed his eyes.

"What I want to see is what Clark is capable of creating. You do have designs for us to look at?"

"We certainly do," Gillian said.

"Well, let's do that, shall we? If we like what we see, then we'll move on to the numbers."

Clark leapt to his feet, put his hand to his mouth, and blew a kiss across the table towards May. "You have no idea how happy I am that you said that."

They left the boardroom, walked back down the hall, and turned left into the factory.

"I apologize in advance for being so amateurish," Clark said. "We've set up a small runway and I've brought in some models. Most of them are friends. I wanted you to see my clothes on real women."

"How long will it take you to set up?" May asked.

"We've been ready all morning."

"You assumed we would want to do this?" Ava said.

"When Amanda said you were coming, I couldn't think of another reason."

"Agreed."

"I like your brother," Ava said to Gillian as Clark ran ahead.

"He will care more if you like his designs," Gillian replied.

As they walked through the factory, the employees left their machines and joined in behind them. Ava felt as if they were leading a parade. Clark led the congregation to a ten-metre-long strip of red carpet that ran along the concrete floor from a black curtain to four folding chairs. The employees took positions on either side of the carpet. They whispered among themselves, some of them eyeing the visitors, others staring at the black curtain, which was strung between two steel poles.

Clark directed the Three Sisters party and Gillian to sit and then disappeared behind the curtain. The cloth moved every time an invisible body brushed against it, and Ava could hear Clark urging everyone to move faster. Then the curtain opened ever so slightly and Clark slipped through the crack. The women lining the carpet clapped, and several shouted his name. He nodded in both directions and then slipped backstage again. A moment later the curtain was drawn.

Standing at the end of the carpet was a tall, thin, fresh-faced young woman, her hair drawn back tightly. She began to walk towards the seated women. She was wearing a frock coat, the upper part fitted, hugging her body, and the bottom flaring out into a skirt. The high collar looked as if it was inspired by the traditional cheongsam. Down the front were four orb-shaped powder-blue glass buttons; two smaller buttons of the same colour and shape were on each wrist. The coat was made of white linen, and even in the factory light it shimmered. As the model drew closer, Ava saw that the collar was trimmed in light blue.

"That is spectacular," May said.

For the next thirty minutes, four young women modelled Clark's work. There were jackets, coats, skirts, dresses, and blouses, all of them made from linen and all of them radiating colour in an array of reds, blues, purples, and pinks, by themselves or in combinations with white. Ava wasn't a fashionista but she was her mother's daughter; she could recognize quality, and Clark's work was quality.

Like the frock coat, the clothes hinted at their Chinese origin: collars she had seen on cheongsams, the voluminous sleeves associated with a man's formal *shenyi*, jackets and skirts that combined elements of a Mao suit with the classic *pien-fu* style, and wide-bottomed pants that flowed as the models walked.

After May's initial reaction to the frock coat, no one spoke. Gillian repeatedly glanced at the other women. But the factory workers weren't so quiet. They greeted each design with applause and shouts of encouragement. When the last model slipped behind the curtain, they knew the show was over and began to clap rhythmically. Clark emerged and stood among the four models, two on each side. He bowed, reached for the hands of the women nearest to him, and walked with them towards his sister and Ava, May, and Amanda.

As they neared, Ava stood and began to clap herself. The others followed. Clark stopped a metre away from them and bowed again, his head almost touching his knees. When he looked up, Ava saw tears in his eyes.

## 7

**THE FOUR WOMEN WALKED BACK TO THE BOARDROOM** and sat around the table. Amanda began to speak but May cut her off. "Is Clark going to join us?" she asked Gillian.

"Yes."

"Had you seen all those clothes before?"

"Only piecemeal, never as a collection, and not on models. I hope you'll pardon me when I say I couldn't be prouder of my brother."

"And so you should be."

Clark arrived a few minutes later, his face flushed.

"Bravo," May said.

"The clothes are wonderful," Ava said.

He lowered his head and Ava thought she detected tears again, but when he looked up, his eyes were dry.

"How would you describe your style?" she asked.

He sat down and took a deep breath. "I love the flowing lines of traditional Chinese clothing. I've been searching for ways to marry the attributes of something such as a cheongsam with a Western sensibility, to create a dress that a Western woman would feel comfortable wearing to a cocktail party in New York and a Chinese woman to a wedding in Hong Kong."

"You use the word *comfortable*," Ava said. "That's how I think your clothes look — things that a woman of any size could wear."

"That is my intention. I don't want to make clothes only for women who have a model's figure."

"Everything seems to be made of linen. Is that deliberate too?"

"I worked with silk at first — Hangzhou silk, of course — but I couldn't get away from its Chinese history and character. I found myself designing clothes that only a Chinese woman would wear. So I switched to linen. That freed my mind, allowed me to cross cultures."

"Isn't the linen Chinese?"

"No. We make linen in this country but it isn't so natural to us, and the quality really isn't that good. I looked to Italy, but the cost was prohibitive. Then I found fabric as good as the Italian in Lithuania, at a cost closer to what we would pay in China."

"How much does it cost?" May asked.

"About twenty U.S. dollars a metre."

"And how many metres in the first coat we saw, or in a dress?"

"Three metres in the coat, two to three in the dresses, and about two in the pants."

"And then you double the material cost to get the finished goods cost," Gillian said.

"So you can make a coat like that for a hundred and twenty dollars?"

"Yes, something in that range," Gillian said.

"A coat like that would easily sell for fifteen hundred U.S. dollars in Hong Kong," Amanda said.

"The margins are healthy," Gillian said. "And if we can get the name Po to mean something, then we can demand a premium."

"It is intriguing," May said.

Gillian picked up one of the binders. "I've prepared a five-year plan."

"We're listening," May said.

For the next two hours, followed by a break for lunch, and then another four hours, Gillian painstakingly took them through the nuts and bolts of creating and growing the brand. It was a slow build, the first year devoted to laying the design groundwork and surrounding it with infrastructure and support systems. She wanted to roll out the brand at the end of that year, paving the way with an extensive public relations, advertising, and marketing campaign. Her plan was to first establish an Asian base and then gradually expand into Europe. She didn't envision tackling the U.S. market until they had a presence and a track record in Europe. By year four she envisioned PÖ as a worldwide brand with sales in excess of US$200 million.

Ava, May, and Amanda listened, often interrupting with questions. Ava made notes, as was her habit. Clark had pushed his chair back from the table, as if he had no interest in the business discussion. Twice he left the room for prolonged periods, but since he was so quiet when he was there, his absence was hardly noticed.

It was late in the afternoon when Gillian closed the last page of her binder. "There, I'm finished. Thank you for your patience. Now, do you have any more questions for us?"

THE KING OF SHANGHAI      55

"Yes, actually, I do," Ava said. "We've heard from you today and from Amanda earlier that many of your clients have a very high opinion of Clark's talents. Why didn't you go to one of them? In fact, why didn't you go to the company that bought your father and uncle's business to bankroll you? It seems to me that they would be a better fit than us."

She saw Clark cast an anxious glance at his sister. Gillian caught it too, and then nodded briskly at him. "We did go to them. We went to the company that bought the business, and then we went to two of the factory's largest long-standing customers. The new owner had no interest at all. Both of the customers were curious enough to kick our tires and then made half-hearted offers."

"Half-hearted?"

"Basically they were prepared to put up a bit of money if Clark agreed to keep designing for their labels."

"I knew what that meant," Clark said through tight lips. "Their labels would have all the priority. I could design my clothes in whatever pitiful amount of time was left over. And as for the money, what they offered was a joke. They were treating me like a child whose whims had to be satisfied so he could be kept under control."

"I don't believe they were quite that condescending," Gillian said. "But the money was totally inadequate, and the demands they would have placed on Clark to produce their own goods would have left him with virtually no time for anything else."

"Did you meet with anyone else?" Ava asked.

"A couple of local people, but the chemistry wasn't right."

"Thank you for being so honest."

"Can we take this plan with us?" May asked. "You have done an excellent job of taking us through it, but now we need to go over it at our own pace. And I'm sure you understand that any decision we make will not be based solely on number projections."

"Of course you can take the plan, and yes, I know the financials are only part of the decision-making process."

"Good. I know we'll have questions when we're finished. Can we agree to touch base again tomorrow morning? We know you don't want to drag this out."

Gillian looked at Amanda, who to Ava's eyes seemed uncomfortable. Had she made some kind of commitment?

"No, I don't want us to be kept hanging," Gillian said. "You know, just as I do, that numbers can be massaged and manipulated, but I think my numbers are an honest representation of where we want to go and what it will cost. But all that aside, I think the big decision is whether or not you believe in Clark."

Ava glanced sideways at him. He was looking at them, each in turn. When his eyes caught hers, she saw something approaching defiance in them. *There doesn't seem to be any doubt*, she thought, *that Clark believes in himself.*

## 8

**THE CAR HAD BARELY CLEARED THE FACTORY GATES** when Amanda spoke. "You both know that I really want to do this. I really believe Clark is a genius."

"He is talented, and the clothes are beautiful," May said. "But?"

"Do you really think we're just talking about ten million? It's ten million to start, but that's a very aggressive expenditure plan she has."

"We could cap it at that."

"No, I don't want to go into this venture with that idea in my head. If we do it, then we have to be prepared to spend whatever it takes to make the venture successful. My problem is that I don't know enough about the clothing business, let alone the fashion business, to be able to put a sensible number against it."

"I'm also uncertain how well we can do without our own stores," Ava said.

"You saw that Gillian has targeted high-end retailers as the initial selling vehicle," Amanda said.

"There's still an entry cost."

"Yes, and truthfully it can be high. Some retailers would want us to provide dedicated staff, take positions in their magazines and in ads, and work with them at supporting margins. And there are always sell-offs and clearances," Amanda said.

"And, high entry costs or not, you still have to convince them that the clothes are worth carrying. The competition for space must be intense, and I'm sure others are just as willing to pay the price."

"That's why, when you go over the plan again, you'll see that Gillian has budgeted a ton of money for public relations and marketing. We need to get the name out there, both directly and indirectly, so we can create a demand that retailers can't ignore. Actually, according to the people I spoke to, all we need is one retailer to champion the PÖ brand. But it has to be a company with a great reputation. We need to take our time laying the groundwork, but when we go to market, it has to be with a big enough buzz to draw that retailer to our side. That's why she wants to spend so much money on a show to launch the brand, buying ads in the major magazines, and paying some celebrities to wear Clark's clothes."

"And we can do all that for ten million?" May asked.

"Gillian thinks so."

"Do you?"

"We need to confirm it."

"How?"

"I was going to recommend that we put Chi-Tze on the file. She did an analysis of the development and growth of the Shanghai Tang chain when she was at business school. She has a good understanding of what's involved in creating a brand. I would like to bring her to Shanghai to sit with Gillian and take all the time she needs to crunch the numbers."

"We told Gillian we'd call her tomorrow," Ava said.

"We could always tell her we have an interest in moving forward with them, but that we need to confirm the numbers."

"Will she be okay with that?"

"We're the only people she's talking to."

"You mean we're the only ones left," May said.

"True enough, but she was honest about that, and she has told me more than once that finding the right partners is almost as important as getting the money. And they did turn down two offers, half-hearted or not, so they're not entirely desperate."

"That doesn't mean she'll have the patience to wait," Ava said.

"There's another question I have," May said. "Assuming we decide to do this, is Gillian up to managing it? I have no worries about the design and production side, but this thing could succeed or fail based on how well they market. This isn't a private label, where the goods you're making are presold."

"I thought that either Chi-Tze or I could assume an active role. Being completely objective, I have to say that Chi-Tze has tremendous credentials."

May smiled. "It's certainly sexier than running a trucking or furniture business."

"It's also potentially far more profitable."

"I know. I was partly joking," May said. She turned to Ava. "What do think? Are you prepared to risk a large portion of our capital on Clark Po? Are you prepared to jump into a start-up when we said we wouldn't?"

"I've always assumed there would be risk in whatever we did, and this is a case where the rewards might just justify it. But we do need to get a rough idea of how much money will actually be needed. I agree with Amanda that we need to bring someone like Chi-Tze into the picture, someone who has a better understanding of this kind of business than we do."

"Do you want to call her?" May said to Amanda.

"I'd love to."

"Then do it as soon as you can, and if she's agreeable, get her here as fast you can."

"She will agree."

"You're sure?"

"Positive. And she could get a flight into Shanghai early tomorrow morning."

"So you've already spoken to her."

"I called her this morning before we met for breakfast."

"Are we that predictable?"

"No, I just asked her to be on standby in case she was needed," Amanda said. "I'll email her Gillian's plans as soon as I get back to the hotel, so she can arrive at least partially briefed."

"Amanda, I like initiative, but don't always anticipate I'll go along with you," May said, and then looked out the window as the Huangpu River came into view. "In some ways Gillian's proposal is exactly why I wanted to get into this business. I just wanted to wait until we had our feet firmly on the ground. Nuts-and-bolts businesses may be predictable and deadly boring, but they pay a lot of bills without a lot of stress. I'm not saying that I won't go into something that provides some excitement, but we need to establish parameters. My appetite for financial risk is not unlimited."

"I agree —" Ava began, and then stopped as her words were overtaken by a yawn.

"Jet lag?" Amanda said.

"Afraid so."

"Are you going to be okay for dinner with Xu?" May said.

"I should be able to stay awake that long."

"And Amanda, you'll work with Chi-Tze tonight?"

"Yes."

"Before you do, I think you should call Gillian," Ava said. "We told her we would get back to her tomorrow. I don't like the idea of her spending the evening wondering what we're going to do and then have to call her to say we're bringing in Chi-Tze to look at the numbers."

"I think you're being a bit too sensitive," May said. "We said we would get back to her, and in my mind that isn't necessarily with a decision. Gillian can't think she can make us a business proposal and then expect instant action."

"I suspect it's Clark who has the expectations," Ava said. "Gillian is simply trying to fulfill them."

Traffic was light and the Oriental Pearl Tower was soon in sight. They crossed the Huangpu River and quickly made their way to the Peninsula.

"Dinner is at seven and the restaurant is about a fifteen-minute walk away. What time do you want to meet in the lobby?" May asked.

"Six forty?"

"Perfect," May said as the car stopped in front of the hotel.

"Will you need us for anything?" Ava asked Amanda.

"No, thanks. You can assume that Chi-Tze will be here first thing in the morning. I'll take her directly from the airport to the plant."

"I'm sure it will go well," Ava said, leading the way towards the elevator.

She said goodbye to the other women at the fifth floor and walked to her room. Her intention was to grab a quick shower, change her clothes, and then check her email. She went into the bathroom, undressed, and was just about to step into the shower when the phone rang. "Hello?" she said.

"Did you get flowers as well?" May asked.

"What?"

"There was huge a bouquet of roses on my bed, with a note."

"I haven't been in my bedroom."

"Go now."

Ava carried the cordless phone with her. "What did the note say?"

"I'll tell you after you check your room."

Ava opened the door and gasped. "I don't have roses," she said. "I have red and purple orchids. The entire bed is blanketed with them."

"Is there a note?"

She approached the bed and saw an envelope resting on top of her pillow. She ripped it open. "It says *Apologies for last night. Call me if you have a chance. Xu.*"

"I just got an apology."

Ava stared at the bed, counting the orchids. She stopped at forty. In Canada it would have cost almost a thousand dollars for that many. "I'll phone him and get back to you," she said to May.

She didn't recognize the number on the card and she assumed it was his mobile. He answered at once with a firm "*Wei*" — an Uncle trait.

"It's Ava."

"Welcome to Shanghai."

"The flowers weren't necessary," Ava said. "Even as a kind gesture you went overboard."

"Buying flowers is something I have not done often in my life. I asked one of my men to look after it. From your remark, I assume he went too far."

"He most certainly did."

"Well, I hope the rest of your day was more pleasing."

"Xu, the flowers aren't unpleasant. It's just that receiving flowers is also not something that's happened often in my life. I'm sorry if I sounded ungrateful."

"Not at all. I understand," he said smoothly. "How was your day?"

"We had a business meeting."

"I trust it went well."

"Well enough. How about your crisis?"

"It has been managed."

"Excellent. So we can have dinner with clear minds all around."

"The reason I asked you to call is that I have made a change in the restaurant reservation and I want to make sure it is acceptable to you and May Ling. Instead of the French restaurant, I have reserved one of the private dining rooms at the Whampoa Club for the entire evening. It has a tremendous view of the Bund and the Huangpu River, and the food is superb. The club is also on the Bund, no more than fifteen minutes from your hotel. Whampoa was my initial instinct, but the room did not become available until earlier today."

"I'm sure we'll be satisfied with whatever restaurant you choose."

"Then it's confirmed."

"Will you be alone?"

"Of course. It will be just me, you, and May Ling."

"And do you want to give me some idea of what we'll be discussing?"

"Does it have to be something in particular?"

"No, but from our earlier phone conversations it seems you have something in mind, and I don't want it to be awkward for either May Ling or me."

"If anyone should feel uncomfortable it is me, around two such beautiful and accomplished women."

"Oh god, what a load of shit that is," Ava said, heading for the bathroom.

"Yes and no." He laughed. "I am rarely uncomfortable."

Ava heard real humour in his voice and found herself smiling. "Let me tell May about the change in plans. We'll see you at the restaurant."

May answered her phone on the first ring.

"I just spoke to our man the florist," Ava said. "He's changed the dinner reservation to the Whampoa Club."

"That's great. They have fabulous food at Whampoa. Still the same time?"

"Yes, seven."

"It's exactly the same distance down the Bund from here, so why don't we meet in the lobby as planned."

"See you then."

**THE WHAMPOA CLUB WAS AT NO. 3, THE BUND, JUST** less than a kilometre from the hotel. Under normal circumstances it would be no more than a fifteen-minute walk away, but at that hour of the warm, balmy evening it seemed as if everyone in Shanghai had decided to go for a walk along the river. It took them almost half an hour to walk the distance.

May wore a pale green Chanel suit trimmed in gold. The skirt came to an inch above her knees, and she wore three-inch heels. She drew stares from men and women alike. In black slacks, a white shirt, and black pumps, Ava felt like the hired help.

They walked nearly to the end of the promenade before crossing the street. "The place is actually called 'Three on the Bund,'" May said.

"You've been there before?"

"Giorgio Armani and MCM have stores on the ground floor."

"Ah."

"And I've eaten at the French restaurant Jean Georges,

which is a floor below Whampoa. That's where Xu was going to take us originally."

They stopped in front of Number Three. Ava looked up at the brown stone building and felt a jolt of déjà vu. Its V-shaped façade looked like a ship's prow, six storeys tall and topped with a cupola. "I feel like I'm in Paris," she said.

"I don't know anything about architecture, but I do remember someone mentioning the Renaissance," May said, and then paused. "Is that our man at the front door?"

The sidewalk wasn't as crowded as the promenade, and Ava had a direct view of the door. It was Xu. He was close to six feet and lean, with tightly cropped black hair. He was wearing a black suit, a white shirt, and a black silk tie. He took a long drag on a cigarette, his eyes glancing right and left. Like Uncle, his age was hard to determine; Ava guessed he could be anywhere from his late thirties to late forties. Also like Uncle, he was fine-featured, with a long, thin nose, high, pronounced cheekbones, and a pointed chin.

When he caught sight of the two women, he smiled, threw his cigarette to the ground, and took several steps forward. He reached for Ava, lightly grasped her upper arms, and leaned forward to kiss her on both cheeks. "I am so glad you came," he said. He turned towards May and extended a hand. "And you too, Madam Wong. We met at Uncle's funeral but we had no chance to speak."

"That's the second time today I've been called Madam Wong. Please don't do that again, and don't call me Auntie either. My name is May."

As May and Xu shook hands, the remnants of the day's sun crept from behind a cloud and lit up the front of the building, drenching them in light. Ava saw that Xu's black tie shimmered with subtle hints of red woven into the silk.

"Shall we go in?" he said. "The entrance is around the corner, on the side street. Let me lead the way."

They rode the elevator to the fifth floor. No one spoke, but Ava and May took turns looking at Xu. Every time they did, he looked directly into their eyes and smiled. *His teeth are unusually white for a smoker*, Ava thought, and then remembered that Uncle's had been the same. The direct gaze was another Uncle attribute that Xu seemed to share. Uncle's internal world was filtered through his eyes, and over the years she had learned to read the emotional nuances in them. All she saw in Xu's was frankness.

When the elevator doors opened, they took a few steps forward before Ava stopped. "My god, this is beautiful," she said.

The entrance hall was massive, its hardwood floor leading past a wall made entirely of beige and tan glass panels overlaid with gold. The other wall was painted a sand colour and lined with narrow vertical light fixtures that glowed like green jade. But it was the gigantic crystal chandelier at the far end of the room that captured her attention. The enormous V-shaped light fixture, tapering to a point close to the floor, looked as if it were made from thousands of diamond drop earrings. Ava was so absorbed in its brilliance that she barely noticed the restaurant host on their left.

"It is wonderful to have you back with us, Mr. Xu," he said. "Your room is ready."

"Then we will go right to it."

The host led them through a full restaurant. Ava took in the art deco decor, the red and gold lacquer wall panels, more gilded glass, matching red leather club chairs, and carved hardwood tables with scroll legs that gleamed even in the dim light.

Their room was furnished with a single round table that could have seated ten but had only three chairs — all of them positioned so their occupants had a view of the Bund and the Huangpu River through the floor-to-ceiling windows. The sun was just about to set, its last flickering rays dancing on the river, and just beyond was the purple and green Pearl Tower in Pudong.

Xu took the seat on the far left, leaving May and Ava to sit next to each other. Ava found that strange until she realized that it allowed him to look at both of them while he was speaking.

"I'll send the waiters through immediately," the host said.

"Why don't you order," Ava said to Xu. "You seem to know this restaurant well enough."

"If you will order the wine . . . assuming that you do not want something else."

"Wine?" Ava said to May.

"Yes, and I'll drink white, since I know you like it."

"White is fine with me too," Xu said.

The door to the room opened and two waiters appeared. They both bowed to Xu. "I will take the menu and Ms. Lee will choose the wine," he said, and then turned to the women. "Any food allergies or particular likes or dislikes?"

"We eat everything," Ava said.

He ordered as if he knew the menu by heart. Ava switched her attention to the extensive wine list. When the waiter turned to her, she asked for a French white burgundy.

"Thank you for joining me tonight," Xu said when the waiters had left the room.

"What could be better than a Shanghai meal with a true Shanghainese?" May said.

"I am hardly that. My father was from Wuhan, like you and Uncle. He came here from Hong Kong after I was born."

"I'm told that he also shared Uncle's old business interests — the ones he was involved in before he met Ava."

"I don't think we have to get into that," Ava said.

Xu glanced at May and then stared directly at Ava. "I do not mind. I have no need to make apologies for my father and what he did, or for what I do or have done. Uncle felt exactly the same."

"I wasn't suggesting otherwise."

"No, but there are times when you seem reluctant to acknowledge the life Uncle led before he met you."

"That didn't seem to matter to him, and I don't understand why it should mean so much to you," Ava answered.

"It matters because that life is not what it appears to people outside it."

"And why should we care?"

"Because I have money I want to put to work in your investment company, and I know you will not permit me to do so unless the money is beyond reproach."

She felt Xu's eyes boring into her. *So much for polite, innocuous dinner conversation*, Ava thought.

Before another word could be spoken, the door swung open and a waiter appeared with a bottle of wine. A heavy silence loomed over the table as he went through the uncorking ritual. He made a move to pour wine into Xu's glass but was cut off. "Ms. Lee will be the judge of the wine," Xu said.

It was the last thing she cared about at the moment, but

she sniffed, took a sip, and then rolled it over her tongue. "Wonderful," she said.

As the glasses were being filled, the other waiter emerged with a tray with two platters on it.

"Bird's nest with minced chicken and deep-fried prawns with a wasabi dressing," Xu said.

The waiters apportioned both dishes and then backed out of the room.

"The food smells fantastic," Ava said. "Unfortunately, I can't get my attention past what you just said about wanting to put money into our company."

"I apologize for bringing it up so abruptly," Xu said. "Let us eat, and then we can resume our discussion."

He reached for a prawn with his chopsticks. He severed the head from the body and split the shell. Then he put the prawn into his mouth, separating the meat and spitting out the shell. He chewed slowly.

Ava's eyes never left him. "I don't want to wait. How can your money be beyond reproach?" she said.

"Thank you for asking. I hope you are actually interested in my answer," he said, plucking a prawn from the platter and putting it in May's bowl, then repeating the process for Ava.

"We had, I believe, the beginning of this conversation over the phone while I was still in Toronto," Ava said, ignoring the food.

"We did, and I handled it very badly."

"Given the subject matter, I don't know how else it could have gone."

"There is a history that needs to be understood — the evolution of what my father began many years ago."

"Evolution?"

"That may be a poor word choice. What I am trying to say is that he began to guide the Heaven and Earth Society along the road back to what it had been and was meant to be. It is a challenge I have taken upon myself, using his experience and the wisdom of men such as Uncle."

"Heaven and Earth Society?"

"People refer to us as Triads, but we are not Triad in the common sense. *Triad* is a term invented by the Hong Kong government. They took our symbol, a triangle with the word *hung* in it — a symbol that represents the union of heaven, earth, and man — and affixed that name to it. We think of ourselves as the Hung Society or the Heaven and Earth Society, and it is to the concepts of those societies I am trying to return."

"Ava may know what you're talking about, but I don't," May Ling said.

Xu smiled and then reached for the bottle of wine, which was nestled in an ice bucket. He refilled their glasses and his own. "We should get another bottle, you think?"

"Yes. I may need it," Ava said.

"And we should eat before the food gets cold," he urged.

The door opened and the waiters reappeared, each carrying a tray. On one Ava saw a plate with a steamed fish, and on the other, sliced beef and noodles.

"Steamed *garoupa* with soy sauce, beef tenderloin, and ba bao, a traditional Shanghai noodle dish," Xu said. He looked up at the waiter. "Another bottle of wine, and keep a third one on ice in case we decide to have more."

May took a spoon and fork and began to dissect the fish. Steam rose from it, carrying hints of ginger and soy.

The thinly sliced beef sizzled on a metal plate. Ava could smell garlic, but the paste on top of the meat was green. "What is that coating on the beef?" she asked.

"Pistachios," Xu said.

As May served each of them a generous portion of fish, Ava's interest in Xu and his money offer was finally overtaken by hunger. They ate quietly, working their way through the dishes. When they had put down their chopsticks, Xu pressed a buzzer on the wall. The waiters appeared so quickly that Ava guessed they had been standing right by the door.

"You can remove our plates," Xu said.

"More wine, sir?" one asked.

Xu looked at Ava and May. They both shook their heads. "If we want anything else, I will call for you," he said.

The door closed, and Ava emptied her glass. "Jet lag and wine are not a good combination," she said.

"I am sorry. I forgot about that," he said.

"I'll survive." Ava shrugged. "Now tell me — before we started to eat you said you weren't Triad."

"Not in the strictest sense, not in the Hong Kong fashion. We call ourselves Yan Yee Tong."

"The people's justice group?"

"Yes, that is a reasonably accurate translation."

"But you have to have an affiliation with 14K or Wo or Sun Yee On."

"We are completely independent."

"How is that possible?"

"The gangs you mention are all Hong Kong–based. My father kept our interests tied to Shanghai. Once in a while the others have tried to stick their noses into our business, but we have more than four thousand loyal, active members, and interlopers were quickly discouraged."

"So you have nothing to do with other Triads?"

"Of course we do. We are part of the international infra-structure, and we work with them when businesses inter-sect and mutual interests can be served. But those are loose and flexible arrangements. In fact, our relationships with the Shanghai government and the government in Beijing are far more structured."

May shot a nervous glance at Ava. "That would worry me as much as the Triads," she said to Xu.

"What would?"

"The kind of government ties you're hinting at."

"It is not what you think."

"And what do I think?"

"That our government relationships are greased by bribes, that we corrupt officials."

"Yes."

"Well, in my opinion that would be a stupid, almost sui-cidal thing to do. There may be some short-term benefits, but that is all they would be — short-term. And whatever good that might accrue would be wiped out, and us along with it, if and when the government decided to act. And in this country, as you know better than just about anyone, they always find out, and eventually they act."

"So how do you maintain these relations of yours?"

"We build factories, we own shopping complexes, we employ tens of thousands of people, and we pay our taxes in full. We contribute to the economic well-being of Shanghai and the country as a whole. And we try never to embarrass or bring grief to any level of government or the officials who work there."

"But you're making knockoffs," Ava said. "Are you saying the government condones that?"

"We prefer to describe it as parallel manufacturing."

"A knockoff is a knockoff, no matter how you spin it."

"The government is quite comfortable for now with the term *parallel manufacturing*."

"You aren't serious," Ava said.

"Of course I am," Xu said, reaching for the wine bottle. "Would you like more?"

Both women shook their heads. He poured some wine, took a deep sip, and then refilled the glass.

"I have a factory about sixty kilometres north of here, just outside a town that has a population of twenty thousand and close to three or four villages that among them have another ten thousand residents. There was once a steel mill in the town; it closed five years ago. The villagers used to eke out a living farming, but as the population grew there was not enough arable land to employ everyone. Three years ago a delegation of government officials, farmers, and former steel-mill workers came to Shanghai to meet with me. The meeting was arranged by my man Suen — you both met him in Borneo, did you not?"

"We did."

"He is from the town, and they approached him first. He came to me and I made some phone calls, including several to some senior people in Nanjing, since the district is within their jurisdiction. They made a simple request: could I find a way to employ these local people? Within a year a factory was built. It now has forty-seven hundred workers making cellphones."

"Knockoffs?"

"iPhones."

"Knockoffs."

"Parallel manufacturing."

"What does the government say about that?"

"They now have a happy town and four happy villages. And in Shanghai they do not have to worry about an influx of more unemployed people from the outlying districts putting extra stress on the social and economic structure."

"A very nice arrangement for everyone but Apple," Ava said.

"They will find out eventually," Xu said.

"And then?"

"The government will deny it knew anything about it and shut us down. If Apple is not diligent in monitoring the factory, we might be able to reopen in a few weeks or months. But if they keep a close watch, then we will be out of that business."

"And move on to the next."

"And repeat the cycle, unless we can break the cycle."

"Break it? How is that possible?"

"I mentioned history before. Can I bore you with some?"

"So far, *boring* is not a word I would use to describe this conversation," May said.

Xu smiled. "Thank you for that. I'll try to keep this short."

"Please. I know you're going to get to the point, and I'm curious as to what it is."

"Okay, some history in short form. The societies came into being hundreds of years ago to help overthrow the Qing Dynasty and restore the Ming. After that finally happened, they lost their initial sense of purpose. Some disbanded; others found new reasons to exist and aligned themselves with martial arts associations, labour unions, or trading groups; and some — but not nearly as many as one would think — turned to criminal activity. A few, such as the Shanghai gang my father eventually took over, were some combination of those things. The overwhelming assumption when people hear the word *triad* is that it is synonymous with *criminal*. That is not the case — not historically and not now," he said.

"Xu, in Hong Kong —"

"Yes, Ava, in Hong Kong it is likely true, but here it is not. My father's cousin began Yan Yee Tong as a way to provide protection and assistance for relatives and friends from Wuhan, from Hubei province. He had many relatives, and maybe even more friends. It became a large organization because every relative and every friend saw the benefit of the assistance and protection they would receive, so they brought in their own relatives and friends. I told you earlier that I have more than four thousand members. What I did not tell you is that attached to them are more than forty thousand dependants."

"Workers?"

"Some are, but it is not an inclusive arrangement," he said.

Ava watched Xu take a gulp of wine. A memory of the way Uncle used to consume his food jumped into her mind. She had often thought that the rushed way in which he ate belied the calm exterior he presented to the world. It seemed to her now that Xu was stressed, despite the fact that his face was composed and his words were measured. "What does that mean?" she asked.

"You have heard of the thirty-six oaths?"

"Yes."

"Do you know them?"

"Not well."

"My father's cousin, and then my father, took them to heart. Not every oath had the same weight, but every one that had an impact on their concept of family had special meaning. The first oath says, 'After having entered the Hung gates, I must treat the parents and relatives of my sworn brothers as my own kin.' And another that I have pledged to uphold is 'I will take care of the wives or children of sworn brothers entrusted to my keep.'"

"So that is how you get from four thousand members to forty thousand dependants."

"Exactly. They are obviously not all dependent, but where it is necessary, we educate the children, employ the adults, and take care of the elderly. And those who do not need our help are still part of Yan Yee Tong and loyal to Yan Yee Tong."

"Including some government officials?" May said.

Xu's head flicked sideways and a smile broke out on his face. "Yes."

"That's clever."

"It is practical. We cannot offer the right kind of work to all those we have educated, and it is shameful to let an education go to waste. So it is inevitable that some of our people will work in the government."

"It seems to me that you've created one hell of a business," Ava said. "Why do you need us?"

He lowered his head and Ava saw his mouth tighten. "We are at a crossroads. The present situation, however stable it looks to the outsider, is not sustainable."

"Why?"

"Part of it is our own doing. Years ago my father decided that we should get out of some of the more traditional society businesses. We gave up prostitution, protection money, and most gambling and drug dealing. These did not entirely disappear, of course. At the street level, some of our people had no other way to make a living, and Yan Yee Tong is not dictatorial. So although we guided those members to find other sources of income, not all of them did. But enough did that we can say, without being cynical, that Yan Yee Tong is not in those businesses anymore. For a few years we struggled financially as we made the transition, but eventually we crossed over, and our income stream grew to ten times what we had earned before."

"Parallel manufacturing?" Ava said.

"Yes, primarily that, and over a wide spectrum. We started with clothes and luxury handbags and then moved on to CDs, DVDs, and computer software from companies such as Microsoft, Oracle, Apple, HP — basically any software that was for sale, we could provide at an enormous discount. And now we have moved even further up the high-tech chain by making iPhones, iPads, iPods, and some of the better-quality products from Apple's competitors such as Samsung and Nokia."

"How do you manage — technically, I mean — to do that?"

"We recruit talent and acquire the information we need from universities, other companies, factories."

"When you say companies, do you mean Apple and Samsung manufacturers?"

"Some of them, but mainly those in the component

business. Do you know what the component costs are for an iPhone?"

"Of course not."

"The latest sixteen-gigabyte version contains one hundred and eighty dollars' worth of component parts: nand flash, display, touch screen, processor, camera, battery, and so on. Apple buys those parts from all over the world — Japan, Korea, the U.S., Taiwan, Germany — and brings them to China, where they are assembled. Now guess what the assembly cost in China is for one iPhone."

"I have no idea."

"Less than seven dollars."

"Cheap."

"That is one word for it; another is *exploitation*. I mean, on every phone they are spending close to two hundred dollars outside China and seven here. So what we do — what we have done — is analyze and break down the components and make them all in China. I think Apple makes its parts in various countries for security reasons. We have no need for secrecy and so we have lowered the component cost to sixty-five dollars, with another ten dollars for assembly. So we make an iPhone — and provide more free apps — for a hundred dollars less than Apple."

"By stealing intellectual property."

"By being nimble."

"Where are your markets? Shanghai can't be big enough to absorb all that production."

"The world is our market. We have been selling our products through the Triad network, through groups such as 14K and Sun Yee On. They have distribution channels throughout all of Asia, and into North America and Europe. For us, it made business simple. All we had to be concerned about was production. The rest of it, they looked after."

"But you're still stealing intellectual property," Ava said.

"And that will come to an end," Xu said.

"You're going to stop?"

"When we have to."

"When is that?"

"When the government decides."

"You make them sound like partners."

"They are, in the sense that we can keep making products like iPhones for as long as they condone it. But there will come a day when we will be more of a problem than an asset. China keeps growing, and as it does, it has to become more concerned about the face it presents. It wants to be a world leader, it wants to be respected, and it cannot be if it knowingly violates international trade agreements and ignores intellectual property rights.

"For now, the need to feed, clothe, house, educate, and employ a billion and a half people still trumps the government's desire to be seen as a responsible player in world affairs, but I can see a day, not so far ahead, when the balance will shift. It is my duty as head of Yan Yee Tong to prepare our society for that eventuality. I must forge the path for our next transition."

"Are you so certain that the government will move against you?" Ava asked.

"They know who we are, they know where we are, and they know what we do. We do not hide," he said, and then laughed. "As if we could anyway. In addition to the factories making software and phones, we have a group of plants about a hundred kilometres from here that, combined, employ close to six thousand workers making clothing. Try hiding that."

"But you're sure they'll come after you?"

"Even if they do not, for me to think otherwise and not take precautions would be irresponsible."

"And we're a precaution?"

Xu leaned back in his chair and looked out the window. The brightly lit Bund was even busier than before. People crowded at the wall, taking in the night skyline of Pudong. Suddenly it struck Ava that there were no sidewalk vendors. "There are no salespeople on the Bund," she said.

"The government prohibits them," Xu said.

"When I came here years ago, there were rows of them," May said.

"Then one day the government said, 'You cannot do this anymore,' and the vendors disappeared. It was as if they had never existed," Xu said. "And that will be our fate if we stand still."

No one spoke for a few minutes, but the room seemed full of noise as each of them sifted through the jumble of thoughts that Xu's words had triggered. May Ling put her hands together in front of her face and pushed the backs of her thumbs against her mouth. Ava knew that sign — Xu had her attention.

"You haven't mentioned how much money you want to give us, and you haven't given us a reason why we are the chosen ones," Ava said.

"We have one hundred and fifty million U.S. dollars put aside — all of it properly accounted for and legal in the government's eyes — and sitting in a bank account here in Shanghai. I want to transfer it to your investment company. I want you to put our money to work."

"Good grief," May said.

"It is all that we have that is totally unencumbered. I wish it were more. In a few more months, if business keeps on as it has been, I may be able to give you that much again."

"You misunderstand me," May said. "That is an enormous amount of money."

"As I said, I wish it were more."

May leaned forward, her fists resting on the table. "Why give it to us?"

"You have expertise that we don't have."

"You can buy expertise."

"Not in China, at least not from anyone with the track record of success that you've achieved. And most certainly not from anyone worthy of the trust we need to place in them."

"You don't know me well enough to trust me," May said.

"I know that you have a reputation as a remarkably astute and respected businesswoman."

"That doesn't speak to trust."

"Ava's involvement does. In truth, we would not be having this conversation if she were not a partner in your business. I do not mean to diminish your role, because it is very important, but if Ava were not your partner, there would be nothing for us to discuss."

"Are you always this honest?" May said.

"No, I am not. I am typically selective in what I say and to whom I speak."

"Why are we so privileged as to hear your truth?"

"I need you, and I have decided I can trust you."

"You mean you trust Ava."

"Uncle trusted her more than anyone in his life. That is all I need to know."

"He still casts a very long shadow."

"And I will be in that shadow for as long as I live."

"We all loved and respected Uncle," Ava said. "That doesn't mean we should be business partners."

"Look, I have a problem that I have tried to outline here tonight, and an opportunity that I think you might like if you take the time to think about it."

"So far all you've said is that you have money you want to put into our investment company. We have no idea what terms or conditions accompany it," Ava said.

"Invest the money for us as you see fit and return fifty percent of the profits the money generates."

"Fifty percent sounds like a partnership. We can't partner with you."

"I know. Your company would own one hundred percent. We do not need our name attached to anything."

"So Yan Yee Tong would just hand us one hundred and fifty million dollars?"

"No, the money would come through a company called Xin Fang Fa. We need Yan Yee Tong to be as far removed as possible from the money and any investments — and that is something I imagine you would like as well. We set up Xin Fang Fa by pooling funds from more than thirty different companies, none of which are legally attached to Yan Yee Tong. Sun Fong Fa is a co-operative with more than a thousand members and a board and chairman who are elected. None of them can be identified as having a Yan Yee Tong affiliation unless someone wants to spend a lot of time digging into their lives."

"But someone might want to do that."

"There is always that chance, but I promise you we have

done everything possible to separate the money's origin from its source."

"If the money is clean, why is that necessary?"

"Because in this country things can be too easily undone. If the day comes when the government decides Yan Yee Tong is no longer desirable, it will eradicate us. What was legal or not legal will not matter."

"That's true enough," May said softly.

"All right," Ava said, glancing at May, who was in turn staring at Xu, "assuming the money is clean, what terms would it come with?"

"I told you, we want fifty percent of the profits."

"Plus interest?"

"No interest."

"What if we lost money?"

"There is always risk. We would not give you the money unless we valued your judgement, but things happen, and we are prepared to live with that possibility."

"So fifty percent of any net profits?"

"Yes, and the Xin Fang Fa board would require that you report investment activity on a quarterly basis. Profits from ongoing businesses can be transferred annually, but if you sell a business they would like to get their share of the proceeds as soon as the transaction concludes."

"You would put this in writing?"

"Only if you need it."

"What, you would prefer a handshake?" May said.

"In your world, is everything always sealed with a contract? Did you and your husband build your business using lawyers and accountants? Did Ava and Uncle conduct their business based on written agreements?"

"Of course not."

"So do not look so surprised when I say we do not need a contract. And I do not need your handshake either. Your word is good enough."

Ava saw May start to bristle and stepped in. "Xu, I need to know — did you discuss this plan of yours with Uncle?"

"I did."

"When?"

"We had been talking for a while about finding a way to protect Yan Yee Tong moving forward, but we did not discuss your business until his last trip to Shanghai."

"And this was his idea, that you come to us?"

"No, it is mine. He thought it had possibilities and that it might be worth exploring, but he never suggested that I make this offer."

"Thank you for saying that."

"It is the truth."

"And it's an entirely remarkable offer," May said. "Why should we accept it?"

Xu slid his forefinger over his upper lip. Ava saw sweat gleaming where the finger touched.

"You get an additional one hundred and fifty million dollars in interest-free, strings-free working capital. Whatever it is you want to do, you can do more of it and you can do it faster."

May nodded. "Xu, I don't want to seem impolite, but who would know we had taken your money?"

"As I said, the money is clean. We're not asking you to launder it or do anything illegal. And it will come to you through the co-operative, not from Yan Yee Tong."

"But an outsider's perception could be different, and my nature is to be cautious."

"I understand that. Only a handful of people in my inner circle know, and whoever you choose to tell."

"And if we tell no one?"

"Then it should not go past this table."

"You don't expect an answer right now, do you?" Ava asked.

"No, of course not."

"We need to talk, and I'm not sure how long it will take for us to decide what to do."

"I have waited this long."

"Yes, you have."

"Whatever your decision, I appreciate the time and attention you have given me."

"How do we get in touch with you?" Ava asked.

He reached into his pocket and pulled out a slip of paper. "Here are my private home number and my mobile number. Please try the home number first; if you can't reach me, call the mobile. I am available twenty-fours hours a day."

May rose from the table. "Whatever we decide, this has been a meal I'll never forget. Thank you for your hospitality, and for your honesty."

Xu stood and extended his hand. "It was my pleasure. Hopefully it will not be the last time we have an opportunity to eat together."

Ava pushed back her chair and took a step towards the door. "We'll call you as soon as we've made up our minds."

"Thanks," Xu said, and then turned to May. "I do not mean to be rude, but I would like to speak privately to Ava for a minute."

May looked at Ava, who simply nodded. May left the room, closing the door behind her.

"I hope this was not an unpleasant surprise," Xu said, still standing at his side of the table. "I debated telling you on the phone before you came, but I thought that would be disrespectful towards May. You are equal partners and you had the right to hear my offer for the first time when you were together. I did not want May to think I had gone behind her back, or that you and I were concocting our own plans."

"That was considerate of you."

"It was practical."

Ava drew a deep breath. "Xu, I have no idea what we're going to decide."

"I am not prying or lobbying. I have stated my case and now it is up to the two of you."

"Is that what you wanted to say to me?"

"Only partially. Mainly I want you to know that I was not phoning you in Toronto for any reason other than to build on the friendship that I think we had started, and that regardless of what the decision is, I want to maintain our relationship."

Ava looked across the room at Xu. He hadn't moved from the table. One hand rested on top of it, his gaze fixed on her. She saw nothing but sincerity in his manner and in his eyes. "Yes, I think I would like that too," she said.

"Good. I'll leave here tonight content, knowing that we will be speaking again."

## 10

THEY SAT IN THE HOTEL BAR, MAY LING SIPPING A martini, Ava nursing a glass of soda water.

Xu had walked them to the restaurant entrance and offered to accompany them back to the hotel. They declined his offer and made their way back alone. May tried to talk as they shuffled through the crowd, but the Bund was still jammed with people and the noise level made it impossible to carry on any kind of conversation. It wasn't until they reached the hotel that Ava could hear May without her yelling.

"I need a drink," May said.

"I'll crash if I have one."

"Then just keep me company."

The bar was quiet and they found a table by the window with a view of the Bund. The waiter was there in an instant. May ordered a martini, Ava a glass of soda water.

"That was quite the dinner," May said when he had left.

"Sorry for the surprise. I told you what he was hinting at earlier, but I wasn't prepared for anything like that."

"It was rather unexpected . . . but fascinating all the same."

"Do you mean you would consider it?"

"From a business standpoint it is one hell of a deal. How many times do you get the chance to more than double your working capital with free money?"

"Assuming the money is unencumbered, and assuming that it really is as far removed from Yan Yee Tong as he says."

"I actually don't doubt that, but nothing was as true as when he was talking about the government's ability to undo things that seem done. There isn't a law in this country that can't be changed in a day or — perhaps even worse — ignored for a day."

"That seems like a case for not taking the money, even if it is clean."

"It is a case for being cautious."

"If — and I do mean *if* — we decide to take it, we could set up a separate company outside China and shift the money there. Canada would work," Ava said.

"So then the money would be four times removed from Yan Yee Tong."

"Exactly. And I don't remember Xu saying that the money had to be invested in China. He might have implied it, but he didn't say it."

"The problem is that most of our investment opportunities are here."

"We could ask Amanda to focus on businesses elsewhere."

May shook her head. "To a degree we could, but this is where our expertise and contacts are, and this is where the greatest profits are to be made."

The waiter arrived with their drinks. May took her martini from the tray and raised her glass. "Partners," she said.

"Partners."

"There was another thing I thought of when Xu was outlining his deal," May said. "There are some synergies we can exploit."

"Such as?"

"He mentioned garment factories. If we did the Po deal, we'd have instant, controllable production capacity. And we could turn Suki loose with her expansion plans and maybe, with the co-operative's help, grow her customer base even more."

"It sounds like you want to take the money."

May took the toothpick from her glass and put the first of three olives into her mouth. "It does have some appeal," she said. "But I have to tell you, I don't think this is my decision to make."

"What do you mean?"

May slid the other two olives into her mouth and then looked out onto the Bund as she chewed. "Xu made it plain enough from his side when he said that without you, there would be no thought of doing a deal. This is all about you and him and Uncle."

"There isn't that kind of bond between him and me."

"He saved your life."

"He did that for Uncle."

"Who knows what motivated him?"

"He told me it was because of Uncle."

"He still acted, and without him the end result would not have been the same."

"What's your point?"

"I'm not sure that I have one," May said slowly. "It was just — when Xu was speaking all I could hear was Uncle. And it isn't just the way he dresses, in that black suit and white shirt. I found that he presents himself like Uncle: calm, soft-spoken, every word calculated. With Uncle there was always the understanding that there were layers, hidden depths, to him, and that his words exposed only a fraction of his mindset. That's all — he reminded me of Uncle and I thought, *That can't be a bad thing*. But you have to decide. If you want the deal, I'm in. If you don't, then I'm out. Either way I am entirely comfortable with your decision. The way I look at it, you knew Uncle better than anyone, and I'm guessing you have a very good read on Xu already. You know, Ava, he was bang on when he talked about contracts. You can paper a deal a thousand times over, but in the end it all comes down to trust."

"And do you trust him?"

"Yes, I think I do. But it isn't my judgement that matters here, it's yours. You have to feel comfortable about him."

"May, one of my problems is that when my business with Uncle ended, I saw it as a turning of the page. Xu reminds me of what I left behind. Even talking to him on the phone when I was in Toronto made me feel like I was still partially in that life. I wanted to make a clean break."

"None of us can escape what we have done and how it has helped form us, but I do know you have experienced extremes, and I can understand why you don't want to go back there."

Ava finished her water, closed her eyes, pushed her head back, and rolled her neck. "I might be making too much of this," she said. "I'm tired, I'm jet-lagged, and my head feels like it's filled with mush. Let me sleep on it. We'll talk more in the morning."

"You should go to bed," May said.

Ava slid down from the bar stool. "And that's where I'm headed."

"I'm going to have another martini. My head is full of Suki Chan, the Pos, and Xu. I need to calm it."

Ava took the elevator to the fifth floor, stripped as soon as she got into her room, and then tried to decide between jumping directly into bed or showering. She opted for the shower, thinking it would relax her and help ease her into sleep. Instead it jump-started her system and left her feeling as if she had downed half a dozen energy drinks.

After tossing and turning in bed for fifteen minutes, her mind running in circles, she got up and sat at the desk. She turned on her computer, checked her email, and fired off a billet-doux to Maria. She then accessed an English-language search engine and for half an hour looked at the websites of various designer clothing brands. She was most interested in their histories and was surprised to find that virtually all of them could be traced back to one creative, often eccentric, young designer.

She then shifted to Xu. She searched his name and those of Yan Yee Tong and Sun Fong Fa in English and then in Chinese. There wasn't a single mention in either language. She liked the name Sun Fong Fa. It translated into "new way" in English and showed, if nothing else, that Xu had a sense of irony.

The room was cold and Ava was dressed in only a T-shirt and underwear. When she began to shiver, she turned off the computer and went back to bed. She slipped under the white duvet, turned off all the lights, and then turned on the television. Hong Kong's Jade Channel was airing a soap opera set in the Ming Dynasty. It brought Xu back into her thoughts again. She willed herself to concentrate on the show. She watched for ten minutes, or an hour — she had no idea. It was a mindless farce but it distracted her, and her mind was calm when she hit the off button on the remote and finally fell asleep.

Her father visited her again in a dream, but this time in a different setting and with a different emotional pull. Rather than just the two of them trying to connect in a hotel or catch a flight, her father was in a restaurant, sitting at a round table surrounded by ten Chinese women. Ava could see them from all the way across the dining room, where she was standing by herself. They were eating and the women were chatting as the lazy Susan spun a series of dishes from chopstick to chopstick. Her father was laughing, and the women seemed to be revelling in his attention. A few of them looked younger than Ava, two could have been in their forties, and the rest were around Ava's age. They were all well dressed and there wasn't a wrist or a throat that was unadorned. Even from a distance she could see green and white jade, platinum, and the rich glow of twenty-one karat gold.

The restaurant was full, but there was an empty seat at her father's table. Ava walked towards it feeling self-conscious and nervous. *I have a right to be here*, she told herself. When she got close to the table, the overhead lights suddenly dimmed.

"Daddy, it's me, Ava," she said, smiling.

He peered at her, the women's eyes following his.

"I don't know any Ava," he said.

"And no one calls him Daddy!" one of the women shouted.

Ava moved closer, thinking that perhaps he couldn't see

her properly in the weak light. "I don't think that's very funny," she said.

He shrugged and turned his head away. The women did the same. The lazy Susan began to circle again, chopsticks plucking food from dishes. Ava felt as if she were watching them through a one-way mirror, able to see but not to be seen.

"Don't let him upset you," a voice said.

She froze.

"He loves everyone in turn, and no one for very long."

He was sitting off to the left, in a green leather armchair pressed against a wall. Beside him was his ashtray stand. He had a lit cigarette in his hand, the smoke curling around his shadowed face. But she knew the voice.

"Why does he do these things to me?" she said.

He crossed his legs and she saw that his feet barely touched the ground. He looked like a child being swallowed up by the chair. The smoke cleared and she could make out his black suit, the white shirt buttoned to the collar, the bottom half of his face. She searched for his eyes but they were lost in shadow.

"He moves from life to life. There is no malice in it, just practicality," Uncle said.

She tried to step towards the chair but couldn't move her feet. "Why are you here?" she asked.

"I miss you."

"I miss you too."

"Don't cry."

She felt a tear trickle down her cheek and her hand shot up to intercept it. "I'm not."

"I also need to talk to you."

"About what?"

"Xu."

"Did he send you?"

"No, he would never ask that of me. And if he had I would have thought so little of him that I would never speak to him again."

"He reminds me of you. Not entirely, but a bit."

He butted out the cigarette in the ashtray, reached into his jacket pocket for his pack, took out a fresh stick, and lit it with a long wooden match. His face glowed in the phosphorus light, the skin taut and unlined, his lips a bit redder than usual. He blew on the match and was plunged into deeper darkness.

"There were rumours that he is my son. Physically we have some resemblance and we share some speech patterns, and he adopted my manner of dress, but the rumours are not true. I am close to him all the same. His father was a friend and a trusted colleague for many years, and after he died I inherited some responsibility for Xu. I did not mind. It made me feel young and purposeful again."

"He seems calm on the surface, like you, but I sense there is turmoil raging inside."

"He has chosen a difficult path, and there are times when he does not think it is the correct one. There are times when he doubts himself."

"You know what he wants of me?"

"Yes."

"And the money is only part of it?"

"You are as beautiful as ever."

"Uncle!"

"And as perceptive."

"Tell me what he wants."

"He needs you."

"That isn't an answer."

"I don't know what more I can say."

"Uncle, please."

"You must talk to him."

"I don't know if I want to," she said.

He took a deep drag on his cigarette. When he exhaled, his face disappeared in the smoke.

"Uncle!" she shouted. Her vision became cloudy and she heard her own voice, the word *Uncle* still on her tongue.

She was sitting upright in her bed at the Peninsula. Across the room, by itself in a corner, was a green leather chair. She sniffed the air. There was a hint of cigarette smoke.

## 11

AVA WOKE AT JUST PAST SEVEN. A THIN STREAM OF morning light had escaped around the edge of the curtains and found her eyes. She burrowed into the pillows but couldn't get back to sleep.

She sat up and swung her legs over the side of the bed. She was still groggy from sleep, jet lag, and wine. Her eyes fell on the green leather chair in the corner, and a sense of loss washed over her. It had been there all the time, she knew. Since Uncle's death she had been carrying around a tight knot in her belly. Now it felt as if the knot had come undone, and whatever it was holding together had been unleashed and was free to course through her body. She blinked as tears began to fall. She wrapped her arms around her chest and shuddered, filling the room with halting, gulping sobs.

At seven thirty the alarm sounded. She was still in bed. The tears had stopped and the ache in her belly had eased. She slid out of bed and went to the window, pulled open the curtains, and looked out onto the garden and the creek. The world was going about its business as it always did, and now she needed to look after hers.

Ava made coffee and sat at the desk, then turned on the computer and checked her emails. A love note from Maria made her smile. She pushed the chair back from the desk, retrieved her notebook from her bag, and opened it to a fresh page. Across the top she wrote *Xu* and in point form summarized the offer he was making. Then she wrote *Pro* on the left side of the page and *Con* on the right. When she was finished, the right side of the paper contained only one word: Triad. She picked up the room phone and dialled May's extension.

"Yes," May said.

"We should do the deal with Xu," Ava said.

"Just like that?"

"Yes."

"What happened?"

"You told me it was my decision. Well, I've made it."

"No doubts at all?"

"Why do you ask? Are you having second thoughts?"

"Not at all. It's just that last night you seemed so tentative."

"My head is clearer this morning. Xu wants to give us the money, so let's take it, let's use it."

"I agree."

"We can use it to fund Suki's expansion."

"Turning Suki loose could chew up a lot of Xu's money."

"As long as we have enough left for the Pos, I don't mind."

"Speaking of which, I just got off the phone with Amanda. Chi-Tze is arriving right about now. Amanda is already at the airport to meet her and will take her directly to the factory."

"I'm glad Chi-Tze is here, but I don't want her to complicate the Po deal. Unless there's something that screams,

'Don't do it,' I want to go into business with them."

"You certainly are a risk-taker this morning."

"I don't think investing in Suki and the Pos is a risk. Do you?"

"No, actually, I don't."

"So please tell Chi-Tze to work as quickly as possible. Let's get this done in the next few days."

"I'll talk to Amanda and I'll give Suki a call as soon as I get off the phone with you. She'll be ecstatic."

"Our profit-sharing structure with her will have to change with this new insertion of capital. The additional money will dilute everyone's percentage."

"I'll get the accountants to put together a spreadsheet so the share structure is completely transparent and traceable."

"But no mention of Xu."

"Of course not."

"I'll have to contact him," Ava said. "Where do you want him to transfer the money?"

"We have two bank accounts for Three Sisters: one in Hong Kong, the other in Wuhan. We funded Suki and the Borneo business from Wuhan, so until we set up other banking arrangements I think we should move Xu's money there. We'll use the Hong Kong account for the Pos once we finalize the amount we'll be investing in their business."

"I'll give Xu the information he needs to do the transfer."

"When you do, mention the possibility of synergy. The clothing factories interest me, and if he doesn't have his own warehousing and distribution network set up, maybe he can arrange to throw some additional business to Suki."

"May, maybe we should wait until we actually have the money and Chi-Tze is finished and we know for sure that

Suki will be okay with the decrease in her profit-sharing percentage."

"Back to being cautious?"

"It's my nature and I can't be any different. You know that once I make a decision I commit to it completely, regardless of the possibility of a negative result, but I hate creating expectations. Once we know that Suki is in agreement and that we're going ahead with the Po deal, then we'll talk synergy."

"You're right, of course. I'm just a touch excited by all this."

"Me too. Now let me call Xu."

"When?"

"As soon as we hang up."

"And I'll phone the girls. Amanda and Chi-Tze can handle the Pos, but I'll have to sit down with Suki. Do you want to join me?"

"No, you and she have a great relationship. It should be easier if you're one-on-one."

"Like you and Xu."

"What do you mean?"

"Well, after you left the bar I thought about our dinner with him. It seemed to me that his sole interest was in how you were reacting to his proposal."

"I didn't get that feeling."

"For someone who's as sharp as you are at reading other people, you can be completely oblivious to the effect you have on them. He was fixated on you. His eyes hardly left you."

Ava felt her face flush. "He knows I'm a lesbian," she said.

"The attraction doesn't have to be sexual. Look at you and me."

"I wish you hadn't said that. I mean about Xu, not us."

"What does it change?"

"I need this to be just about business," Ava said.

"And so far that's all it's been. There's no reason we can't keep it that way."

"Uncle didn't come to your room last night," Ava said under her breath.

"What are you mumbling?"

"Nothing."

"You'll call him?"

"Right away."

"I have to say I have a very good feeling about this."

Ava looked at her notebook and her list of pros and cons. The word *triad* suddenly seemed more ominous. "Me too," she said.

## 12

AVA SHOWERED, DRESSED, DOWNED ANOTHER COF-
fee, and then looked through her bag and found the card
Xu had given her the night before. She dialled his home
number.

"*Wei*," he answered.

"I hope it isn't too early for me to call," she said.

"Not at all. I have been up for a while."

"May and I just finished talking about your offer."

"Yes?"

"We've reached a decision —"

"That is either wonderful or dreadful," he interrupted.
"But whichever it is, I do not feel comfortable speaking
about it over the phone."

"What do you suggest?"

"Have you had breakfast?"

"No."

"Then why not join me?"

"May has other plans."

"We do not need May."

"I'm not sure that's a great idea."

"*Mei mei*, I would like you to see my home, and my house-keeper can make us breakfast."

"I'm not your little sister."

"No, but you are the closest thing I have to one. Besides, I think you might like my house. It is in the French Concession, not too far from you. Have you been to the French Concession?"

"No."

"Then you must come. It is like no other part of Shanghai, like no other part of China."

He spoke in the matter-of-fact way she had come to associate with him, and she felt slightly foolish for having let May's opinion colour her own view of him. "Is it within walking distance?"

"Yes, but it is a complicated route that has many twists and turns through small streets. I will send my driver for you. He will be in a silver Mercedes."

"Okay, tell him I'll be at the front of the hotel in half an hour," Ava said. "I'll be wearing a black T-shirt and Adidas training pants."

"I am sure he will find you. Now, the housekeeper has a pot of congee on the stove. Will that do?"

"That's perfect."

"See you then."

Ava hung up and pushed her chair back from the desk. So far in their relationship, it seemed to her she had done just about everything Xu wanted. She would have to draw some lines, although to create boundaries around what she wasn't exactly sure.

She went into the bathroom and looked at herself in the mirror. Her hair was pulled back and secured with her favourite ivory chignon pin. She removed the pin and tied up her hair with a simple elastic. She slipped on a black T-shirt and the Adidas pants and then pushed her sockless feet into her running shoes.

She sat at the desk and looked through her computer files for the Wuhan bank account number. She recorded it in her notebook and then on a piece of hotel stationery that she would leave with Xu. She put the notebook and the paper into her Chanel bag and then called May.

"I'm meeting him for breakfast," she said.

"How did he react to our decision?"

"He didn't want me to talk about it over the phone. That's why we're having breakfast."

"That's cautious. But given his line of work, I guess it's also prudent."

"He's sending a car for me. I have no idea how long I'll be there."

"There's no rush. I've spoken to Suki and set up a meeting. I imagine I'll be with her for most of the day. We can catch up later."

The hotel lobby was crowded with a lineup waiting to get into the coffee shop. Ava circled the line and was halfway towards the front entrance when she heard her name being called. She turned and saw Suen sitting next to the fireplace in one of the red velvet chairs. He looked enormous squeezed into it.

"Hi. So we meet again," she said.

"Under much nicer circumstances," he said, putting his hands on the chair's arms and pushing himself up. He smiled and walked towards her with his hand extended. He was wearing grey slacks and a sky-blue golf shirt; like all of Xu's people that she had met, he had no visible tattoos. When she took his hand, he bowed his head ever so slightly — a subtle sign of respect.

"Are you my driver?"

"No, he's outside in the car."

"Both of you didn't have to come."

"Xu wanted you to see a familiar face."

They started towards the entrance. Ava could feel eyes on them, and she knew that Suen was the attraction. There couldn't be many men in Shanghai larger than him. He was at least six foot six and had to weigh close to three hundred pounds, she guessed, with arms that were thicker than her thighs.

The driver, in black slacks and a white golf shirt, stood by the rear passenger door of a Mercedes S-Class. He opened the door and stood to one side. Ava climbed in and slid across to the other side, expecting Suen to join her. Instead he tipped the doorman with what looked like two one hundred–renminbi notes and walked around the car to the front passenger seat.

The car pulled away from the hotel, drove down the Bund, and turned right, then right again. Ava almost immediately lost her sense of place. At one point the car travelled along Huaihai Road, a major boulevard in the Concession, but it veered off again, cutting through a series of streets and lanes. Neither of the men spoke, so Ava was able to concentrate on the passing neighbourhoods. The Concession, she knew, was more than 150 years old, but even after passing through French, Chinese, Japanese, and now Chinese control, the area had managed to retain some of its original charm. There were the inevitable high-rise condos and office buildings, but low-rise buildings predominated, with rows of boutiques, restaurants, and antique shops inter-mingled with street-vendor carts and stalls. The tree-lined smaller streets were lined by a mixture of English Tudor and French colonial houses, Spanish-style villas, and rows of bungalows hidden behind stone walls and iron gates.

At the end of one of the small streets the car paused in front of a fruit stall. Suen raised his index finger in the direction of the vendor. The man nodded, Suen nodded back, and the car turned left into a narrow laneway that threatened to scrape the paint off both sides of the Mercedes. Three-metre-high stone walls were broken only by the occasional iron gate. They drove for about a hundred metres — almost to the end of the lane — before the car stopped just in front of a gate. The driver squeezed out of the car, punched a code into the security system, and the gate swung open. Then he turned and looked towards the opposite end of the lane. Ava saw another fruit stall positioned there. That vendor was looking at the car and nodding his head.

The car pulled into a paved courtyard that had room for two or three more vehicles. On her left was a Japanese-style garden with a pond fed by three small waterfalls. The house looked like an English country bungalow, with red-brick walls, a red tiled roof, a large oak door with a brass knocker, and one immense leaded window with wavy glass. It was hardly the kind of place she had envisioned him living in.

The door opened and Xu stepped into the courtyard. He was wearing black slacks and a white shirt unbuttoned at the neck.

"Welcome," he said.

"This is surprising," Ava said.

"My house?"

"The entire neighbourhood."

"If you have the time, you should take a tour. Within walking distance are the former homes of Sun Yat-sen, Soong Ching-ling, and Zhou Enlai. They are museums now, but you can sense that they were really lived in."

"How long have you lived here?"

"Ten years. I needed a place where I could have privacy."

"Is that why you have lookouts at the ends of the lane?" she asked, thinking of the fruit vendors.

"And two-and-a-half-metre walls all around the house that are topped with a metre of electrified razor wire."

"Is all that necessary?"

"Not so far," he said with a smile. "Now, please come in."

Xu's home went from English-style cottage on the outside to classical Chinese decor on the inside. The living room was furnished with carved wooden benches and chairs that had thin, flat seat cushions. An old tea chest doubled as a coffee table, two corners were occupied by stone lions, and the walls were decorated with paintings of rushing waterfalls, rice paddies, and dragons.

"*Mei li de nu ren*," a voice said. Ava saw a slight, small woman with grey hair standing in the doorway.

"This is Auntie Grace. She was my father's housekeeper and now she is mine," Xu said. "Auntie, this is Ava Lee, the woman you heard Uncle Chow speak of."

"He said you were pretty. He didn't lie," Auntie Grace said.

"He wasn't always objective where I was concerned."

The woman waved her hand dismissively. "You need to learn how to accept a compliment."

"Yes, Auntie, you may be right," Ava said.

"Speaking of compliments, I have to say that Auntie Grace makes the finest congee in Shanghai," Xu said.

"And it's waiting for you," she said, turning and leading them to the kitchen.

Ava was startled by its plainness. The appliances looked as if they were twenty years old. The white-tiled floor was stained and chipped, and a folding table — the kind brought out for a game of mah-jong — had been set up in a corner with two folding chairs. Xu guided her to one of the chairs. As soon as they sat, Auntie Grace placed two big, steaming bowls of the boiled rice porridge in front of them. Between Xu and Ava she placed smaller plates of fried dough, salted duck eggs, bamboo shoots, lettuce, and pickled tofu, a bottle of soy sauce, and a shaker of white pepper.

"I ate breakfast with Uncle many mornings in Tsim Sha Tsui," Ava said. "He loved congee, especially with duck eggs . . . though at the end all he could manage was the porridge. Did he try yours, Auntie Grace?"

"Once. He said it was the best he'd ever tasted," she said, and then chuckled in disbelief.

"Now who can't take a compliment?" Ava said as she shook white pepper into her bowl.

Xu poured tea into both of their cups, and Ava tapped her middle finger on the table in thanks. "I do not think I can eat until I know what your decision is," he said.

Ava had a stick of fried bread in her hand, ready to dip into the congee. She paused, holding it in midair. "We're going to take your money," she said.

"Just like that?"

"Yes. Unless your terms have changed since last night."

"They have not."

"Then after breakfast I'll give you our banking information and you can make the transfer."

"That is wonderful."

"To be fair, you may not say that when you see one of the investments we're thinking of making with the money. It's quite speculative."

"You mean when the co-operative sees?"

"Sure."

"That sounds like it could be fun."

Ava smiled. "Actually, it might be."

Xu raised his teacup. "To an exciting new venture."

"Yes," Ava said, raising hers.

They ate silently, Ava staying with plain congee and bread while Xu ate duck eggs, tofu, and bamboo shoots. The moment her bowl was almost empty, Auntie Grace was at her side. "More?"

"Yes, just a little," Ava said.

"Not for me," Xu said, pushing his chair back from the table. "I need a cigarette. But even here in my own house I have to go outside, because Auntie disapproves. Join me in the garden when you are finished."

Ava watched Xu walk through the living room and out the front door. He held himself erect, almost stiffly.

"He was very pleased when you agreed to come for breakfast," Auntie said, her eyes glittering.

"I'm not his girlfriend, you know, and there isn't any chance of my becoming one. We're going to be business partners, and that's all."

"He has a girlfriend — several, actually. They come and go as he needs them. I hear them in his room making noise.

Sometimes they stay for breakfast, but I don't mind as long as they're dressed properly. More than once I've had a girl sitting in your chair without any underwear on," Auntie Grace sighed and shook her head.

"I don't need to know those things," Ava said.

"It doesn't matter to me, and I know it won't matter to him that you do."

"And why is that?"

"Because I know you like women."

"How do you know that?"

"He told me."

"And why would he do that?"

"When he said you were coming for breakfast, he told me about who you are. I mean, I already knew things about you from Uncle, but nothing that private."

"So tell me, Auntie, what motivated Xu to share that information with you?"

"He wanted me to understand that you aren't like the others, that you are someone I have to respect as much as I respect him. He said he hoped you would be in his life for a long time, but that I shouldn't start dreaming about children because you are a lesbian."

"I don't know whether I feel pleased or offended by that."

"Please don't tell him I told you."

"Why not?"

The older woman looked towards the living room, and Ava turned to see if Xu was there. He wasn't. Still, Auntie lowered her voice as she said, "He doesn't share his thoughts very often, or very easily. I wouldn't want him to think I repeat what he says."

"I won't say a word."

"Thank you. And now maybe you should join him in the garden. He likes to go there in the morning, while the air is still fresh."

The car was still in the courtyard, the driver seated behind the wheel. Suen was standing at the entrance to the yard, looking both ways down the lane. Xu sat by the pond on a wooden chair. An empty one was next to it.

"Ava, come," he said, pointing to the seat.

She walked towards him, then stopped short, looking down into the pond. Four giant goldfish were snapping at food pellets that dotted the water's surface.

"My horoscope for this year said that fish will bring me luck but that I need an even number of them," Xu said.

"I wouldn't have thought of you as superstitious."

"Why tempt fate, especially when it costs so little to keep it appeased?"

Ava reached into her bag and took out the paper with the Wuhan banking information. "Here — this is where the money should be transferred."

"I will look after it today. Now please sit."

The empty chair was directly across from Xu. She turned it slightly so she could watch the fish.

"I was thinking about Fanling, about Uncle's funeral," he said.

"It was a wonderful tribute to him that so many came."

"That is true, and you earned tremendous respect for the way you organized it and for how you conducted yourself. The most senior Triads were particularly pleased when you took time at the funeral dinner to thank them individually for coming, and for their contributions. Not everyone is willing to acknowledge them so publicly."

"I'm not naive enough to think it really meant that much to them."

"No, perhaps not," Xu said, staring at her. "But maybe Auntie is right, and you do need to learn how to accept a compliment."

Ava avoided his eyes. "I sense that you're trying to make a point that has nothing to do with my modesty."

He lit a cigarette, inhaled deeply, and turned his head to blow the smoke away from her. "Do you remember the short conversation we had in Fanling, while we were walking back from the cemetery?"

"Only vaguely. I was quite caught up in grief."

"I see. I was hoping I would not have to explain myself quite so thoroughly again."

"Sorry."

"No matter. It is important enough to bear repeating."

"If this has to do with business, I have to say I would prefer that May Ling also hear what you have to say."

"It is a different business."

"I have only one business."

He inhaled, and this time the smoke swirled around their heads. "In Fanling I started to tell you that I am engaged in a project that is very complicated and has far-reaching implications, some of which could be dangerous. Well, it has become more complicated since Fanling."

"And dangerous?"

"I think so."

"What is this project?"

"I want to become chairman of all the Triad societies," he said. His face was impassive. Then his hand went to his mouth and the cigarette slid between his lips. She saw traces of dried saliva in the corners of his mouth. Was he nervous?

"I would hardly call that a project."

"Call it what you want."

"And Uncle was involved in this plan?"

"The idea was his. I began to warm to it only after several months of talking and thinking."

"Uncle told me about his life in Wuhan and how he came to Hong Kong, but he never spoke to me in any detail about his Triad years. I did hear him referred to as a Dragon Head, and Sonny once mentioned that Uncle had been chairman of the societies for consecutive terms. That's the extent of my knowledge, so I'm not sure what I could possibly contribute to any discussion about Triads or the chairmanship."

"Yes, Uncle was a Dragon Head or Mountain Master or Mountain Lord or whatever title you want to use for the gang leader . . . we still cling to those old names. He started out as a forty-niner — a regular gang member — and worked his way up. He was a White Paper Fan — an administrator — for a while, and then he was a Vanguard and actually ran operations. He obviously excelled, because he was quite young when he became a Dragon Head."

"Those titles mean nothing to me."

"There is no reason why they should. Did Sonny say anything other than that Uncle was chairman?"

"He said that during Uncle's terms the gangs were at peace with one another. When his last term ended, infighting erupted again."

"And that caused him considerable pain."

"Why were they fighting among themselves?"

"There are eighteen major gangs in Asia. Some are concentrated in and control one city, such as Yan Yee Tong in Shanghai and Li's gang in Guangzhou. Some cities, like Hong Kong, are split among several gangs. Then there are gangs that have branches or affiliations all over Asia and in Europe and North America. When you add them up, there are about one hundred different groups. It is a very large, complex structure without any real central core. Disputes are inevitable, in the same way that regular businesses go at each other over sales territories and market share."

"If it's normal behaviour, why worry about it?"

He tossed the cigarette butt into the pond. One of the fish swam to it and then left it to float. "The Triads cannot keep following that path."

"This sounds like the discussion we had last night."

"Taken to the next level, and then past it."

"If you secure a future for Yan Yee Tong, why should you care about anyone else?"

"Because we cannot be separated quite so easily from the rest of that world. I spoke about the government and its ability to shut us down whenever it chooses. Well, right now we have less to fear from the government than we do from our fellow Triads. In fact, the same is true for every society — we spend more time defending ourselves from our brothers than we do from the police or the authorities. Everyone wants to expand their business, and the easiest way to do that is to grab someone else's. Sometimes there are direct attacks — they have tried to kill some of my people, and the plant where we make the iPhones has been bombed and the workers threatened.

"Other times they are more subtle. I had a phone call

from one of the Hong Kong gangs wanting to know if they could invest in the factory, offering me in exchange secure and guaranteed access to their markets. I already sell into those markets, so what they were really doing was threatening to cut me out of them. I declined, because the moment I let them in they would learn the business and then copy it and cannibalize it. They went away unhappy but I kept the market, because they need my products and because they have not yet been able to put us out of business."

"The danger of making knockoffs."

He smiled. "I do see the irony, of course, but if things keep going the way they are, I know that eventually we will hurt each other's businesses, and that can only lead to more violence among the gangs. And when inter-society conflict becomes a visible public menace, we will give the authorities no other choice but to come after us."

"You make it sound as if the societies are determined to self-destruct."

"They do not think about it that way, but then they rarely think much past next week. That is the problem — this intense focus they have on the now instead of trying to create a structure that will be sustainable into the future."

"And you're the man who can lead them into the future?"

"Maybe, maybe not, but I am prepared to try."

"For reasons . . ."

"That are primarily in my own self-interest."

"Yes, it does sound that way to me."

"That does not mean that the end result cannot benefit everyone."

They heard a commotion in the laneway, the sounds of men yelling. Ava looked towards the gate and saw that

Suen had moved out into the lane. He stood with his legs far apart, his shoulders squared, as if ready for a challenge. The noise stilled. Suen turned and walked back to the gate without looking in Xu's direction.

"I think I should go back to the hotel," Ava said.

"I am going to run for chairman," Xu said.

"So you've said."

"The election will be in six days."

"Good luck."

"It is rather fortunate — or maybe the right word is *fortuitous* — that you are in Shanghai right now. It gives me an opportunity to discuss it with you."

"I don't see how I could contribute anything useful."

"Let me be the judge of that," he said, taking a cigarette from the package.

He bent at the waist and leaned towards Ava, his head down, the unlit cigarette held between his fingers like a small spear. All she could see was the top of his head, but then it rose and his eyes caught hers. For a second she had a memory of the picture she had placed by Uncle's coffin: him as a young man sitting in a chair with his legs crossed, an unlit cigarette dangling between his fingers and his eyes locked onto whoever was taking the photo.

"I owe you my life," Ava said.

"No," he said, shaking his head. "I told you in Fanling that I sent my men to Borneo to rescue you for reasons that were incidental to your situation. Because of that I will not accept any obligation on your part."

"You said you did it for Uncle, and he wanted it done for me, and in that there is a connection that I can't deny."

"Yes, I did it for Uncle, but equally true is that I needed

to send a message to my brothers in places such as Hong Kong and Guangzhou. You were taken only a few weeks after the bomb went off at my factory. There was a suspicion, I heard through my colleagues, that I was not tough enough to safeguard my interests. The bomb was a test, and I knew others would be coming. I did not want to go to war, but I had to send them a message that I am entirely capable of doing whatever is necessary to protect myself. That idiot Wan in Borneo gave me the chance."

"I do remember you telling me that in Fanling."

"To get you back, all I had to do was make a phone call. Instead I put Suen and Lop, who is my Red Pole — do you know what that is?"

"Unfortunately I do. I had a run-in with one in Macau. He was an enforcer, what Uncle called 'the sharp end of the stick.'"

"That is accurate, although I prefer to think of Lop as my minister of defence. Anyway, I put him and Suen and twenty of my men on a private jet and sent them to Kota Kinabalu with instructions to destroy Wan's gang. We killed twelve of them. Wan had no formal alliances with any of the Hong Kong or mainland gangs, and only a slight attachment to one in Kuala Lumpur. Before my men left Shanghai, I called Kuala Lumpur and told the Dragon Head there what I planned to do. I told him not to warn Wan and not to interfere in any way or I would send another plane to KL.

"When we were finished in Kinabalu, I called him and thanked him for his neutrality. He asked me why we had to kill so many men. I told him that you were Uncle's granddaughter and that we were related almost by blood. I told him that this was how I would react every time anyone or anything close to me was threatened. I knew the Dragon Head belonged to the 14K gang and that he would talk to his 14K colleagues in Hong Kong. That is when the harassment stopped. And that is when the friendly phone calls started."

"People doing the right things for the wrong reasons, and on more levels than one," Ava said.

"Yes, Uncle's favourite saying, and one of the truest things I have ever heard. It is my maxim."

"And mine."

"So now we are bound by Uncle and by a philosophy. Does this mean you will make yourself available to me?"

"Again, I'm not sure how I could be of help, and —"

"I said let me be the judge of that."

"But I know nothing about this election, and my understanding from Uncle is that the chairmanship is mainly an honorary position."

"*Mainly* is the key word. There is power attached to it, but it can be used only in certain circumstances. I find myself on the edge of some of those circumstances."

"How does the vote work?"

"The heads of the eighteen major gangs in Asia will meet in Hong Kong to vote for the chairman. Each gang has one vote and every vote is equal. To succeed, I need a simple majority. Right now I have one opponent: Li, from Guangzhou. Li is no friend of mine, but that aside, he sees himself as our elder statesman and thinks the chairmanship should be his by right. The vote will be close — how close I'm not exactly sure; my colleagues tend to be noncommittal. They whisper words of encouragement without actually telling me how they are going to vote. So I am treating it as if I have to find nine more votes to add to mine."

"Why are you a better man for the position than Li?"

The question seemed to catch Xu off guard. Ava was sure that was because it came from her, not because he didn't have an answer.

"Li is yesterday's man. His only interest is in supporting the status quo, and his definition of that is keeping the old businesses intact and letting gangs grab what they can from each other," he said slowly. "It was Uncle's opinion that the position is what each man brings to it. If I win the vote, it will be because I have convinced the others that the vision I have for the future is the correct one. It will then fall on me to implement that vision, and I will have ready-made allies to support me."

"And what is this vision?"

"We must act in a unified way. We need to develop businesses that governments will . . . if not support, then at least be able to ignore. It is the best chance we have to make the future sustainable for our people."

"And you think I have a role in this?"

"I need an objective set of ears, a subtle mind, and an honest tongue."

Ava grimaced in disbelief. "Your flattery is overwhelming," she said.

Xu smiled and reached out to Ava, his hand resting lightly on her knee. "In all seriousness, I may need help to bring these men to my side. Uncle said he knew no one who could read people as well as you, and that once you had some understanding of them, you could find the means to persuade them to do as you wanted. Let me consult with you, let me use your talents."

Ava closed her eyes and tilted her head back. *How real is any of this?* she thought. "Why should I be the recipient of so much trust? You have men here who would die for you," she said.

He turned his head. "It is true that I have men like Suen and Lop who are completely loyal, but they have no sense of strategy, no ability to negotiate without a gun in their hands, no subtlety. I do have men who are smarter, but their primary loyalty is to themselves and their own ambitions."

Ava looked at him. His head was turned to one side, his eyes averted and slightly hooded. He looked like a man in pain.

"I will take your phone calls and I will listen to whatever you want to discuss, but beyond that I can't make any promises."

"Thank you. I could not ask for — and did not expect — anything more."

Ava stood. "I feel like going for a walk. I need to clear my head, and it would be a shame to be here and not see some of the neighbourhood."

"You will need a map. Suen has one he can give you."

"Thanks."

"Before you go, there is one more thing I would like to say. I was reluctant to mention it until we had concluded our discussion about the chairmanship."

"Why?"

"It might have coloured your response."

"Again, why?"

Xu rose to his feet, took a step towards Ava, and reached for her hand. "For as long as I knew Uncle, he was the calmest and the most collected man in any situation. I saw him truly emotional only twice. The last time was when you were kidnapped in Borneo," he said.

"And the first time?"

"When he urged me to run for the chairmanship."

"Why would that generate so much emotion?"

Xu squeezed her hand gently. "He felt he had failed as chairman. He saw the future then the same way I see it now, but he was not able to bring about change. I told him that the economics of those times were different and that back then there was no compelling reason for the gangs to change. He saw my logic but it did not seem to ease the depth of his regrets. He said that the Triads had been the only way for him and men like my father to escape poverty, and like my father he saw it as a brotherhood, as his family. He wanted to protect it. He wanted to ensure that it had a future. He passed that obligation on to me."

"I understand," Ava said softly.

"Ava, with your help, I am determined to fulfill his legacy."

## 13

AVA LEFT XU'S HOUSE ON FOOT, WITH A MAP IN HER pocket on which Suen had drawn the route back to her hotel. He had argued with her quite forcibly when she said she wanted to walk, but she was even more insistent.

Her desire to clear her head was now more intense than when she had first told Xu she needed to take a walk. His parting words had shaken her. In her mind, Uncle was forever calm and collected. Even when she confronted him in hospital and he confessed to the existence of cancer and his imminent death, he had done so in the most matter-of-fact manner. The thought of his being overcome by emotion was hard for her to grasp.

But she didn't doubt Xu. His words had triggered a memory of Sonny telling her how Uncle's strength and composure had left him when he found out she had been kidnapped and would almost certainly die. She was glad she hadn't seen him so vulnerable. She wanted to think of him as the wise, cool, and consoling man who had come to her in her dream the night before, the one who had nudged her to work with Xu. He had done that, hadn't he? She recalled the last fragment of the dream, when Uncle had been so mysterious about the help Xu needed. Could it have been about the chairmanship? Was Uncle asking her to do this for him? Maybe Xu wasn't the only one who wanted that legacy fulfilled. She felt a chill on her neck and shivered. She'd do what she could, limited though that might be.

She turned right when she left the courtyard and walked down the alley. As she neared the street, she saw the fruit vendor staring at her. Then he looked past her in the direction of the house. She imagined that Suen was standing in the entranceway, watching her progress. She nodded at the vendor and he lowered his head in acknowledgement.

"Is this cart always here?" she asked.

"Every hour of every day," he said.

"With someone tending to it?"

"Of course."

"Who buys fruit at three in the morning?"

"You would be surprised," he said, smiling.

Ava figured she had a long, quiet day ahead of her, with May tied up with Suki and Amanda with Chi-Tze and the Pos. She hadn't relished the idea of spending it alone in the hotel. Besides, she needed a distraction, and what could be better than roaming the French Concession? She turned right onto a street that was lined with restaurants and shops, most of which wouldn't have looked out of place in downtown Toronto. She stopped at an antique store, a shoe store called Louis, and several jewellery stores. She bought a white jade bracelet for Maria and a set of ivory mah-jong tiles for her mother. The tiles came with a certificate stating that they were more than two hundred years old, which made them legal to import into Canada. Ava hoped the certificate was authentic. The last thing she wanted when she got home was to be suspected of smuggling ivory.

If the street hadn't been filled with Chinese merchants and shoppers, Ava could have been in Paris. The architecture was almost entirely European, the buildings fronted by trees and red cobblestone sidewalks. She tried to imagine the neighbourhood a hundred years before, a Western atoll in the middle of a gigantic Chinese sea. What had life been like for the Europeans? Did they live in isolation or did their interactions with the locals go beyond commerce? *I need to read more*, she thought.

As she continued to walk, thoughts of Xu and May and Amanda took turns occupying her mind. Xu's talk about the chairmanship had rattled her and pushed aside thoughts about the dollar transfer, but now the money began to intrude. She wondered if they had been entirely wise to take his investment offer — not that the decision could be easily reversed. By now May had committed to Suki, and Amanda and Chi-Tze were negotiating in good faith with the Pos. There was no backtracking now.

May Ling was proving to be a steadfast partner. She was consistent and solid, and Ava found that comforting. It was almost like her relationship with Uncle. No recriminations, no second-guessing, just total support. And Amanda and Chi-Tze were cut from the same cloth — well-educated, committed, hard-working, conscientious, and loyal. How lucky she had been to fall into the company of such accomplished women. And the Po deal offered up the opportunity to take advantage of the girls' skills.

Her thoughts were random and her wanderings equally so. Several times she left the main thoroughfare to explore side streets, and it was early afternoon when she found herself on Sinan Road, looking at a knot of people standing in front of a gate about halfway down the street. Curious, she went to see what the attraction was. The house number was seventy-three and a sign on the gate read RESIDENCE OF MR. ZHOU. The house was closed to tourists until one o'clock, which was five minutes away. Ava got in line behind six others.

She knew very little about Zhou Enlai, other than that he had been premier under Mao and was supposedly a moderating influence on the chairman in his later years. From what she knew about those years from her mother and Uncle and from watching Gong Li films about the Great Leap Forward and the Cultural Revolution, Zhou couldn't have had that much effect on Mao — about twenty-five million people had died during those two calamities.

At exactly one o'clock the gate swung open. Ava went to a booth on the left and paid the admission price — the equivalent of twenty-five American cents — and was handed an information pamphlet. She stepped into the front yard and found herself looking at a house that seemed as unlikely a home for Zhou as Xu's seemed for him.

The brochure said the house's architecture was in the French style, but it seemed to Ava to have elements of Swiss or German design. The structure was three storeys high and the ground-floor entrance was under a small arch. The enormous windows contained at least fifty panes of glass. There was a white wooden structure like a picket fence below each window, a feature she identified with German homes. The house was constructed of grey brick and stone, its walls barely visible beneath thick layers of ivy.

A guide stood at the front door. She waited until all the tourists had congregated and then launched into a well-rehearsed presentation. It turned out that the house had never really been Zhou's home. It was actually the Shanghai office of the Communist Party of China, and Zhou had bunked there during his visits to the city in 1946 and 1947. The guide went on for more than fifteen minutes, describing Zhou's conversion to Communism and his rise in the party. He had also spent time in Shanghai in the 1920s as a spymaster, but he didn't live at 73 Sinan Road; in fact, he had changed his address virtually every day.

They were then led through a series of small rooms with bare wooden floors, plain walls, and odd pieces of unadorned wooden furniture. Zhou had stayed on the ground floor. The guide led them into his bedroom, where the furnishings consisted of a chair, a small dresser, and a single bed. She picked up two threadbare blankets that were on the bed and held them to the light coming from the window. The other tourists oohed, and one said it made him proud to see how the country's first leaders had made so many sacrifices. Ava decided she'd had enough.

Back on the street, she realized she was lost. In her wanderings she had strayed into an area that Suen hadn't mapped. She put the map in her pocket and started to walk in the general direction of where she thought she had been. After ten minutes she came to a bakery that had the sign BOULANGERIE above the door and a rack of baguettes in the window. The aroma of freshly baked bread wafted out onto the street. She couldn't resist.

A baguette, butter, jam, cheese, and two double espressos later she asked the woman behind the counter how she could get to the Bund. She left the store with a map drawn on a napkin.

It took her close to an hour to get to the Peninsula. As she stepped into the lobby, her phone rang for the first time since she had left that morning.

"Yes?"

"Ava, it's Amanda. Where are you?"

"I just walked into the hotel."

"Are you alone?"

"Yes."

"I'm in Pudong and we have a big problem. I need you to come here if you can."

"What's going on?"

"Things sort of blew up."

"Is Chi-Tze there?"

"That's part of the problem. When I called Gillian last night to say we needed more time to review the plan and that we were bringing in Chi-Tze to help, she didn't say much. I knew she wasn't happy about it but I thought she understood that it was necessary. Later I emailed all the plans to Chi-Tze and we spent a good part of the night going over them. When I picked her up at the airport this morning, she was primed for the meeting. However, Chi-Tze does not have the best social skills. I had barely introduced her to Gillian before she started grilling her on some details in the plan."

"And Gillian reacted badly?"

"Not immediately, but Chi-Tze kept at her and I could see that Gillian was getting upset. Clark was in the room too, but not saying anything. I should have read his body language better."

"What happened?"

"He exploded. He told Gillian not to answer any more questions. He yelled that the plan and his designs spoke for themselves, and either we wanted to do the deal or we didn't. Gillian tried to calm him down but he stormed out of the room. At that point she said she wants a decision today and that it has to come directly from you or May."

"May is with Suki Chan."

"How soon can you get here?"

"I'm hardly dressed for business."

"That won't matter to anyone."

"I'll get a taxi right now."

"Thanks. I'll let everyone know."

Ava turned and headed back towards the hotel entrance. A minute later she was in a taxi headed for Pudong. She called May Ling, but her mobile rang five times and went to voicemail. "This is Ava. Call me."

She leaned back her head and shut her eyes. Things were moving quickly and she felt slightly overwhelmed. Maybe she just needed time to adjust to the rhythm of the new business. Maybe six months of being idle had dulled her instincts. Whatever the cause, for the first time in years Ava felt she lacked control of the situation.

The sound of her phone ringing broke her thoughts. "Ava, it's May. Did everything go well with Xu?"

"The money will be transferred to our bank account today."

"So, no nasty surprises?"

"None."

"That's great. Suki's been on the phone with Beijing and we have a conference call set up with them for this afternoon.

It looks like there's a deal to be done there quickly."

"She's okay with the dilution?"

"All she cares about is growing the business. She'd rather have a small slice of a big pie than a big slice of a small one."

"I wish things were as settled with the Pos."

"What's going on? Did Chi-Tze get here?"

"Early this morning. She and Amanda went directly to Pudong for a meeting with them. It didn't go well."

"What's the problem?"

"Evidently Chi-Tze aggravated the Pos. She was asking Gillian questions when Clark took offence and left the meeting. The end result is that Gillian is saying they want an answer today about what we're going to do."

"That is sudden."

"We shouldn't have told them yesterday that we would get back to them so soon. We raised expectations. Now, by adding Chi-Tze to the mix, we've muddied the waters and are looking indecisive."

"Still, Gillian is being unreasonable."

"Whether she is or not, we have to deal with it."

"What's your plan?"

"I'm on my way to the factory right now. I'll sort it out as best I can."

"Ava, do whatever you think is right."

"What is your instinct telling you? Should we do this deal?"

May paused. "If we do, it's a leap of faith."

"That isn't answering my question."

"I want to do it, but not at any price."

"Does the ten million bother you?"

"No, I'm more concerned that the Pos treat us as true

partners. That when it comes to any major expenditures or financial commitments, we have the control we discussed."

"Do you have a threshold in mind?"

"Something that would be larger than their normal monthly operating expenditure. We don't want to impede the running of the regular business."

"Okay."

"Ava, what do you want to do?"

"Close the deal."

"Just like that."

"Yes. I don't see any rational way to quantify the cost or the business's potential. We either believe in his talent or we don't, and obviously I am a believer. The only thing that might give me pause is if Gillian gets sticky about agreeing to the financial controls or if Chi-Tze finds something fundamentally wrong in their proposal."

"Clark's behaviour doesn't alarm you?"

"He's temperamental — we saw that yesterday, to a lesser degree. I would like to know what's behind this outburst, but I don't think we can expect him to be any different moving forward. It's part of the package."

"Do what you think is best," May said.

"I will."

## 14

**THE GUARD SALUTED AND SWUNG OPEN THE GATE FOR** the taxi. Amanda was standing in front of the main door, looking worried.

"Where is Chi-Tze?" Ava asked as she got out of the cab and started up the steps.

"In the boardroom. She's by herself. Clark has left the building and Gillian is in her office with the door closed."

"Tough morning for you."

"A surprising one, anyway."

"Tell me about it in a bit more detail before we go inside."

Amanda sighed. "I had forgotten how formidable Chi-Tze can be. I know she's tiny and looks like she's barely out of her teens, but when it comes to business and business analysis, she can come across like a two-hundred-pound bully. That's what happened with Gillian. Chi-Tze was super-aggressive with her questions, and I could see that Clark was getting agitated. I should have stepped in. But I didn't and Chi-Tze kept going at Gillian until Clark exploded and left. Gillian ran after him. When she returned, she told us he isn't coming back and that they need a decision today."

"Do you still want to do this deal?" Ava asked.

"Yes, I do."

"Their behaviour didn't sour you on it?"

"We had some miscommunication we need to fix. I wasn't clear enough with Chi-Tze about our intentions, and that's why she went at it the way she did. She treated it like a case study at Brandeis — her objective was simply to find fault. If I had explained better . . ."

"Okay, I understand."

"I think Gillian wasn't pleased about her being here in the first place, but as I said, she did bite her tongue and try to co-operate until Clark got involved. She's terribly protective of him."

"I noticed that yesterday."

"So what I'm saying is that I don't put the blame on Gillian or Clark."

"Let me ask you again. Do you still want to do this deal?"

"I do."

"Chi-Tze had time to go over the proposal and the due diligence. What did she think?"

"That's the crazy thing. She thinks developing the Po brand is a tremendous idea. She says there's no Chinese designer who's really made a mark on the world stage, and the timing is perfect to launch someone."

"She hasn't seen the clothes."

"She took my word that we were all impressed with them. What she's looking at is the soundness of the proposal and how Gillian wants to execute the plan."

"And you obviously think highly of her judgement."

"Absolutely. And she's completely sold on Gillian's business model."

"She didn't tell Gillian how she felt, though."

"No. As I said, she didn't have the chance. Things blew up before she could get there."

"Okay, I understand. Let's go inside and see what we can salvage."

Amanda opened the door and they stepped into the small foyer. The offices were quiet, people hunkered down at their desks as if trying to stay out of harm's way.

"Does Chi-Tze understand why things went sideways?" Ava asked.

"Yes, and she feels awful."

"Have you mentioned to her that we might want her to be our person inside this business?"

"No."

"Good. Now you go and talk to her and I'll speak to Gillian."

Ava could feel eyes on her as they walked down the corridor. In an office that size there wasn't much that could be said and kept confidential. At the far end Ava saw Chi-Tze watching her though the glass wall of the boardroom. Ava waved and gave her a little smile. "I'll come and get you when things are sorted," she said to Amanda.

She knocked on Gillian's door. "Just a moment," she said. Ava heard her end a phone conversation.

The door opened and Gillian stood directly in front of Ava. "I'm sorry we had to drag you all the way here," she said, her face set firmly.

"I was pleased to come. I just wish it were for a different reason," Ava said.

"Things got out of hand."

"So I heard."

Gillian backed into her office. "Here, take a seat."

"Is it okay to talk in here?"

"The offices on either side of me are empty."

Ava nodded and sat down. "Amanda has explained to me what happened and why it happened."

"I have to say we were disappointed."

"Surely you didn't think we wouldn't have more questions after hearing your proposal."

"I told you that you aren't the only people we've spoken to about the business," Gillian said sharply.

"You did."

"Well, aside from the fact that most of them wanted Clark to keep designing for their own labels, the chemistry just wasn't right. All they could see was numbers and all they wanted to talk about was numbers. When I met Amanda and she told me about you and May Ling, I thought there might finally be a fit. I have to tell you, Amanda conducted a very thorough, professional, discreet, and sensitive due diligence on our business."

"I'm sure she'll be happy to know that you think so."

"And in the talks I had with her, she came across as someone who cares about the soul of the business. I know *soul* might be a funny word to use, but Clark and I see the business as a living, breathing entity, full of people we've grown up with and love."

"Amanda was raised in a family business. She understands that kind of emotional attachment."

"Exactly — that's how she came across. So when I realized we might have found the right the fit, I did some due diligence of my own, on your business."

"Of course."

"I knew of May Ling by name and reputation — what Chinese woman in business doesn't? I was really happy when I discovered how respected she is. As for Amanda, well, she has a terrific education and background. You were a bit of an enigma, but I thought that if May Ling Wong wanted you for a business partner, that was recommendation enough. That's when we decided to make a serious pitch."

"And that's how we took it — seriously. But I can't help saying again that it was naive of you to expect an instant decision."

Gillian closed her eyes, pressed her lips together, and sighed. "My brother rarely gets involved in business matters."

"I sensed that."

"When I said that we'd talked to other companies, what I didn't mention was that this has been going on ever since the day my uncle sold the firm. We must have talked to ten potential buyers. Clark has been getting impatient. Actually, *impatient* is an understatement," she said. "He's bursting with ideas, and not being able to transform them into reality wears on him. He gets emotional, even neurotic, at times. One of my main challenges is to keep him calm and keep him focused on the business at hand."

"Did he also meet with the other companies?"

"Some of them, but it was always strained. Either they were put off by his personality or he wanted nothing more to do with them. He liked Amanda, of course, which is why yesterday happened."

"Yesterday was a good thing all around."

"We thought so too, which is why the insertion of Chi-Tze into the process was a bit of a shock. She was acting exactly like every other bean counter we've met. It was as if all the due diligence Amanda did and all our conversations didn't matter. We felt like we were back at square one."

"There was some miscommunication within our team. Chi-Tze is not to blame."

"So you say. Our fear is that she's the tip of the iceberg."

Ava shrugged. "Clark is not the only person whose feelings need to be considered."

"What do you mean?"

"Chi-Tze has gone through hell over the past six months. This assignment — which so far has consisted entirely of her reading Amanda's briefing notes and flying into Shanghai this morning — is a way for her to put a lot of misery behind her. She wants to impress us. She doesn't really need to, but in her mind she thinks it's necessary. So she overdid things. She is very bright, very analytical, and as well trained as Amanda. She has studied how to build a brand, so we thought her input would be useful. We didn't expect her to go back over old ground. It was our fault that we weren't more specific."

"She was very aggressive, to the point of being rude."

"I apologize for that. That wasn't our intent."

"What was your intent?"

"We wanted her to confirm our belief that investing in the PÖ brand isn't a far-fetched idea."

"Confirm?"

"We like your plan. So does Chi-Tze."

"She never even hinted at that. She was all doubt and skepticism."

"As I said, there was a misunderstanding."

"So where does that leave us?"

"Where is your brother?"

"Why?"

"I have a proposal for you."

Gillian pushed her chair back from the desk, as if distancing herself from Ava. "If this is a business discussion, you should be having it with me," she said.

"What I have to say, I need to say to the two of you."

"I would like to hear it first."

"No."

"You can't dictate —"

"I'm not," Ava said, her voice rising. "We have a proposal. I want you and your brother to understand, directly from me, what we are prepared to do, why we are prepared to do it, and what our expectations are."

"He's left and he won't come back."

"How can you be sure?"

"I've been through this before."

"So what do you suggest?"

"Are you serious about making an offer?"

"Yes," Ava said.

"Then give it to me in writing. I'll review it with my brother and our lawyer and I'll get back to you."

"How long will that take?"

"That depends on the complexity of the offer."

"We're prepared to give you most of what you want."

Gillian blinked, and Ava thought she saw her catch her breath. "You used the word *most*," she said.

"Yes. You may have some questions about the financial controls we need to put in place, but I can assure you they're not there to impede the running of the business."

"I want to see the details."

"Of course."

"Is that all?"

"No. We want to put someone into the business full-time. That person would represent our interests, and we'd make sure they had skills that would be of benefit."

"We don't need anyone. One reason we want to do this is to have control of our own destiny. We've had enough of working for other people."

"I'm suggesting someone you would work with, not for."

"Amanda?"

"I don't have a name yet."

"Whoever it is would have to be compatible with Clark."

"That's a given."

"Would the person be Chinese?"

"Why do you ask that?"

"It's no secret that my brother is gay. With our European and North American customers it's completely inconsequential. China is another matter. Even in cities the size of Shanghai there is widespread intolerance. I said earlier that some of our potential buyers were put off by Clark's personality. *Personality* is a euphemism — all those buyers were Chinese. Some of them even asked if we would hire someone to be the public face of the brand."

"I understand."

"It isn't a small matter."

"And it won't be treated as one."

Gillian looked across the desk at Ava. "So where does this leave us?"

"We'll prepare an offer and send it to you."

"Fine."

"And you'll explain to your brother about Chi-Tze's behaviour?"

"I'll try."

"That's all we can ask. Now I'd better get Amanda and Chi-Tze." Ava stood. "We'll be in touch."

As she walked along the corridor she could see two faces staring at her from the boardroom. Their expressions couldn't have been more different. Chi-Tze looked distraught; Amanda's face was full of questions.

"We should leave. How soon can you get us a taxi?" Ava asked.

"Five minutes," Amanda said.

"Then do that," Ava said.

While Amanda called a cab, Chi-Tze pulled her papers together, her eyes cast downwards.

"We'll talk when we get outside," Ava said. "The two of you have some work to do."

"So —" Amanda began.

"Outside," Ava said.

When they walked out the factory door, the cab was waiting for them. Ava motioned for the two women to get into the back seat. She sat in front. "The Peninsula Hotel," she said to the driver. As he pulled away, she turned to face Amanda and Chi-Tze. "Gillian and I had a decent talk, so let's not dwell on what happened earlier."

"Great," Amanda said. Chi-Tze bit her lower lip and gave a slight nod.

"What I need to know from the two of you is whether or not you're absolutely on side with our getting into this business — and by that I mean buying into Clark Po's dream. So let's hear it. Can this really work, and are you both prepared to get into it up to your chins?"

"Are you saying you want both of us to be actively involved?" Amanda asked.

"Yes."

"Do you think Gillian and Clark will be okay with that?" Chi-Tze said.

"Let's not get ahead of ourselves trying to anticipate what they'll like. Let's concentrate on what we want."

"I want to do the deal, and I'll do everything I can to make sure it's a success," Amanda said.

"Me too," Chi-Tze said, just as forcefully.

"Good. When you get back to the hotel, I want you to create an offer sheet. I'd like it done by tonight so we can run it past May Ling and then send it to Gillian and Clark."

"That's quick," Amanda said.

"Is that a problem for either of you?"

"No, we can do it, as long as we have some guidance."

"Give them the share structure they want, but we have to have right of first refusal if they want to sell even one share," Ava said. "Detail and insist on the financial protection May Ling thinks we need. Commit us to putting in ten million dollars immediately and whatever else is needed if the business's performance matches the projections in Gillian's plans."

"Ava, if those projections are met, we'll have to come up with another twenty or thirty million quite quickly. Currently we don't have that kind of availability," Amanda said.

"May and I talked about this last night. The money will be there if it's needed."

Amanda looked surprised but simply said, "Okay."

"Now in addition to those points I'm sure there's a lot of boiler-plating you learned at business school and will want to add. Feel free to do that, but remember the sensitivities you're dealing with."

"Is that all?" Amanda asked.

"No. We want you to be the partner who sits on the board and the executive committee and is the official point of contact for all things PÖ."

"Gladly."

"And we want Chi-Tze to be our eyes and ears and brain in the business."

"What does that mean?" Chi-Tze asked.

"Are you prepared to move to Shanghai?"

"Yes."

"Then you'll be our in-house manager. Use whatever title you want. All that matters is that you run day-to-day operations with Gillian."

"Do you really want that spelled out in the offer sheet?" Amanda asked.

"Yes."

"They won't like that," Chi-Tze said.

"I don't care. It's our money, and we have a responsibility to make sure that it and the business are managed in a way that makes us comfortable."

"I would hate to see you lose the deal because of me," Chi-Tze said.

"Look, we're a relatively new company and we're small, but the one thing we'll always do is cover each other's backs. There are more important things than closing a deal."

Chi-Tze glanced at Amanda, who was staring at Ava. "Thank you for your trust," she said.

"We're a team. Thanks aren't necessary."

## 15

**IT WAS NINE THIRTY BY THE TIME THEY SAT DOWN FOR** dinner.

As soon as they got back to the Peninsula, Amanda and Chi-Tze had taken over a small boardroom in the hotel's business centre to begin drafting the offer. "Call me if you need me or when you're done," Ava said. Then she went to her room to get her own thoughts organized and to call May Ling.

May answered almost immediately. "How did it go?"

"Well, we're all still talking and the Pos have agreed to consider an offer. They want it in writing, and the girls are drafting it now."

"That's fantastic."

"Don't say that until you see it. I wasn't exactly hard-nosed."

"I've just spent two hours on the phone with Beijing, and we're scheduled to be back at it in a few minutes. After listening to Suki and the guy there negotiate, I can only say that I have a different view of *hard-nosed* than I did before. They beat the hell out of each other, and then they gladly agreed to do it again."

"Is it going well?"

"We're close to a deal in principle. It may take a trip to Beijing to finalize it, but that's a small matter. We still need to do our due diligence, but Suki already knows a lot about the internal workings of that company, and after listening to her grill the guy, I'll be shocked if there are any surprises."

"What is it going to cost us?"

"Close to eighty million U.S."

"About double what we gave Suki for the shares in her company."

"He has substantially more assets in terms of warehouses and trucks."

"That eats up our initial investment fund and then some."

"Yes, so thank goodness for Xu. And by the way, his money is already in our bank account."

"On this end we're going to be out of pocket ten million."

"Do we really have to front that ten million so soon?"

"After this morning, we need to demonstrate our confidence in the Pos. We were going to put up the money eventually, so why not do it now and get credit for it?"

"I see the sense in that, as long as we have our controls in place."

"We will or there's no deal."

"How about operationally?"

"I like Amanda's idea of putting Chi-Tze into the business full-time. Clark will obviously be the creative boss, and it makes sense to leave Gillian in charge of day-to-day operations such as procurement and production, but I don't believe they have enough expertise in actual brand building. Chi-Tze can fill that void."

"Will the Pos be okay with that?"

"I don't know. I'm more concerned about our best interests."

"And you're not worried that it might be too much for Chi-Tze to take on?"

"No. I know she's young, but she's certainly smart enough, and she's conscientious. Mind you, you never really know if someone is ready to take on a responsibility until you actually give it to them. But Amanda thinks Chi-Tze can handle it, and I trust her judgement."

May laughed, catching Ava by surprise. "What's so funny?" she asked.

"I was just thinking how crazy the past twenty-four hours have been."

"Isn't that the truth."

"I find it exhilarating."

"I felt that way when I left the Po factory, though I didn't let the girls know."

"Yes, don't ruin your image."

"Image?"

"The girls think you're the coolest thing around — the unflappable Ava Lee."

"I wish."

"Anyway, that's what they think, and I don't think you should try to dissuade them of that idea. It's good when there's that much respect for the boss."

"I hardly think of myself as that."

"Well, you'd better start, because that's what you and I are now. If we close these deals we will have five companies under our control."

Ava paused. The thoughts that had been rumbling around in her head during her walk in the French Concession, and later in the taxi, returned. "I can't help finding it strange. For ten years it was just Uncle and me, and for a lot of that time, especially when I was on a job, it was me alone. I've developed a mindset and habits that reflect that experience. It's going to take me some time to get used to all this interdependency."

"Nonsense."

"Anyway, be patient."

"*Momentai*," May said, and then quickly added, "Ava, I have to go — Suki is waving at me. I'll be back at the hotel sometime in the early evening. Save dinner for me."

Ava yawned. She was exhausted and feeling the effects of residual jet lag and the previous night's disturbed sleep. It was late afternoon. She wondered if the Bund was negotiable for a run, but a quick glance out the window told her it wasn't. She turned on the television, skipped past news shows, and found herself looking at a young Chow Yun-fat in the movie *Hard Boiled*, John Woo's last Hong Kong gangster/cop film before he went to Hollywood. Ava had seen it before and thought it was one of Woo's best. Chow and Tony Leung were both sexy and moody in it, though Ava thought the female lead, Teresa Mo, was a bit plain for either of them; but then, women were usually incidental in Woo's films.

She went to the room bar, found a bottle of white burgundy, fluffed her pillows, and lay down on the bed to enjoy some wine and watch the film. She didn't make it past the first few minutes, waking to the hotel phone ringing and a different film on the screen.

"Ava, this is Amanda."

"Hi," Ava mumbled.

"It's nine o'clock."

"God, I fell asleep."

"We're downstairs waiting for you. We have a table at Sir Elly's Restaurant, on the thirteenth floor."

"See you there," Ava said, and then groaned. She showered quickly, brushed her teeth and hair, and threw on a pink shirt and black skirt. As she was walking towards the elevator, her cellphone rang. Before she could retrieve it from her bag, the elevator doors opened. She stepped inside, and as the doors closed the incoming call was cut off. She checked for missed calls and saw a vaguely familiar Hong Kong number. *Well, whoever it is*, she thought, *they'll call back.*

Sir Elly's may not have had the dramatic setting of Whampoa, but it was spectacular in its own way. The room was long, with a high arched ceiling, and terminated by a massive, speckled black marble fireplace. Floor-to-ceiling windows looked out onto the Bund, the Huangpu River, and Pudong. May Ling waved to Ava from a window table.

May, Amanda, and Chi-Tze stood as she approached. They were all smiling. Ava saw an open bottle of champagne on the table.

"We're having a little celebration," May said, extending her arms for a hug. "Our man in Beijing finally agreed to Suki's basic terms. She and I are flying there tomorrow to continue the due diligence, shake hands, and put together an offer sheet."

"Wonderful," Ava said.

"And the offer letter is done for the Pos. I think it expresses exactly what you want," Amanda said.

"I'll read it later. Right now, I'm famished."

"Champagne okay for you?" May asked, pointing the

bottle towards Ava's empty glass.

"Please."

"Here's the menu," Amanda said, passing Ava a thick red leather tome. "The chef is quite famous. His name is David Chauveau. He's French, of course."

"You've all decided?" Ava asked, scanning the menu. "Let's order."

Ava was awed by the quality of the food. They had all ordered kumamoto oysters, which were served in shot glasses with arugula gelée, fennel, lemongrass, and pickled Granny Smith apples. For her main course May had chosen pork belly coated in masala spices and mango chutney. Both Amanda and Chi-Tze opted for wagyu beef tenderloin. Ava had grilled octopus and crispy pig ear. The pig ear was particularly spectacular, its light, crunchy exterior giving way to a luscious fatty interior.

They chatted as they ate, May entertaining them with stories about Suki's negotiating style, which was highly emotional — and obviously effective. "And that damn woman," May said. "We had no sooner reached the agreement with Beijing than she started to talk about a company in Guangzhou!"

When the table had been cleared, Amanda reached down into her briefcase and pulled out four sets of paper, three pages each, neatly stapled. "Shall we go over this now?" she asked.

"I think my head is clear enough," May said.

They read silently. Ava noticed Chi-Tze and Amanda exchanging glances as they tried to gauge the other women's reactions. Keeping her face expressionless, she said to May, "Well, what do you think?"

"Although it says that Three Sisters will play an active role in the business, it doesn't mention that Chi-Tze will have a permanent senior position."

"Why doesn't it?" Ava asked the two younger women.

"I thought it was a bit presumptuous," Chi-Tze said.

"Don't you feel up to the job?" May asked.

"It's what I'm trained to do."

"You're not answering the question," Ava said. "We know you have the education. The point is, do you feel strong enough to take this on? I've obviously made the assumption that you are, but if you feel otherwise, now is the time to say. We don't want to throw you into a situation that you can't handle."

"I can do this."

"Are you sure?" May asked.

"Yes. I know I will have to manage Clark as well as the nuts and bolts of assembling a business, and I know that Gillian will be watching me like a hawk, but I'm up for it. I'm up for all of it and I won't let you down."

"Then rewrite the letter to reflect the fact that you will be working there full-time and making decisions for us in relation to the PÖ company," Ava said.

"We will," Amanda said. "Do you have a particular title you want us to use?"

"Senior vice-president of marketing and branding," Ava said. "That's the only change I can see that we need. So when that's done, send it to Gillian."

"And if they accept our terms?"

"Then Chi-Tze had better start looking for a place to live in Shanghai. And she should talk to Clark about what kind of space he'll need to operate in."

"What about papering it?"

"We'll use our Hong Kong lawyers," May said.

Ava's phone rang, catching her by surprise; she thought she had turned it off. She looked at the incoming number. It was the same as before, but this time it dawned on her who was calling.

"Sonny?" she said.

"Hi, Ava. Are you still in Shanghai?" he asked.

"Yes, I am," she said, standing and moving away from the table.

"Are you somewhere you can talk?"

"Yes. What's going on?"

"Carlo called me earlier tonight."

"Carlo?" Ava repeated.

"He sounded nervous."

Ava knew Carlo very well. He had worked for Uncle for years, usually in tandem with a partner, Andy. The two men had done jobs with Ava and had always been efficient and loyal. Without their help the year before, she doubted she would have been able to extract her brother's business partner from Macau. "Did he want anything in particular?"

"He wanted to know where you are."

"Did you tell him?"

"No. Then he asked me to ask you to call him."

"Why would I call Carlo?"

"I have no idea, but he was insistent."

"What's he doing these days, anyway?" Ava asked.

"He's gone to work for Sammy Wing in Wanchai. Do you remember Sammy?"

"Yes, he helped us track down Jackie Leung when that creep contracted to have me killed."

"That's him. He and Uncle became close after that, and when Uncle died, Wing offered jobs to Carlo, Andy, and me. Carlo was the only one who took him up on it."

"What does Carlo do for him?"

"I don't know and I don't ask."

"Yes, it's better that way," Ava said. Uncle had wanted Sonny to stay as far away from his old Triad roots as possible.

"Anyway, now I've passed on his message like I said I would."

"Do you have a number for him?"

"Yes, but Ava, don't feel that you have to call him. You don't owe him anything. He was paid well enough for what he did over the years."

"Actually, Sonny, I owe him quite a bit."

"You sure?"

"Give me the number."

"After you talk to him, let me know if there's anything strange going on," Sonny said. Ava heard the menace in his voice and couldn't help but smile. At well over six feet and more than 250 pounds, Sonny was the fastest, most vicious man she had ever encountered, one of the few men she doubted she could best physically. Not that she'd ever had to worry about that — he was completely loyal; she knew there wasn't anything he wouldn't do for her.

"I'm quite sure it's nothing out of the ordinary," she said.

"Still . . ."

"I know, Sonny. Thanks for the concern."

"Is there any chance you'll be coming to Hong Kong this trip?"

"I don't know."

"You would let me know?"

"Sonny, if I do go to Hong Kong, you'll be the first person I call."

"I thought so, but I just like to hear it. I've missed you."

"Me too."

## 16

SHE FORCED HERSELF TO SLEEP WITH THE HELP OF A cognac and two melatonin tablets. After she had woken at two, three, and then five thirty, she knew afternoon naps would have to be banished if she was ever going to overcome the jet lag. It was just past seven when she finally gave up and crawled out of bed. She made a coffee and settled at her computer to read emails.

Amanda had sent their offer to the Pos the night before, copying her and May. Ava read it over and was pleased by how precise it was. There shouldn't be any confusion about their intentions.

There were also several messages between May and Suki Chan confirming flight and meeting details for Beijing. May's flight was at nine, and Ava was certain she was on her way to the airport now. She thought about calling her and then wondered what she could say other than "Good luck." In any event, if things went according to Suki's plan, Three Sisters was about to more than double the size of its logistics business.

Ava scanned the rest of her mail, reading the short, newsy

notes from her mother and her sister and a longer one from
Maria that was filled with yearning. She fired off answers
to Jennie and Marian and then sat back and thought about
her girlfriend. They'd been together for more than a year,
and with the exception of a one-night stand in the Faeroe
Islands, Ava had been completely faithful. It was the lon-
gest relationship she'd ever been in. The question wasn't
whether she wanted to maintain it, but could she live with
someone — with anyone — on a full-time basis? She had
been living alone for more than fifteen years without feeling
lonely. Maybe it was her personality, maybe it was a result
of her previous career, but she was comfortable with her
own company. She didn't need people around her to make
her feel complete. In fact, spending a prolonged period of
time with anyone — her mother, her sister, her best friend,
Mimi — left her feeling suffocated. It was as if they were
sucking the air out from around her.

Maria didn't generate quite the same reaction, but after a
weekend together Ava was happy to see her leave for work.
She was, she thought, ready to commit to Maria, but she
knew, deep down, that she wasn't prepared to live with her.
She read the message again and then wrote: I miss you too.

She pushed the chair back from the desk and went to
the bathroom. Half an hour later she emerged shiny clean
and refreshed. She looked at her cellphone. There hadn't
been any calls, and in Ava's world that was usually a good
thing. She checked past calls, saw Sonny's number, and
then remembered she had promised to phone Carlo.

His phone rang four times before she heard a croaky
"Wei."

"Carlo, it's Ava."

"Ava?"

"Sonny said you wanted to talk to me."

"Are you still in Shanghai?"

The question caught Ava off guard. "Why do you ask?"

"Because if you are it will be easy enough for you to come to Hong Kong."

"And why would I come to Hong Kong?"

"You know Sammy Wing, right?"

"I know of Sammy Wing."

"I'm working for him."

"I heard."

"He co-operated with Sonny as a favour to Uncle when Jackie Leung was gunning for you."

"I know."

"He wasn't the one who actually threw Leung into Victoria Harbour, but he helped finger him."

"Carlo, where is this leading?" Ava asked.

She heard him draw a deep breath. "Sammy wants you to come to Hong Kong to meet with him."

"For what reason?"

"He didn't tell me."

"And you didn't ask?"

"Ava, you know me. I'm small-time. I'm running a book-making operation for him. I'm not part of the inner circle."

"So why are you the one who's calling me?"

"I guess he thought you would take my call."

"That was a reasonable assumption."

"So will you?"

"Go to Hong Kong to meet with Sammy Wing?"

"Yeah."

"Carlo, I don't know why I should."

"You do owe him a bit of a favour."

"I don't know him, I've never met him, and I don't feel any obligation, despite Jackie Leung. As I remember, that was nearly all Uncle's doing."

Carlo became quiet. Ava could imagine his tightly compressed eyes and lips — classic Carlo in thinking mode. "Then would you do it for me?" he said, his voice cracking slightly.

Ava hesitated. There wasn't any doubt that she owed Carlo. "You must have some idea of what he wants."

"Ava, I told you, I don't have a clue."

"Earlier, you asked me if I'm still in Shanghai. What made you think that?"

"That's what Sammy told me."

"How did he know?"

"Again, I don't have a clue."

"Carlo, I don't know what to say. Part of me knows I owe you, but another says that Sammy Wing's request is very strange and not such a good idea."

"I'm trying to make my way in this organization. So far it hasn't been bad, but the jobs I get are all chicken-shit stuff. This is the first real chance I've had to make any kind of a mark . . . Ava, I think this is kind of important to Sammy or he would never have asked me to reach out to you. That's all I know."

She sighed. "Okay, Carlo, I'll come to Hong Kong. But when I meet with Wing, I'm going to tell him that the only reason I'm there is because of you."

"That's fine. In fact, that's more than fine."

"When does he want me to come?"

"As soon as you can. How's today?"

"Good god."

"I'm just saying."

Ava thought about her day. May was en route to Beijing. The girls would be waiting for the Pos' response. "Where does he want to meet?"

"Your choice."

"How many people?"

"It sounded like just you and him."

"Call him and make sure of that, will you? In the meantime, I'll talk to my partners and make sure I can get away from here today. I'll phone you back in half an hour or so."

"Ava, thank you."

"I haven't said yes yet."

"I know, but you will. One of the things Andy and I always admired about you was your loyalty to your friends. And even though we worked for you, we still felt like friends."

"Just call Sammy Wing," she said.

"Yes, boss."

Ava got up from the desk and walked to the window. The sun was high in the sky and the early morning dew had already evaporated from the lawn below. The garden was a jewel and, like the French Concession, a reminder of foreign occupation. Both were such unique creations that even the Maoists couldn't bring themselves to rip them down, nor the next wave of Communist developers. *Why would Sammy Wing want to meet with me?* she thought. *How did he know I was in Shanghai?* She reached for her phone and called May.

"I'm at the airport," May said.

"I know. I saw from your emails last night," Ava said. "May, I've just talked to Carlo in Hong Kong. Do you remember Carlo?"

"Funny little guy who thinks he's every woman's fantasy?"

"Yes, that Carlo. He called for Sammy Wing. You wouldn't know Sammy, but he's Triad and runs Wanchai. Carlo is working for him now. Sammy wants me to go to Hong Kong to meet with him."

"That's odd."

"I thought so too, but the thing is, I owe Carlo quite a few favours. I think it will help his status with Sammy if I go."

"What does Sammy Wing want?"

"I don't know, and Carlo doesn't either. Whatever it is, it shouldn't be something that I can't handle."

"So you're thinking of going?"

"Yes, but not if it interferes with anything we have going on."

"Truthfully, it might be beneficial to have you in Hong Kong. If things go as planned in Beijing, we should be able to fire off instructions to our lawyers there tonight. And — who knows? — Amanda and Chi-Tze might hear from the Pos. It would be almost ideal if you were there to work with them to get both deals papered as fast as possible."

"Well, I guess that settles it. I'll let Amanda and Chi-Tze know what the schedule is and then I'll book a flight."

"I love it when plans come together the way they should," May said.

"Yes, me too," Ava said. *But how and why did Sammy Wing become part of this plan?* she thought.

## 17

**AVA CAUGHT THE NOON CATHAY PACIFIC FLIGHT FROM** Shanghai to Hong Kong. Two and half hours later the plane began its descent over the South China Sea into Chep Lap Kok airport. An armada of freighters, container ships, and tankers was waiting for its chance to enter the port and unload. Moving past them, another armada, fully loaded, was making its way to the four corners of the world. Darting among the ships were fishing boats and junks with more local but just as pressing business. She had made this particular flight many times, and the sea was always as busy as a highway at rush hour. If Suki Chan had her way and things went well in Beijing, their own containers would soon be on those ships.

It was close to three o'clock by the time she had cleared Customs, collected her bag, and walked into the cavernous arrivals hall. Sonny was standing, as he always did, under an arrivals sign. She had called him the moment after she booked her flight. Ava figured he must have come directly to the airport after their call ended. In the past he had waited six, eight, ten hours, or however long he was needed, for Uncle. It was one of the few areas in his life where he exhibited patience.

He took a step forward when he saw her and then stopped. He was wearing a black suit with a white shirt and a black tie. The suit was unbuttoned, and Ava saw that his stomach was stretching the shirt and the jacket seemed tight around the shoulders. Months of doing nothing but driving Michael had taken their toll. His brow was furrowed and his manner seemed grim, but then he gave a little smile, placed his hands together and raised them to his chest, lowered his head, and slowly moved his hands up and down in a sign of respect.

She hadn't seen him since shortly after Uncle's funeral, when she told him she was returning to Toronto for a while. She had asked him to drive for her brother and Amanda during her absence and to protect them both. "But you're still the boss?" he had said then.

"Yes, of course. But when I'm not in Hong Kong, I need you to do these things for me."

"I will. But you'll be coming back?"

"Yes, but I don't know when or how often, or for how long."

How long, Ava thought as she reached Sonny, had turned out to be the most time in ten years she had spent away from Hong Kong. "So good to see you," she said.

He smiled awkwardly. She put down her bag and, holding onto one of his arms, got on the tips of her toes to kiss him gently on the cheek.

He seemed embarrassed by her show of affection. "Hey, boss," he said.

"Hey, Sonny," she said.

He reached for her bag. "Where are we going?"

"The Mandarin Oriental in Central."

"I didn't really have to ask," he said, then turned and pointed. "The car is parked in that direction."

He walked towards a door that opened onto a no-parking, no-stopping zone that was reserved for Hong Kong's elite. That was where Uncle had left his car when he came to meet her. She was surprised that the privilege had been extended to Sonny.

A policeman stood near the front fender. Ava thought he was writing a ticket, but when he saw them, he stepped back, placed his hands together, and bowed. "Thanks," Sonny said, extending his hand, which held a Hong Kong hundred-dollar note.

Ava went to sit in the front passenger seat, but Sonny walked past her and opened the rear door. "That's where Uncle always sat," he said. "It seems right to me."

The car left the airport and eased onto the Tsing Ma Bridge, whose six lanes of traffic and two rail lines connected the man-made island airport to Kowloon. The Ma Wan Channel was two hundred metres below, its water carpeted with even more ships.

Traffic was light. Sonny was across the one and a half kilometres of bridge into Kowloon and leaving the Cross-Harbour Tunnel by the time Ava spoke. "Sonny, what do you know about Sammy Wing?"

"He runs Wanchai."

"So I gather. But tell me, what's he like?"

"He's big, fat, and looks like a bit of a slob. Some people assume he must be sloppy. He's not. Uncle didn't like him but he had time for him. He thought he's maybe the shrewdest of all the Triad bosses in and around Hong Kong."

"How does he operate?"

"He smiles a lot when he talks to you, like he wants you to think he's your best friend. That works, until he puts a knife in your back."

"Not uncommon."

"Well, as long you keep doing what he wants, he'll be nice enough. The moment you resist, you can expect him to turn into a monstrous prick."

"How did he and Uncle get along? I mean really."

"Like I said, Uncle never liked him. He went out of his way to avoid him."

"Yet Wing helped you find Leung."

"Only because Uncle paid him."

"I see."

"Paid him a lot."

"I see. Did he and Uncle have unfinished business?"

"No, I don't think so. Why do you ask?"

"I can't figure out why he wants to meet with me."

"So why do it?"

"I'm here because of Carlo."

Ava saw Sonny look at her in the rear-view mirror. "Carlo doesn't think much beyond what's going on for a particular day."

"I know, but whenever I needed him, he was there for me."

"He was good that way," Sonny said, nodding.

"So I'll meet with Sammy Wing."

"Where?"

"A noodle shop two blocks from the Mandarin, where Uncle and I used to go."

"Do you want me to go with you?"

"We agreed that it should be just the two of us."

"That figures. He's secretive as well as being a prick."

"But I don't see any reason why you can't walk there with me and wait outside until I'm finished."

"Yeah. That will work."

They ran into the beginning of rush hour as they drove deeper into the city. Ava checked her watch — it was almost four. She had agreed to meet Wing at six, so even with the traffic she would have time to check in, change her clothes, and prepare herself.

They reached the hotel half an hour later. "I'll meet you in the lobby at five to six," Ava said.

"I have a parking spot near here," Sonny said. "I'm no more than two minutes away if you need me before then."

*That won't be necessary*, Ava thought, then caught herself before the words were spoken. "That will be perfect," she said.

The doorman smiled when he saw her. "Welcome back, Ms. Lee," he said.

"Thank you."

She had stayed at the Mandarin so many times over the years that she knew most of the staff by name and knew her way around the hotel as well as she did her Toronto condo. Within five minutes she was checked in and walking into her suite on the twentieth floor. She unpacked her case, put her toiletries in the bathroom, set up her computer on the desk, and then went over to the window. Her room overlooked Victoria Harbour, across which she could see Tsim Sha Tsui and the rest of Kowloon beyond. When she was staying in Hong Kong during Uncle's illness, every morning she had taken the Star Ferry across the harbour, from Central to Tsim Sha Tsui, to meet Uncle for a congee breakfast. The harbour was as busy as usual, outgoing and incoming ferries passing each other as they dodged the array of traffic. There had been a time when she could look out over the entire expanse of Tsim Sha Tsui's waterfront from the hotel; now all she saw were swatches between the high-rise towers and office buildings that formed a wall flanking the Hong Kong side. It was the world's tallest sky-line, larger by far in both numbers and size than New York City's, and still growing. Ava often thought of the towers as citadels protecting the core of Central — Hong Kong's financial heart — from invasion.

She turned from the window and went into the bath-room. She brushed her teeth and her hair and put on a light touch of red lipstick and black mascara. She stripped off the black T-shirt and Adidas training pants she had worn for the flight, and in her underwear went to the bedroom. She put on a white shirt with an Italian collar, securing the cuffs with the blue enamel links she had bought at Shanghai Tang. She debated between a skirt and slacks, and opted for the pants.

Her phone had been off since she left Shanghai. She turned it on and saw a text from Amanda. They hadn't heard from the Pos. May had left a voicemail that said sim-ply, "Check your email."

Ava turned on her computer and opened May's mes-sage. The news from Beijing couldn't have been better: the offer sheet had been returned to them with only minor modifications. May had attached the document for Ava to review. She had also sent a copy to their Hong Kong law firm, Burgess and Bowlby, advising them that

Ava was in Hong Kong and would be the company's point of contact as the deal memo made the transition into formal contract.

Ava had met Brenda Burgess when Three Sisters was incorporated. She was a *gweilo*, as was her partner, Richard Bowlby. May, like Uncle, felt more comfortable working with Western-trained, Western-minded lawyers. It wasn't that their Hong Kong Chinese counterparts weren't as smart; it was that *gweilo* lawyers moved in entirely different social and business circles. Both May and Uncle believed that there was less chance of their affairs becoming public, however inadvertently or innocently. Uncle did not want anyone to know even who his lawyer was, and even the most discreet Chinese lawyer would have found it difficult not to divulge the fact that Uncle was a client.

Ava opened the attachments May had sent. It would be costing them $85 million to take control of the Beijing operation. She shook her head at the thought of so much money. She knew they had it, but the fact was still too new to fully absorb.

At the end of her message May wrote that she and Suki probably had a week of due diligence ahead of them, in and around Beijing, but that Ava should proceed with the lawyers as if everything had already checked out. Ava forwarded the email to the law firm, advising them that she was indeed in Hong Kong and staying at the Mandarin Oriental in Central. Their office was no more than a ten-minute walk away.

She checked her watch and saw that it was ten to six. It was time to meet Wing. She debated taking a notebook to the meeting and then discarded the idea. She couldn't imagine he would have anything to say that would be worth writing down.

It was close to dinnertime, so she had to wait a couple of minutes for the elevator, which made five stops on the way to the lobby. It was almost six when she finally got there. Sonny was standing by the main entrance, his back against a wall, his eyes darting in all directions. *Old habits die hard*, Ava thought. He straightened when he saw her, and he reached for his tie and gave it a tug to tighten it.

"I'm a bit late. Sorry," she said.

"That's no problem for me."

The noodle shop was only two blocks from the hotel, uphill from the harbour on Ko Shing Street near Des Voeux Road, but it was a long two blocks to walk. The surrounding office towers were beginning to empty. Ava and Sonny walked side by side, almost pressed into the backs of the people in front of them, the breath of the people behind on their necks. "I'd forgotten how bad the foot traffic can be," she said as they reached an intersection and were forced to stop five metres from it.

When they got to Ko Shing, Ava turned right and the pedestrian flow eased. They were still about twenty metres away when Ava saw Carlo and another man standing in front of the noodle shop. Carlo was small and wiry. He was dressed in a tight white T-shirt and black jeans that didn't add any substance to his build. His head was cleanly shaven and he was still wearing the scraggly beard and wisp of a moustache he'd had the last time she had seen him. The other man was not quite as big as Sonny but there wasn't an ounce of fat on him. He wore a black T-shirt that showed off the tattoos covering both his arms.

Ava saw Carlo look in their direction and waved at him. He glanced sideways at his companion and muttered something, then both men turned to face them.

"Good to see you again, Carlo," Ava said.

"And you. Thanks for coming," he said.

She waited, expecting him to offer his hand, or even his cheek. Instead he motioned at the bigger man. "This is Bobby. He's one of Sammy's key men." Bobby nodded at her. He seemed bored to be there.

"Hi, Sonny," Carlo said.

"How are you doing?"

"Well enough. You?"

"Working for Ava."

"Yeah, I sort of knew that."

"Now you know for sure," Sonny said, his eyes now focused on Bobby.

"Sammy is inside. Let me take you in and make the introductions," Carlo said.

Bobby moved to one side, clearing the entrance. Carlo leapt forward to open the door and then stood aside to let Ava pass. As she did, he whispered, "I can't thank you enough for doing this."

The restaurant was small — ten tables with steel tube legs and Formica tops. The air inside was thick and humid from the steam rising from bowls of soup and noodles, and it was jammed with customers. Carlo touched Ava gently on the elbow and guided her towards the rear. In the far corner, a short, heavyset man wearing a red Ralph Lauren polo shirt stood as they neared. Next to him a large, very fat man remained seated at the table.

"I'm Jimmy Tan," the standing man said, offering his hand.

"And I guess you know I'm Ava Lee."

"I saw you at Uncle's funeral."

"I'm sorry, I don't remember you. The day was a complete blur."

"That isn't a surprise," he said. "And in case you don't remember, this is Sammy Wing."

She looked down at a round face and a double set of jowls. He had a full head of black hair parted in the middle. He had fine features — a small nose, thin lips — but they were almost swallowed up by mounds of flesh flowing like layers of melted wax. His eyes were large and round and flickered from side to side like those of an owl. He pushed himself up from his chair. It was a laborious process, hindered by a huge belly that hung over the waistband of his jeans.

"Thank you so much for coming. Please take a seat," Sammy Wing said. His voice was surprisingly soft.

There were three chairs at the table. "I thought we agreed that it would be just the two of us," Ava said.

"Jimmy is my deputy Mountain Master," Wing said.

"I told Carlo that I would meet with you alone. When he called me back, he said you were okay with that." She felt Carlo stiffen behind her and wondered if he had misled her. If he had, she had enough reason to turn and walk out of the restaurant.

"I was," Wing said. "I just don't see how having Jimmy sit in should make that much of a difference."

"Look, I don't know what you want with me. I agreed to sit with you out of appreciation for the help you gave Uncle last year and out of respect for Carlo. But if you can't honour a simple agreement, I don't feel obliged to stay."

Wing reached down and extracted a toothpick from

the jar on the table. He closed his eyes and jabbed the pick between his lower middle teeth. "Jimmy, go wait outside," he said.

As Carlo and Jimmy moved away from the table, Sammy Wing smiled. "Now will you sit?"

Ava chose the chair directly across from him. "I'm sorry if I seemed rude," she said. "But I have no idea why you want to speak to me, and whatever it is, I prefer that it be between the two of us."

"Are you always this cautious?"

"Yes, I am."

"I am as well, which is why I've lasted this long. It's also why I wanted to meet with you in person. There are — Oh, forgive me, I haven't offered you anything to eat or drink yet."

"I don't want to eat. Tea is fine to drink."

He raised his hand in the air, his eyes not leaving her. *They aren't unkind eyes*, she thought.

"Yes, Sammy?" a voice said.

Ava looked at the restaurant owner, a man she had met many times while in the company of Uncle. He ignored her, all his attention focused on Wing.

"Tea for the lady."

"Jasmine," Ava said.

Wing lowered himself back onto his chair. It disappeared under his bulk. "How was Shanghai?" he asked.

"It's a wonderful city."

"I mean, how was your business in Shanghai?"

"Mr. Wing, I'm not sure why my business there — or anywhere else — is of any interest to you."

"Please, call me Sammy," he said.

"Sammy, what is going on here?"

"Ah, your tea is here," he said, reaching for the bottle of Sing Tao in front of him. The owner hovered, a pot in one hand, a cup in the other.

When they were alone again, Wing wiped his mouth on the sleeve of his shirt and then leaned ever so slightly towards her. The move, though not particularly abrupt or intrusive, caught her off guard, and she flinched.

"Have you heard of Li Kai?" he asked.

"No, I don't think I have," she said, gathering herself.

"He thought you might remember him. He runs Guangzhou. Jackie Leung contracted his gang to kill you."

"I only knew the name Li and the name Ko. Ko was the one they sent to do the job."

"But Li called him off before he could."

Ava began to correct him and then stopped. What did it matter if Li's message hadn't got to Ko before he tried to kill her? What did it matter that she'd fought him off, and another thug? This had nothing to do with the reality of the past. "I think you're implying that I owe Li a debt of gratitude for cancelling the contract — one that he initially and readily agreed to — only after his contractor ended up floating face down in Victoria Harbour."

Wing shrugged. "He had other choices."

"At the time there was only one that made any sense. I can't give him credit for doing what best served his interests."

"We all value our self-interest, don't we? It would be a strange and unpredictable world if we didn't. I'm sure you aren't any different than the rest of us when it comes to that. I know for a fact that Uncle wasn't — except maybe when it came to you. He put you ahead of most things in his life.

That was never clearer to me than when he asked me to help find and put away that pig Jackie Leung."

"I'm told he paid you well enough to do that."

"That was just the business side of things. The hard part for him was asking me in the first place. We had fallen out years before. There was, I admit, bad blood between us — mistrust, a taste for revenge — but he put all that aside and came to me, cap in hand, to ask me to help him find Leung. Now, I could have said no. I could have taken the opportunity to make him squirm. Instead I greeted him as an old colleague. I shook his hand and I agreed to do what he asked. The fact that I took money for it was a way for him to save face and not be so openly beholden to me."

"That's your story," Ava said quietly.

"That's what happened."

"And I have no way of knowing otherwise."

"Why would I lie?"

"Why do men breathe?"

"Are you always so skeptical?"

"It reduces disappointment."

"You're too young to be so skeptical and cynical."

"Uncle taught me that you can't be enough of either."

"Like your friend in Shanghai?"

"I'm not aware that I have a particular friend in Shanghai," Ava said quickly, and reached for her tea.

"He's a problem, you know."

"I don't know who you're referring to."

Wing leaned in closer. Ava found herself staring at the part in his hair: the roots were grey.

"He's not just a friend anymore, is he. I hear he's become a business partner," Wing said.

Ava felt her face twitch. She took a deep breath as she tried to regain her composure, the word *how* dancing on her lips. Instead she said, "I'm still waiting for the name of this friend and business partner."

Wing sat back with a slight smile on his face. "I know you're surprised that I know and that I knew so fast, but that's the way it is in my world. People you think are friends may not be. People you think are enemies may have only your best interest at heart. It isn't always easy to sort things out, even for the most experienced of us. I'm sorry for you if Xu betrayed your trust, but that's the nature of the man."

"Why am I here?" Ava said.

"Did you know that he's running for chairman of the societies?" Wing wielded the toothpick again, covering his mouth with his hand, his eyes never leaving Ava. "Li Kai is running as well," he said through the hand. "It's going to come down to the two of them. I support Li, but I'm prepared to live with whatever the result is. The problem is that your friend has decided to sabotage the democratic process."

"I beg your pardon?" Ava said. "Democratic process?"

He shrugged and placed the toothpick on the table. "We vote. The majority rules. What would you call it?"

"It's beyond definition."

"You're being cynical again. Frankly, I don't think it suits you. I think if you heard me out you might agree with me."

Ava shook her head. "Mr. Wing, why did you invite me here?"

"I need you to talk to your friend."

"Since you seem to know him so well, why don't you speak to him yourself?"

"I've tried. Li, myself, and others have tried, but he bobs and weaves. He's a hard man to pin down. He tells you what you want to hear and then goes off and does whatever he wants. The problem may be — and I'm being kind here — that he doesn't listen very well. When we talk to him, it's as if he thinks every word is designed to mislead and undermine him. He's programmed to disbelieve. We're all very frustrated with him, and in our business frustration sometimes leads to overreaction. I would like to avoid that."

"That's hardly my concern."

"Ms. Lee — Ava, we need to find someone he'll actually listen to. My opinion is that you could be that person."

"And why would I volunteer to do that?"

"Who mentioned volunteering? I will pay you, and I will pay a lot."

"To do what exactly?"

"I want you to listen to me and then I want you to reason with Xu. We need an honest broker."

"You overestimate my talents. And you're making some very large assumptions about my relationship with Xu. I'm afraid I would disappoint."

"I'm prepared to take that chance."

"Mr. Wing, what I said about my talents and my relationship to Xu was also my way of politely telling you that I want nothing to do with any of this."

"We'll pay you well to make the effort."

"I don't need or want your money."

Wing closed his eyes, tilted his head back, and breathed deeply and audibly through his nose. He looked to Ava like an angry man, and she braced herself for a tirade and readied herself to leave the restaurant.

Wing's eyes opened, the light seemingly gone from them. "You remind me of Uncle," he said in a whisper.

"Thank you."

"I don't mean it as a compliment."

## 18

THEY SAT QUIETLY, LOOKING AT EACH OTHER ACROSS the table. The moment lasted not much more than ten seconds, but it was a heavy silence, filled with discomfort.

"I apologize if I offended you with my remark about Uncle," Wing said finally.

"Accepted," she said.

"Now please, may I take a few minutes to explain why someone has to talk to Xu?" Wing said.

"I've already made my position clear."

"I know, but you should understand the depth of the consequences of this situation in which we find ourselves."

"Why?"

"Because if something unfortunate — terribly unfortunate — should happen, it might be important for you to understand the circumstances that led to it."

"I don't think I want to hear any more," Ava said, rising from her seat.

"Wait. Please, I'm not trying to be anything but honest with you," Wing said.

"But you don't speak plainly. What the hell does 'terribly unfortunate' imply?"

"Nothing that need be inevitable."

Ava shook her head. Every instinct she had was telling her to leave. But then what? Like it or not, now she needed to know. "Explain to me the circumstances that you've alluded to," she said as she lowered herself back onto the chair.

"Thank you."

"What are the circumstances?" she repeated.

"He is very clever, your friend. We all understand that, and many of us have benefited from it. And the fact that he spent the past year or two scheming with Uncle only advanced his education."

"Scheming?"

"Sorry. Let me say that he's taken Uncle's counsel for the past year or so and it has helped contribute to his growing success. Are you more comfortable with that description?"

"Go on."

"The first thing you need to understand is that Xu has made us all a lot of money. He understood very quickly the profits that can be made from software, electronic devices, and designer fashion labels, and most of us went along for the ride. And why not? The profits are almost as good as they are with drugs, and they come without the head-aches we have to endure with most of the other traditional businesses, like prostitution and gambling. The fact is, the police don't really care that much if you're ripping off some big American or European corporation. Once in a while they'll raid one of our street markets or shopping centres, but we usually get some notice. We load up the vendors with old inventory for the police to seize and make a big splash in the media as they destroy it." He laughed. "My man Jimmy says that letting the police grab that inventory is almost cheaper than having to truck it to a dump and get rid of it ourselves."

"So he's making you money and doing it in a way that keeps the police off your backs. That's a hell of a problem to have."

"*Momentai.* But a problem I do have is that your friend is manufacturing the majority of the goods we're selling."

"You said you were making all kinds of money."

"True, but what happens if the supply dries up?"

"Has that happened?"

"No, not yet."

"So what makes you think it's a possibility?"

He shrugged. "You have to understand that there's more involved here than just the supply line. As that business grew over the past few years, we began to move away from our more traditional pursuits. We let them go or we pushed them down to the bottom rungs of our gangs. It will be very hard, if not impossible, to rebuild what we had if your friend decides to play god."

"Is he playing god?"

"I think he's testing the idea."

"What makes you think that?"

"Shipments that were always on time are now sometimes late. Orders that were always filled properly now come up short."

"Perhaps demand is outstripping supply."

"That seems a logical explanation, but I'm attentive, and I've noticed that people who support him for chairman don't have those kinds of problems."

"How would you know?"

"There's talk."

"It sounds more like gossip."

He smiled. "Exactly. We gossip like young girls, except it isn't boys we talk about. It's about how much product reaches who and when," he said. "We have created — and it's our own fault — a dependency on those products. It's much like a drug addiction. All we can think about is when the next shipment will be coming in, because we know the one on hand will soon be gone."

"Why didn't you create alternative supply lines?"

"Ah, an excellent question."

"So you didn't."

"My excuse is that my dependency snuck up on me. One day selling software and iPhones was a sideline, six months later it was half my business, and now . . . I don't want to tell you. The world moves so fast today that even the Triads can't keep up with it."

"Xu does."

"Yes. I give him full credit for that. He has the technology, the engineers, and the factories, and he keeps buying more, hiring more, and building more. We tried to figure out how he did it but we couldn't. Oh, here and there we found an alternative supply, but there was never enough product and, truthfully, the quality was never good enough."

"It sounds to me as if you need to accommodate him until you're in a position where your need isn't so great."

"We've tried."

"My understanding is that the attempts to accommodate came only after threats and violence didn't work."

Wing sat back, his hands folded across his belly. "I was told you're smart. I know Uncle wouldn't have felt the way he did about you unless that was the case. I mean, I know there were rumours that you kept his bones warm, but I never believed them. That kind of behaviour wasn't typical of his character. He was a man who kept everything separate — he would never mix business and pleasure. So he kept you by his side for business, and for you and him to be partners for ten years speaks well of your intelligence and abilities. So I'm going to believe you'll act as smart as I think you are."

"Is that meant to be a compliment?"

"Only if you're smart enough to understand that Xu can't have everything."

"Everything?"

"He can't ransom his way to becoming chairman. It doesn't work. The end result, I mean. It's one thing for him to have economic leverage over us and to use it as any gang leader would, to further the interests of his own people. It's another thing to combine that leverage with the prestige and powers and perks that come with the chairmanship. He could — he would have us all by the throat." His hands went to his knees and he leaned forward, the smile disappearing. "He must drop his attempts to become chairman."

"You still haven't told me why."

He looked hard at her across the table, any hint of conviviality gone. "The chairman mediates," Wing said. "Eighteen organizations form our brotherhood, and from time to time there are territorial disputes, arguments about payments or financing, disagreements about who has the right to do what. The chairman is the man who decides who is right."

"Is the decision binding?"

"Yes, at least as long as everyone wants to stay in the family."

"If they don't?"

"When the chairman makes a decision, he communicates it to everyone and we proceed accordingly. It's possible that a gang might choose to ignore a ruling that went against them and try to go their own way, but they would very quickly find themselves cut off from the brotherhood. As a punishment, isolation can be very powerful. As formidable as any one gang may be — even Xu's — none of them would last very long without the support of the brotherhood's infrastructure."

"I see."

"It's a practice that goes back hundreds of years. No one, not even me or Xu, would go against it without expecting the consequences to be dire."

"Why do think Xu would not be even-handed if he was chairman?"

Wing pressed his hands against the seat of his chair and pushed. Slowly, painfully, he rose to his feet. "He might have no reason to be. He already has enough economic power, and now he's in the process of building a small army in Shanghai."

"Don't exaggerate."

"That episode in Borneo — there was no need for it. He just wanted to show us that he has the gun-power. It's been quite some time since any gang attacked another like that."

"He saved my life there."

"And I saved your life here."

"So why should I take sides?"

"Because there isn't any other choice. We can't let him

have the kind of absolute control he seems to want. Either you'll talk to Xu and get him to step down or we'll do everything we can to stop him."

"How do you expect him to react to a threat like that?"

"That depends on how you tell him. He doesn't need the chairmanship; he has enough influence and power. He talks and talks about preserving the societies but he's doing everything he can to cut the guts out of every society but his own. In Xu's perfect world, only Shanghai matters. The rest of us are peasants working for the king."

"Then vote against him, and get the gangs who feel the way you do to do the same."

"It's an open vote."

"What are you saying? That people are scared to vote against him because he'll withhold product as punishment?"

"That's how he's already acting. It can't go on like this."

Ava shook her head. "You keep talking about things that are beyond my knowledge."

Wing hovered over her, his eyes now tiny slits. He wiped the sweat from his face with a paper napkin and let it drop to the floor. "You need to understand that when I speak of consequences, they would not be restricted to Xu alone," he said. "Our reach would extend to people who consider him a friend, and even more surely, to those who are his partners."

"Just a minute —" Ava said as Wing brushed past her and lumbered towards the door without looking back.

## 19

SONNY WAS WAITING FOR HER OUTSIDE THE RESTAU-rant. Night had fallen. Ten metres away, illuminated by a 7-Eleven sign, Wing was climbing into the back seat of a Bentley, its door held open by the man Carlo had intro-duced as Bobby.

"Where are Carlo and Jimmy Tan?" she asked.

"They left together after you went into the restaurant," Sonny said, his attention divided between the Bentley and her. "Do you need either of them?"

The evening rush hour was now in full force. Even the sidewalks of the street where they stood were crammed. "No, I guess not. I think I'd just like to go back to the hotel."

"Are you okay?"

"Yes."

"You look either pissed off or worried. Did that prick Wing try anything?"

"Let's walk," Ava said.

Sonny led the way, Ava tucked in behind him like a small boat trailing an ocean freighter. When they reached the Mandarin, she paused by the entrance. "I'm going to stay in tonight," she said. "If I need you I promise I'll call, but I think it's quite unlikely."

"What happened with Wing?"

"Nothing," Ava said. "Nothing at all." The big man sighed and she saw the doubt etched in his face. She also knew he was too devoted to challenge her. "Tomorrow I expect I'll be going to see the lawyers in the morning. Their office is only a few streets from here, so I'll walk. After that I might need you, so I would appreciate it if you were on standby," she said.

"I'll be here."

Ava gave him a little wave and then turned and went in, his eyes boring into her back.

Her room had been serviced by the maid, the bed turned down and a small orchid and a Godiva chocolate left on her pillow. The curtains hadn't been closed, and the skyline was now lit up in all its brilliance, the water of Victoria Harbour gleaming along the shoreline under the skyscraper light show. She could see Tsim Sha Tsui in the distance, the Pacific Mall glowing like a giant beacon.

She rolled the desk chair over to the window and opened the mini-bar. She took out a miniature bottle of California Chardonnay, twisted off the cap, and carried it to the window. She had no need for a glass. She sat down, took a large swig, and extended her legs so they rested on the window ledge. *What a mess*, she thought. *What an awful fucking mess.*

She had to get her emotions under control. Then she had to think things through. The problem was that she hardly knew where to begin.

When she left the restaurant, she had been filled with an anger that bordered on rage. She was furious with herself for having been sucked into the meeting and then losing control of it, with Sammy Wing for his clumsy threats, and maybe most of all, with Xu. Who had he spoken to? What had he said? Less than forty-eight hours after making their supposedly confidential business agreement, it was now already in the open. What the hell had she gotten herself into? Worse, what had she involved May Ling and Amanda in?

The first idea that had come to her as she followed Sonny back to the hotel was to return Xu's money. Now she thought about the consequences. Without Xu's money they could still go ahead with the Po deal, but if the PÖ line suddenly took off, they might not have enough to properly finance its growth. And they certainly wouldn't have enough money for Suki to acquire the Shanghai business unless they put a lot more of their own capital into Three Sisters. Even if they did, May had been adamant that they should always retain some flexibility, some cash reserves, and trying to do both deals without Xu's money would leave them hamstrung. *We could pull back from the investments*, Ava thought, and then felt almost nauseated at the prospect. No matter what excuses she invented, they would lose all their credibility with Suki while having to continue dealing with her as a partner in the Shanghai business. That would not be fun. She would have to explain to Clark and Gillian that she hadn't actually lied to them about her willingness to fund their business. She doubted they would care either. And how would Amanda and Chi-Tze react? She couldn't tell them the truth, so it would be a case of saying she had changed her mind about the deal. She knew that would devastate them. How much of their trust and respect would she lose?

May was another factor. Ava knew the money could not be returned without her involvement and agreement, so she would have to be told about Xu's indiscretion and Wing's threats. Ava wasn't worried about recriminations or damage to their friendship. She expected her to be understanding and to go along with whatever Ava wanted to do, regardless of how it would damage May's relationship with Suki Chan. There would be disappointment, though; voiced or not, Ava hated the idea of being the cause of it.

But what nagged at her even more was the thought that giving back the money would make not one bit of difference to Sammy Wing. He might choose not to believe they had done it; he could decide he didn't care even if they did. They were leverage. The money didn't matter; it was the relationship — or what he thought was the relationship — between Ava and Xu that he was exploiting. He thought Ava would go running to Xu looking for protection, and he was gambling that Xu would do whatever was necessary to protect her. Would Xu withdraw from the contest for chairman if she asked him? She had no idea.

Without noticing, she had finished the small bottle of wine. She went to the bar and took out its twin. She knew she should eat, but she had no appetite.

She resumed her position at the window. Wing, she decided, was clever. The threats directed at Xu were just posturing. Xu sat in his safe haven in Shanghai, surrounded by his men, and had already proved himself capable of repelling attacks. The women, though, were completely vulnerable. She doubted that Wing would stoop to physically harming them, but that still left a wide range of options he could use to terrorize and damage them. She could imagine his goons warning their clients about the dangers of doing business with them, late-night threatening phone calls, cars and houses spray-painted with obscenities. Maybe May was beyond their reach in Wuhan, but Ava didn't doubt that they could reach her in Toronto, and she knew for certain they could make life a living hell for Amanda in Hong Kong and for Chi-Tze wherever she was. How much abuse could those two young women tolerate? Not much, Ava guessed. The beatings in Borneo had damaged their psyches as much as their bodies.

They were leverage, she thought once more. Wing had probed, looking for a crack in Xu's armour. The women were it — or so he believed.

*How did he know we were in Shanghai? How did he know about the business arrangement?* The questions came at her again, but this time with more urgency. The only two people who could answer them were Wing and Xu, and she knew that at least one of them wouldn't tell her. She reached for her cellphone.

"*Wei*," Xu said after his mobile rang twice.

"We have a problem," Ava said.

"Ava? You did not receive the money?"

"More like I wish we hadn't."

"I do not understand."

She drew a deep breath. "I'm in Hong Kong. I just met with Sammy Wing."

"I did not know you were in Hong Kong. And why would you meet with Wing?"

"An old friend asked me to do it as a favour. I saw no harm in it."

"What did Wing want?"

"First of all, he wanted to know how I enjoyed my visit to Shanghai. And then he asked me why I had become a business partner with you."

The line went quiet. Uncle would have known from the terse, clipped way she had spoken that she was furious. If Xu lied to her, that control would vanish. "What are you telling me?" he said quietly.

"He knows about the money," she said.

"You are certain?"

"Yes."

"Did he tell you how he knows?" Xu asked calmly.

"No."

"I did not think he would. I will have to find that out from this end."

"Xu, this was supposed to be a confidential arrangement."

"It is — was. There are only five people other than us who know anything about it. They are all part of my organization. Someone has let this out through some slip of the tongue . . . or maybe not a slip. Either way, I will find out who did it."

"It's a bit late for that," Ava said, more loudly than she had intended.

"I am sorry. I regret if it has caused you any embarrassment or inconvenience."

"That's the least of my worries."

"How so?"

"Wing threatened me."

"With what?"

"He wasn't specific, but then he didn't have to be. He just made it clear that I and my partners and our business could be a target of his displeasure. He knows I know the kind of shit he can throw our way."

"Why? Have you ever done anything to offend him?"

"Nothing at all, except for the fact that we're in business with you," she said.

"Why would he care about that?"

"He doesn't. He wants you to withdraw from the election for the chairmanship. He said that he and Li Kai from Guangzhou don't want you to become chairman. He said you already have too much power. He said they'll do whatever it takes to stop you. His animosity is directed entirely at you, but since he can't get to you, he's threatening to come after us. We are convenient, we are reachable, we are easy to intimidate. He obviously figures that I'll come to you and you will feel compelled to do something about this situation."

"My running for the chairmanship is not what this is all about," he said softly.

She sipped her wine. "I'm listening."

"They want more of my product and they want to buy into my businesses."

"So you told me when I was with you in Shanghai."

"Well, now they obviously think they have found a different way to get what they want."

"Then why bring up the chairmanship?"

"They will be talking to all the other gangs, but just about the chairmanship, about how I will use it to expand my base and my markets. They will not say a word about wanting a piece of my action. Opposing me for chairman is simply a cover."

"And threatening me and my partners?"

"He thinks that I will step in and cut a deal to prevent that."

Ava waited. She was not about to ask.

"Let me go and make some phone calls," he said. "I want to find out who said what to whom, and I will make sure it never happens again. And then I will call Sammy Wing."

## 20

**AVA DIDN'T MOVE FROM THE WINDOW. SHE NEEDED A** distraction, and the activity on and around the harbour, even at night, always held her interest. But after a few minutes of watching boats move across the water, her mind started to wander. In her head she replayed her conversation with Xu and found her anger returning. He had misled them, or at least overstated the amount of discretion he could command. Now she found herself doubting that he had the power to make things right. If he didn't, then what?

She would talk to May. Between the two of them they might be able to find a solution — even if they had to come up with the money to honour their commitments.

Her cellphone rang. She glanced at the incoming number and saw that it was May. "Hey," Ava said.

"How is Hong Kong?" May asked, her voice full of enthusiasm.

"Same as ever."

"I wish you were here in Beijing."

"Me too."

"I wanted to call before I join Suki and Zhang and some of

his senior people for dinner. It will be a late night, I think —
everyone is in a mood to celebrate. Zhang has built a tremendous business here, and we're so damn lucky he has no family
to hand it off to and that he adores Suki. The only downside
is that he doesn't want to stay in it much longer. He's in his
seventies, and he says he's ready to spend the rest of his days
chasing young women in Thailand," she said, laughing.

"With the money he'll be getting, he can capture whoever he chooses to go after."

"He's agreed to stay for another twelve months," May
said. "Suki will have to find someone to take over the day-
to-day running of the business. Zhang hasn't set up much
of a support system, and Suki's opinion is that the people
who are in place won't be able to keep up when he's gone."

"Does she have anyone in Shanghai she can transfer?"

"No. She runs her business the way he runs his," May
said. "I may have to pull in someone from Wuhan."

"And if you do that, how will Changxing react?"

"He'll complain, and then I'll mother him until he gets
over it."

"May," Ava said.

"Yes?"

"We need to hire more people for our business. We
should tell Amanda to start recruiting more of those bright
young things she went to school with."

"I know. How exciting is that?"

"Probably more than I can handle right now."

"What do you mean?"

"Oh, nothing," Ava said.

May paused, and Ava wondered if her friend sensed her
discomfort. "Is that all?" May asked.

*Should I tell her?* Ava thought. If she did, what purpose would it serve except to spread anxiety?

"Yes, that's all," Ava said. "I'll call the lawyers in the morning and get them started on things."

"Good. Now I have to get on the phone to Wuhan before going to dinner. I still have a business there that needs my attention, and a husband who needs it even more."

"Stay in touch."

Ava put down the phone, reached for her wine, and then was overcome with hunger. She debated going upstairs to Man Wah, but if Xu called she didn't want to have a conversation with him in the middle of a restaurant. She wandered over to the desk, read the room service menu, and ordered a bowl of hot and sour soup, Cantonese fried noodles with barbecued pork, shrimp, and scallops, and a plate of steamed Chinese broccoli with oyster sauce. She glanced at the room bar and asked for two small bottles of wine to be brought with her food.

She threw herself on the bed and turned on the television. The Jade Network was airing *Life Is Beautiful*, a soap opera set in the Ming Dynasty that revolved around the love life of a perpetually confused king. It was one of her mother's favourites, and despite its being almost slapstick at times, Ava found herself enjoying it. The episode ended just as her doorbell rang.

A waiter rolled her meal into the room and set it up near the window. She tipped him, opened another bottle of wine as soon as he left, and settled in to eat with another episode of *Life Is Beautiful* for company. When she finished her meal, she pushed the cart back into the hallway. She was thinking about taking a shower and getting ready for bed when her cellphone rang.

"This is Xu," he said.

"That was fast."

"I found out what happened."

"Yes?"

"I have an accountant named Deng who supervises the books of many of the firms attached to the co-operative. He has a cousin who works for the gang in Tianjin, also an accountant. Evidently, during the course of a conversation with his cousin the day we transferred the money, he mentioned that we had found a wonderful way to put the co-operative's money to work. He is not sure if your actual names came up, but he does remember mentioning Three Sisters. It was in passing, he said. He did not think anything of it."

"And he told you all this voluntarily?"

"I asked him the question; he answered it. My people understand that there is no value in trying to hide things from me. The truth always emerges, and they know that the severity of the repercussions is in direct relation to the amount of trouble I have to go through to get it."

"I see."

"I made Deng phone his cousin and I listened in on their conversation. The cousin said he had told his boss, who is the White Paper Fan, about our investment. From there it was obviously passed to the top. Deng thinks, in unfortunate hindsight, that the Tianjin gang is tight with Guangzhou."

"Yes, very unfortunate."

"What do you want me to do with him?"

"With Deng?"

"Yes."

"What would you normally do?"

"Nothing. It is at least partially my fault for not stressing strongly enough that the information had to be kept in-house. He is very loyal and normally tight-lipped."

"Then do nothing."

Ava heard someone shouting in the background over Xu's phone. "Wait a second," he said, and the line went quiet. She imagined he was covering the mouthpiece with his hand. "That was Auntie. One of my men walked into the house without taking off his shoes."

"So we know how the information leaked. But you still haven't said how you're going to handle the fallout."

"I talked to Sammy Wing," he said.

"That's a start."

"Yes, and only a start. It was a five-minute conversation."

"That's not what I wanted to hear."

"It is not as bad as you think. I asked him to meet with me. I told him that face-to-face we can sort things out. He agreed to the meeting. And truthfully, it is about time I did something like this. We cannot keep taking potshots at each other from a distance. It is neither healthy nor productive."

"You mentioned that Guangzhou knows about us as well. Does that mean Li Kai has to be involved?"

"I am meeting with Sammy only. There was no suggestion from his side that Li would take part. Still, I do assume that Sammy is talking for both of them, and whatever concessions I give to Sammy, Li will eventually expect."

"What about the chairmanship?"

"It was not discussed and I did not expect it to be. As I told you, this is about money."

"When is the meeting?"

"Tomorrow. "

"Thank you."

"Do not thank me yet. All we have done is agree to meet."

"Where?"

"He wanted me to go to Hong Kong. I wanted him to fly to Shanghai. We decided that a neutral site would have to do. We chose Shenzhen."

"That's so close to Hong Kong."

"Yes, but it is neutral enough."

"So, tomorrow?"

"Yes, I am flying there in the morning. We are scheduled to meet with Wing at one."

"We?"

"Yes, you and me. That is another reason I did not object to Shenzhen. I thought it would make it easier for you."

"Xu, why would Wing want me at the meeting?"

"He does not care one way or another. I am the one who insisted. I want you to see and hear that I am sincere in my efforts to make things right with him. I have an offer to make to him that is more than fair. It should pacify him and Li."

"If he doesn't think it is fair?"

"Then I have a sweetener. I will get an agreement."

Ava had been sitting on the corner of the bed during their talk. Now she stood and walked to the window. "Where is the meeting location?"

"I insisted on a public place. Wing chose the Imperial Manor Restaurant. It's on Nongyuan Road, in the Futian district."

"Xu, do you trust Wing?"

"What do you mean?"

"They attacked you in Shanghai."

"They attacked the factory and not me personally. There is an agreement — unwritten, but an agreement all the same — that no Dragon Head will ever personally attack or order an attack on another. It is a code that has not been violated in my lifetime. So I am not worried."

"I see," Ava said.

"So, will you be at the Imperial Manor in Futian?"

Ava, who had been to Shenzhen more times than she liked to remember, knew the area. "I will do the best I can. If I come, I'll have Sonny drive me."

"He cannot come into the restaurant. That is the deal. Just Wing, his man Jimmy Tan, you, and me."

"You'll travel alone?"

"No, I am bringing Suen. He can hang around outside with Sonny."

Ava sighed. "Okay. I want this resolved more than I hate going to Shenzhen. Barring any other crisis in my life, I'll see you at the restaurant tomorrow."

## 21

**AVA AND SONNY TOOK THE TRAIN FROM HUNG HOM** to the Lok Ma Chau MTR station, just across the river from Shenzhen. It was Sonny's choice to take the train, which surprised her. When she had phoned him the night before to say she needed him to drive her across the border, he hesitated and then asked if she really wanted to take the car.

"Is that a problem?" she asked.

"The lineups at the border are completely unpredictable. We could be waiting hours to get through, and then when we do, we'll have to contend with the Shenzhen traffic. There are always traffic jams, and worse than that, no one there knows how to drive — and that's not a joke. I read in *Sing Tao* last year that Shenzhen has a million unlicensed drivers. They drive like they're in bumper cars."

"What do you suggest?"

"Where's your meeting?"

"Futian."

"The train from Hung Hom goes directly to the station there. A forty-five-minute ride, tops. Do you have a Hong Kong ID card?"

"Yes."

"We get out of the train, swipe the card, and we're in Shenzhen. We can catch a cab from the station to wherever you're going."

"The meeting starts at one, but I want to be there a few hours earlier."

He didn't ask why. Sonny had worked with Ava enough times to understand that she liked to be prepared for anything, and being early sometimes prevented nasty surprises. "I'll pick you up at the hotel at nine. I'll park at Hung Hom. We should get to your meeting place by eleven."

They reached Hung Hom at nine thirty. As they walked from the parking lot to the station, Ava was aware that they made an odd couple: diminutive Ava and the hulking Sonny. In Borneo Ava at one point had found herself standing between Sonny and the even larger Suen. She had never felt quite so small. As if conscious of the height disparity, on the way to the station Sonny walked a couple of paces behind her, his eyes flitting in all directions.

Ava bought two first-class tickets for the nine-fifty train, which left the station on time. *Hong Kong trains always seem to leave on time*, Ava thought. "You know, I met Uncle for the very first time because of a case in Shenzhen," she said as the train headed north on its thirty-kilometre trip towards the Pearl River Delta.

"I remember. I was still working for him in Fanling. He hadn't cut off all his old connections yet. He told me he had a crew in Shenzhen chasing down a debt and they had run into you. They had no idea how to handle you."

"Or me them."

"I heard you wrapped them around your finger," he said, smiling.

"They felt sorry for me."

"And then you managed to get enough money out of the guy to look after everyone. That's when Uncle said, 'I need to meet that girl.'"

"And the rest is history."

"Shenzhen was smaller then," he said.

"Still had to be five or six million people."

"Yeah, and now it's over fifteen million."

"What a place."

"I knew it before it became the first special economic zone. It was the late seventies and I was dating a girl from there. It was all farmland and fishing villages back then — maybe a couple of hundred thousand people spread across the entire area. And it was pretty, with Shenzhen Bay on the coast and all rolling hills and orchards inland. Shit, what a change. I don't think there's a hill left."

"I've never seen anything but the ugly side of it," Ava said. "I've been there five or six times. I don't know why those thieves thought it was a good place to hide; it never really worked out for them. But every time I came, there were two more skyscrapers, another highway, another industrial park filled with factories that weren't built to code and were prone to blowing up or falling down."

"Half an hour from Hong Kong but a world away," Sonny said.

"Sonny, that is profound."

He smiled. "Uncle used to say that. He never got over his hatred of the Communists. Whenever he heard people talking about Shenzhen as a symbol of the new China, he would start ranting."

"I never heard him rant."

"Did you ever say Shenzhen is a symbol of the new China?"

"No."

"Then that's why."

The train arrived at Lok Ma Chau on schedule. They got a taxi and drove to Nongyuan Road. The ride took them through neighbourhoods that were a mixture of soaring apartment buildings and commercial towers. Nothing was small in Shenzhen. The architecture wasn't quite as boxy as Ava remembered, but even the odd design gem couldn't take away the oppressive feeling inspired by the line of buildings looming over the highway.

The restaurant was in the middle of a block of shops and eateries that ran down both sides of the street. Every building was the same height and every façade was the same distance from the street. Only the store signs and windows offered any visual variety.

It was just past eleven when they got out of the cab in front of the restaurant. Ava scanned the street. "There's a coffee shop that has some decent sightlines," she said, pointing across the street and to the right.

"I'll meet you there in a while. I want to take a walk," Sonny said.

Ava nodded. She knew he would walk down and around several blocks. In all her years with Uncle, she couldn't remember him going to a meeting with Sonny where Sonny didn't case the area. At first she thought he was being overly cautious, but after a meeting in Sha Tin went sideways and they had to make a hurried early exit, she never questioned his preparation again. Her insistence on arriving early for meetings mirrored that caution. People who were supposed to be alone arrived with henchmen. Secure locations turned out to be anything but. The only thing she ever wasted by arriving early was time. And the thing she saved more than once was her well-being.

The coffee shop had a rack of Chinese newspapers. She picked up three and then bought a black coffee. She sat at a table near the window that gave her a clear view of the Imperial Manor and most of the street. She had read one newspaper and was on her second coffee when Sonny entered the shop. He nodded at her, ordered a tea, and then sat at another table with a slightly different view.

The street was busy with a steady stream of traffic, both automotive and pedestrian. By twelve they had seen nothing out of the ordinary. At twelve fifteen a black BMW with tinted windows parked almost directly in front of the Imperial Manor. The driver's window opened just far enough for a cigarette butt to be flicked out.

"Can you see anyone in the BMW?" she asked Sonny.

"No."

After five minutes had passed, she thought about asking Sonny to take a walk past the car. Just as she was about to, the BMW pulled away from the curb and drove down the street.

The coffee shop was filling with the lunch crowd, and Ava saw the manager eyeing her and Sonny with their empty cups. Just as it looked as if he was about to approach them, Ava caught sight of a black Range Rover pulling up in front of the Imperial Manor. Xu stepped out of the passenger side and Suen from the driver's. They looked around and then Suen accompanied his boss inside.

"There's Xu and Suen. I'm going over to the restaurant now," she said.

"I'll go with you," Sonny said.

As they crossed the street, Ava saw a panel truck in a no-parking zone beside a raised manhole surrounded by orange cones, almost directly across from them. Five men stood over the manhole. The truck had no markings. The men were wearing blue safety helmets and yellow fluorescent vests. Ava saw two of them turn when she and Sonny approached. One of them looked startled. He had a row of rings in each of his ears.

When they were well past them, Ava said, "I think I know one of those guys."

"How?" Sonny asked.

"I think his name is Ko. If it is, he works for Li. He was the one they sent to London to kill me."

Sonny stopped and looked back quickly towards the workmen. "Three of them are wearing running shoes. What kind of maintenance workers wear sneakers?"

Ava turned and stared at them. They were focused on the manhole, chatting among themselves. The man with the earrings was in profile, and now his resemblance to Ko didn't seem so apparent. "Let's not jump to conclusions. It might not be Ko, and running shoes may be what workers wear here. But tell Suen about them all the same," she said.

"Speaking of Suen . . ." Sonny said, pointing ahead.

The big man was in front of the Imperial Manor, leaning against the Range Rover. When he saw them, he straightened up.

"Hey," Sonny said, extending his hand.

"Good to see you," Suen said, then lowered his head in

Ava's direction. "The boss is inside already. I went in for a few minutes — it looks clear."

"Well, I guess I'll join him. You two boys behave yourselves out here, okay?"

"We will," Suen said.

"Sonny, just a word," Ava said, motioning for him to join her near the door. "Your phone is on, right?"

"Yeah."

"Mine too. If you see anything suspicious out here, you call me right away."

"Count on it."

Ava squeezed his arm, turned, and walked into the restaurant. She was instantly enveloped in an aromatic cloud of garlic and ginger. *They're cooking seafood*, she thought, then saw the row of tanks full of geoduck and Manila clams, spiny lobsters, crabs, shrimp, eels, *garoupa*, and snappers. "I'm here to meet with Mr. Wing," she said to the hostess.

"You have a private room in the back. Let me show you the way."

The restaurant was full, and Ava had to fight off hunger pangs as she walked past tables loaded with steamed and fried seafood.

The private room wasn't much more than a cubicle with enough space for one circular table. Xu sat in a chair against the back wall so that the door was in his direct line of sight. He was wearing his usual black suit, white shirt, and black tie. He stood when he saw her. "I am glad you decided to come, *mei mei*," he said.

"It was hard not to."

There was a teapot on the table and four cups. Xu poured tea into the cup next to his. "They should be here soon."

Ava checked her watch. It was five to one.

"Did you bring Sonny?" he asked.

"Yes, he and Suen are outside."

"Precautions. There was a time when they were not necessary," Xu said.

"And there was a time when having a fax machine and a mobile phone that weighed five pounds was considered high-tech."

Xu smiled. They were standing next to each other. Ava stretched out her arms and gave him a small hug, then they both sat.

"I have to tell you that, despite the way it came about, this meeting was long overdue and is probably a very good thing. I had been putting off having to deal with Wing, but as a long-term strategy it was never going to work. So we will get things settled and move on," Xu said.

"You seem confident that he'll agree to your offer."

"I am hopeful more than confident, but if I read him correctly, he will agree."

Ava glanced at her watch again. It was one o'clock. The door was open and she could see into the restaurant. There was no sign of Sammy Wing or Jimmy Tan. She felt a flutter of disquiet in her stomach.

"Wing did say one o'clock?" she asked.

"Yes."

Her phone rang. It was Sonny. "Yes," she said.

"Three of those workers just got into the truck and drove away."

"Where did they go?"

"Down the street and around the corner."

"What are the others doing?"

"Looking down the manhole."

"Have they done anything other than that?"

"No."

"Any sign of Wing?"

"No."

"Thanks." She looked at Xu. He held a cup of tea to his lips, seemingly relaxed.

"I'm starting to get uncomfortable," she said.

"They are only a few minutes late."

"I'm giving them another five minutes, no more than that."

"I spoke to Wing this morning when I got in. He said he was driving here from Hong Kong. He could be tied up at the border or in traffic."

"If he is, why doesn't he call?"

Xu shrugged, but Ava saw his eyes narrow and knew she had his attention now. "I will phone him." She watched him search for Wing's number in his log and then press the call button. A few seconds later he put the phone back in his pocket. "The call went to voicemail," he said.

"I think we should leave," Ava said, rising from the table.

They heard a clatter of dishes from outside the room, raised voices, and then a woman's scream. Ava slid around the table. Xu moved even faster and reached the door before her, blocking her view for an instant. She wasn't sure which she saw first, the flash of a yellow vest or the bare arm with a knife in its hand. She moved to the right and saw the knife catch Xu's upper chest near the left shoulder. As Ava tried to get past him, the knifeman struck again, his blade catching Xu's side.

Ava finally found space and struck. With the middle

knuckle of her index finger extended, she smashed her right fist into his face. Blood exploded as the assailant's nose crumbled into a mass of bloody pulp. The man lurched back, falling to the floor and blocking the path of the two men who stood behind him.

"We don't want you. All we want is him, but if you get in the way I'll fuck you too," the man who Ava now knew for certain was Ko said. "Move out of the way."

Xu was slumped behind her. She stared at the two men holding long, lethal stilettos.

"No," she said.

"I should have killed you in London," Ko said.

"You couldn't do it then and you can't do it now."

"Bitch," he said.

Ko rushed her from the left. Ava swivelled as he thrust the knife towards her neck. She moved her head back a few inches, and as the weapon hissed past her she drove her foot into his groin. He gasped and folded forward. Her knuckle rocketed into his ear, and then she raised her foot and drove the heel of her shoe into his forehead.

She turned to face the remaining man. The knife was in his left hand, and in his right he held a gun. Ava looked at Xu. He was leaning against the doorframe, clutching his side, half of his shirt soaked in blood. She saw the man raise the gun and aim at Xu. Before she could move, a shot rang out. Wing's man looked at her in shock and then crashed to the floor. She looked down at what had been the back of his head. All she could see was blood spreading around him like a halo.

"We need to get out of here," Sonny said, still holding his gun at shoulder height.

Ava turned towards Xu, who was slipping to the floor. She leapt forward and caught him by the right arm. He groaned and his eyes rolled back. "You'll have to help him," she said to Sonny.

Sonny crossed the five metres between them in two steps. He slipped his arm under Xu's good arm, lifted him partially off the ground, and pressed him against his side. "These guys obviously came in through the back door. We should leave that way. Four more of the guys in yellow vests just arrived. They were walking towards the restaurant when I came in to warn you."

"Where's Suen?"

"I told him to drive the Range Rover around to the back alley. He should be there by now."

"Okay, let's go."

Sonny looked down at Ava's two victims. They were still alive but barely moving. "Is one of these the guy who tried to kill you in London?" he asked.

"The one with the rings in his ears."

Sonny pointed the gun at his head.

"Don't bother. It's not worth it," she said, just as he pulled the trigger.

## 22

**THE ROOM WAS AT THE REAR OF THE RESTAURANT, SO** all they had to negotiate was the kitchen and its staff. Six chefs were manning more than a dozen giant woks, and the noise was intense from steel spatulas hitting cast-iron pans and the sizzle of food in oil. No one gave them more than a passing glance, out of indifference or fear or simply because they hadn't heard the shouting and gunshots over the noise.

The back door was open. The idling white panel truck the thugs had used was blocking their view. Sonny poked his head out and looked up the alley. "Here comes Suen," he said.

The Range Rover drove past the truck and then eased in front of it before stopping. Ava knew Suen was using the truck as cover in case he had been followed; she also knew it would provide serious cover for only a few seconds. She opened the truck door, reached over, turned off the engine, and put the key in her pocket. She saw no point in leaving the men an easy way to follow them.

Sonny opened the back door and lifted Xu onto the seat.

Ava ran around the car to the other side and climbed in beside him.

"I'll drive," Sonny yelled. "I know my way around this town."

Suen nodded and slid into the front passenger seat. His eyes never left Xu, and a look of worry, bordering on panic, was etched across his face.

Sonny closed his door and gunned the car, speeding to the end of the alley. He hesitated for a second, then executed a hard right turn and raced to Nongyuan Road, shooting through an amber traffic light. Suen glanced down the road towards the restaurant.

"Those four new guys in vests arrived in a black BMW," he said. "It's still there."

"Anyone visible?" Ava asked.

"No. They must still be in the restaurant or in the alley," Suen said. He looked back at Xu, whose eyes were shut and whose breathing was laboured. "Was he shot?"

"Stabbed," Ava said. "Once in the shoulder and I think the second one caught him in the side."

"I am okay," Xu said softly. "Get us out of here."

For ten minutes Sonny weaved through traffic, turning down street after street until Ava had lost all sense of where they had been. Suen kept his eyes locked on Xu.

They were in a residential area, the street flanked by rows of towering apartment buildings, when Sonny finally slowed and looked carefully at their surroundings. "There's a shopping centre near here called Emperor's Landing," he said. "Everyone look for it."

During the drive Xu had remained still, his head slumped against the back of the seat. His breathing seemed less strained, but when they hit a bump on the road, he groaned. Ava was relieved that he was still conscious.

Suen turned to Sonny. "What happened to the guys who did this?" he snarled.

"Two of them are dead," Sonny said. "Ava obliterated the other one's face."

Suen's rage seemed to subside, but only slightly. Ava knew that worry about his boss would be competing with thoughts about Sammy Wing, as it was for her.

Sonny drove the Range Rover for another two blocks before Ava spotted the shopping complex, two streets down and to their left. Sonny circled the parking lot until he found an isolated spot. He turned off the engine and leaned forward over the steering wheel. "I haven't had to drive like that in years," he said.

"Great job," Suen said.

"Well, we lost them," Sonny said.

"But we can't stay here, not with the boss hurt," Suen said.

"I know."

"We need time to think. Sonny has bought us that," Ava said, reaching towards Xu. She slid back his jacket. The entire left side of his shirt was soaked in blood.

"We need to get him to a doctor," Suen said.

"I don't know any here. Do you?" Ava asked.

"No."

"Sonny?"

"No."

"We can't take him to a hospital," Ava said. "There would be too many questions, and we have no idea who to trust."

"Ava is right," Xu said, his eyes opening.

"We're less than an hour from Hong Kong," Sonny said.

"I know a doctor there who has a fully equipped clinic. It's as good as any hospital."

"Is he affiliated with the Triads?"

"He's my girlfriend's brother. I'm the only Triad he knows."

"We're agreed, then, that there's no way we can go to a hospital here or risk looking for a doctor?" Ava said.

"Hong Kong is our best bet," Sonny said.

"Yes, take me to Hong Kong," Xu said.

"We have to get through the border crossing," Suen said. "How can we when he looks like that?"

"We need to patch him up," Ava said.

"We can buy some bandages, ointment, wraps in the mall," Sonny said.

"Suen, did you guys bring a change of clothes?"

"No, we thought we'd be flying back to Shanghai tonight."

"Okay, go and buy Xu an undershirt and a dress shirt — a black one if you can find it. Get a size bigger than he normally wears. Sonny, you pick up a jug of water, whatever painkillers you can get over the counter, and some towels, along with the bandages and ointment."

Suen hesitated. Ava guessed he was reluctant to leave Xu.

"Let's go," Sonny said.

The two men clambered from the car and walked quickly across the parking lot. Ava turned to Xu. "How are you doing?" she asked.

"Not well, but I can talk," Xu said.

"That was a mess back there."

"I walked us right into it."

"You couldn't have known."

"I should have figured that Wing's approach to you was

just a ploy. It was careless of me to think he would honour our code," Xu said. His voice was fading.

"What are you going to do?"

He took several careful breaths. "Destroy Sammy Wing," he finally said.

"You need to know that at least one of the men who attacked us works for Li."

"Are you sure?"

"I'm certain. I've met him before."

Xu shook his head and closed his eyes. "I cannot say I am surprised."

"What will you do if Li is actually involved in this?"

"I have no doubt that he is. I am also beginning to think that this is more about the chairmanship than money."

"So what will you do?"

"Nothing. At least, nothing right now. His organization is much stronger than Wing's, and even if it was not and I went after him without having certain proof, it would look as if I was trying to seize the chairmanship."

"But you think Wing and Li are partners."

"Yes. But it is a partnership that has not really been tested."

"And you will test it?"

"I will go after Wing with more firepower than he can imagine. We will know soon enough what kind of partner he has in Li."

"And what do you suspect?"

"Li will stand by and let events unfold. He will let us fight, hoping that Wing wins but knowing that if Wing loses, he can still blame me for instigating the conflict. I imagine he thinks that whatever the outcome, he is the only one who will emerge with his gang and his reputation intact."

"And if you're wrong?"

Xu groaned and shifted his weight. "Then instead of a battle in Wanchai it will be all-out war as far as Guangzhou." He paused, closed his eyes. Then he said, "I am going to turn Suen and my man Lop loose on Wing. When we win, and if I am in no shape to negotiate, you will have to handle it. Suen and Lop are soldiers and they will have blood in their eyes. They will want to kill Wing. I want him alive. I have uses for him."

All Ava could think of was reasons why she shouldn't get involved, but then she remembered her conversation with Xu in his garden in Shanghai and knew this was hardly the time to argue with him. "Why do you want Wing alive?" she asked.

"If I have him under my control, I can protect my best market. If we kill him, that will give Li an excuse to turn as many other Dragon Heads against me as he can. A dead Wing would cost me votes."

"How can you control Wing from Shanghai?"

"I would leave men in Hong Kong to protect my interests."

"It sounds like you've been thinking along these lines for a while."

He shook his head. "Not specifically, but when you leave desperate men with no options, they will always do desperate things. We need to give Wing a way out that also suits our needs, and then we need a plan to neutralize Li."

"By the time we get to that point, I'm sure you'll be able to handle things."

He threw back his head and groaned, biting his lower lip.

"No more talk," she said.

"Things will move fast. You know now what I want as an end result."

"Be still."

"Ava, promise me. I can't leave this to Suen or Lop."

"Enough."

"Promise me."

"Xu, that's enough. You need to preserve your strength so we can get you across the border." He became quiet.

Ava turned away from him and focused on the parking lot. Everything seemed normal. Everything except for the fact that the wounded man next to her was waiting to cross the border from China to Hong Kong so he could unleash a war. And somewhere in Guangzhou was a man named Li who had twice tried to kill her.

## 23

**SUEN WAS BACK FIRST. HE STOOD OUTSIDE THE CAR,** occasionally looking at Xu and then at Ava. Every time he did, Ava smiled and gave him a thumbs-up.

Finally Sonny arrived with two bags. The two big men were talking when she opened the door and slid out of the car.

"We know what to do," Suen said.

"I believe you," she said.

She watched as Suen put a couple of pills between Xu's lips and gave him some water. Then he and Sonny went to work. It took twenty minutes for them to strip off his shirt, wipe away the blood, apply ointment, layer bandages, add tape, and then put on the new undershirt and black dress shirt. When they were done, Xu looked drawn but he didn't look wounded.

"Put all the bloody stuff in those garbage cans," Ava said.

When they returned and were settled in the car, Suen asked, "What do we do when we get to Hong Kong?"

"See the doctor," Ava said.

"I'll call him as soon as we cross the border," Sonny said.

"Xu will need blood," she said.

"The clinic has everything," Sonny said.

He drove more carefully now but he kept looking in all directions. Ava could see the tension on his face and in his shoulders. He was ready to react to whatever came their way. Suen had the same edgy look.

"We're close now," Sonny said. "The lineups shouldn't be too bad. Why doesn't everyone pass their passport or ID card to me."

Xu's head was resting against the back of the seat, his eyes still closed. He reached into the left breast pocket of his jacket and took out his passport. Ava took it from him, half expecting to see it coated with blood. It wasn't discoloured, but it was damp to the touch. She passed it to Suen. "Wipe it well," she said.

The customs and immigration booths came into view. Three lanes of traffic fanned out to line up at fifteen booths. When they finally reached theirs, the customs officer stepped outside to take the documents from Sonny. He scanned them, checking the photo IDs against the occupants of the car. Xu didn't open his eyes and didn't move. *He looks like he's sleeping*, Ava thought. Without a word, the officer handed the documents back to Sonny and motioned him to move along.

Driving across the border between China and the Special Administrative Region of Hong Kong wasn't just a matter of dealing with Customs and Immigration. As they left the booth, Sonny's immediate challenge was to move the car into the proper lane without getting hit. In China they drove on the right side of the road; in Hong Kong it was on the left. Sonny had to make the transition in a criss-cross fashion and hope that everyone in front of him knew to do the same. After a few nervous moments he had the car at the speed limit on the Shenzhen–Hong Kong Western Corridor Highway.

"Call the clinic," Ava said to Sonny as soon as the road was clear.

"I was going to call my girlfriend instead and get her to arrange things with her brother. I think it would be easier that way."

"Whatever you think is best."

Sonny pulled his phone from his jacket and hit the speed-dial button.

"As soon as Sonny is finished, I want to talk to Lop," Xu said to Suen.

"Lop?" Suen said, his head swivelling to stare at his boss.

"Yes, Lop," Xu said, his eyes still closed.

Sonny's conversation with his girlfriend was quick and to the point. When he had finished, he put away the phone and said, "We can go directly to the clinic. She'll make sure they'll be ready for us."

Suen was now on his mobile. "Get me Lop," he said, and then paused. "Go get him. The boss needs to talk to him."

Xu pulled himself upright. Ava saw him flinch and knew the pain was worse than he was letting on.

"Wait a second, I'm passing my phone," Suen said.

"Put it on speaker and hold it in front of me," Xu said.

Suen turned and leaned over the front seat, his huge arm extended.

"Lop, things did not go well in Shenzhen," Xu said. "I will be staying in Hong Kong to sort things out. How soon can you get here with sixty men?"

Sonny glanced sideways at Suen, whose eyes were locked straight ahead, his face impassive.

"What do you mean 'not well'?" a strained voice said.

"I have been hurt, but it is nothing for you to worry about."

"Those fucking sons of bitches!" Lop yelled so loudly and harshly that Ava flinched.

"Lop, I need you to control your temper. This is strictly business. Do not get the men all pumped up."

Ava could hear Lop breathing into the phone and knew he was deeply agitated. "If I use private planes, I can have the men there tonight," he said finally.

"No, I do not want you to use private planes. Send the men separately on commercial flights and then book them into different hotels. We do not want to raise any alarms or give any warning. But I do want you to move them here tonight," Xu said. "Sonny, we will need weapons. Can you do anything from the Hong Kong side?"

"Not for sixty men. Not even for ten men — I don't have those sorts of contacts."

"Lop, you will have to figure out how to get weapons into Hong Kong. We have a shipment of phones and tablets scheduled to be flown here today. Find out the specifics and see if you can piggyback some guns with them. We are paying some people at the airport to turn a blind eye on the shipment, so a few extra boxes should not make that much difference."

"I'll look after it."

Xu nodded. Then he slumped back against the seat.

"Boss!" Suen said, alarmed.

"What's going on?" said Lop over the phone.

"He's in pain," Suen said. "We're on the Hong Kong side and headed for a clinic."

"I am getting tired," Xu said softly. "Let us wrap this up. I want you to take out enough of Wing's men that he will come begging on his knees to get me to stop. Keep him alive, and do not hurt him — I have uses for him. If I am out of circulation after you are done, I want Ava to handle any discussions with him. Do you understand?"

Lop said nothing. Suen stared at Xu.

"Did you hear me about Ava?"

"Yes," Suen said.

"Lop?"

"Yes, boss."

"And Lop, if Wanchai is more than sixty of our men can handle, bring in sixty more. In fact, have them ready and on standby."

"I will.

Beads of sweat had formed on Xu's forehead and upper lip, which was almost white. The effort of the phone call seemed to have sapped his strength.

Suen ended the call. "We'll need somewhere to stay in Hong Kong," he said.

"The clinic has beds," Sonny said.

"Perfect."

"And Ava, you shouldn't stay at the Mandarin. Wing knows you're there."

"I'm not going to stay at the clinic," Ava said.

"Uncle's apartment in Kowloon is empty for the next month," Sonny said. "Lourdes is in the Philippines. I can't imagine anyone would think of looking for you there."

"Let me think about it," Ava said.

They were in the New Territories now, heading south to Kowloon. They drove through Tai Po and had just entered Sha Tin when Xu found the strength to speak again. "Sonny, we must find out as much as we can about Wing's operations. Do you know anyone who can identify his men? We need to know who they are and how we can get to them."

"The only person I know well enough to recommend is Carlo. He used to work for Uncle and helped Ava more than once. The only problem is that he works for Wing now."

"Would he help?" Xu asked.

"Only if Ava asked him."

"Ava, what do you think?"

"He hasn't been with Wing very long and might not know that much. I don't want that held against him."

"I understand."

"I mean absolutely no recriminations."

"I understood what you meant. So, will you ask him?"

"I might, but not now. Let's get you to the clinic first. Sonny, where is it exactly?"

"On Argyle Street in Mong Kok."

Ava groaned. Mong Kok was a district near the centre of Kowloon. It was densely populated, and not an easy drive at the best of times.

She had expected they would be delayed at the Lion Rock Tunnel, which separated the Territories from Kowloon, but they sped through and were soon into the outer edges of the district. They kept moving at a steady rate of twenty to thirty kilometres an hour until they reached Argyle Street, where they ran into gridlock. For ten minutes they inched forward, Sonny muttering under his breath; Ava could see the tension in his neck. Xu seemed to have lost consciousness, and Suen cursed every time they stopped.

"How far are we from the clinic?" Ava asked. "Close enough to carry him?"

"About half a kilometre, and you can see how crowded the sidewalks are. I think we're better off staying in the car," Sonny said.

They finally got past the intersection that seemed to be causing the delay, and a few minutes later Sonny parked in front of a women's clothing store. "The clinic is above the shop," he said. "I'll go upstairs to let them know we're here."

Suen jumped from the front seat and opened the back door. He slipped an arm under Xu's legs, the other around his back, and lifted him clear. "I'll be right behind you," he said.

"I'll stay here," said Ava, who wasn't fond of hospitals or clinics. She watched Sonny open the door and then stand back so Suen could pass with Xu. When the door closed behind them, she reached for her phone.

"*Wei*," Carlo said hesitantly.

"It's Ava."

"Are you okay?"

"You're alone?"

"Yeah. I'm at home."

"Did you hear what happened?"

"I just got a call. All kinds of crazy rumours are flying around," he said in a rush. "Who knows what's true?"

"What's being said?"

"Someone tried to kill Xu and fucked up."

"Who tried?"

"No one seems to know, or else they don't want to say."

"Well, it was Wing and Li."

"How do you know?"

"I was there. They tried to kill me too."

She heard him breathing, and even in that she could feel his fear. "Carlo, we need to meet. Is that possible?"

"Ava, I had nothing to do with this."

"My friends from Shanghai want to meet with you too, but they thought I might be your better option. Carlo, I'm not blaming you. I just want to talk."

"I'm not sure that's a good idea."

"Are Wing's men watching you?"

"Why would you ask that?"

"They know we're close."

"I don't mean shit to them. They think I'm an idiot."

"So what's your problem?"

"Does Xu know I phoned to ask you to meet with Wing the first time?"

"Yes."

"Fuck."

"But he'll do what I want," Ava said.

"And what do you want?"

"Right now I want you to meet with me. Why don't we start with that?"

"Ava, you know I would never do or say anything to hurt you."

"Carlo, we're going in circles. Let's stop, because neither of us has time to play around. I have no intention of hurting you or letting anyone else hurt you — we're old friends. So tell me, how long would it take you to get to the Kowloon MTR station?"

"Fifteen minutes."

"I might be a bit longer, but let's say I'll meet you there in half an hour, at Andy's restaurant. Call and ask him to set up a small table in the kitchen. I had a meal or two there with Uncle. It's as private as you can get in Kowloon."

"Okay, I can do that."

"Good," Ava said. "See you there."

## 24

**SHE DEBATED WHETHER TO GO INTO THE CLINIC OR**
simply phone Sonny. In the end she called him and got
his voicemail. "Sonny, this is Ava. I'm going to meet Carlo.
When I'm finished, I'm heading back to the hotel to pack. I
haven't decided about Uncle's apartment yet. I'll be in touch."

She searched in her purse and found a piece of paper
and a pen. *I'm checking out of the hotel*, she wrote. *I'll call
you later.* She left the backup note on the dashboard and
hailed a cab.

The traffic was as brutal leaving Mong Kok as it had been
getting there. Ava got out of the taxi three blocks from
the Kowloon MTR station and walked the rest of the way.
When she was a block from the station, her phone rang.
The screen said BURGESS AND BOWLBY. She let the call go
to voicemail; this wasn't a time to be distracted. She would
get in touch with the lawyers after she was finished with
Carlo — after she had some notion of how deeply she was
immersed in Xu's war.

Ava hesitated near the door to the restaurant, making
sure no one was following her. When she went inside,

both Andy and his wife, Winnie, were at the hostess stand. Winnie smiled and bowed her head in Ava's
direction as Andy walked towards her, his face grim and
full of worry. He had been Carlo's partner for many years
as an occasional employee of Uncle's, and he had helped
Ava from time to time. The restaurant was his father's,
but now he had passed it on to Andy and Winnie, and
Andy was mainly out of the old life. Ava knew him well
enough to trust him, and she knew that setting up a table
in the kitchen where she and Carlo could talk wouldn't
be an issue. Andy was small and wiry, like Carlo, but
didn't have as many tattoos. His head and face were now
completely clean-shaven.

Ava kissed him on both cheeks. "Is Carlo here?"

"In the kitchen." He turned and started towards the back
of the restaurant. "I've never seen him so panicked."

"We have a bad situation to deal with."

"He should never have gone to work for Wing."

"It's the only life he knows."

"I told him he could come here and work with me."

Ava couldn't help but laugh. "You're a good friend to
him, but Winnie would have a fit and he would scare off
half your customers."

Andy pushed the door that swung into the kitchen.
Through a veil of steam she could see Carlo, sitting on a
folding chair at a card table set against the wall. He stood
when he saw her, his shoulders slumped, his face downcast.

"There's tea on the table. If you want anything else, just
ask one of the chefs," Andy said.

"I'm not hungry," Ava said.

"Neither is Carlo."

As she approached, Carlo took two steps towards her. She shook her head. "Just sit down," she said. "Let's make this as businesslike as possible."

He eased back onto the chair, his eyes darting around the kitchen.

She sat across from him and poured herself a cup of tea. "The last time I had a cup of tea, I was in Shenzhen with Xu," she said.

"I told you, Ava, I had nothing to do with any of it."

"I believe you. This was all Sammy Wing, with maybe a little help from Li Kai. He was clever — or he thought he was being clever."

"So now what?"

"You don't know?"

"Will it be that bad?"

"I think so."

"Fuck."

Ava sipped her tea. "You have to decide where your loyalties lie."

He pushed back from the table. His head tilted skyward and all she could see was the whites of his eyes. "Am I dead whichever side I choose?"

Ava took a deep breath. "Carlo, there's only one side you can choose, and that's my side. Xu is going to crush Wing, and everything and everyone associated with him. I would like it to happen as quickly as possible, and for that to be the case, some help is needed. That's why you're here."

"What can I do?"

"I want information."

"I don't know anything."

"I don't believe that. All you need to do is think. For

example, how many men does Wing have? I mean how many men who will fight for him."

"Forty or fifty maybe. I'm not sure."

"Think about it some more. Take your time."

"Well, Jimmy Tan works the bars and clubs in Wanchai and he has about ten men," Carlo said. He was actually counting on his fingers. "His cousin Marlon runs the street markets. He has a lot of people, but I don't think many of them are forty-niners or even blue lanterns."

"Just a second," Ava said, reaching into her purse. She took out a sheet of paper and a pen and placed them in front of Carlo. "Let's do this a different way. What I would like you to do is write down the name of everyone you know who works for Sammy, and next to their name, where they are most likely to be found. Concentrate on the main guys: Sammy and Jimmy and Marlon and whoever else runs things. Can you do that?"

"Ava —"

"Listen, Carlo, I know you don't like being a rat, but think about what these guys tried to do."

"What about me? What will happen to me?"

"I want you to write down everything you know. Do that and you can leave. You'll have to go underground, more to protect yourself from Wing than from Xu. When this is over, I'll make sure you have a life and a future."

"How can you do that?"

"You doubt me?"

He sighed. "No, I'm not saying that."

"What are you saying?"

"I'm not sure."

"Look, do you have somewhere you can go?"

"If anywhere, it would be Macau."

"Good. Give me what I want and then head for Macau. I'll make sure your name isn't on any of Xu's lists and that when this is over, you can come back to Hong Kong and get a decent job."

He picked up the pen and looked across the table at Ava. "My life is in your hands."

"Can you think of anyplace safer?"

He shook his head. "Life has been shit since Uncle died."

"For all of us."

"This will take more than a few minutes. I need to really think."

"I'll go and chat with Andy. I'll be back in a while."

When she walked into the dining room, Andy was only a few metres from the kitchen door, leaning against a wall. He was smoking. The restaurant, like all the others in Hong Kong, had a government-imposed no-smoking policy. And the restaurant, like all the others in Hong Kong, treated the policy as a guideline that could be waived for special customers or, in this case, owners. He straightened when he saw her, threw the cigarette to the floor, and stomped on the butt.

"Let's sit," she said.

The restaurant was quite busy for late afternoon and they had to sit close to the front door. Winnie was in listening range, so Ava lowered her voice. "Carlo will be going to Macau today. He needs to hide out for a while."

"What's he done?"

"Nothing."

"Then why does he have to take off?"

"He's accidently put himself in the middle of a turf war between Sammy Wing and Xu. You've heard of Xu?"

"Who in our life hasn't?"

"Well, it's going to be messy and Carlo runs the risk of being collateral damage. He works for Wing but he's loyal to me, and my loyalties are with Xu."

"What does Xu want with Hong Kong?"

"Wing tried to kill him earlier today in Shenzhen. He failed."

"Fucking hell."

"Anyway, Carlo has decided to help me with some information about the Wing organization. There's no way he can go back to work with them, so staying in Hong Kong is a non-starter."

"That makes sense."

"Andy, do you have any customers who work for Wing?"

"A few," he said without hesitation.

"They might know we worked together."

"They might."

"They would certainly know that you and Carlo were partners."

"Everyone knows that."

"So they might come around asking questions. I think, for your sake, you should be prepared for that eventuality."

He shrugged. "I haven't seen you since Uncle's funeral, and I haven't heard from Carlo since he went to work for Wing."

"Perfect."

"Thanks for the heads-up."

"*Momentai*. Now I should go back to the kitchen and see how Carlo is doing."

"Ava, if he does go to Macau, tell him not to stay with that mama-san whose place he usually goes to. She has a big mouth, in more ways than one," Andy said, smiling at his little joke.

Despite herself, Ava found herself smiling as well. "I'll tell him," she said.

Carlo was still hunched over the table when she walked back into the kitchen. The paper was almost completely covered with his handwriting. He looked up when he heard her heels striking the concrete floor. "I'm done, I think," he said.

Ava sat down and reached for the paper. "This is long on names and short on everything else," she said.

"Well, they don't exactly have an office or a clubhouse," Carlo said.

"If you were going to look for them, where would you go?"

He sighed and ran his fingers through the stubble on his scalp. "The Hong Kong Jockey Club has three betting centres in Wanchai: one on Hennessy Road, one on Jaffe Road, and the third on Spring Garden Lane. Some of them hang around in the vicinity. There's a street market near the MTR exit on Hennessy. Look for the stalls selling phones; they'll be nearby."

"How about bars and clubs?"

"On Hennessy and on Gloucester Road, but mainly Hennessy. They like to operate out of bars close to hotels like the Metropark."

"Where can we find Sammy Wing?"

"I have no idea."

"How about Jimmy Tan?"

"There's a bar called Oasis on Hennessy. He hangs out there at a table in the back. Though with all this shit going down, he may have decided to relocate."

"Marlon?"

"He's at the street market every night. There's a 7-Eleven about twenty metres from the MTR entrance. He's usually standing by the front door."

"Describe him."

"He's tall and skinny with bleached blond hair."

"That's distinctive."

"He thinks of himself as a ladies' man."

Ava had been making her own notes as Carlo spoke. The last detail she ignored. "This is all helpful, and hopefully it will never have to be actually used," she said. "Still, I think you need to get to Macau as fast as possible. Today wouldn't be too soon. Don't tell anyone you're going and don't contact anyone from there, including me. When I think it's safe for you to come back, I'll call your cell and leave a voicemail. If you don't hear from me, stay there and keep quiet."

"I got it."

"Andy says you'll probably stay with a mama-san."

"Well, if I'm going to lie low, I might as well take advantage of it. She gives amazing blow jobs."

Ava rolled her eyes. "Make sure that's the only thing she does with her mouth. Andy says she blabs."

"All he knows about her is what I've told him, and I never told him that."

"Okay, enough said."

Ava folded the papers, put them in her purse, and then stood to leave. Carlo started to stand and then hesitated.

"What is it?" Ava said.

"I hope you don't get too involved in this feud. I don't pretend to understand the reasons for it, and even if you explained it, I still might not make sense of it. All I know is that Sammy Wing is a cruel son of a bitch. He sees insults in everything and carries grudges like nobody I've ever met. He doesn't care who gets in his way. Man, woman, or child, he'll whack anyone."

"Thanks for the concern."

He looked down at his feet. "I still like to think of us as a team, you know — me, Andy, Sonny, and you. We may have different interests from day to day, but when things matter, we cover for each other."

She put a hand on his arm. "Which is why you need to get on a jetfoil to Macau."

## 25

AVA CHECKED HER PHONE AS SOON AS SHE LEFT THE restaurant. There was nothing from Sonny and nothing from May Ling or Amanda. She listened to the message that the lawyer, Bowlby, had left. He wanted to set up a meeting. She thought about calling him and then quickly decided it would have to wait.

She caught a taxi at the MTR station and took it to the ferry terminal in Tsim Sha Tsui. Fifteen minutes later she had stepped off the Star Ferry and was walking from the waterfront in Central to the Mandarin Oriental. When she got to her room, she hesitated and contemplated packing her bags. The thought held no appeal. She hated the idea of running from anyone, but she was not a careless person. Ignoring the possibility that Wing might target her, if only as a way to get to Xu, would be careless in the extreme. The hotel was too accessible, and no matter how tight the security, too many employees had master keys — employees who could be threatened or bribed.

She walked over to the window and looked out onto Victoria Harbour. Her mind was spinning with possibilities,

and none of them seemed to work in favour of her staying at the hotel. She moved away from the window and
methodically repacked her bags. As she did, she weighed
her options about where to resettle.

She knew she could always stay at Amanda and
Michael's apartment in the Mid-levels, or even out in Sha
Tin with Amanda's father, Jack Yee. But how could she
put them at risk? She thought about moving into another
hotel. The trouble was, she hadn't brought her alternative
ID and credit cards with her. There had been no need, she
had thought as she packed her bags in Toronto, for Jennie
Kwong on this trip.

Uncle's apartment in Kowloon was the most logical, saf-
est choice. What she didn't know was whether she could
handle it emotionally. She reached for her phone and called
Sonny's line. Still no answer. "Sonny, I'm at the hotel. Call
me when you can. I need to know how things are going."

She sat on the edge of the bed. In the past at times like
this, a phone call to Uncle would have brought calmness
and certainty. Now she felt alone and vulnerable.

Her phone rang and she almost leapt at it. The screen
said PRIVATE NUMBER. *Who could that be?* she thought. On
the third ring she hit the answer button. "Yes."

"Ms. Lee?" an English voice said.

"Yes."

"This is Richard Bowlby. I'm sorry if I'm disturbing you."

"No, not at all. I was just expecting another call."

"I phoned earlier."

"I know. I didn't have a chance to get back to you."

"We have all the paperwork related to the acquisition in
China and I'm about to assign it to someone on staff to draft

the agreement. Before I do, I would like to sit down with you and review it. I spoke with Ms. Wong after I couldn't reach you and she gave me a bit more detail about the Beijing offer. Frankly, it isn't that complicated, so I think we are probably good to proceed."

"I would be happy to sit down with you," Ava said.

"Excellent. It will be good to meet the third partner in what promises to be a substantial and impressive business."

"Today isn't very good," Ava said.

"Nor for me. I do have an opening tomorrow at eleven a.m. Will that suit you?"

"Where is your office?"

"We're in the Bond Building, on Queen's Road West in Central. We occupy three floors. I don't know which boardroom we'll use yet, so come to main reception on the thirty-first floor and we'll take it from there."

"That sounds fine."

"You'll be meeting with me, Ms. Ma, and Mr. Ong. And I expect that my partner, Brenda Burgess, will poke her head in to say hello."

"Okay, I'll see you then."

There was no reply, and Ava wondered if Bowlby had hung up. Then he said, "Ms. Lee, you do still intend to go ahead with this acquisition?"

"Of course. Why do you ask?"

"If you don't mind my saying so, you sound rather hesitant."

"I have another issue to deal with that is pressing, Mr. Bowlby. Hopefully by tomorrow it will be less of a concern."

"Would you rather put off our meeting?"

"No, not unless I have no choice," Ava said quickly. "This

is very important for us. The sooner we can close, the better. But if there's any change in my plans, I'll let you know."

"All right then. So I'll either see you or hear from you tomorrow."

She placed the phone on the bed and went to her computer to turn it off. First she checked her email and saw that both May Ling and Amanda had sent several messages. May Ling and Suki were now burrowing deep into the financials of the Beijing business and continued to be pleased with what they found. Amanda wrote that she hadn't heard from Gillian Po but wasn't worried. She and Chi-Tze were taking advantage of their time together in Shanghai to review other business proposals that Three Sisters had received. *Well, no bad news,* Ava thought. *At least one part of my life is on an even keel.*

Ava wrote an email to May: I have spoken with Richard Bowlby and I will be meeting with him and some of his associates tomorrow. It doesn't seem that there are any reasons not to go ahead at full speed. So unless you tell me to slow down, that's exactly what I intend to do. Then she paused and added: I am moving out of the Mandarin today. I didn't want you to phone the hotel and find that I'd checked out. I'll explain when I see you.

She sent the message and then composed one for Amanda. While I appreciate that Gillian and Clark are probably consulting with their lawyer and accountant, our offer isn't any different from what you discussed with them and I reiterated. I don't want this dragging on. Call Gillian tomorrow if you haven't heard from her by then. We need to know where their heads are. Don't press her, though. Treat it as a friendly enquiry.

After she had sent the message, Ava closed her computer. Now all she had to do was wait for Sonny. She hadn't eaten since breakfast, so she looked at the room service menu. Before she could decide between nasi goreng and fried noodles with shrimp and squid, her cellphone rang. It was Sonny. "Finally," she muttered.

"Where are you?" she said.

"Standing on the street outside the clinic."

"How is he?"

"The doctor said we got him there just in time. He'd lost so much blood he could have died. He's just come out of surgery. He's been patched up and now he's getting another blood transfusion. He's going to be completely out of commission for at least a few days."

"Thank goodness he's alive," Ava said. "What do you mean by 'out of commission'?"

"He's going to be sedated until his condition stabilizes. When it does, the doctor wants to keep him under observation until he thinks he's well enough to leave on his own two feet. He won't be able to use that arm for a while. He'll need physio and the arm will be in a sling."

"You said the doctor is your girlfriend's brother?"

"Yeah."

"Thank him."

"I'll thank her instead. The brother is more than a little nervous about having us here. He's keeping us at arm's length."

"Just as well."

"I think so."

"Sonny, I met with Carlo. I thought it would be better than having him grilled by Suen, or any of Xu's men."

"I thought you might do something like that."

"He gave me as much information about Wing's operation as he could. It's sketchy, but it's a start."

"Knowing these Shanghai guys, they won't be hanging around waiting for more."

"What makes you say that?"

"Suen has been on the phone with Lop. They'll have some people in Hong Kong tonight, and it looks like they've already solved the weapons problem. They're itching to go. I've never seen people move so fast. And Ava, I have to tell you that this Lop is a piece of work."

"What do you mean?"

"He even makes Suen nervous. Three times in one phone conversation, Suen had to tell him to calm down."

"Can Suen control him?"

"I think so."

"I need to get this information to them but I don't want to go to the clinic. I've had enough of hospitals and clinics to last me a lifetime."

"What do you want to do?"

"I've decided to stay at Uncle's. I need you to meet me there with a key. I'll brief you and you can pass along the information to them."

"Okay."

"I'm still at the hotel but I'm packed and ready to go. How long should it take me at this time of day to get to Uncle's if I take the Star Ferry and then grab a cab in Tsim Sha Tsui?"

"No more than forty-five minutes."

## 26

**UNCLE'S APARTMENT WAS ON KWUN CHUNG STREET,** near the Jordan MTR station in Tsim Sha Tsui, northeast of the Star Ferry terminal. As her taxi pulled away from the terminal and started north on Canton Road, she looked out the window at Victoria Harbour, barely visible behind the Gateway towers and the Royal Pacific Hotel. On her right was Kowloon Park, thirty acres of greenery in the middle of one of the most densely populated places on earth. Some mornings, after eating congee in a restaurant near Pacific Place, she and Uncle would cut through the park to get to his apartment. Whenever they did, he liked to find a spot to sit for five or ten minutes.

The taxi continued along Canton until it reached the northwest corner of the park, turned right on Austin Road, and then made an immediate left onto Kwun Chung. The Range Rover Sonny had driven from Shenzhen was parked outside the four-storey building. Both sides of the street were lined with older apartment buildings, with laundry hanging from small balconies or on poles below windows, and a store or restaurant on the ground floor. The restaurant in Uncle's building was Nepalese, which Ava had found strange until Uncle explained that until 1970, Kowloon Park had been Whitfield Barracks, an important military base for the British. When the barracks were closed down, the Ghurkha soldiers — indigenous people from Nepal — had remained.

Ava pointed out the building to the taxi driver and he pulled in behind Sonny. Before she even had time to pay him, Sonny was at her door. When she stepped out, he took her bags. "I feel better seeing you here," he said.

The building didn't have an elevator, so they walked up the narrow staircase in single file. Ava let Sonny go ahead, and she was astonished by how enormous he looked from behind.

Uncle's apartment — which he had left to Lourdes, his long-time housekeeper — was at the far end of the fourth floor. All the entrances had wooden double doors plus a heavy-duty metal screen. Ava had never understood why Hong Kong apartment dwellers felt they needed that level of security, but right then she was happy they did.

Sonny unlocked the outer screen and then the bright blue main door.

"Lourdes painted the door," Ava said.

"She's done more than that," Sonny replied.

The apartment was close to one hundred square metres, which was rather large by Hong Kong standards. It had two bedrooms, a bathroom, a tiny kitchen, and a living room that Uncle had furnished sparsely, with an easy chair set by the window and next to it a table that held his ashtray and racing forms. His old twenty-inch television had sat against the wall next to his bedroom door, and just outside the kitchen was a wooden table with two chairs. The apartment had been so sparsely furnished and decorated so plainly that it looked huge.

Now that illusion had vanished. The pale wood floor hadn't changed and the walls were still off-white, but that was all that was the same. As Ava stepped into the apartment she saw that the easy chair was still there, but sitting by itself in a corner. The old television was gone, replaced by what looked like a fifty-inch high-definition flat-screen. Lourdes had also added a plush red brocade couch, loveseat, and chair and a long glass coffee table. The old dining setup was gone; in its place was a dark wooden table with scrolled legs and six padded chairs.

"Good god," Ava said.

"Well, it's her place now, and she has a right to do what she wants," Sonny said. "Besides, I always thought Uncle's taste was a little too simple."

"True enough."

Sonny put her bags on the floor and handed her the keys. "We should talk before I leave," he said.

"Yes, we need to," Ava said. They sat down at the table facing each other. "You seem a bit jumpy."

"It's been a while since I've been involved in anything like this."

"Sorry for being the cause of it."

"Not your fault. I know you got sucked in."

"I was a bit of a fool."

Sonny shook his head. "No."

"Wing played me to get to Xu — I should have seen the signs. But that's done now. I can't go back, so let's move forward," Ava said. She reached into her purse and extracted Carlo's list. "This is all I know about Sammy Wing's operations." She slid the paper across the table to Sonny and then summarized its contents. When she was done, she said, "I know that doesn't give Xu's men much to go on, but I'm hoping you can fill in some of the blanks."

"How?"

"I was thinking about the time you were hunting down those guys Li sent to kill me. Uncle arranged for Wing to help, and my understanding is that you and he co-operated. You must have met him someplace. You must have some idea of where he hangs out."

"Yeah. I'll tell Suen."

"Good. And I'd also like you to talk to Uncle Fong. He must know Sammy Wing and Jimmy Tan."

"Yeah, he does."

"So talk to him and find out where he would go if he wanted to find them."

Sonny nodded.

"So that's a start, yes?" Ava said.

"Yeah, but that's all it is."

"This is out of our hands, Sonny. All I want to do is get past this and get back to my regular life. If I thought I could do that just by walking away, I would. But I suspect I'm still in Sammy Wing's sights."

"That stupid fat fucker."

"Tell me, do you think he has a chance against Xu?"

"No."

"Then let's stay out of the way and let Xu's men do their thing."

"I need to get rid of that car. They might be looking for it," Sonny said. "And you need to stay around here. Don't wander."

"I won't, at least not tonight. I do have an appointment with our lawyers tomorrow. I'll decide in the morning whether to go or not."

"I'm going back to the clinic now," Sonny said as he stood up. "I'll call Uncle Fong on the way and see what he knows about Sammy. Then I'll pass along Carlo's information and anything else I can think of."

"Sonny, what are you going to do?"

"What do you mean?"

"Don't play dumb."

He smiled. "I've been thinking about it ever since we left Shenzhen. Part of me — the old part — wants to rip Sammy Wing apart for what he tried to do to you. The newer me says I should let Xu and his men handle it. It's their fight, but . . ."

"But what?"

"I may tag along with Suen. You know, to keep an eye on things. I do know Hong Kong better than they do, and they may need me at some point."

"I don't want you taking any risks," she said.

"Look who's talking."

"I didn't go looking for trouble."

"It found you all the same, just like it always seems to find me. If I'm with Suen, then at least I'm prepared for it."

"I hope this doesn't drag on. Uncle's apartment is not my preferred place to stay."

"Who knows? By this time tomorrow it could be all over and you can move back to the Mandarin Oriental."

"Do you think there's a chance?"

"I saw Xu's men tear apart that gang in Borneo in about two hours. They were completely unforgiving. Wing's men have never had to take on guys like these."

"Well, I just want this to be over as fast as possible."

"Okay, boss. I'll do what I can to make that happen," Sonny said with a smile.

Ava looked around the room, her eyes drawn to the old easy chair. "Try not to get directly involved, and keep in touch. I want to know about any significant change in our position. My phone will be on."

He nodded, then turned and left. Ava stood by the door until she couldn't hear his footsteps any longer. She picked up her bags and without thinking took them into Lourdes's room. Her old single bed had been replaced by a king-size that almost touched the walls. Directly above its head hung a wooden crucifix flanked by images of Mother Teresa and Jesus with a pulsing red heart. Ava opened a bag and took out her toilet kit, a T-shirt, and underwear.

A bright blue duvet and six throw cushions covered the bed. Ava piled the cushions in one corner and pulled back the duvet so the bed could air. Then she wandered back into the living room.

She felt hunger pangs. It was almost five o'clock and she hadn't eaten since breakfast. The fridge was empty except for some bottled water and various condiments. There were tons of restaurants within easy walking distance, but Sonny had asked her not to wander — advice she would take because it was advice she would have given. She decided to go to the Nepalese restaurant, which she could access through a side door from the apartment lobby and not have to go outside.

As she opened the restaurant door, she was greeted with the aroma of curry and other, unfamiliar spices. She took a look around before committing to stay. The place was narrow, with two rows of tables along the side walls and an aisle down the middle. The floor was white ceramic tile, the walls were painted white, and the tables were covered with white tablecloths. It was all quite pristine — more Toronto than Hong Kong.

A Southeast Asian couple seated by the front window were the only customers. Ava walked to the back and took the table farthest from the door. She had to wait a few minutes before a waiter emerged from the kitchen. He seemed startled to see her, and Ava wondered how many Chinese customers they had.

When the waiter brought the glass of white wine she'd ordered, she asked him what he recommended, and that prompted a five-minute description of Nepalese cuisine. Ava chose a pumpkin soup with coriander; chicken breast marinated with saffron, curry, and cashew nut paste and cooked in a clay oven; and prawns stir-fried in a tomato and almond gravy. None of it disappointed, and she was happy to take the leftover chicken and shrimp upstairs with her, along with a bottle of Pinot Grigio.

She turned on the television and saw that a marathon showing of *Forensic Heroes* — the Hong Kong equivalent of *CSI* — was scheduled for the evening. She opened the wine and settled into the couch.

One episode turned into two and then into three, and she kept pace with a glass of wine for each one. Whatever was happening on the streets of Wanchai or at the clinic in Mong Kok became less important by the hour. By ten o'clock, when she turned off the television to go to bed, all that seemed a world away.

## 27

**THE FIRST PHONE CALL CAME JUST AFTER 12:30 A.M. IT** was Sonny, and he was almost breathless. "More than forty of them arrived in Hong Kong from Shanghai during the evening. Their weapons got in at nine o'clock, as part of a shipment of iPads," he said.

"That was fast."

"They're operators."

"Are they going to wait for the others?"

"Not a chance."

"It's late."

"The bars are still open and the street market is just shutting down. Suen is going to pick up that guy Marlon and Lop has gone to the bars on Hennessy. They want Tan and Wing."

"They should be so lucky to find both."

"They'll start at the bottom and work their way up. Sooner or later they'll get to them."

"I'm surprised that Suen left Xu."

"Two men from Shanghai are outside the clinic. No one is going up those stairs unless they're friends. Besides, Suen has got serious revenge in mind. He's not as crazy as that little fucker Lop, but he has a mean streak that runs just as deep when it comes to protecting his boss."

"Where are you?"

"I'm in my car, following Suen."

"Sonny, like I said before, I want you to stay out of it. Those guys can go back to Shanghai when this is done, but you can't. You don't need problems with the Hong Kong police or with the local Triads. Even if Xu's men take down Wing, some people here will remember that you played a part in it."

"I have my own mean streak, and I have my own boss who was threatened."

"Yes, a boss who happens to be safe in Kowloon."

He paused, then said, "I promise I won't do anything stupid."

Ava lay on the bed with her eyes shut and tried to force herself back to sleep. After ten minutes she knew that her mind wasn't going to co-operate. It was in overdrive, bouncing from one Wanchai scenario to the next. The speed at which Xu's men could move had startled her. They were as efficient as Sonny had claimed, and she had no doubt they would be equally ruthless. How many men would die in the next few hours? The thought made her shiver. She wasn't a stranger to death, but it seemed to be becoming a more constant companion. In her early days of debt collecting there had been occasions when she, usually with her friend Derek alongside, had been forced to kill in self-defence. How many men over the years? She strained to remember, and realized she had pushed those men deep into the recesses of her mind.

The violence had never been personal — it was work, but some resolutions, almost of their own accord, had been more tragic than others. When it was over, she always felt drained and saddened; even the satisfaction of recovering the money and restoring a client's life and livelihood couldn't overcome her depression. Now more men were going to die, and even though she understood rationally that it wasn't her battle and that it hadn't been brought on by her, even marginally, she still had a cold, clawing sensation in her belly.

She swung her bare legs out of the bed and felt chilled. She wrapped the duvet around her and dragged it like the long train of a wedding gown into the living room. The blinds were partly open and light from neon signs flickered across the walls. Ava bundled herself into Uncle's easy chair and looked out at the street. Some restaurants were still open and the street was still busy with traffic, the distinctive red-and-white Kowloon taxis outnumbering regular cars. It all looked so normal.

Uncle had lived in this chair. Its brown leather was cracked and the recliner had stopped working, but she could still see him lying back in it, his feet well off the floor, as he watched the races from Happy Valley. When Xu came to Hong Kong, had he and Uncle met in the apartment? She doubted it somehow. Uncle wasn't a man to mix personal affairs with business. He had let a handful of people into his life, and she and Sonny may have been the only two who knew him in his entirety.

Her mind flooded with memories of Uncle. She thought of his funeral and struggled to remember those who had journeyed to Fanling to pay their respects. One by one they came back to her — all the clients whose fortunes and lives they had saved, all the hard men from his previous life. Then she saw Sammy Wing. He was there, standing in the doorway of the funeral home talking to Uncle Fong. Next to him was Jimmy Tan. They looked sombre and respectful, and whatever malice Ava felt towards them began to ebb.

A phone rang. *Who would bring a phone to a funeral?* Ava thought. And then she realized it was hers. She pulled it from the depths of the duvet.

"Sonny."

"They have Marlon," he said.

"And?"

"He's talking up a storm. I think he knows that it's pointless not to co-operate."

"How about Jimmy Tan?"

"No word yet, but for the last ten minutes we've been hearing a lot of police sirens in the direction of Hennessy Street. I can only assume that Lop is the cause."

"So now what happens?"

"When they've squeezed Marlon for every bit of information he has, they'll go hunting. That's what they did in Borneo. Eventually they'll get to Wing and Tan. When they do, it will be over. Ava, these guys are lethal. This isn't like any gang I've ever seen. I thought they were good in Borneo — well, they're better now. If I was Sammy Wing I'd be suing for peace."

"On Xu's terms?"

"Completely."

"Sonny, despite what Xu said, do you think they'll kill Wing and Tan if they find them?"

"I don't know about Tan, but I heard Suen stress to Lop that Xu wants Wing alive."

"Good."

"Xu doesn't let his emotions rule. He reminds me of Uncle — that and the way he thinks ahead."

"I wish you hadn't said that," Ava exclaimed.

"I'm sorry, but it's true — wait, Suen is waving at me. I have to go. I'll call you when I can."

Whatever chance she had for sleep had vanished. She curled into a ball and pulled the duvet more tightly around her. The nights could be chilly, particularly since Uncle's apartment had no central heating. It was late afternoon in Toronto and she thought about calling Maria or her mother. To say what? That she was staying in Uncle's apartment until a Triad war finished? When she had been on collection jobs, she had made it a policy to shut out what was happening at home. This wasn't a job, but the feeling that she should keep them at arm's length was just as strong.

Ava let her mind wander. She thought about the Pos and the deal Three Sisters had offered. She was anxious to learn their reaction to it. The offer was fair but she wondered if their lawyer was picking holes in it, as lawyers were inclined to do. She hoped not, because there weren't many changes she was prepared to make. Ava's main worry was that Clark Po had lost faith in them. Well, they'd have a better idea after Amanda spoke to Gillian.

Gillian and Clark were good people, and so were Suki and Chi-Tze. And Amanda and May Ling — she couldn't have found better partners. After caring for Uncle and then grieving for Uncle, it was time for Ava to step up and play her part.

As the first signs of dawn crept across the street and lit up the apartment window, her phone rang again.

"Sonny, is it over?" she said.

"This is Sammy Wing. I need to talk to you."

## 28

**"HOW DID YOU GET MY NUMBER?"**

"From Carlo."

"When?"

"Ten minutes ago."

"Where are you?"

"I'm in Hong Kong. Carlo is in Macau, with two of my men and that old whore he likes to hang around with. He shouldn't have run out on us. He shouldn't have told you what he did," he said calmly.

"Is he okay?"

"For now."

"What do you mean by that?"

"Let's talk about that later. Right now what I want is for you to set up a meeting between me and Xu."

"We tried that before. It didn't work out too well."

"And now I'm paying for it."

"And you think you shouldn't?"

"What does that matter? I'm paying and I want to stop."

"You should have thought of that before you tried to kill us."

"The men were told to leave you out of it."

"I'm sure the fact that Xu was the only target will make him feel more charitable."

"Call him. I've tried but his phone is off, and I don't know how to reach Suen."

"You haven't even asked if Xu is well enough to speak."

"My man who survived that mess in Shenzhen said Xu was wounded but alive. I assume that's still the case."

"He is alive, but in no condition to talk. So you're going to have to deal with me."

He paused and then laughed. "You're joking."

"Sammy, I want you to count to ten. When you get to ten, the phone line will go dead, and Xu's men will continue to round up and kill as many of your men as they need to until they get to you. If, somewhere between one and ten, you decide that I'm serious, then we'll choose a place to meet."

"If I can't talk to Xu I'll have Carlo killed," Wing said.

Ava drew a deep breath. "Is Carlo still alive?"

"You don't trust me?"

"No."

"How do you want me to prove it to you?"

"I want you to put Carlo on a jetfoil back to Hong Kong and then I want him to call me from the jetfoil and tell me he's okay."

"I won't send him alone. I won't lie to you about that."

"I want him out of Macau and I want to hear his voice."

"And if I do that?"

"Then you can decide if you want to talk to me or if you want the carnage to continue. Because, Sammy, you won't be talking to Xu, today or tomorrow. I'm the only person who can stop this."

"I don't believe it."

"Put Carlo on the jetfoil. When I know he's safe, we can arrange a meeting. In the meantime, let's just hope Xu's men don't find you."

She could hear his deep, raspy breathing and she wondered what thoughts were bouncing around in his head. What was controlling him, fear or rage?

"Are you really calling the shots?" he finally said.

"Yes, I am."

"He'll be on the fucking boat," Wing said. "And if you're really speaking for Xu, then call off the war. I've lost more than ten men tonight, and not all of them were armed. Another fifteen are being held hostage. I'm not a threat to anyone."

"We didn't start this," Ava said.

The line went silent.

"Now give me a phone number where I can reach you after I talk to Carlo," she said.

He hesitated and then very slowly and precisely recited the number.

"I'll contact you when I'm satisfied," she said.

"I'll be waiting," Wing said, and then gave a painful laugh. "I have no other immediate plans."

## 29

**AVA PUSHED HERSELF OUT OF THE CHAIR.** *I SHOULD GET dressed*, she thought. She stopped at the kitchen on the way to the bedroom. A check of the cupboards revealed an unopened jar of Nescafé instant coffee. Ava turned on the hot water thermos and then went to the bedroom.

She pulled out her track pants, a black T-shirt, and a clean bra and underwear. She dressed quickly and then went to the bathroom to wash her face and brush her teeth and hair. If she decided to see the lawyers later, she would shower and change into something more businesslike.

The kettle's light indicated that the water had boiled. She made a strong cup of coffee, sat down at the dining room table, and called Sonny. He answered on the fourth ring.

In the background Ava could hear men yelling. "What's going on?" she said.

"We've just rounded up four more of Wing's men. They all know what happened during the night. None of them want to fight."

Ava noticed his use of the word *we*. Sonny hadn't been

as neutral as he had promised. "How many men are dead?" she asked.

"I don't really know. Suen and his guys took out three. I have no idea about Lop — the two of them are still operating separately. They talk by phone, but the only thing Suen has told me is that as of an hour ago they hadn't found Tan or Wing."

"Wing called me."

"Fuck."

"He wants to negotiate."

"No fucking wonder."

"And he's holding Carlo hostage to make sure I do."

"How did he get Carlo?"

"What does it matter?"

"And you'll be the one negotiating with him?"

"Unless Xu makes a miraculous recovery, who else is there?"

"He made it clear enough in the car that if he was out of action you were to handle it."

"I know Suen and Lop agreed, but do you think they'll still feel that way?"

"I don't think you have to worry about them. They'd never go against Xu's wishes. I'd be more concerned about Sammy Wing believing he has to meet with you and not Xu."

"I was direct with him."

"Did he buy it?"

"Reluctantly."

"Do you trust him?"

"Not particularly. But I'll have you, Suen, Lop, and as many other men as we need alongside."

"Jesus, Ava, I hate to see you getting so involved in shit like this."

"We need to protect Carlo, and I owe Xu. Besides, I'm a big girl and I'm no stranger to shit."

"When's this supposed to happen?"

"As soon as I hear from Carlo and I'm convinced he's well."

"Suen and Lop are still going at these guys."

"Tell them not to back off until I give the word, and don't say anything about Wing just yet."

"Okay, boss."

"And Sonny, it doesn't sound like they need you there anymore. Why don't you go home?"

"In a while."

"Sonny —"

"Ava, after five months of driving your brother to business meetings it's been good for me to get my juices flowing again. I'm too pumped to sleep, and I want to see this through to the end."

"Don't —" she said, and then swallowed the rest of her scolding. She wasn't his mother, she wasn't his wife. "Just be careful."

She made herself another coffee and went over to the window. Uncle had always kept the blinds raised during the day. His chair was positioned so he could look out onto the street and, as he always said, "feel the life out there." She pulled up the blinds now and was amazed at how quickly Kowloon had come to life. Nearly all the stores and restaurants were open for business, the sidewalks were jammed, and three double-decker buses and two minibuses were on the street. She checked the time: more than thirty minutes since she had spoken to Wing. The jetfoil terminal in Macau was a fifteen-minute car ride from just about anywhere in the territory. Had Wing been playing her? Maybe he didn't yet have his hands on Carlo. As that thought crossed her mind, the phone rang, and she saw Carlo's number.

"Carlo, are you on the jetfoil?" she said.

"Got on two minutes ago."

"You okay?"

"Yeah. Just embarrassed."

"What happened?"

"When I got to the terminal in Central, I met a couple of guys who work for Jimmy Tan. They asked me where I was going, and since I was in line to get the boat to Macau, I couldn't lie. When all hell broke loose last night, they started calling everyone to come in. I had left my phone on but didn't answer when I saw who was calling. That was stupid. Someone got suspicious, and of course Tan and Wing know we're close, so they sent some guys to look for me. I wasn't hard to find. Ava, I had to tell them what I told you. It was either that or —"

"Did they hurt you?"

"No, but they were ready to. Fuck, Ava, I'm sorry."

"I understand, Carlo. No harm has been done."

"What's going to happen to me?"

"I'm doing a trade. I'll get you back."

"Jesus. What does Wing want for me?"

"A meeting."

"That's it?"

"Do you have any idea what's been happening?"

"Not in any detail. The two guys who grabbed me said it was bad, really bad. They're as jumpy as hell."

"They should be. Xu's men arrived in Hong Kong last night. They've decimated Wing's organization."

"Holy fuck."

"Now listen to me, Carlo. I'm going to call Wing and make some arrangements. You need to keep in touch. I want to know when you land in Hong Kong. If things go smoothly, you should be able to say goodbye to those two guys at the terminal."

"Thank you."

"You're welcome. But you know what? When I think of all the things you did for me over the years, all this does is make us even. Take care of yourself, and wait for my call."

She hung up and went back to the kitchen to make herself another coffee. She knew that Carlo would be safe and that she could call Wing — except as a pre-negotiating strategy it didn't make sense. The longer they hammered Wing's organization, the more receptive he would be to accepting Xu's deal. But she knew she couldn't let it go on indefinitely or there wouldn't be any organization left. Still, she first wanted to know for certain that Carlo was back in Hong Kong. Another hour shouldn't make that much difference.

Neither Wing nor Sonny had mentioned Li, Ava thought. And Li hadn't come to Wing's aid. She assumed that, despite being only a few hours away, he might not have had time to react. Or maybe he just didn't care enough. Either way, without him Wing was helpless.

She took her notebook from her Chanel bag and returned to Uncle's chair. The front of the book was full of notes about Suki Chan and the Pos. She turned to the back and on the last page wrote *Sammy Wing*.

It had been a rule when she worked with Uncle that they took on only one job at a time, and she only ever carried one notebook. It struck her as odd, almost disquieting, that she was now listing issues that would have to be discussed with Wing in the same book that contained details of the beginning of her new life. She worked slowly and several times closed the book, but then she began again, unable to shake the promises she'd made to Carlo and Xu.

She checked the time, counting down the minutes until Carlo should have arrived safely. It was only a few minutes short of the scheduled docking when the phone rang.

"Lop has caught Jimmy Tan," Sonny said.

"Where?"

"In Central. He was hiding in a closet at his girlfriend's apartment."

"Is he alive?"

"So I'm told."

"What does he actually do for Wing?'

"He's the street operator. He's the one who knows the nuts and bolts."

"Make sure he isn't harmed. We may need him."

"I'll pass the word."

Ava's phone lit up again and she saw Carlo's number on the screen. "Carlo is calling. Let me talk to him and I'll get right back to you."

She switched lines, and as she did she couldn't help but notice a jump in her adrenalin level. "Are you okay?" she said.

"I've landed and the two guys who were with me have left."

"Anyone else lurking around?"

"Not that I can see. I have to tell you, the guys were anxious to get as far away from me as possible, so I'm not worried."

"Still, go home and keep your head down. This isn't over yet."

## 30

**SHE LOOKED AT THE CONTACT LIST ON HER PHONE AND** dialled a Kowloon number. "Andy, it's Ava. Are you at the restaurant yet?"

"I'll be there within an hour."

"I'm sorry, but I need to use the kitchen again."

"No problem."

"I'll need a table that can seat up to six people. Can you set it up in the kitchen as far from the cooks as possible? I need to have a private conversation."

"I can do that."

"We'll be there just before noon. I'll be arriving with Sonny and some Shanghai men."

"Okay."

"Sammy Wing will show up as well. I'll tell him to check in at the hostess stand. You can bring him into the kitchen."

"He'll be alone?"

"If he isn't, don't let him in. If you see anyone suspicious hanging around, let me know and leave Wing at the entrance until we can confirm who they are."

"Okay."

"Okay? That's all you have to say? Andy, you are the least curious person I know."

"My phone has been ringing constantly since last night. All anyone can talk about is the beating that Xu is laying on Wing. I didn't have to ask."

"It's more than a beating."

"I'm not surprised. Is Carlo all right?"

"He's fine," Ava said, seeing no reason to elaborate.

"Good. I was thinking about him all night."

"So we'll see you around noon?"

"My kitchen is your kitchen."

She looked at Sammy Wing's name in her notebook. *He must be anxious*, she thought. He would be sitting by his phone, waiting and worrying, wondering if she would get back to him. *Let him sweat a while longer*, she thought as she called Sonny.

"*Wei.*"

"Carlo is back and safe, and I've just arranged to use Andy's restaurant for the meeting with Wing, at noon. Tell Suen and Lop to meet me there about fifteen minutes before. They should bring Jimmy Tan and some of their own men with them. Can you pick me up at Uncle's at eleven fifteen?"

"Yes, boss, I'll be there," he said, and then paused.

"Is something wrong?"

"Lop worked Tan over before Suen could talk to him."

"But he's alive?"

"Yeah, just bruised and battered."

"Is Lop always that violent?"

"He's a bit crazy, but he follows orders."

"Well, what's done is done," Ava said. "Now there's one more thing I need you to do for me: give me the number for the clinic. I'm going to see if I can talk to Xu."

"He's probably still out of it."

"I know, but I want to try anyway."

Sonny rhymed off the number without another comment.

"And what's the doctor's name?"

"Lui."

"Thanks. I'll see you here in a while."

She thought again of Wing as she phoned the law offices of Burgess and Bowlby. The receptionist said Mr. Bowlby was in a meeting and asked Ava to leave a message. When Ava gave her name, the receptionist said, "Excuse me, but I think I can interrupt for you. Wait just a minute."

"This is Richard Bowlby. Ms. Lee, I trust that you are calling to confirm our meeting," he said when he came on the line.

"Actually, I'm not. I have to postpone."

"That's unfortunate."

"I know, and I apologize, but something's come up. Can we reschedule for tomorrow?"

"Let me look at what's in the planner," he said.

"I'm available from early morning to late evening."

"My younger associates don't like to hear that — they think I work them hard enough as it is. But let me see . . . How is eleven a.m. again?"

"That will work just fine."

"Fantastic. In the interim we'll keep working away at trying to turn your quite basic agreement into something quite incomprehensible."

Ava laughed. It came from God knew where and caught her off guard. "I have the same tendency," she said.

"Then we should get along just splendidly."

"Tomorrow, then."

Ava ended the call. It was finally time to call Sammy Wing.

He answered halfway through the first ring. "Ava Lee?"

"The same."

"Did you hear from Carlo?"

"You have your meeting. It will be at noon in Kowloon at the Three Clouds noodle restaurant, in the MTR station. Wait at the front door. Someone will come and get you."

"I want to bring some people with me."

"No."

"They need to know what —"

"No."

"Then just Jimmy Tan."

"Xu's men have caught Tan."

The line went quiet.

"So I'll see you at noon," Ava said.

"Is Jimmy alive?" Wing said, the control in his voice surprising her.

"Yes."

"Good."

"The thing you need to understand is that Xu's men won't stop until the meeting is over."

"Why not? He's won already. You know that he's won. Why go on?"

"You may not be agreeable to his conditions and we don't want to give you a chance to regroup."

"As if I could."

"Or give Li a chance to arrive from Guangzhou."

"Li has nothing to do with this."

"Then why was his man Ko at the restaurant in Shenzhen?"

"He was a hired gun, nothing more than that." He said it quickly, and Ava wondered if he'd been waiting for her to mention Li.

"It's hard for me to believe that Ko isn't still Li's man. Either way, he tried to kill me twice and he wasn't doing it on his own initiative. And don't pretend you're not tied to Li."

"Don't make things so complicated."

"Fuck your concern about complications, Mr. Wing. You have your meeting. You know where and when. Show up or don't — the choice is yours."

"I'll be there," he said, the words sounding as if they were being forced out of his throat.

"See you at noon then," she said, and ended the call.

She leaned back in the easy chair and felt her muscles collapse. She hadn't realized how tense she had been. With Wing sidelined, she could go back to the Mandarin Oriental. She considered it for a moment and then decided to wait until the meeting was over.

She went into the bedroom and made Lourdes's bed. She was actually glad Lourdes had changed things. This wasn't a place where Uncle would have been comfortable; it wasn't a place she could see him in. It was just an apartment in Kowloon now, not a shrine.

She went into the bathroom and took a shower, turning the stream to maximum power. When she was done, she wrapped herself in a thick towel and stared into the bathroom mirror as she dried her hair. The past forty-eight hours had been like a dream from which she had just woken, except that when she stepped outside, she would walk right back into it. Could she be faulted for anything that had happened? She thought not, at least not overtly, though her willingness to maintain contact with Xu had set off a chain reaction. Or had it? From what she had seen and heard, the collision between Xu and Wing had been almost inevitable. She had simply been an excuse, and if it hadn't been her it would have been someone or something else.

She brushed her hair, pressing the bristles deep into her scalp. When it was completely dry and hung like a curtain of black silk, she pulled it back with her ivory chignon pin. After she had applied lipstick and mascara and dabbed perfume on her wrists and collarbones, she was ready to get dressed. She pulled on a pair of black slacks and then chose a white button-down shirt, fastening the sleeves with green jade cufflinks. Ava was superstitious. Over the years the chignon pin and the jade cufflinks had become good-luck charms. This was the first time on this trip that she had worn them at the same time.

It was almost eleven o'clock, and she began to feel nervous about the meeting that was about to take place. She picked up her phone and called the number Sonny had given her.

"The Lui Clinic," a woman's voice said.

"Doctor Lui, please. This is Ava Lee. I'm a friend of Sonny's."

"Just one moment."

The moment became one, and then two, and then five. Ava was about to hang up when she heard, "This is Doctor Lui."

"My name is Ava Lee. I'm a friend of Sonny's and of Mr. Xu."

"Sonny told me you want to talk to Mr. Xu."

"I do, if that's possible."

"He's heavily sedated."

"Is he awake?"

"Off and on."

"When he is awake, does he understand what's being said to him?"

"Some of it. I'm not sure how much."

"How long will he be like this?"

"At least another day, maybe more. And when he becomes less dependent on the pain medication, he still won't be very mobile. He was lucky, you know. The knife wounds just missed his organs."

"Thank goodness for that."

"Yes. Now I assume you would like me to see if he is able to chat with you."

"That would be wonderful."

This time only a minute passed before she heard another voice. "This is Xu." He spoke in a whisper, his name trailing off.

"It's Ava. I don't want to bother you, but I'm meeting with Wing in less than an hour."

"Is it over?"

"The worst part."

"You mean the easy part."

"If you say so. Xu, are you up to telling me again what you want from Wing?"

The line was silent, and then she heard him say, "I'll try."

## 31

SHE CARRIED HER BAGS DOWNSTAIRS AND STOOD inside the door, waiting for Sonny. When this was over, she would go back to the Mandarin. Tomorrow she would see Bowlby and then get ready to leave Hong Kong.

Sonny arrived right on time, double-parking in front of the building. When he saw Ava's bags, he popped the trunk and ran to get them.

"How is traffic?" she asked as she slid into the back seat.

"Okay. We should be there in fifteen to twenty minutes," he said as he got behind the wheel.

He looked at Ava in the rear-view mirror. She saw that his eyes were lined and his mouth was sagging. Even Sonny was finding it harder to handle all-nighters.

Ava waited until they had cleared the street and were headed towards the Kowloon MTR before she asked, "Tell me about this Lop character."

"I've only met him twice, once in Shanghai and then in Borneo."

"What was he like?"

"I didn't speak to him, just saw him in action. Like I said

to you earlier, he's a bit crazy."

"Did you ask Suen about him?"

"Yeah, but not until last night. And I had to ask more than once before I could get anything out of him."

"What did he have to say?"

"Lop has been with them for less than two years. He was an officer in the Chinese army, the head of some kind of elite squad. Suen wasn't specific but he hinted that the squad was special operations. And that kind of figures, because he's in charge of Xu's guys on the ground and he's trained them to operate like a well-oiled army unit."

"So how did he find his way from there to Xu?"

"I have no idea, but however it happened, Xu evidently holds him in very high regard."

"Is Suen jealous?"

"A bit, I think."

"Is that a problem?"

"Not that I can see. Suen says Lop worships Xu, is completely loyal, and will follow orders to the letter."

"Until the day he doesn't."

Sonny looked back at Ava, his eyes hooded. "Is that a prediction?"

"I don't know the man well enough."

"I think you're just being cynical, and after all the crap you've had to put up with over the past few days, I don't blame you. The truth is that Xu has a way of inspiring loyalty in his people. It reminds me in many ways of —"

"Don't compare him to Uncle again," Ava snapped.

Sonny half-turned, his face serious. "I was going to say you."

Ava blinked. Then she closed her eyes and shook her

head. "All I want is to get this mess behind me so I can go back to what I should be doing."

Traffic wasn't nearly as bad as it had been the day before in Mong Kok, and Sonny quickly found his way to the Kowloon MTR. "We're early," he said.

"So are they," Ava said, motioning at Suen and four other men standing in front of the station.

"I'll drop you off and then go park," Sonny said as he pulled up at the curb.

Suen saw them and walked immediately to the car. Ava opened her door before he got there. He stood to one side as she climbed out. "I brought six men," he said. "I thought I'd leave two out here, two inside by the restaurant's front door, and two around the back."

"That sounds fine," Ava said, wondering if he really wanted her approval. "Where's Lop?"

"He's on his way with a few more men."

"And Jimmy Tan?"

"Yes, Tan is with them."

"Was he badly beaten?"

"No."

"I wish he hadn't been harmed at all, but I guess I should be congratulating you and Lop for a job well done."

"It was hardly a fair fight. They weren't much tougher than Wan's men in Borneo. We expected more resistance, but these guys have been getting by here for years without any real opposition. They've gone soft."

"Evidently," Ava said.

As they entered the station, Ava saw Andy and Winnie standing at the front door of their restaurant. They both bowed. "The table is set for you, Ava," Andy said.

"Thank you, Andy. Let me introduce you to Suen, one of our Shanghai visitors. He's going to leave some men out here as a precaution."

"It's an honour to meet you," Andy said.

"Not everyone in Hong Kong thinks that," Suen replied.

"I guess they'll learn," said Andy.

"Sammy Wing should be here shortly," Ava said. "He's supposed to come alone."

"You told me that earlier. I'll keep my eyes open for anyone who looks suspicious."

"Thanks."

"Sonny is right behind us and Xu's man Lop is coming a bit later. You'll recognize him because he'll have Jimmy Tan with him. You can show them to the kitchen," Ava said.

"Will anyone want to eat?" Andy asked.

"No," Ava said.

"But this is for the inconvenience we're causing you," Suen said, handing him a roll of Hong Kong dollars.

Andy hesitated for a second, then took it. "I'll have tea and water brought to your table. Would you like anything else to drink?"

"That's all that I need," Ava said. "Let's go to the kitchen. I don't want to be hanging around when Wing gets here."

When they walked into the kitchen, she looked automatically at the spot where the table had been set for her and Uncle, and then for her and Carlo. The area was empty.

"I moved our vegetable crates to another area and set you up in the back," Andy said.

They trailed him to a spot near the back door, where a table for six was tucked into a corner. Ava sat with her back to the wall. Suen went to the door and checked to see if it was locked. When he returned, he sat next to her.

The kitchen door swung open and Sonny walked in. Behind him was Sammy Wing. From the door the table was difficult to spot, and Ava saw Sonny straining to find them.

"Suen, go and get them, please," Ava said. She took several deep breaths and tried to compose herself. It was, she told herself, just another negotiation.

She watched as Suen ran his hands over Wing's body, searching for a weapon. Suen then stood back and the three large men walked through the kitchen towards them. The chefs kept working, seemingly oblivious of everything but their woks.

Sammy was between Suen and Sonny, dwarfed in height but not in girth. He looked calmer than he had sounded on the phone, a man resigned to his fate. When they neared the table, Ava stood and extended her hand.

"Sammy, it's good to see you," she said.

"Is that a joke?" the fat man said.

"No. We're past jokes."

Wing slid his hand over Ava's, not gripping it.

"Sit, please," she said.

Wing sat down directly across from her and then turned to see if anyone was behind him. He started to speak, but Ava cut him off.

"Sammy, I'm sorry things have come to this," she said. "None of this had to happen — it was all completely unnecessary. You and Xu should have been able to resolve your differences in a more amicable way. You should have gone to Shenzhen yesterday instead of sending your men."

"It was stupid of me," Wing said.

"I also have to tell you that I resent the fact that you used me as bait."

"The men were instructed not to harm you."

"So they said, but that didn't stop them ultimately from trying to."

"What can I say? I misjudged the situation."

"You will understand if I regard that as an understatement."

"Yeah, I can see that. Look, I took a chance because I thought I had to, and I lost. So here we are."

"Tell me, Sammy, what the hell was running through your head? What logic led you to try to kill us?"

"I told you when I met with you before," he said.

"I know what you said, but I still don't understand. What real threat is Xu to you?"

"I don't want to go over that shit again. Whatever reasons I had don't matter anymore, do they."

"No, they don't, and now we find ourselves in this uncomfortable situation. Sammy, what would you do if you were in Xu's place?"

Wing shook his head and then looked at Suen and Sonny in turn, as if they had influence. "I'm not playing that game," he said. "You're calling the shots. Whatever I have to say doesn't mean a damn."

Ava nodded and leaned back in her chair. "Did you talk to Li last night?"

"No."

"I don't believe you."

"I didn't talk to him."

"Not even when your men were first attacked and you knew it was going badly?"

"What does it matter if I did or didn't? He isn't here and he isn't coming."

"Did you reach out to anyone else for help?"

"There was no point."

"How many of those men who attacked us yesterday were Li's?"

Wing shook his head so vigorously that his jowls flapped. "They were all my men. I paid Ko separately."

Ava's right arm flew through the air, her open palm crashing onto the table with such force that it shook. Wing flinched, and Ava saw the first real sign of fear cross his face. "Don't tell me that," she said. "You can offer up any kind of bullshit justification for what happened, but don't lie to me about Li. I know he sent Ko. Now, how many others?"

Wing looked at Ava and then shrugged. "One more."

"So it was a partnership between you and Li."

"Call it what you want."

"And now your partner won't come to your aid. You need to be smarter when it comes to choosing sides."

"I'm at least thirty years older than you, twenty years older than Xu, and I've been in this business my whole life. One of the first things I learned — and never doubted — is that the only side you can count on is your own. Li knows that too. That's why his men didn't leave Guangzhou last night."

"Ko and the other one shouldn't have left the day before."

"That's for you and him to sort out. "

"Yes, I guess it will eventually come down to that. In the meantime, what is to be done with you?"

Wing's chins dropped. There were beads of sweat on his forehead and upper lip, and Ava noticed that his polo shirt was getting wet across the chest and at the armpits. It could have been the heat in the kitchen that was causing it, but she could see the tension in his face and in his wandering eyes.

Suen leaned over to her. "Lop is here," he said.

Ava looked towards the door and saw Andy, Jimmy Tan, and a man dressed in khaki pants and a pale blue golf shirt. The man she assumed was Lop wasn't much taller or more muscular than Andy, who pointed them towards the table. As Lop came closer, she could see that he was clean-shaven and his hair was parted on the right. He had no scars, no tattoos, no memorable facial features. It wasn't until he was almost at the table that his eyes caught her attention. He was blinking rapidly, like a man caught suddenly in a blinding light.

Lop held Tan by the elbow, and from the pained look on Tan's face, the grip was strong. Tan's hair was dishevelled and his shirt hung over his pants, but it was the dark bruising around his eyes and the traces of blood under his nose and around his mouth that held Ava's attention.

"Do you want him to sit?" Lop asked.

"No. He won't be here that long," Ava said.

Tan trembled. Ava could only imagine the outcomes running through his head.

"Jimmy, do you have any family living outside Hong Kong?" she asked.

Tan nodded.

"Don't make me guess."

"I have a daughter living in Guangzhou and another one in Vancouver."

"Good. Vancouver sounds perfect. Now, how long will it

take you to brief Lop on the part of the business you run and get him up to speed on your men?"

"Why?"

Ava raised her right hand. "No questions. Just answers."

"A day or two," Tan stammered.

"Two days, then. I'll give you two days. On the third day I want your ass on a plane to Vancouver. When you get there, stay there. You aren't to come back here for any reason."

"I have property, investments, businesses here. How —"

"Get rid of them, keep them, run them from Vancouver — I don't care. Just don't come back. If you do, Lop will bury you here."

Tan glanced at Sammy Wing. Wing was staring at the wall. It was as if Tan didn't exist anymore. "Okay. I'll make it work," he said.

"I thought you might," she said. "Now I'd like you to go into the restaurant and wait for Lop. He won't be long. Sonny will escort you."

Lop released Tan's elbow. Tan shook his arm and grimaced. "Get out," Lop said, grabbing him by the collar and turning him towards the door.

"Jimmy, you'll have some of our men for company until you actually get on the plane. So don't get any ideas about doing something stupid," Ava said to his back.

He swivelled towards her. "I have things to do, personal things. If you want me out of here in three days, how can I do them with those guys hanging around my neck?"

"Your wife and girlfriend will understand. And if they don't, that's too bad."

He started to speak, but Sonny moved in front of him and stared down at him. Tan's head dropped and he resumed his walk towards the kitchen exit.

"Take a seat, please," Ava said to Lop.

He took a chair next to Wing, directly across from her. He sat ramrod straight, his hands intertwined and resting on the table. Ava noticed that his eyes weren't blinking quite so fast, but now his shoulders seemed to be twitching.

"Now we need to talk about you," she said to Sammy Wing.

"I'm not leaving Hong Kong unless it's in a box," Wing exclaimed.

"There's no need to be so dramatic," she said. "Xu is prepared to consider the events of the past few days the result of a misunderstanding. He thinks he could have been a bit more sensitive to the economic pressures you felt were imminent, and he thinks you would have been better served by going to Shanghai to discuss things with him face-to-face. Can you agree with that?"

"A misunderstanding?"

"Yes. Why not?"

"What are you trying to say?"

"He doesn't see any reason why you shouldn't keep running Wanchai." She didn't know who looked the more surprised, Wing, Suen, or Lop.

"What?" Wing said.

"You have the infrastructure and you have the street connections, and, I assume, the right police connections. Why would he want to disrupt one of the best markets for his products?"

"Then why did he dump Jimmy?"

"Lop will be replacing him. He is your new deputy Mountain Master. Xu is going to leave him here with about twenty of his men. They'll make sure none of the local gangs try to take advantage of you in your current weakened state. They'll make sure there isn't a repeat of what happened yesterday. Can you live with that?"

"As a figurehead, a straw man?"

"Call it what you want. Lop will take over the day-to-day business. That will free you to spend some time thinking about how to make everyone even more money. Mind you, Sammy, Xu doesn't want you making any decisions without consulting Lop."

"I'll be — what, a fucking servant?"

"Think of yourself as the chief executive officer and Lop as the chief operating officer."

"And Xu?"

"He's the new chairman of the Wanchai board. Though it will be better for everyone concerned if that's kept between you and the people at this table. Xu doesn't want his colleagues to get paranoid about his involvement, and we have your face to worry about."

"Of course, my face — the little I have left."

"Sammy, you need to adjust your sense of reality."

"It was adjusted several hours ago . . . Okay, I'm CEO, Xu is chairman, and Lop is COO. Now, I don't mean for this to sound negative," Wing said, "but what actual experience does Lop have running a business like ours? Until six months ago I hadn't even heard his name. Where does he come from?"

"Do you remember Fen Ying?" Suen asked.

"He worked for Xu's father," Wing said, almost startled by the interruption.

"Well, Lop is his son."

"Shit. That apple didn't fall far from the tree."

"Xu's father urged Lop to join the People's Liberation Army and arranged for him to attend military academy for officer training. He reached the rank of captain in the special operations force. You have heard of that force?"

"Who hasn't?"

"About two years ago Xu decided he needed Lop's talents and asked him to join the family in Shanghai. He agreed immediately. He's been training a select group of our men. Our aim was to strengthen our defences, but as you saw last night, we are also quite capable when on the attack."

Wing's head swung towards Lop. "For you, taking us on must have been like fighting children," he said.

Lop shrugged. "We take nothing for granted. A gun doesn't know if there's a trained professional holding it or a fat old man."

"Sammy, Lop has Xu's complete trust and I am assured that he is very capable. Do you agree to the proposal?" Ava said.

"What choice do I have?"

"You can say no."

"I'm not a fool."

"Then we have an understanding?"

"That's a polite way of putting it," Wing said.

"You may not be aware of it, but that's how Xu likes to conduct all his affairs. There's no reason why things have to be acrimonious."

"Speaking of which," Wing said, turning to Lop, "how many of my men are dead? How many are you still holding and what is going to happen with them?"

Lop looked at Suen and then at Ava.

"Tell him," Ava said.

"Eleven men are dead. We have seventeen still under our control," Lop said.

"The eleven are dead because they resisted," Suen added.

"What are you going to do with the seventeen?" Wing asked.

"Do you anticipate anything but full co-operation from them?" Ava said.

"No. All most of them care about is that money finds its way into their pockets every week. Where it comes from isn't a huge concern."

"Where are the men being held?" she asked Suen and Lop.

"We took them all to a restaurant on Hennessey Road," Lop said.

"Perfect. When Sammy and I have concluded our business here, Suen can take him there to tell them about the new arrangements, and then you can release them."

Wing slid back his chair, placed his hands on the table, and started to push himself to his feet.

"Wait a minute, we aren't finished yet," Ava said. "I want to talk to you about the chairmanship."

Wing froze, his bum just inches from the seat. "Xu wants my vote?"

"He doesn't have it?"

Wing tried to smile but his lips barely moved. "We'll be sitting around a table together. There will be a show of hands. How can I not vote for my new silent partner?"

"What we really want to know is where you think the overall vote stands."

"Xu doesn't know?" Wing asked, sitting down again.

"He has a rough idea, but he also understands that people like to keep their options open."

"Before last night, I think he was trailing Li."

"Was?"

"He has my vote now, which means he and Li are probably tied — unless you've pissed off someone else over the last couple of days."

"Not unless you have another friend like Li."

"It isn't smart to be detached from what's going on in the south."

"Well, Xu has a foothold here now and a reason to be more involved," Ava said. "Tell me, if you thought Li was ahead in the vote, why did you try to kill Xu?"

"Shit, you already won. Why do you want to keep talking about yesterday?"

Ava ignored him. "Xu told me about the bombs in Shanghai, and now we've had knives and guns in Shenzhen."

"The factory was bombed in Shanghai. Xu wasn't the target."

"Still, it seems that every time someone wants to damage his business or kill him, you're involved."

"Like you said, people keep their options open. We weren't a hundred percent — maybe not even sixty percent — sure that the others would vote the way they said they would. We didn't want to take the chance that Xu would win, or that if Xu lost he would take it out on the gangs that didn't vote for him."

Ava nodded, her face impassive. "So your best guess is that he and Li are tied now?"

"The gangs in Hong Kong, the New Territories, Macau, and Guangzhou support Li. Xu has Malaysia, Taiwan, and most of the mainland."

"Who do you think might be persuaded to switch?"

Wing shrugged. "Off the top of my head, no one."

"Really?"

"They all respect Li. They've known him for years. In their eyes, Xu is a new and maybe dangerous player, and they aren't quite so committed to selling his goods."

"They're still peddling Li's drugs, I assume."

"For some of them that's their main business."

"A risky one."

"Old habits die hard."

"Especially a habit that's backed by a reliable track record. None of them will budge?"

Wing grimaced and then shrugged.

"Would you talk to them on Xu's behalf?" Ava asked.

"Is that a demand or a request?"

"A request."

"I could, but I'm not sure what kind of credibility I'll have with them. I mean, you can talk about 'secret partner' all you want, but the word will be out about what happened in Wanchai. Li, if no one else, will make sure of that."

"Then what about Li?"

"You want Li to vote for him?"

"No, we were thinking maybe you could ask him to withdraw his candidacy."

Wing shook his head in disbelief. "That's crazy."

"Maybe it was yesterday, but now I'm not so sure. I certainly think it's something worth exploring."

"Under what pretext?"

"He tried to kill us."

"Who knows that?"

"He does, and he needs to understand that we do as well."

"You know only because I told you."

THE KING OF SHANGHAI    283

"We know that, and I'm sure he does too. He's no fool.
Do you think he believes you stayed quiet?"

"Believe what you want."

Ava slowly leaned forward. "As you said, Li knows what
happened to you last night. Maybe he'll feel the need to
make Xu a peace offering."

"Guangzhou isn't Wanchai, and Li has at least ten times
more men than I do."

"We can match him in numbers, and I know that our
men are better trained than his," Suen said.

"I don't doubt anything you say; I just don't know why
you're saying it. I don't believe you'll ever attack Li, and if
I'm smart enough to figure that out, then so is he."

"Humour me, Sammy. Call him and find out where his
head is," Ava said.

"I don't have to call him to know that. He'll be organizing support against Xu, and not just in Guangzhou. He'll
be calling all the societies that support him and enlisting
their aid."

Ava reached for the cup of tea that had been in front of
her since she sat down. She sipped and then grimaced. "I
hate cold tea," she said.

Suen took the cup from her and threw the tea onto the
floor. He poured a fresh cup. "This should be better, boss,"
he said.

"Just leave it on the table," she said, her eyes trained on
Sammy Wing.

"This thing with Li — if I was you I'd leave it alone,"
Wing said.

"Why?"

"He's stubborn and extremely hard-headed. He'll already

have an idea, an opinion about what Xu did, why it was done, and what Xu is going to do next. Nothing I say will change him."

"That attitude isn't healthy for business."

"He cares less about business than any of the other leaders. He's an old man now. It's all about power and prestige."

"He has a huge market for Xu's products. That must matter."

"More to Xu and to some of Li's people than to him."

"Like who?"

"What?"

"His people. Which of them cares about the business?"

Wing shrugged, pressed his lips together, and slowly shook his giant head. Ava couldn't tell if he didn't have an answer or was just reluctant to give one.

"Give me a name," she said.

"Well, Lam is the man who runs the day-to-day operations."

"I've met him," Suen said. "Tall, thin guy with long hair who likes wearing bright-coloured glasses."

"Yeah," Wing said.

"Does he have any influence with Li?" she asked.

"Some."

"Then talk to him."

"I know Xu wants me to do this, and I know it may be dumb to seem like I'm resisting, but I have to say there's no one — not me, Lam, Gong Li, Mao Zedong, or God — who could persuade Li to withdraw his name for the chairmanship."

Ava leaned back in her chair. Wing rubbed his eyes with his right hand, and Ava could see he was beginning to tire. The past twelve hours had taken their toll.

"Maybe you're right," she said. "And maybe we've done all we can here." She turned to Suen. "I would like you to go with Lop, Sammy, and Tan. Make sure everyone understands that the game stays the same but there are some new players in it. Sammy, I expect you to introduce Lop as your new right-hand man."

"*Momentai.*"

"And you'll also be rooming with him or one of his men until the vote is over."

"What!"

"Did you expect anything else?"

He grimaced. "I guess not."

"Nothing has to change, Sammy. Xu wants you to understand that he's not putting his hand in your pocket. What you earn, you keep. He does want you to pay Lop what Jimmy Tan would have made, and the rest of the men left here should get the traditional cut. He thinks that's fair."

"And the supply line will obviously be kept open."

"You can count on that."

"I figured I could."

"Well then, we're done for now. It would be nice to have the transition completed and business humming along by the time the election is over."

"I'll look after it," Lop said.

Ava looked at Sammy Wing. His face was impassive, his eyes focused on some spot above her head. His stillness struck her as odd. What was churning through his mind?

## 32

**AVA PULLED SUEN ASIDE AS LOP ESCORTED SAMMY WING** out of the restaurant. "Please make sure Wing is never left alone until the election is over," she said.

"Someone will be with him even if he's crapping."

"Good."

"Will you call the boss to tell him how the meeting went?"

"I'll try. I spoke to him this morning, but he's weak and I don't want to overtax him."

"I'll go over to the clinic later today, after things are completely settled in Wanchai," Suen said. "My plan is to sleep there as long as the boss is there. Will you be coming too?"

"Not unless it's really necessary. I have other business to look after, and besides, hospitals and clinics make me nervous."

He looked down at her and smiled. "It's nice to know that something does."

They caught up with the others in the restaurant. Sonny moved behind Ava, trailing her several paces to the rear. Tan was at the entrance between two of Lop's men. Andy and his wife stood nearby.

"You're coming with us now," Lop said to Tan. "You and Wing."

Ava waited until the Shanghai group had dispersed before turning to Andy. He and Winnie bowed.

"Thanks, Andy," Ava said, kissing him on the cheek. "I hope this is the last time I ever have to use your restaurant this way."

"It's the least I can do for you."

"Andy, I have a favour to ask," Sonny said. "I have to go and get the car. Could you stay with Ava until I come back?"

"Sure."

"Do you want my gun?"

"I have one," Andy said, patting his pocket.

"That isn't necessary," Ava said. "I'll walk with you."

"No, you can't. Xu would kill me — or try to — if anything happened. It's still too soon to take chances."

As she watched Sonny's back recede, Andy asked, "Everything okay?"

Ava shot him a glance. "Andy, I don't think I should discuss this with you."

A bus stopped in front of the station and unloaded. As the flood of people moved past them, Ava backed up against a wall. Andy stood in front of her, his hand in his pocket. When the bus moved off, Sonny's Mercedes slid into its spot. Ava said a quick thanks to Andy and then walked to the car, where Sonny waited, holding the rear door open for her.

As the car pulled into traffic she said, "What did you think of the meeting?"

His eyes flickered in the rear-view mirror. They looked uncertain, as if she had sprung a trick question on him.

"They'll have to keep a lid on Wing, and I wouldn't let Jimmy Tan leave Hong Kong until the election for chairman is over," he said.

"You knew about the election before?"

"Who doesn't?"

"I didn't until a few days ago."

"No reason for you to know."

The traffic slowed and Ava replayed in her mind the meeting with Wing, searching for any mistakes she might have made.

"And boss, you shouldn't ignore Li," Sonny said. "Just because he didn't rush to Wanchai doesn't mean he isn't coming. He knows Xu is hurt. He may take a gamble and try to finish him off. He may think there isn't any other leadership in place."

"I'm not ignoring him," Ava said quietly.

Again his eyes flashed in the mirror. "Sorry if that was out of place."

"Don't be," she said. "And since we're speaking of Li, do you have any good contacts in Guangzhou?"

"What do you mean by 'good'?" he said.

"People who are connected and discreet."

"No, not really, but Uncle Fong does. He was in and out of there for years."

"Doing what?"

"We had bits of business there. Fong was the man on the ground for Uncle."

"So he knows Li?"

"Very well."

"I wouldn't want him to talk to Li."

"Of course not."

"Does he know Lam?"

"Even better than Li."

"Sonny, how mentally alert is Uncle Fong these days?"

"I don't understand what you're getting at," he answered.

"I need someone to talk to Lam who I can absolutely trust. I trust Uncle Fong, but what I don't know is how capable he is these days of handling something this delicate."

"Why talk to Lam?"

"I want to convince him that Guangzhou should negotiate with us."

"Li will make that decision. And from what Wing was saying, it doesn't sound likely."

"I know it's Li's call, and I can't imagine him responding positively to a direct approach from us. But Wing said this Lam character is more pragmatic. If I can persuade him that it's in everyone's best interest, maybe he can sway Li. Do you know Lam?"

"I've met him."

"And?"

"He's solid. Not a man who gets overly emotional."

"So, someone we can do business with?"

"Only to a point. Li makes all the final decisions."

"I would never ask Lam to talk to Li about an agreement unless he had something firm in hand, something that would satisfy Li's needs."

"Ava, you're losing me."

"I want to talk to Lam, and Lam alone. I want him to know that Xu is prepared to cut a deal."

"Ava, have you discussed this idea with Suen or Lop?"

"No, I haven't, and given Xu's wishes, I don't think I have to. Do you?"

"No," he said quickly. "I'm sorry for even asking the question."

"I didn't mean to snap," Ava said. "It's just that things can't keep going like this. Wing and Li were stupid to attack Xu, but enough revenge has been taken on Wanchai. The bloodshed has to stop and business needs to get back to normal."

"No one likes war — except maybe Lop," Sonny said.

"So let's bring an end to it."

"But Ava, I have to tell you that what you want done sounds very complicated. For starters, you'll have to explain things to Uncle Fong very clearly. He'll be eager to please, but alert or not, I worry about his ability to relay your message to Lam. Truthfully, it might be better for me to tell Uncle Fong what you want."

"Will Lam trust him? He must know that Uncle Fong and I are friends."

"Yeah, he'll know, but Uncle Fong has been Triad his whole life. He took the oaths and he honours the traditions. Lam also knows that Fong is retired and has no particular axe to grind."

"So you're saying that we can use Uncle Fong as our go-between and you'll brief him?"

Sonny's head bobbed, and she knew he was pleased with himself. How often had Uncle used him as a sounding board? It was a question she'd never considered.

"I think we will do it that way," she said. "Uncle Fong should contact Lam and say that he's been talking to me and that I requested he make an approach. We want to do a deal and we're prepared to make concessions. The first step towards reaching an agreement is for Lam to contact me directly. Uncle Fong has to make it absolutely clear that it's too early to involve either Li or Xu. Lam and I will need some time to feel out each other's positions and find a middle ground that we think will be acceptable to the Mountain Masters. When he and I are satisfied, then we'll bring the bosses into the picture."

"Lam will have lots of questions."

"And Uncle Fong won't have any answers. Lam will have to talk to me."

"He'll be suspicious."

"I want just one phone call from Lam to tell me he's prepared to talk. Nothing more than that. We'll take it from there."

"He may run directly to Li."

"Uncle Fong must stress that if the bosses are brought in too soon there will never be a deal — their egos will get in the way. Lam and I need to lay the groundwork."

"So all you want is for Lam to agree to meet with you?"

"Yes, so make sure Uncle Fong has my cellphone number. He can also tell Lam I'm staying at the Mandarin Oriental." Ava looked into the rear-view mirror and saw that Sonny was staring straight ahead, his brow furrowed, his lips moving. "How soon can you meet with Uncle Fong?" she asked.

"As soon as I get you back to Central, I'll call him."

"How will he contact Lam?"

"He'll phone him, but only to arrange a meeting between the two of them. There's no way something this sensitive can be discussed over the phone."

"If Lam agrees to see him, how soon can we get him to Guangzhou?"

"I'll drive him myself. It's a two-hour trip unless the border is clogged."

"You haven't slept in more than twenty-four hours."

"In the past I've gone seventy-two."

"Sonny, if Lam agrees to meet Uncle Fong, schedule it for early tomorrow."

"That might be best."

"We don't want Lam to think we're too eager."

## 33

**AVA CALLED THE CLINIC FROM HER HOTEL ROOM AND** got Dr. Lui. "He's resting," he said.

"When he wakes up, please tell him I called."

"It may be a while. He had a very restless night and morning and I've upped the dose of sedative. He needs sleep."

"Of course. There's no urgency to my call."

She unpacked her bags and then turned on her computer. With the Wing issue resolved, she thought for a second about calling Richard Bowlby to try to set up a meeting for that afternoon, but she knew her head wasn't in the right space. Neither was her body. She was tired. The sleepless night, combined with the adrenalin drain after the meeting with Wing, had left her feeling limp. She glanced at the bed, but she knew that climbing into it would be the worst thing she could do. A two-hour nap would screw up her body clock for days. She needed to do the opposite, she thought, and reached for her running gear.

It was a typical hot and muggy Hong Kong summer afternoon. Ava didn't mind the heat, but Hong Kong's humidity and perpetual cloud cover made the air thick and everything seem gloomier, more oppressive. But she was an outdoor runner, and at least she could run in Victoria Park.

She walked from the hotel to the Central MTR station and took the train three stops east to Causeway Bay. Victoria Park was a tiny oasis of green nestled in a concrete jungle. It had been built in the 1950s, on land reclaimed from what had been a typhoon shelter for the yachts, fishing boats, and junks that now anchored at the nearby Royal Hong Kong Yacht Club and docking sites along the bay. It wasn't particularly large; its forty-six acres paled in comparison to New York's Central Park, at nearly eight hundred acres, and the combined 630 acres of London's Hyde Park and Kensington Gardens. The Victoria Park jogging path was just over six hundred metres, a quarter the length of her favourite run at Lumpini Park in Bangkok. But everything is relative; given the population density of Hong Kong Island and the pressure on the government to use every square metre of land, Ava was grateful there was a jogging path at all.

The park was open twenty-four hours a day. Early morning and evening were the peak hours. Ava had once tried running in the morning but had given up because the track was so jammed she could barely walk, let alone run. But that afternoon she was able to manoeuvre her way around the track without having to stop. There were also fewer distractions, such as the tai chi practitioners with their fans and swords and the old men with their caged birds, than there were in the morning. She was able to focus on the run, getting past the pain in her thighs and steadying her breathing until she was on cruise control, knocking off each lap in about three minutes. By the second lap she was drenched in sweat. She used a hand towel she'd brought from the hotel to wipe her face.

She tried to think about May Ling in Beijing with Suki, and Amanda and Chi-Tze waiting in Shanghai for the Pos, and then her meeting the next day with Richard Bowlby. But almost without her realizing it, the names Lam and Li came to mind, and she was soon replaying that morning's meeting with Wing and her talk with Sonny. It wasn't over, she knew, not by a long shot. There were too many moving pieces, too many men still in the shadows, and she had to put her plan in the hands of Uncle Fong. *That was stupid*, she thought suddenly. How many years had he been retired? How senior had he actually been? How sharp was he? How could she expect him to get a meeting with Lam, let alone convince him to meet with her?

The realization caused her to miss a breath. She felt her chest tighten, her pace slowed, and she came to a halt in the middle of the track. She had done ten laps, six of them while obsessing about Wing, Lam, Li, and Uncle Fong. But she felt energized and her mind was more alert. She'd call Sonny when she got back to the hotel, she decided.

Rush hour had started by the time she went down the stairs into the Causeway Bay MTR station. She was still sweating profusely when she got into the train, which was almost full, and her presence in the car wasn't welcomed. The people heading home from work didn't appreciate being crushed against someone so sweaty. She did the best she could to be unobtrusive, but there was no escaping the masses inside the cars. By the second stop she found herself pressed so tightly that her arms were pinned to her sides, leaving her sweat to roll unchecked. The ride back to

Central took only about ten minutes, but her discomfort was so extreme that it felt like half an hour, especially since, in addition to being wet, she had to put up with looks of disgust and muttered curses from the other passengers.

Back at the hotel, she stripped and wrapped herself in a thick white terry cloth robe. When her body cooled down, she'd shower. She made herself a coffee and sat at the desk. Her worries didn't seem quite so extreme now that she was in a different, calmer environment.

Ava turned on her cell and saw that she hadn't missed any calls. She opened the computer. Her inbox contained a long list of unread messages, most of them from May Ling, keeping Ava up to date on her progress. In the first she responded to Ava's news that she was checking out of the hotel by writing: I don't like the sound of that. Be careful. In the last she said they'd just finished lunch and were going back to work.

The phrase *to work* implied structure and routine, which Ava found rather strange. The debt-collection business had been anything but regular. Jobs were intermittent, sometimes months apart, and when they did come, they often involved days of endless slogging punctuated by moments of enormous stress and, as she had told Amanda, occasional terror. Could she handle the routine? The first job she had had was with a large accounting firm in Toronto — she didn't last six months. She wasn't good at blindly taking orders, she had a low threshold for boredom, and she had been quietly, almost subversively, insubordinate. *Three Sisters won't be as mundane*, she told herself. May Ling and Amanda were so passionate and committed that she felt stimulated just being around them. And it was nice, for a change, to feel like part of something bigger than herself. With Uncle, Ava had been on her own more often than not. This was different. Whatever they accomplished would be the result of a group effort.

She responded to May's emails, telling her that she would be meeting with the lawyers the next morning and that she was back in the hotel and life was good.

There were no messages from Amanda. Ava wrote: Have you heard from Gillian? If not, please call her.

She headed for the bathroom and took another long, hot shower. She checked her cellphone when she came out and saw she'd missed a call. The red light on the room phone was blinking as well. *Xu*, she thought.

It was Sonny, and in his message he sounded pleased with himself.

"It's me," Ava said when he answered.

"I just left Uncle Fong. He was thrilled that you want him to do something."

"I'm glad I made him happy."

"You'll be gladder still. He called Lam and the two of them talked. Lam is going to meet with him tomorrow morning."

"In Guangzhou?"

"On the outskirts, so we won't have to go all the way into the city."

"That's thoughtful of him."

"Also he might not want anyone to know he's meeting with Uncle Fong."

"And why not?"

"You said to keep Li out of this. There's a better chance of that if they meet on the edge of the city. Besides, these guys are all naturally suspicious."

"Were you with Uncle Fong when he spoke to Lam?"

"I was."

"And how did Uncle conduct himself?"

"As you wanted. In fact, better than I could have imagined. I'd forgotten how smooth and persuasive he can be. He was Uncle's Straw Sandal, and that job was all about communicating."

"Lam didn't wonder why Fong wanted to meet with him alone?"

"Yes, but Fong just said it was about something too important to discuss over the phone."

"And Lam didn't push for details?"

"No, he didn't push for details. I don't know him that well, but Uncle Fong says he's very smart and subtle. I'm sure he's reading something between the lines."

"What time is the meeting tomorrow?"

"Nine."

"I'll be at the lawyer's office from eleven on. Call me anyway on my cell the moment you can."

"Okay."

"And thank Uncle Fong for me. Tell him I'm sure he'll do well tomorrow." Ava hung up with the sense of satisfaction that comes when a decision is vindicated.

## 34

**SHE SLEPT FOR TWELVE HOURS, HER DREAMS CALM**
and fleeting and the outside world kept at bay. When she
woke, the room was bathed in almost complete darkness.
But when she opened the drapes, the morning sun had
climbed well up in the sky and the streets below were full
of cars and pedestrians.

She did a bathroom run, grabbed the *Wall Street Journal*
and the *South China Morning Post* from the door, and
made a coffee. She hadn't set an alarm or asked for a wake-
up call, and with only an hour to get ready before leaving
for the lawyer's office, she knew she shouldn't procrastinate.
Still, she couldn't help leafing through the *Journal*, making
another coffee, and turning on her computer to check her
email. There were more updates from May Ling but still no
word from Amanda. She turned to the *Post* and scanned it
quickly, looking for any mention of violence in Wanchai.
There was nothing. She pushed aside the paper and went
back to the washroom to shower and get herself presentable
for her meeting at Burgess and Bowlby.

May Ling's description of Burgess and Bowlby had been

a revelation to Ava. Her experience with lawyers had been primarily with those who represented the thieves and scumbags who had stolen money from her clients, lawyers who as a rule were as slimy as the people they were trying to shield. They would lie and threaten, and when that didn't work, they would resort to the legal system to slow things to a crawl. But Ava and Uncle didn't acknowledge the system when it came to bear on their clients' situations — going to court wasn't how they operated. They preferred a more direct, hands-on approach.

It was May Ling who had discovered Burgess and Bowlby about a year earlier. One of her and Changxing's businesses had become involved in a dispute with a Hong Kong–based supplier that B&B represented. When the firms, together with their lawyers, met to resolve their issues, May Ling had been impressed by Richard Bowlby. She told Ava that he was smart, calm, analytical, and even-handed, and — unlike other *gweilo* lawyers she'd dealt with — he spoke fluent Cantonese and passable Mandarin and really seemed to understand the Chinese mentality. She had used his firm to incorporate Three Sisters and then hired him to paper their Borneo Furniture and Suki Chan acquisitions.

Before leaving the hotel, Ava called the clinic. "Mr. Xu had a peaceful night," Dr. Lui told her. "He was awake quite early and was able to speak to a couple of his colleagues. But that did seem to tire him, and he's sleeping again. I think I'll ban visitors and phone calls for the rest of the day. If he has complete rest today, by tomorrow he should be able to get out of bed."

"Please tell him I called and that I won't bother him until you give the green light."

"Something else you should know — one of his men insisted on sleeping here last night, in the bed next to him," Lui said.

"That would be Suen."

"Yes, that's his name. He makes me rather nervous. We mustn't have any problems at the clinic."

"There won't be any trouble, Doctor. Suen is just naturally overprotective."

"Then I won't say anything."

"That's best," she said.

Ava left the hotel at ten to eleven, took a right turn, and within five minutes was walking into the lobby of the Bond Building. As she waited for an elevator, her mind flitting between details of the business agreements and thoughts about Uncle Fong and his meeting, her cellphone rang.

"It's Sonny. How soon can you get to Guangzhou?" he asked.

"Lam's agreed to talk to me?"

"Yeah."

The elevator doors opened but Ava stayed rooted in the lobby. "I'm just about to go into a meeting with some lawyers."

"How long will that meeting take?"

"I really don't know."

"Ava, you can't make Lam wait all day. When Uncle Fong talked to him on the phone, he stressed how urgent it was that they talk, and I know it was his plan to push for a quick meeting between you two. Now that he's got an agreement, I think you'd better get here as fast as you can."

She knew he was right, but that didn't make her feel any better about cancelling on Richard Bowlby again. On the other hand, she wasn't sure how well she could concentrate on legal matters with Lam dominating her head. "I can get a limo at the hotel," she said.

"Yeah, they always have some available on short notice. The drive is about an hour and a half. How far are you from the hotel?"

"Ten minutes on foot."

"You should be able to get back to the hotel, get a limo, and be on the road by eleven thirty. That'll get you here by one o'clock. Just to be safe, I'll tell Uncle Fong that you'll be here before two p.m."

"Where is 'here' specifically?"

"The Pearl Dreams Hotel in Huangpu. It's half an hour southeast of Guangzhou, so it's that much closer to Hong Kong. Tell your driver to take the Huangpu Bridge over the Pearl River to the National Road East exit. From there he should go south on Kaifa Avenue. The hotel is on the avenue just before you reach the river again."

She hesitated.

"Ava, do you need me to repeat that?"

"No. I'm just thinking about the lawyers."

"They'll still be there tomorrow. You can't count on Lam being so accommodating."

"I get it."

"So?"

"I'm heading back to the hotel right now. I'll let you know when I have things organized."

"Ava, I have to tell you, Lam's guys are real thugs. Two of them went upstairs with Uncle Fong when he got here. There are at least two more outside and two sitting with me in the lobby."

"Are you worried about them?"

"No, I just thought you should know. I don't want you to get here and be spooked."

"Thanks," she said, and then glanced at her watch. "Look, I have to go. I'll call in a while."

She searched her contacts list and found the number for Richard Bowlby. She called him as she was walking out of the building. The receptionist said he was in a meeting.

"I'm the reason for the meeting and I'm not there, so there isn't any meeting going on. Could you please connect me?"

A moment later she heard, "This is Bowlby."

"Mr. Bowlby, this is Ava Lee. I'm terribly sorry about this, but I can't make it to your office today," she said quickly.

"Ms. Lee —"

"And I apologize for the short notice, but something urgent arose when I was literally about to step into one of your elevators."

"I understand," he said in a tone that implied he didn't. "Do you have any idea when you'll be available?"

"No, I don't, so I think I'd better call May Ling. Perhaps you could work directly with her until I'm available."

"I'll be pleased to work with whomever the company designates."

"Thank you," Ava said, noting the stiffness in his voice. "And again, my apologies." She ended the call less than satisfied with the conversation and walked towards the Mandarin, thinking about what she would tell May. She called her cell, not expecting her to pick up, and was mentally preparing a voicemail when May answered.

"Are you alone?" Ava asked.

"Yes. I stepped outside to call Wuhan. There are some issues there I have to deal with."

"And I have one here, I'm sorry to say."

"What's going on?"

"I've just cancelled the meeting I had planned with Richard Bowlby."

"Did something happen? Are you displeased with him?"

"No, he's fine."

"Are you having second thoughts about these deals?"

"It's Xu," Ava said.

"Has he become a problem?"

"No, he's wounded. He's in a clinic here in Hong Kong — in Mong Kok, actually."

May gasped. "My god. Is he going to live?"

"Yes, and he'll be mobile in a few days. But May, there's no denying it's a mess, and I'm in the middle of it."

"How —"

"That doesn't matter right now. What does matter is that I have a plan to extricate both myself and him from the situation. It will take a day or two, though, and I can't focus on anything else until it's done."

"Is there anything I can do to help?"

"Manage the Beijing closing with Bowlby," Ava said, stopping at a red light.

"What about the Po investment?"

"Amanda hasn't heard from Gillian, so there's nothing to be done yet. Frankly, it's becoming a concern, but I think we should leave it to Amanda to sort out."

"I agree, and of course I can handle Beijing, but what I meant was do you need help with the Xu problem?"

"No. It's something I have to do."

"Are you going to tell me about it?"

"Yes, I will, just not right now."

"Why not?"

Ava closed her eyes and felt her shoulders tense. It was a fair question, and Ava realized there was no answer that wouldn't sound like *I don't trust you enough to tell you.* "Xu was attacked two days ago in Shenzhen by Sammy Wing's gang from Wanchai and another from Guangzhou," she said.

"When did you find out?"

"I was with him when it happened."

May became quiet. Ava could only imagine the kinds of questions that were now in her friend's mind.

"The gangs used me as bait to draw him there," Ava said in a rush. "When I met with Sammy Wing in Hong Kong, he said he knew about our financial relationship with Xu and he made some threats about disrupting our business. I went to Xu and told him to fix the problem. He went to Shenzhen to do that."

"Threats?"

"All they wanted was to get to Xu, and we were a convenient route."

"And they did get to him."

"To their regret. Wing's gang has already been decimated and is now controlled by Xu's men. We're just starting negotiations with Guangzhou to restore stability."

"You said, '*We* are starting.'"

"Yes. I'm handling some of the talks for Xu. I'm leaving in a few minutes for the first session," Ava said, the hotel coming into view.

"Do you know how crazy that sounds?"

"It isn't quite that bad. I have a plan that I think is workable. This could be all over by tomorrow, or the day after."

"You never cease to amaze me. You say that as if it's the most common thing imaginable."

"It isn't much different from other situations I've had to deal with."

"I thought those days were behind you."

"Me too."

"Oh, Ava, now I'll be spending the next few days worrying."

"I'd rather you spent them getting the deal done."

"That won't be a problem. It's what I've been doing for more than twenty years."

"And sorting out the problem of Xu and Guangzhou is something I know how to do."

"Yes, I guess you do," May said, and then paused. "Ava, who else knows about this?"

"No one."

"Then I'll keep it close."

"Thanks, and if you don't hear from me for a day or two, don't get paranoid."

"I remember very well how you like to operate."

"Look, I just got back to the hotel. I have to speak to the concierge about getting a car to take me to Guangzhou."

"Be careful. Don't take any risks when you get there."

"I always am."

"Remember, you have friends who love you and worry about you."

"And I love you too," Ava said.

"Thanks for sharing this with me."

"Sure," Ava said. When she ended the call, she realized that May hadn't asked her a single detailed question about the threats or Xu's money. She smiled.

## 35

**THE LIMO WAS A MERCEDES-BENZ S-CLASS, THE SAME** as Sonny's and Xu's, and the driver also wore a black suit with a white shirt and black tie. But unlike Sonny, he kept up a steady stream of chatter, and Ava finally had to ask him to stop so she could take time to think. She had to plan the pitch she wanted to make to Lam. She opened her notebook, turned to the back, and began to list options. She was still adding and subtracting ideas when the driver said, "There's the Huangpu Bridge."

The Mercedes passed over the Pearl River, continued to speed along a four-lane highway, and then exited sharply onto another. Ava lifted her head from time to time to note that development in Huangpu was as rapid as in the rest of China. The car slowed and began to make its way down Kaifa Avenue, which had a mix of low-rise shops, restaurants, and office buildings. The only tall building in sight loomed on the left, and that was where the driver took them.

The Pearl Dreams Hotel was twenty storeys of grey concrete, glass, and aluminum sheathing. The driveway was packed with late-model German and Japanese luxury cars, and the Mercedes was forced to stop well short of the entrance. Ava thought about getting out and walking the rest of the way, and then decided to wait. She didn't want to appear too eager or look too rushed. So wait she did until the Mercedes was directly in front of the entrance.

"This has been charged to my room?" she said to the driver.

"Yes, miss."

"Thanks, and this is for you," she said, passing him an HK thousand-dollar note.

She walked through the revolving doors into the lobby. The concierge was on the right and a carpeted strip ran directly down the middle of the tiled floor towards the elevators. On the left was a sitting area with leather chairs and sofas and glass coffee tables. Towards the rear of this lounge, next to the elevators, Ava saw Sonny. He was sitting in a chair facing in her direction. Across from him she saw the backs of the ponytailed heads of two men.

Ava started to walk across the lobby towards Sonny, but she hadn't gone more than ten steps before he saw her and leapt from the chair. He moved quickly towards her, his right arm extended. "Hey, we should go right upstairs. They gave me the room number when I said you were on your way," he said.

As they walked past the sitting area, the two men on the sofa stood and moved in behind them. They made Ava uncomfortable, and she threw a questioning glance at Sonny.

"They're my shadows, not yours. Don't worry about them," he said.

The four of them rode the elevator to the seventeenth floor and walked down the hallway to a corner suite. Sonny knocked. Ava heard voices from inside and the shuffling of furniture. When the door opened, its frame was filled by a man who was as broad as Sammy Wing and several inches taller. When he stepped aside, Ava saw Uncle Fong sitting at a round table set against the window. Across from him stood another man. She paused, expecting Fong to greet her, but he didn't move. Ava took two steps inside the room and stopped. The negotiations had already begun.

She watched as Uncle Fong struggled to his feet, his hands pressing down on the table for support. At one time he had been close to six feet tall, but he was in his eighties now and the years had shrunk him. He looked so frail that Ava wondered how he walked without a cane. She clasped his hands with both of hers and then kissed him lightly on the cheek. "Thank you for all of this," she whispered.

"For you, anything," he said.

Fong was a contemporary of Uncle not only in age but also in the lives they'd led. Like Uncle, he had fled China as a young man and joined a Triad society to secure some kind of future. He didn't start out working with or for Uncle, but by the time he was in his forties he had joined the Fanling society, which Uncle headed. Ava wasn't certain when he had retired — he had been retired for as long as she had known him — but she did know that he was dependent on Uncle financially, a dependency that had been passed on to her. When she had asked Uncle how Fong came to be in that situation, he'd shrugged and said, "He was convinced there was a system that could beat the roulette tables in Macau. He spent most of his adult life proving himself wrong."

"Will you introduce me to Mr. Lam?" she asked.

Fong turned and signalled with a flick of his finger for Lam to come over. Ava was startled by the apparently rude gesture, but Lam simply nodded and came towards them.

He was tall, thin, and wiry and had long hair. He was in his mid-forties to early fifties, she guessed, but when he moved she saw that he was supple, lithe even, and there was strength in that slender body. His long, narrow face was just starting to show age, in lines at the corners of his eyes and a slight sag along his jawline. His hair was white, combed back and tied in a ponytail. Some strands hung loose on the right side of his face, giving him an almost boyish look, a look that was accentuated by a pair of round blue-tinted wire-framed glasses. He was wearing a long-sleeved black shirt, black jeans, and a pair of Ferragamo loafers. In his own way he was as unlikely a Triad as Xu, she thought.

"Thank you for agreeing to meet with me," Ava said before he had reached her.

"Do you remember me?" he asked, extending his hand.

"No, I'm sorry, I don't."

"I was at Uncle's funeral, so this is our second encounter."

"I don't remember much about that day."

"Uncle was a great man, and Fong here was as good a Straw Sandal as ever I've met — something he's just proved again today."

"I owe him my gratitude."

"Maybe we both will by the time the day is over," Lam said, his face solemn. "Why don't we sit by the window."

"Yes, I'd like that," Ava said.

"And I'd like everyone else to leave," Lam said to the other men, who were still standing near the door. As they started to back out of the room, Uncle Fong hesitated. Lam touched him lightly on the arm. "That means you too, I'm afraid. You've done your job. Now Ms. Lee and I need to talk alone."

"I'll wait for you downstairs with Sonny," Fong said to Ava.

"Please. And don't leave without me."

Lam motioned to Ava, and she took the seat that Uncle Fong had vacated.

"Tea or water?" Lam said. "Or I can order whatever you want from room service."

"Water is fine."

He poured her a glass and then one for himself. "I have to say that I was surprised when Fong called and asked to meet with me."

"I understand."

"He was quite vague about the reasons, although he did drop some interesting hints. I didn't put much stock in those hints, I must say."

"So why did you agree to meet with him?"

"Out of respect mainly. When Uncle was still running Fanling, we did some joint ventures together and Fong was the go-between. He is an honourable man, and I couldn't imagine he would want a meeting for frivolous reasons. I just didn't think it really had anything to do with the war between Wing and Xu, which is what he was implying."

"And why did you think that?"

"Because what could that possibly have to do with us?"

Ava ran her finger down the side of the glass, her eyes moving between the water and Lam's face. She looked for telltale signs of tension, for any clue that he was lying. He didn't know that she knew about Ko. "If that's the case, why did you agree to meet with me?"

"I could say that I was simply curious, but that wouldn't be entirely true. I mean, I can't deny there are issues between Guangzhou and Shanghai, and Fong made it clear that's what you want to discuss."

"Issues like Xu controlling the supply of software and various devices?"

"Yes."

"And the fact that Li and Xu are both contesting the chairmanship?"

"Yes."

"Then of course you know that Xu was wounded in an attack that was designed to kill him. You must have some interest in his condition, in his ability to defend his turf."

Lam's right hand reached for the strand of hair that hung loose. He stroked it, and for a second he reminded Ava of Clark Po. "From what I've heard, Sammy Wing has paid dearly for his rashness," he said. "I can also assure you that there was no doubt about Xu's strength either before or after the attack. He has a formidable force."

"Wing must have known that as well, so why did he try to kill Xu?"

"You would have to ask Sammy that question."

"Maybe he thought if he lopped off the head, the body would obey."

"Ask Sammy."

"I did. He said the attack on Xu was for the benefit of Li."

Lam smiled, but his eyes narrowed. "Ms. Lee —"

"Call me Ava."

He nodded. "And I'm Ban. Ava, I don't believe Wing said anything of the sort."

"And if he did it was a lie?"

"If you wish to insist that he said it was for Li, well then, yes, it was a lie."

"So how do you explain Ko?" she said.

His immediate response was to speak, but he caught his words before they were fully formed. Slowly he sat back in the chair, his eyes not leaving her face.

"He tried to kill me in London, more than a year ago now. I recognized him, of course, when I saw him at the restaurant in Shenzhen," she said. "You never quite forget the face of a man who's tried to kill you. Sammy Wing told me Ko was freelancing, but when I pushed him, he admitted that Ko was still working for Li, and so was at least one of the other men who tried to kill Xu and me. So, you know, that's twice your boss has tried to kill me. I have no idea what I've done to offend him."

Lam poured himself another glass of water. As he drank, his eyes wandered to the Pearl River below. "I know you don't remember me, but do you remember meeting Li at Uncle's funeral?"

"No."

"He was quite taken with you. He told me that in London you fended off Ko and another one of our men even though you were unarmed. He was convinced that Uncle was sleeping with you. He thought he might take a run at you himself if the opportunity came."

"Instead he tried to kill me."

He smiled. "Tell me, if you and Xu have assumed that Li was somehow involved in the attack in Shenzhen, why did you only go after Sammy Wing?"

"It's early days."

"Bullshit," he said. "And speaking of bullshit, it's just

occurred to me that I'm sitting here talking to you based on the assumption that you speak for Xu. The only backing for that claim is Uncle Fong."

"Do you know Suen?" Ava said.

"Of course."

"And Lop?"

"No, though I've heard of him."

"Do you have a phone number for either of them?"

"Suen."

"I'll leave the room and you can call him. When I come back, I want an apology."

He shook his head and smiled again. "What do you want from me?"

"I want you to help me avoid a war."

"What makes you think there's going to be one?"

"As things stand, it's inevitable."

"Why?"

"Li has tried to kill Xu at least once, and I think more than once. In any event, once is enough, wouldn't you agree?"

"I would if you could prove it."

"Let's not do that dance again."

"Okay, we'll leave it alone."

"Then we have the fact that Wing was fighting to get Li the chairmanship and was willing to participate in the killing of Xu to make it happen. Even between friends, that's a bit excessive. So our view is that Wing and Li are partners, not just friends."

"I'm told that Sammy has paid a price for what he did."

"Do you know to what extent?"

"No."

"About a third of his men were killed and Xu has taken

control of Wanchai. Sammy is alive, but he'll do what he's told. So now Li finds his enemy parked on his doorstep, less than two hours away by car from Guangzhou. How long will it be before Xu decides to seek his revenge here?"

"It would be suicidal if he tried."

"I couldn't agree more. But as things stand, he will try, if for no other reason than to prevent Li from trying to kill him again."

"That will never happen."

"Explain that to Xu," Ava said. She leaned forward. "Or better still, explain it to Suen and Lop."

"This isn't Wanchai."

"I know. From everything I've heard, you're probably as strong as Shanghai. It would be an even match, which in this game means everyone would lose something, and they would keep losing until there was a winner. And what would the winner have when it was over? Not much of anything, I suspect."

"So why do it when the outcome is so uncertain?"

"Because right now there isn't any other choice on the table."

"And you're going to put one there?"

"Yes, because in addition to everything else, I'm also rather tired of Li trying to kill me."

Lam stared hard at her. "You obviously have something in mind."

"I do, something that I think is reasonable."

"It sounds like you want to deal."

"Why else would I be here?"

"You have my undivided attention," Lam said.

## 36

**IT WAS CLOSE TO NINE O'CLOCK WHEN THEY REACHED** the outskirts of Kowloon. Ava sat in the back of the car alone. Uncle Fong slept next to Sonny in the front, his head collapsed against the window. There hadn't been much conversation since they'd left the Pearl Dreams. Ava was exhausted from her meeting with Lam — not as physically tired as Fong but drained mentally and in no mood to talk.

Both Sonny and Uncle Fong had waited in the lobby. When she came down, they almost ran towards her as she exited the elevator.

"It went well enough. At least it's a start," she said before they could ask. "Lam and I agreed we'll keep this between the two of us until we get a chance to talk to Xu and Li. So please, let's leave it at that."

When she got into the car, she turned on the reading light. In her notebook she recorded the train of her conversation with Lam. It hadn't run in a straight line, which was predictable, given the nature of what they were discussing, but it was even more complicated than she had anticipated. Lam was subtle and incredibly intelligent, and he preferred asking questions to providing answers. Since Ava shared that last quality, finding common ground proved to be a tortuous exercise. But she hadn't lost her patience. She'd prodded him and fended off his probes with increasing confidence as she began to realize that, despite being abstruse, they were of the same mind on most matters.

"Do you want me to take you directly to the Mandarin?" Sonny asked.

The question caught her by surprise. Ava had lost track of time as she worked on her notes and shuffled scenarios. "Where are we?"

"In Kowloon."

"Let me make one phone call and I'll tell you," she said, taking her cell from her bag. She called the clinic. "This is Ava Lee. Can I speak to Doctor Lui?"

"He's gone," a female voice said.

"How about Mr. Xu?"

"He's sleeping."

"Mr. Xu's friend, Mr. Suen?"

"Just a minute."

"Yeah, who is this?" Suen snapped.

"Ava."

"Oh. Sorry if I sounded rude."

"How is Xu?"

"Better. He ate something tonight and walked around for about five minutes."

"Do you think he might be up for a meeting outside the clinic sometime tomorrow?"

"I'm no doctor but I'd be surprised if he could handle that."

"I see. But just in case, does he have a change of clothes?"

"No."

"Then tomorrow I want you to buy him a new jacket, white shirt, and tie. Take his old jacket with you so you get the size right."

"Okay."

"And when he wakes up, tell him I called and that I'll be at the clinic by midmorning," she said. "How are things going in Wanchai? Are Wing and Tan under control?"

"Lop has them."

"I guess that says it all."

"I'll tell the boss that you called and you'll be by tomorrow," Suen said. "I already told him how the meeting with Wing went. He couldn't have been happier. He'll be pleased to see you."

*I wonder how pleased he'll be after I tell him about Guangzhou,* she thought.

## 37

**SHE SLEPT FITFULLY, HER MIND CHURNING OVER THE** conversation she'd had with Lam and preparing for the one she was about to have with Xu. At six she gave up and slid out of bed. After a quick coffee, she put on her running gear and headed for the MTR and the short ride to Victoria Park.

The night before, she'd ordered room service when she got back to the hotel. While she waited for the food, she started up her computer. There was an email from May Ling saying she'd talked to Bowlby and that the law firm was working on the Beijing agreement. Another from Amanda said she'd finally contacted Gillian. Their conversation had been brief and lacking in detail, but Gillian had promised to respond to their offer within forty-eight hours.

There was one message on Ava's phone. Jennie Lee wanted her to call her father and arrange a dinner. Her father would have to wait until things were more settled, Ava thought. He tended to interrogate her, and she didn't fancy either lying or being evasive.

The park was almost quiet when she got there. The jogging track was busier than its perimeter, where the exercise clubs and tai chi groups were just beginning to set up, but she was able to get in five quick laps before it got congested. She did three more laps, starting and stopping, before she became frustrated and walked back to the Causeway Bay station.

She made another coffee when she got back to the room and sat down at the desk with the *South China Morning Post*. She read the front-page stories and then skimmed her way through the rest, almost missing a headline that riveted her. "Gang War in Wanchai," it read. The short article was buried near the back. It reported that a gun battle had broken out in Wanchai two nights before and several people had been killed or wounded. A spokesperson for the Hong Kong Police Special Investigations Unit was quoted as saying that two rival Triad gangs were involved and that the SIU was in the process of identifying and arresting suspects. Ava had no idea how much truth there was in that claim, but the fact that the SIU had gone public was bad. She was sure the story had made the front pages of the local Chinese papers; the only thing they loved more than a sex scandal was anything Triad-related.

She put down the paper and phoned the clinic. Dr. Lui came on the line almost at once.

"It's Ava Lee. I'm calling to see how Mr. Xu is doing this morning."

"Much better."

"So he can speak to me if I come over?"

"Yes."

"How about his mobility?"

"What do you mean?"

"How soon do you think he can leave the clinic?"

"I think he needs at least another twenty-four hours of

rest and care. And frankly, that won't be soon enough."

"Doctor, did something unpleasant happen?" Ava asked, surprised by his tone.

"My nurse brought me a fistful of newspapers this morning. They're full of stories about a Triad gang war. In two of them Mr. Xu is mentioned by name."

"I see."

"You do understand that I did this for Sonny? Actually, for my sister."

"Well, your help has been much appreciated. The last thing anyone, especially Mr. Xu, would want is for his presence to cause you any problems. I'll be at the clinic in about an hour. We'll start organizing his departure, and the moment you say he can leave, we'll take him home."

"Thank you."

"Now, could you let him know that I'm on the way?"

"I will."

Ava hung up. The election was two days away. If the doctor's prognosis was correct, it seemed that Xu would be in good enough condition to attend. What she had to ensure was that, whether he attended or not, the outcome would be the same.

Ava jumped in and out of the shower, dressed, quickly applied some makeup, and left the room with her bag in hand. She waved off the doorman's offer of a taxi and headed for the Star Ferry terminal. Rush hour was in full flow, and the ferries to Hong Kong Island were jammed with commuters. She had her choice of seats going to Tsim Sha Tsui and took one that gave her a view of the receding Hong Kong skyline. She took out her notebook and began to review the notes she'd made the night before.

When the ferry docked, she went over to the taxi stand. The driver hesitated when she gave him the clinic's Mong Kok address. She passed him an HK hundred-dollar bill. "That's your tip in advance," she said.

They crawled through Kowloon, and Ava felt her patience beginning to fray. She knew it was her eagerness to talk to Xu rather than the traffic that was the cause, but that didn't stop her silently cursing the motorists around them. When the cab stopped again about a hundred metres from the clinic, Ava had had enough. She passed the fare to the driver and climbed out.

The sidewalk was crowded, and she was almost at the clinic door before she saw the two men standing on either side of it. They were trying to appear casual, but as she moved towards the entrance, both stepped directly in front of her.

"I'm Ava Lee. I'm here to see Xu. Call Suen," she said sharply.

"Oh, you're Ms. Lee. Sorry, I didn't actually know your face," one of them said, and leaned forward to open the door for her.

She started up the narrow wooden stairway, which smelled of disinfectant even before she got to the door. The clinic had the same smell as every hospital she'd ever been in, and she hated it. In Ava's mind these were places where people went to die. She knew it was illogical, but it was a visceral response she'd never been able to get rid of. And spending months with Uncle at the Queen Elizabeth Hospital in Kowloon hadn't helped.

The door opened into a small reception area with about ten chairs surrounding a large coffee table stacked with Chinese magazines. Ava walked to the reception desk.

"My name is Ava Lee and I'm here to see Mr. Xu. Doctor Lui knew I was coming."

"Just one second," the nurse said, reaching for her phone.

There was a woman with a small child and an elderly couple in the waiting room. She heard the older woman say something curt to her husband. Ava turned to her. "I'm not here to see the doctor, so I'm not cutting in front of anyone." The woman looked embarrassed, and Ava felt ashamed for having spoken that way to an elder.

Before she could apologize, she was greeted by Dr. Lui. "Pleased to meet you, and thank you again for everything you've done," she said.

"Come inside," he said, standing back so she could pass. "Mr. Xu is in a private room at the end of the hall. Go left — you can't miss it."

She walked down the hall to a closed door and knocked.

"Who is it?" Suen said.

"Ava."

"Come in."

"You should know that your man downstairs let me in because I said I was Ava Lee. I might not have been," she said.

"I'll talk to him," Suen snapped.

Xu was propped up in bed with an IV in his arm. Suen sat near him in a blue leather chair.

"You look good," Ava said.

Xu shrugged, and then grimaced from the effort. "Well, I am twice as good as I was yesterday and ten times better than the day before. I have some energy back and my head feels less like mush."

"Are you up for a talk?"

"Sure."

"I think it might be best if it's just between the two of us for now."

Suen turned and looked at his boss, who nodded. "I was about to go buy you some clothes anyway," he said. He slid by Ava and left the room.

She stood near the door, fidgeting, shifting her weight from foot to foot. "I should tell you I'm very uncomfortable in hospitals."

"This is a clinic."

"Not much different."

"Come and sit down," he said.

She settled into Suen's chair, her head at the same level as Xu's. "I have to say you look better than I expected. The doctor sounded rather gloomy, but you have colour in your face and your eyes are alive."

"You should see what is under the gown. I have never seen so many bandages. I feel like a mummy."

"Well, he's done a hell of a job."

"I think so, although when he saw me this morning, he was quite nervous. I wondered if something had gone wrong with me."

Ava shook her head. "He was reacting to the local Chinese newspapers. The police have been talking up the Wanchai attack. They say it was a Triad gang war, and you were named in a couple of papers. I guess Sonny didn't tell the doctor everything when he brought you here."

"I hate publicity," Xu said. "In all my years in Shanghai I have never been mentioned in any of the media."

"Hong Kong is a different place. But the good thing is that when something new comes along, they'll forget about you soon enough."

"I hope it is not too late. Some of the brothers may see it as well, and they do not like publicity either. You know that the vote is in two days. I do not need to give them a reason not to support me."

"I doubt that a couple of small news stories in local Chinese papers would upset anyone."

"You do not know these guys."

"That's true."

Xu pulled himself up, groaning from the effort. Then he looked at Ava and smiled. "Suen and Lop were impressed with the way you handled Sammy Wing and Jimmy Tan. I owe you thanks for that. I meant to say it the moment I saw you, and then we got sidetracked."

"All I did was what you wanted."

"Do not be so modest."

It was Ava's turn to shrug. "When you said a minute ago that you don't want to give your brothers a reason not to vote for you, did it occur to you that going after Sammy Wing might already have done that?"

"I do not think so, or at least I hope not. The attack on Wanchai, given the provocation, will be something they all understand as a reasonable response. What they will not grasp is why I let Sammy live and why I am letting him continue to pretend he is in charge of Wanchai."

"Why did you?"

"I thought it was a good short-term business strategy."

"And the others won't see that?"

"They may not. Some may even think I am soft."

"That would be foolish of them."

"Foolish or not, it may give them a reason not to vote for me."

"What if it didn't matter who they voted for?" Ava said.

## 38

**"I DO NOT KNOW IF IT IS THE PAINKILLERS I HAVE BEEN** taking," Xu said slowly, "but I am having problems understanding you."

Ava leaned forward and put her hand on the edge of the bed. A memory flashed of her laying her head on Uncle's hospital bed, of his hand covering hers.

"I went to Guangzhou yesterday," she said.

Xu became still, his face impassive. "Why?" he said.

"To meet with Lam."

"Not Li?"

"No."

"Lam asked you to go?"

"No, I approached him through Uncle Fong. I requested a private meeting."

"And he agreed?"

"He did."

"What compelled you to do it?" Xu said, shaking his head.

"I'm not very good at sitting back and letting things happen."

"You were safe here."

"I wasn't so sure. We had Wing under control but Li was

still out there. You were here in this bed and Li would know you were badly hurt. So in my mind it became a question of what was better — to sit and hope Li wouldn't come after either of us again or to do what I could to make peace. I'm fed up with Li trying to kill me, however incidental he claims the attempts have been."

"I understand your frustration," he said. "But how did you think you would resolve anything by going to Guangzhou?"

"I had some ideas I wanted to discuss. I was told that Lam was reasonable and had influence with Li. I thought it was worth a shot."

Xu stared at her. "Well, you made it back, so either you did not have the meeting or Lam was as approachable as you thought."

"I had the meeting."

"And was he reasonable?"

"I think so, although the next twenty-four hours will tell the tale."

"What tale?"

"Will it be peace or war."

"Not making peace does not mean going to war."

"I don't believe that where you and Li are concerned. He's tried to kill you several times, and he has to figure you'll want revenge sooner or later. Will he wait for you to take it or come after you first? Either way, the violence will linger. Then there's the question of the chairmanship. No matter how the vote goes, nothing will get resolved, Xu. If you lose, you spend two years hunkered down in Shanghai figuring out how to kill Li. If you win, you could spend two years fighting off a vengeful Li and his friends. Tell me, how many votes have actually been committed to you?"

Xu paused. "Seven."

"Well, I would assume that if someone isn't prepared to declare their vote for you, they're prepared to vote against you. So that leaves you a lot of votes short of a win."

"And did you share that opinion with Lam?"

"I was hardly that direct, and neither was he. In fact, we spent close to three hours just fencing verbally and trying to find common ground."

"And did you?"

"Well, we finally agreed that to have Shanghai and Guangzhou battling each other was ultimately and inevitably counterproductive and probably destructive."

"There is nothing shocking about that conclusion."

"No, but then we tried to pinpoint the reasons for the animosity driving the conflict."

"I am interested to hear what he thinks they are."

"Two of the reasons are obvious enough: the contest for the chairmanship and the insecurity Guangzhou is feeling about becoming economically dependent on Shanghai."

"I can understand that the chairmanship race is making Li crazy, but how would killing me or starting a war help them economically?"

"Lam says Li believes your lieutenants would be more inclined to co-operate."

"Then he doesn't know my lieutenants."

"And, in truth, Lam doesn't share that view either. He said that Li is old school, content with running drugs, women, and gambling. Lam is the one who values your products and respects your business acumen."

"They are making enough money with them."

"That's only part of it. He says the police don't care if

they're selling your devices and that a lot of his men have come to like a life without constant pressure from the law. His problem is that if the Guangzhou gang gives up some of the old business for the new and there's a supply issue, they'll have a huge problem with their members. In some ways he sounds like you when he talks about business."

"So did you promise to keep the supply lines open?"

"I promised nothing other than I'd talk to you. He promised nothing in return, other than to talk to Li. We share some views, Lam and I. If you don't want to hear them, then you won't. If you do listen and then reject them, I'll take myself completely out of the picture and you and Li can have at each other."

"What did you discuss about supply?"

"Lam tells me that Guangzhou is your single largest market."

"It is."

"He wants you to commit to keeping them supplied on a prorated basis. He understands there will be shortages from time to time, but when there are, everyone should be affected equally."

"How will they verify that? Am I supposed to send them production reports?"

"According to Lam — and I heard something similar from Sammy Wing — the territories talk to each other. They all know what everyone else is getting. It doesn't take a math whiz to figure out if someone is being shorted."

"And committing to this prorated deal would make Li happy?"

"It would make Lam happy, and that would be a good enough start. Let him worry about Li."

"You have that much faith in a man you have met once?"

"Who said anything about faith? He has his self-interest, as we all do. I'm counting on him to look after his."

Xu smiled and gently shook his head. "Despite all the paranoia about supply, we have been trying to treat everyone fairly. If Lam needs my personal commitment, he will get it. I am as anxious to secure my markets on a long-term basis as he is about getting supplied."

"I thought that would be your reaction."

"So that leaves the other issue you mentioned — the chairmanship. What did you and Lam come up with that could possibly satisfy both me and Li?"

"I'm not sure we have anything workable."

"But you have something you want to talk about?"

"Yes, but first let me give you some background," she said. "When I met with Sammy Wing and then with Lam, I tried exploring the idea of Li withdrawing his name. Both of them said that would never happen — Li is determined to win. Lam said it's almost an obsession. He's an old man and he thinks it's his time. The chairmanship would be the crown of his career. Lam said he's been making at least ten phone calls a day, every day for weeks. He's offering whatever he thinks it will take to get a vote."

"And how many votes does Lam think Li has?"

"He could have enough, but there is no certainty in the numbers. Lam says Li is as unclear about the outcome as you seem to be."

"And where does that uncertainty leave us?"

"Maybe he's prepared to strike a deal."

"You have lost me again."

Ava took a deep breath. The case she'd been constructing

on paper seemed less plausible now that it was time to voice it. "Lam told me that the last four chairmen were acclaimed. He said this kind of contested election is unusual to begin with. Add in the fact that it's between two powerful men who dislike each other intensely, and that makes for an uncomfortable environment for all your colleagues. None of them wants to make enemies, but it sure seems that's what will happen, no matter who they vote for."

"I would never hold a grudge against anyone who voted for Li," Xu said sharply.

"Maybe not," Ava said, surprised by the force of his assertion. "But I'm talking about their mindset, not yours."

"I can see how they would expect an angry reaction from me."

"And from Li if he lost."

"Of course."

"Anyway, as Lam was explaining this situation and talking about how confused Li is about the final vote, it struck me that instead of being on this path of certain alienation, you and Li should try to find a way to work together in harmony."

Xu leaned forward. "How can harmony emerge from this set of circumstances?" he said quietly, calmly.

"It can't. We have to change the circumstances."

He collapsed back on his pillows, looked up at the ceiling. "I cannot imagine what you have in mind."

"It isn't my idea alone," Ava said. "Lam warmed to it and helped me flesh it out."

"I am listening."

"Well, we believe that a joint chairmanship might be the solution."

"What?" His face was still impassive, but for the first time Ava saw a flash of anger in his eyes.

"I know it sounds far-fetched, but as Lam and I talked about it, it began to make perfect sense," she said quickly. "You and Li head up the two most powerful societies. If you worked together, there wouldn't be any question of whether you'd have the complete respect and loyalty of your colleagues. You'd be giving them stability instead of uncertainty."

"They want more than stability."

"Things like growth and profitability and a way to carry their organizations forward for a new generation to take over?"

"My words from our meeting in the garden come back to me."

"If they were true then, they're true now. The way I see it, you and Li span two very different generations. The two of you represent the old and the new ways of doing business. You said in Shanghai that you need to find a way to build a bridge from the present to the future. What better way than having a man who represents the past working with a man who epitomizes the best of the present and the future?"

"There is a lot of wishful thinking in those remarks. You are discounting Li's character."

"No. What I just said is the message that you and Li would have to take to your colleagues. My understanding from Lam is that they have to agree to any major change in the way the chairman is chosen. That is a rationale we thought could be used."

"And do you honestly think they will believe for a second that Li and I could actually work together? It is quite a stretch to expect those guys to accept the idea of the two of us discussing and analyzing problems side by side, let alone reaching some kind of consensus."

"Yes, we know it's an unlikely scenario. In fact, Lam said it was a complete non-starter."

"So why are we talking about it?"

"We're not. What we're suggesting is that you alternate the chairmanship, each man taking one year. Both of you would agree to consult with the other during his term, but the final decision would rest with the man whose term it was."

"That is too complicated."

"Not really. All it takes is the willingness to say yes."

"And why would Li do that?"

"Because he isn't sure that he has the votes to win. So why would he risk losing when he has a chance to settle for something certain that will save his face? Besides, from what Lam told me, Li is very smart — maybe *shrewd* is a better word — but smart or shrewd, I bet he thinks he could manage you and that ultimately he would come out on top. Lam says that Li would most definitely want to be chairman for the first year. So all you'd have to do is get past that year, assume the chairmanship, and in a heartbeat Li is yesterday's man. When it comes to politics, people have short memories."

"What if he will not step down?"

"Do you really think that's realistic? The two of you go to your colleagues, propose a deal that makes everyone feel secure, and then Li takes it upon himself to renege? I can't believe for a second that it would be tolerated. That is, as long as you are still running Shanghai and Wanchai."

Xu closed his eyes and was quiet for a long time. Ava waited. One minute, two minutes, three minutes passed.

Finally he said, "What you and Lam have come up with has some appeal."

"If you are in agreement, I'll phone Lam. He was going to speak to Li this morning."

"What were his expectations?"

"He thought Li would go for it."

"That gives me pause."

"You have thirty years on him and a pipeline full of products. You are the future. Why not throw Li a bone? Give him his year. It will be a year of peace for you, a chance to grow your business without having to look over your shoulder. There's a certain irony to that, isn't there. You give him what he thinks he wants, and then he's done."

"Will you be talking to Lam?"

"Our plan was to touch base after I spoke to you and he spoke to Li."

"When you reach him," Xu said, "tell him I will call him."

Ava blinked.

"I know Lam very well, *mei mei*. Eventually he will want to hear directly from me that I agree. We might as well make it happen now."

## 39

**AVA TOOK A TAXI FROM THE CLINIC TO THE STAR FERRY** terminal. Thirty minutes later she was in Central, where she bought a disposable phone and a SIM card from a shop near the Mandarin. She called Sonny as soon as she stepped outside.

"I have a new phone. Lam needs to know the number — Uncle Fong should pass it along."

"Okay."

"Ask Uncle Fong to confirm when he's done it."

"I will. Is there anything else I can do?"

"Not right now, but please stay available."

She walked to the hotel filled with a sense of anticipation. She'd fulfilled her side of the deal and now it was up to Lam to conclude his, and he couldn't call her soon enough. She checked the new phone to make sure the ringer volume was set to maximum. As she did, her regular phone buzzed. She glanced at the screen and saw a text from Amanda. Spoke with Gillian again this morning. No decision yet, and I think we have a problem. Call me if you can, it read.

"Shit," Ava said softly. "Why now?"

She entered the Mandarin lobby and was almost at the elevators when the new phone rang. "Uncle Fong spoke to Lam. He has your number. He told Uncle Fong that you shouldn't expect to hear from him till later," Sonny said.

"Thanks," Ava said, her anticipation turning into impatience.

When she got to her room, she went directly to the desk. She turned on her computer, and while it was booting up she placed the two phones on the desk within easy sight and reach. She checked her email and saw that Amanda had sent the same message as in the text. Ava called Shanghai on the room phone.

"Amanda Yee."

"It's Ava."

"Thanks for getting back to me, and I'm so sorry I have to bother you," Amanda said in a rush. "May said you were into something complicated and that we should leave you alone unless there was no other choice."

"What's happened?"

"I spoke to Gillian yesterday and then again this morning. Yesterday she was hesitant when I asked her what they thought about our offer. Today our conversation started the same way, until I pushed. She finally told me they had some reservations."

"What specifically?"

"Our direct involvement in the running of the business."

"Is it Chi-Tze who's the issue?"

"She's obviously part of it, but I don't think it would matter who we wanted to put in there."

"Why do you say that?"

"I think Chi-Tze rattled them. The questions she asked

really zeroed in on how demanding and difficult it will be to create this business from scratch. I believe they hadn't grasped the full extent of it. They may be getting cold feet — this is a huge leap into the unknown. There's no built-in customer base, there are no guaranteed orders, and there are no private label buyers and designers to give them direction."

"And they're using our active participation as an excuse not to go ahead?"

"Not directly. Gillian didn't say anything negative about us. She just kept stressing that she and Clark are capable of running the business on their own and don't need any help."

"Maybe she also sees this as a way of protecting him," Ava said.

"What do you mean?"

"Well, he's been in a controlled and comfortable environment ever since he started working, first with his father, then with his uncle, and then with the company that bought the business. They and the customers have provided him with structure and some degree of certainty. Maybe the reality of what he's about to undertake has hit home. He's going to be under tremendous pressure — it will all be on him. That may have brought out his insecurities. He might be feeling a need to be surrounded by people who are familiar and nonthreatening."

"And we're threatening?"

"They might see it that way."

"And Gillian's definitely familiar."

"Yes. Now, aside from the issue of our involvement, are there any other problems with our offer?"

"No."

"So where does this leave us?"

"At an impasse until you talk to Gillian."

"Why me?"

"She requested it. She liked the approach you took the other day in her office."

"What does she expect? I'm not going to tell her anything different."

"Maybe you can put it differently."

"Have you discussed this with May?"

"Yes. She offered to call Gillian herself, but I told her I don't think that's a good idea, given Gillian's frame of mind. May said if I couldn't reach you that I should go back to Gillian and tell her we aren't going to change our mind about Chi-Tze, even if that means losing the deal."

"Where is Gillian?"

"At the factory," Amanda said.

"Is Clark there?"

"I think he was listening on the speaker phone when I was talking to her."

"Okay, I'll call. Give me the number."

"Thanks," Amanda said.

"For what? I haven't done anything yet. And I'm not sure anything can be done, because I'm not going to change our position either."

"Ava, I have to tell you that Chi-Tze is still blaming herself for this. If it doesn't go through she'll be devastated."

"I understand."

"Okay. Good luck."

Ava sighed as she put down the phone. There weren't many things more frustrating than trying to close a deal with a reluctant second party. She and Uncle had gone through it more times than she could remember. Her initial response was usually negative, but he counselled patience and urged her to find and then directly address the source of the reluctance. It worked more often than not. What was the source this time? There was quite a list to choose from.

*Oh, what the hell*, Ava thought as she picked up her phone. When the receptionist came on the line, she asked to be put through to Gillian and then waited for several minutes.

"Sorry for being slow," Gillian finally said, sounding breathless. "I was in the plant."

"And where is Clark?"

"He's there as well."

"Could you get him, please? I want to speak to both of you."

"Is that necessary?"

"Gillian, I'm in Hong Kong on other business. I didn't want to get involved in this negotiation, but now that I am, I'd like to conclude it one way or another as quickly as possible. That means speaking to you and Clark together."

Gillian hesitated. "I'll get him."

While she waited, Ava almost absent-mindedly drew a chart on the desk stationery. Every line led to her and May Ling.

"We're here," Gillian said.

"How are you, Clark?" Ava asked.

"Well."

"And so you should be," Ava said. "It isn't every day that someone offers you ten million dollars and the chance to fulfil your dream."

"The money is not the problem," Gillian said.

"Amanda says neither are the share structure or the financial controls."

"They're reasonable."

"So what's at issue?"

"We want to run our own business within the framework you've laid out. We don't need or want any other help."

"Meaning Chi-Tze?"

"Anyone that we don't hire ourselves."

"Okay, here's the thing," Ava said, drawing a deep breath. "You're being idiots."

"What!" Clark said.

"You have no real idea who you could be getting into business with. If you did, you'd be saying a prayer of thanks."

"We know your backgrounds," Gillian said.

"You don't know mine," Ava said.

"Amanda said you were in some kind of finance business."

"I guess you could call it that. What I did was chase down bad debts. I did it for more than ten years, with a partner whom I trusted with my life. And when I say my life, I'm not exaggerating. I've been shot, stabbed, and attacked with just about any weapon you can name. Through it all, I never had to worry about his not being there for me."

"He's not involved in Three Sisters?" Gillian asked.

"He died of cancer several months ago. The old business went with him. Three Sisters is my new venture, and I'm blessed to have partners whom I trust as much as I trusted him. They're smart, they're strong, and we'd go through hell for each other. Passing up the chance to work side by side with us is why I think you're being idiots."

"We don't want to give up our independence," Gillian said.

"Who's asking you to do that? No one will be telling you what to think or what you can say and do. Our intention is to support Clark, and that's it. You've never run a business on your own. Our people have. You've never started up a business. They have. They're there to support you."

"I don't know . . ." Gillian said.

"Look, let me make this very easy for you," Ava said sharply. "We're offering to put ten million dollars behind Clark without a single guarantee that he'll be successful. We could lose the money, but we're willing to make the commitment because of Amanda and Chi-Tze and the faith they have in his talent. To make this work, though, you need to have faith in them."

"Is there any kind of compromise —" Gillian began.

"No. The deal on the table is the only one you're going to get. No Amanda and no Chi-Tze means no ten million."

The line went quiet, and then Ava heard Clark whisper something to Gillian.

"Can we get back to you?" Gillian said.

"No, I want you to call Amanda when you decide what you want to do."

"Is there a deadline?"

"Call her by the end of day tomorrow. It isn't complicated — either you want to work with us or you don't."

Ava ended the call, then pushed back her chair and walked to the window. Dark clouds had moved in over Victoria Harbour and it looked as if it was going to rain. The weather suited her mood. She turned back to the desk to call Amanda just as the disposable phone rang. She ran to answer it. The number on the screen wasn't one she recognized.

"This is Lam," he said.

"I didn't expect to hear from you so soon," she said.

"I wanted to know what Xu had to say."

"Xu is on side. He said he'll call you to confirm."

"Did my number show up on your screen?"

"Yes."

"That's the number you should give him. I bought the phone this morning."

"I hope you're also calling to tell me about Li."

"I talked to him last night and then again this morning."

"And was he difficult?"

"It went more or less the way we discussed."

"So some options are still open?"

"That's how Li likes to operate — he never likes to close a door. He says he has questions."

"How many options are there?"

"Three or four, and that's right now. I told you that's what to expect."

"And how will we resolve those?"

"He's agreed to a meeting."

"Do you have any idea which way he's leaning?"

"I don't want to guess."

"When do you think you'll know?"

"It could be at the last minute, it could be when we meet."

"When and where does he propose to meet?"

"We're coming to Hong Kong tonight."

"Hong Kong is fine, but I would prefer to give Xu another night's rest. He's recovering, but he'll be stronger by tomorrow."

"Tomorrow morning will work. How is eleven o'clock?"

"That's fine. Where in Hong Kong?"

"There's a small hotel called the Montrose in Happy Valley, which is neutral territory. We'll meet in the coffee shop."

"I still have to talk to Xu before I can confirm, but I don't expect a problem."

"You'll call me with his answer?"

"I will."

"Good. Now let me go over what you can expect from Li and how I think we should respond."

## 40

**AVA PHONED SONNY AS SOON AS SHE ENDED THE** call with Lam. "I heard from Guangzhou and I'll need you tomorrow morning," she said. "How long will it take us to get from Mong Kok to Happy Valley by car?"

"Half an hour in decent traffic."

"Then we'll play it safe. Pick me up at the hotel at nine thirty. We'll go to the clinic and get Xu. You can drive us from there to the Montrose Hotel in Happy Valley."

"There's a meeting?"

"Yes, and I'll want you to stay there until we're done."

"How about Suen and Lop and Xu's other men?"

"They can meet us at the Montrose."

"So you cut a deal."

"Sonny, I can't talk about it. It isn't that I don't trust you; it's more that I'm superstitious. Uncle always used to caution me about assuming that a job was done until it was well and truly done."

"I understand. Will you need me for anything today?"

"I don't think so. I'll see you tomorrow."

She called the clinic, asked for Xu, and found herself

talking to Doctor Lui. "I was just about to call Sonny," he said. "Mr. Xu's condition is stable enough for him to leave."

"That's good news. My plan was to pick him up tomorrow morning anyway. Thanks for everything you've done."

"It's my job," Lui said, and then paused. "Despite the fact that his condition has improved, he shouldn't be taking on too much for a while. He still needs rest."

"What about the stitches?"

"He should wait for another couple of weeks before seeing his own doctor. If the wounds are sufficiently healed, the stitches can come out."

"You've told him all this?"

"I will."

"Thank you. Now could you please transfer me to his phone?"

Suen answered with a gruff "*Ni hao.*"

"This is Ava."

"He's been waiting for your call."

"Before you give him the phone, did you have any luck finding a jacket and shirt?"

"One jacket, two shirts. I brought them here for him to try on. Then I had to exchange them for larger sizes because of all the bandages."

"That was smart of you."

"I'm not just a pretty face."

"No, I guess you're not." Ava laughed. "Now let me speak to him."

"*Ni hao, mei mei,*" Xu said.

"I just spoke to Lam."

"And?"

"Li seems prepared to make a deal."

"Seems?"

"He needs some clarification on a few points and he wants it to come directly from you. He told Lam it was time for the intermediaries to get out of the way."

"And Lam thinks that is a positive sign?"

"On the surface, yes, he does," she said. "They've proposed a meeting tomorrow morning at eleven at the Montrose Hotel in Happy Valley."

"Do you know the place?"

"No, but I assumed that Suen or Lop could check it out tonight."

"One of them will. And how many people can we bring tomorrow?"

"No limits as far as I know. In the actual meeting it will be me, you, Lam, and Li. We can surround the place with fifty men if we want."

"How many will they have?"

"Lam said they were bringing ten men in total to Hong Kong for the meeting of the Mountain Masters. I imagine they'll all be at the Montrose as well."

"There is not a lot of time to reach an agreement with Li. If we cannot finalize things tomorrow, then the Triad meeting the next day will be interesting. I was talking today with some people and they tell me that Li is still working the phones. He has also invited them to a dinner in Hong Kong tomorrow night."

"Are you having second thoughts about doing the deal?" Ava asked.

"And third and fourth. But I keep coming back to the idea that things cannot continue as they are. We need to at least make an effort to broker a peace deal without totally abandoning our position."

"Neither of you can see this as capitulation. It has to be win-win, or eventually it will be lose-lose."

"I know, and that is why I am prepared to do it."

"I spoke to the doctor before I spoke to you," she said. "You're strong enough to be released tomorrow, so you should get someone to book a hotel for you for the next few days. How long do you think the meeting of the Mountain Masters will be?"

"We are scheduled to meet at one. There will be a lot of general discussion, then a dinner, and then we will have the vote in the evening. No matter what the outcome is, I have other business to do with some of the organizations, and that will take at least another day or two. So I think I will be here at least another four or five days."

"You aren't to overdo it. You still need rest. And you'll need your bandages changed."

"Suen is handy with bandages."

"I'm sure he is."

"Ava, just a second," Xu said, and his line went quiet. "You still there?" he said a moment later.

"I am."

"The doctor is here."

"Okay, I'll call Lam and confirm that we'll be at the hotel tomorrow. My plan is for Sonny and I to pick you up between ten and ten fifteen."

"That sounds fine."

"If anything changes, I'll phone."

"The same from this end."

After Ava had given Xu Lam's number, she put down her

phone and took a deep breath. Then she called Lam. He answered on the second ring.

"We'll see you at the Montrose at eleven," she said.

"If I need to talk to you before then?"

"Call my new cell."

"See you tomorrow," he said.

She reopened her inbox and started reviewing the messages with a less cluttered head. May had copied her on all the correspondence between Richard Bowlby and the lawyers in Beijing and Shanghai. The questions and comments were minor. There wasn't anything that May thought Bowlby couldn't handle quickly and completely. Ava emailed May. Thanks for keeping me in the loop. It all looks very encouraging. Things here are as well.

She pushed the chair back from the desk and went to the mini-bar to get a bottle of wine. Then she walked over to the bed and lay down with her back against the wall of pillows, turned on the television, and searched for something mindless. *By tomorrow*, she thought, *I may finally be able to get on with my new life.*

## 41

**AVA WOKE UP FEELING ALERT AND BURSTING WITH** energy. She made a coffee and drank it while she read the *South China Morning Post*; there was no mention of Wanchai or the Triads. She showered and took her time drying her hair, then pulled it back and fastened it with the ivory chignon pin. This was a day for looking her best. She put on a white shirt, fastened the cuffs with her favourite green jade links, and slipped on a black pencil skirt. She completed the outfit with her alligator stilettos, bought the year before at the Brooks Brothers outlet in the Pacific Mall in Tsim Sha Tsui.

She went to the desk and checked her email. There was nothing of any importance. She turned on both phones — no messages.

It was eight thirty when she left the room and went downstairs for breakfast at the Mandarin Grill and Bar, a Michelin one-star restaurant. She got a table overlooking Statue Square and perused the breakfast menu, which offered dim sum alongside duck eggs from the United States and organic chicken eggs from Wales. Ava ordered congee with abalone, which cost four times more than the plain version served at Uncle's favourite restaurant in Kowloon. She left the restaurant satisfied that it was the best congee she'd ever had.

She saw Sonny at the hotel entrance and wondered how long he'd been there. He nodded as she approached. Through the glass doors she could see the Mercedes parked in front — he still had *guanxi*.

"Hey, boss," he said.

"Hi, Sonny. Let's head for the clinic."

They were in line at the Cross-Harbour Tunnel when he said, "I made some calls about that Montrose Hotel. It has a reputation for being a dump."

"We're not sleeping there."

"No, boss." He looked at her in the rear-view mirror. "Sorry. I thought you might like to talk, but I don't think you do."

"No, Sonny. Maybe after the meeting. Until then I'm sort of preoccupied."

They inched into Kowloon and then worked their way towards Mong Kok. It was only a few minutes past ten fifteen when Sonny pulled up in front of the clinic. The door opened almost the instant they stopped. Xu emerged, with Suen in front of him and a man on either side.

Xu's face looked much thinner than it had the day before. Ava felt a twinge of alarm until she remembered that he was wearing a larger shirt and jacket to accommodate the bandages. He walked slowly to the car and took some time climbing into the back seat.

"Are you okay?" she asked.

"I never imagined that a sling could be so cumbersome."

Suen stood by the side of the car, peering in.

"You should head over to the hotel with the men," Xu said to him. "We will meet you there."

"He looks anxious," Ava said as the car pulled away.

"Yes, anxious to take a run at Li and his men. He cannot understand why I am going to this meeting. Whatever my reasons, I think he and Lop both secretly hope that things fall apart, so they can work out some of their anger."

Happy Valley was on Hong Kong Island, directly south of the Cross-Harbour Tunnel exit from Tsim Sha Tsui. Sonny drove through the tunnel and started along Canal Road. Ava checked her watch and saw that they had plenty of time to spare. Just as that thought registered, her regular phone rang. She answered without thinking

"It's Amanda."

"Hey. I'm in a car heading to a meeting and I shouldn't be on the phone."

"Just wanted you to know that Gillian called me ten minutes ago. They've accepted our offer sheet as written."

"How was her manner?"

"She was gracious, and then Clark came on the line and was as well. They both said they were looking forward to working closely with us."

"Congratulations."

"Ava —" Amanda began, only to be interrupted by the sound of the disposable phone ringing.

"I have to go. I'll call you when I can," Ava said quickly, and then picked up the other phone. "Ava Lee."

"This is Lam."

"Where are you?"

"Happy Valley."

"We are too, maybe ten minutes from the Montrose."

"There's been a change in plan."

"I'm listening," she said. She heard background noise and guessed she was on speaker phone.

"Instead of the Montrose, Li would like to meet at the Lucky Man mah-jong parlour on Wong Nai Chung Road. It's just south of the racetrack, about five minutes from the hotel."

"We'll tell our men."

"No, Ava, no men. The boss is afraid that ten or twenty Triads will attract unnecessary attention from the cops. He thinks that, after the events in Wanchai, we'd be better off keeping a low profile."

"So what are we talking about?"

"Me and him, you and Xu."

"I'm not sure we'd be willing to put ourselves at risk like that."

"We'll be next door to Wanchai, and that's your turf now. We're the ones who should be nervous."

"Still, I need to clear it with Xu."

"I'm waiting."

She covered the microphone. "It's Lam. They want to change the meeting place to another spot in Happy Valley, and they want only you and me there with just him and Li."

"That is fine," he said, his face impassive.

"Are you certain?" she said, looking closely at him.

"I trust Lam. But ask him if this means Li is serious about making a deal."

Ava hesitated and then said to Lam, "Xu wants to know if Li has made up his mind now. I mean completely."

"Yeah. That's why the change in meeting place."

"Lam says yes," she whispered to Xu.

Xu nodded. "Good."

"So we'll see you there?" Lam asked.

Xu sat back in his seat. He appeared relaxed but she could see that his attention was focused on her and the phone conversation. "Yes, we'll see you there," she said.

"What is the excuse they used to change the meeting place?" Xu asked after she ended the call.

"Li thinks too many Triads in a place as public as the hotel will attract the wrong kind of attention. He wants a more private setting."

"He is not wrong."

"No gang members included, inside or outside. Just the four of us."

"Let us hope that this works out better than the last time we scheduled a meeting for four people," Xu said.

"We're on home territory, with a small army close by. We'll let everyone know where we are. We can put Suen and Sonny on standby."

"Yes, we need to do that."

Ava saw Sonny's shoulders tense and knew he was feeling uneasy. "Sonny, do you know the Lucky Man mah-jong parlour on Wong Nai Chung Road?" she asked.

"Not the place, but I know the street."

"I want you to drive us there and stay in the area, then phone Suen and tell him we've changed the meeting venue. He and Lop and some men should be close at hand."

"Yes, boss."

Ava turned to Xu. "Are you really okay with this?"

"I am. I trust Lam. As long as he is there, I have no worries."

## 42

**WONG NAI CHUNG ROAD WAS JUST SOUTH OF THE** Happy Valley racetrack, which was as much a fixture in Hong Kong as Victoria Peak or the harbour. Sonny drove along Ventris Road, the track dominating the skyline on their right. When he reached Wong Nai Chung, he turned right and then drove slowly, searching for the mah-jong parlour. He spotted it halfway along on the other side of the road.

"We'll get out and walk," Ava said.

Sonny didn't stop. He drove farther, turned left, and headed down an alleyway behind the building. Ava knew he was checking for a back entrance, but there was none. He turned left at the end of the alley and then left again onto Wong Nai Chung. He did a U-turn and stopped in front of Lucky Man, a storefront with a single wooden door. The windows on either side were cloaked by black curtains, and a long hand-painted sign extended over the windows and door.

"Are you sure this is the place?" Sonny asked.

"This is it," Ava said. "Stay close and keep your phone on. If you see anyone other than Li or Lam go through that front door, you call Suen and then me, and you do whatever you have to to get inside."

She saw Xu and Sonny exchange glances, but before either of them could speak she slid out of the Mercedes and walked directly up to the Lucky Man entrance. She tugged at the door handle, expecting resistance. To her surprise, the door swung open.

"We are a little early," Xu said from behind her.

"We might as well go in."

They walked into a dimly lit room that was about twenty metres square. Rows of folded chairs were stacked against a wall and a few mah-jong tables were set up on the floor. The air was thick with dust; Ava guessed it was a while since mah-jong had been played there. There was a closed door at the far end, a ray of light leaking through the crack at the side.

Ava walked to the door and knocked. "This is Ava Lee," she said.

"Come in," an unfamiliar voice boomed.

"Li," Xu whispered.

The room was as large as the one that fronted the street, and as badly lit. A small square table was set up in a corner, with four metal chairs. A tall, thin man sat by himself, his back against the wall, smoke from a cigarette curling around his head. "Right on time," he said.

Ava looked around the room, searching for another exit, but there wasn't one. *No back-door or side-door surprises this time*, she thought as she and Xu approached the man.

Li's features were indistinct in the dimness and smoke until they got up close. He looked to be in his seventies, his grey hair combed straight back, exposing a receding hairline.

His face was drawn and deeply lined, as if someone had taken a knife and cut crevices into his cheeks and along his forehead. He stared at Xu and then at Ava with pale, watery brown eyes. She had trouble reconciling the man in front of her with the man who'd tried to have her killed — twice.

"You are by yourself," Xu said.

"Lam is outside, making sure you came alone. He'll be along in a minute," Li said. "Both of you should sit."

Ava was surprised by his abrupt tone, which bordered on rudeness. Xu didn't seem bothered and took the chair directly across from Li. Ava took the seat to Xu's left, so she could have a better view of the door.

Li focused on Ava. His eyes moved from her chest to her face and back again. She felt as if she were being evaluated for sale or rent.

"I met you at Uncle's funeral," he said.

"Like many other people, it seems, none of whom I remember."

"He was a great man in his time. But his time had passed, as it does for all of us — at least, for those of us who allow time to dictate our lives."

"And you obviously don't," Ava said.

"I'm young in heart, young in mind, and some days still young enough to please a woman." Li smiled, baring yellowed, stained teeth. "How are you feeling?" he asked Xu.

"Well enough."

"It was stupid of Wing to try what he did. If he had discussed it with me, I would have told him he was digging his own grave. But he and I don't talk much anymore."

"I heard you were best friends. How unfortunate that relationship did not last," Xu said.

Li shrugged, butted his cigarette in an ashtray, pulled a pack from his shirt pocket, and lit a fresh stick with a gold lighter. He inhaled deeply, raised his head, and blew smoke high into the air. "So many rumours about Sammy and me, most of which he started. I told him more than once, 'Don't mess with Xu. Those Shanghai boys are tough.' He didn't listen."

"And so here we are."

The door opened and light flooded the room. Lam walked in, closing the door behind him.

"My man is here," Li said.

The three of them watched him approach. Lam looked relaxed and confident, just as he had when Ava met him in Huangpu.

Xu stood and held out his hand. Lam took it and then turned to Ava, who was struggling to her feet. "I'm glad you were able accept the change in meeting place. This is much more private."

She shook his hand. "No one likes prying eyes."

As the three of them settled into their chairs, Li coughed, hacked, and then spat on the floor. "The dust in here is going to kill me. Can we get down to business before it does?"

Lam looked at Ava and she turned towards Xu.

"Between our two organizations there has been a lot of — I do not know quite how to describe it," Xu said.

"Unpleasantness?" Lam said.

"That will do, thanks," Xu said. "I am not sure how it started, but I know that it culminated when someone tried to kill me in Shenzhen."

"Sammy Wing," Li said. "I told you that had nothing to do with us."

"Sure, it was Sammy Wing, but whether he did it alone or with help, the point is that the time has come for calmer heads to prevail. We cannot keep going at each other like this. It is not healthy for business."

"You're always full of talk about business," Li said.

"What else matters to the people who depend on us?"

"Your father didn't always talk like that."

"Times have changed."

"Not always for the better. I was saying to Lam and some of my other men that all these new ways of making money you've come up with make me nervous. The old ways may not be perfect, but despite all the headaches that come with them, they are dependable. What are you selling that will last hundreds of years?"

"We have to adapt. As long as we are prepared to keep changing, there will always be business."

Li took a long drag of his cigarette. Ava noticed that the skin around his fingertips was dark brown. He coughed again, water leaking from the corners of his eyes.

"The boss is right," Lam said. "We can't just throw out the old businesses. We need a balance."

"I am not telling anyone how to run their organization," Xu said. "I have products to sell. If you want them, you can buy them."

"Yeah, but I'm sure Ava has explained our dilemma to you. We're uncomfortable about building a market for your products when we have no control over the supply side," Lam said.

"I cannot guarantee unlimited supply," Xu said quickly. "You understand that I have to deal with powers in and around Shanghai that I do not control?"

"I know that."

"That aside, what I am prepared to do is make sure that everyone gets their fair share, no matter how small or large the number is. If we reach an agreement on the other things we need to talk about, then I will tell my people to open the production books and sit down with your people to work out a formula."

"I'm satisfied with that," Lam said, turning towards Li.

"Good. That is one piece of business concluded," Xu said. "Is there anything else we must resolve between Shanghai and Guangzhou before we move on to the chairmanship?"

"What are you going to do with Sammy?" Li asked.

"Nothing. He is still in charge of Wanchai. We had a falling-out and now we have put that behind us."

"I can't reach him or Jimmy Tan."

"I believe Jimmy has decided to retire and emigrate to Vancouver to live with his daughter. Is that right, Ava?"

"It is."

"And I do not know why you cannot reach Sammy. Maybe he does not want to talk to you. Ask him yourself — he will be at the meeting tomorrow."

"Will he be wearing a leash?"

"You seem very concerned about a guy who you told me earlier was a pain in the ass."

"He's a neighbour."

"As the world shrinks, are not we all?"

"Fuck. Do you always go on like this?"

"No. I am just waiting for an answer to the question I asked you. What other issues must we resolve before we talk about the chairmanship and then make some kind of peace?"

"None."

Ava saw Lam shifting in his chair, but it wasn't their place to speak. The two of them had laid the groundwork as best they could. Now it was between Xu and Li.

"I want to be chairman," Li said.

"We both do," Xu said.

"I've often been approached over the years to take the post and I've always declined. Not because there were better men. It's just that the timing was never right."

"What makes it so right now?"

"The job needs an elder statesman."

"Or a younger man with a vision for the future."

"You're not going to back down, are you."

"No."

"Neither am I."

"Well, that leaves us with a vote tomorrow that could go either way. Or we agree on the compromise that Lam and Ava worked out — a compromise I thought you had already agreed to."

Li smiled. "You can't blame an old man for trying to improve his position."

"Are you prepared to share the chairmanship?" Xu said.

"Maybe."

"That is not the answer I was expecting."

"It's the one you're getting."

"You have different terms than those I was told?"

"What were you told?"

"We would each be chairman for a year, with you serving first."

"That's right." Li smiled again. The man seemed to be enjoying himself.

Ava shot a glance at Lam. He was staring at his boss, his face devoid of any expression.

"What else do you want?" Xu said.

Li put out his cigarette, took the gold lighter from his pocket, reached for the package, and then put both on the table. "When Lam explained what you had in mind, he said he thought you wanted us to consult with each other, no matter who was chairman."

"That was the general idea."

"I don't like it."

"Why not?" Xu said calmly.

"I like things to be clear-cut — if I'm chairman, I'm chairman. And I can tell you, the other leaders would agree with me on that point if we asked them. No one wants confusion, muddy waters. The chairman has to have the authority to make decisions as he sees fit, not run around taking a vote every time someone wants to shit."

Xu shrugged. "Given the quality of consultation that might take place, I think you may have a point."

"What does that mean?"

"I can agree to it as long as the others go along also."

"What's it got to do with them? This is me and you reaching a deal."

"They still need to understand how it will work."

"That's another thing. I don't want to tell them upfront about the deal."

A heavy silence descended on the room. Ava wasn't sure how long it lasted, but if it was a minute it felt like ten. She wasn't going to break it, and from the look of resignation on Lam's face he wasn't going to either. Her attention flitted between Xu and Li. Xu's lips were tightly drawn and his eyes were slightly hooded. He looked like a man ready to erupt, except that he didn't. He stared at Li, who still had that slight smile on his lips but whose eyes couldn't maintain contact with Xu's.

"Is this the old man trying to improve his position again?" Xu finally said.

"No, it's the man who's been running Guangzhou for more than twenty years being practical," Li snapped. "I don't want a shadow hanging over me. I need my chairmanship to be as free of outside influence as yours would be."

"Then let me have the first year and you have the second. I can live with you looking over my shoulder."

"No. The deal I outlined is the only one I want. Lam and the girl can be witnesses to it. I'll put it on paper if that will make you happy."

"I would have to withdraw my candidacy to allow that to happen."

"Yeah, you would."

"I told you earlier that I will not."

"You don't trust me?"

"That is a stupid question, especially coming from you," Xu said. "But I am curious. Did you actually believe I would go along with this?"

"I thought it was worth a try. You're the one who's always talking about building bridges and co-operation. Truth is, you're as selfish and greedy as the rest of us."

"Fuck off," Xu said softly. He turned to Ava. "Call Sonny. We need to leave."

"Wait. I want you to know that this is the last offer you'll get from me," Li said.

"Fuck off," Xu repeated. "I will see you tomorrow and I will win the vote."

"No, you won't," Li said, his eyes staring past them.

Ava swivelled. Lam stood three paces away. She had been so engrossed in the conversation between Xu and Li that she hadn't seen him move. Now Xu turned and saw him as well.

He held the handgun at waist height. It was a Glock that would have slipped easily into his pants pocket, Ava thought. And then she realized how strange it was that she knew what kind of gun it was, and that she should think of it at that very moment.

She started to rise but Xu put his hand on her shoulder. "It is better to stay put," he said.

The gun fired, and fired again. The first bullet caught Li in the middle of the chest and threw him backwards. The second hit him near the throat. He spun violently to the left before crashing to the floor.

## 43

**THEY STOOD AT ONE SIDE OF THE ROOM. THE BODY** was barely visible in the dim light and dust-filled air. Xu leaned against the wall, Ava next to him, her arm hooked through his and her fingers gripping his wrist.

Lam faced them, his hands shaking and his face still contorted. "I gave him a chance to do the right thing. He just couldn't bring himself to do it," he said.

"What will you do with the body?" Xu asked, the calmest of the three.

"My men from Guangzhou are nearby. They'll get him," Lam said. "And the men are mine, not his."

"He was so stupid," Xu said. "But then he was never a man to compromise, and the older he got, the less flexible he became. This was not necessary."

"No, but it was almost inevitable. You were right about how he would react," Lam said. "I didn't completely believe you."

"When did he tell you?"

"This morning. He went back and forth about doing a deal but every time he thought about you becoming chairman, even for a year, he'd lose control. So he decided to push you hard in this meeting. If you agreed to everything he wanted, he said he'd take the deal and find a way to cut you out. And if you didn't go along, then . . ."

"This wasn't our plan," Ava said.

"Yes, it was," Lam said. "We took the plan you and I agreed on as far as we could, until Li rejected it and created his own. Then it was time for Plan B."

"My intention was to broker peace," Ava snapped. "That was the plan."

"And we gave it our best shot," Lam said. "I swear to you, I did everything I could to persuade him. I didn't want it to come to this any more than you did."

"The change of meeting location was a signal that Li had a different idea about how to resolve our differences," Xu said. "And even though I knew what the intent was, I was hoping it would not happen."

"What if he had agreed to do what you wanted with the chairmanship?"

"I would have been happy to go along with him. But he did not want me to agree. He wanted me dead," Xu said.

"So pointless."

"He knew only one way to do things. Maybe it worked twenty years ago, but not now," Lam said. "If I'd let him do what he wanted, it would have brought death and chaos into everyone's lives. I couldn't let that happen to my men. They're more secure now than they've ever been."

"What will we say about this?" Xu asked, pointing at the body.

"He had a heart attack in Guangzhou."

"Wasn't he in contact with the other society leaders who are in Hong Kong for the meeting? We were told he had a dinner with some of them planned for tonight. Won't they suspect something?" Ava asked.

"He told them he wasn't sure when he would be arriving, that he wasn't feeling well. If he had been successful in killing Xu, the plan was to leave here right away and head back to Guangzhou before Xu's people had a chance to react."

"Pretending he'd never left?"

"Yeah."

"How clever."

"I thought so when I suggested it to him."

Xu moved away from the wall until he was almost nose to nose with Lam. "Will you go to the meeting tomorrow in his place?"

"No, that would be disrespectful. I'll return to Guangzhou with the body. But I will take time when I get back to phone his allies and let them know that his health finally failed. I don't imagine you'll have any other opposition for the chairmanship."

"I think not."

"Then, congratulations."

"Thank you," Xu said. He turned to Ava. "Lam will be the new Mountain Master in Guangzhou. You will be happy to know that he will be accepting the deal you proposed about my products."

"Aside from that," Lam said, pointing towards the body, "some good things happened this morning. And none of them would have happened without you."

She shook her head, not sure what to believe.

Xu bent forward and kissed her gently on the forehead. Ava still had her back pressed against the wall. "*Mei mei,*

Lam and I seem to have got everything we wanted. Tell us what we can do for you."

She closed her eyes. "All I want is to go back to my life," she said softly.

"What makes you think you ever left it?"

**COMING SOON**
from House of Anansi Press
in February 2016

Read on for a preview of the next thrilling
Ava Lee novel, *The Princeling of Nanjing*

**IT WAS EARLY EVENING WHEN AVA LEE AND MAY LING**
Wong exited the elevator on the eleventh floor of the
Peninsula Hotel in Shanghai. Ava had arrived in the
city that afternoon, and now she and May were going
to a reception that was a prelude to the launch of a new
clothing line called PÖ. Ava, May, and Ava's sister-in-law
Amanda Yee had financed the creation of PÖ, the brain-
child of Clark and Gillian Po, through their Three Sisters
investment firm.

"How many people are we expecting?" Ava asked as they
followed the signs directing them to the Palace Suite.

"More than a hundred."

"Can we get them all into the suite?"

"Maybe not all of them indoors, but there's a wraparound
terrace that can comfortably accommodate two hundred people. Amanda had a marquee put up outside in case it rains."

Ava spotted Amanda standing just inside the doorway
to the suite, talking to a group of familiar-looking women.
"Are those the women I saw working at the old sample factory?" Ava asked.

"Yes, we hired them to work in the new one. Clark invited them. I'm quite sure that they and Clark and Gillian's friends are the early arrivals," May said.

"That was considerate."

"Chi-Tze wasn't so sure it was a good idea, but she was sensitive enough not to say anything to Clark. He adores those women and they love him to death. They're also coming to the show tomorrow."

"How many fashion industry types are you expecting tonight?"

"At last count we had about thirty people from various publications, websites, and social media, and I'd say about twenty who either own major chunks of various retail chains or work for them. There are also some real estate agents who control the malls, in case we decide to go with stand-alone PÖ boutiques."

"How many of them are your friends?"

"Acquaintances more than friends, but a fair number of them," May said. "I see Gillian. I'm going to go say hi."

Ava followed May into the suite. She had taken only a few steps before Amanda was by her side. She noticed the long, thin scar that ran across and just above Amanda's eyebrow. It was the only physical evidence of the brutal beating she had endured in Borneo. In Ava's opinion it enhanced rather than detracted from Amanda's delicate beauty.

"I just got off the phone with Michael," Amanda said. "He sends his love. He wanted to come, but things are crazy for him and Simon right now."

Michael Lee was Ava's half-brother from her father's first wife, and Simon To was his business partner. "Crazy good or crazy bad?" Ava asked.

"They don't need you to bail them out of trouble, if that's what you mean," Amanda said with a smile.

"That's kind of what I meant."

Amanda laughed and then stopped and stared. "With the exception of my wedding, I've never seen you in a dress before. You look so damn sexy."

"It's a gift from Clark. It was in my room when I arrived."

"I figured as much, but I only saw the outside of the garment bag. He told me not to peek."

"This is snug but still very comfortable," Ava said, pointing to the form-fitting bodice of the black silk crepe dress. Then she moved her hips, and the lower half of the dress floated out around her knees. "I'm not used to wearing clothes this loose — it makes my legs feel completely naked. I have to say, though, I think I could get used to it."

"Clark said he also left a special message for you."

It was Ava's turn to smile. "Inside the dress, just below the neckline, there's a thin red ribbon with words stitched in gold."

"What does it say?"

"*Ava Lee has my heart.*"

"He does think the world of you."

"No more than he thinks of you," Ava said. "Now, how was he today at the rehearsal?"

"Excited but in control, and still being critical about his designs."

"You've obviously seen them all."

"Several times, and please don't ask me for an opinion. I find it impossible to be objective."

"We're all eager."

"None more so than the factory ladies. They're here to scream and shout, and they'll do the same tomorrow."

"Did you meet your friend from *Vogue*?"

"Yes. She's just sent me a text saying she'll be here in about fifteen minutes."

"May has just finished telling me about Lane Crawford."

"My god, how terrific it would be to get our clothes in there," Amanda said. "It almost gives me chills thinking about it. Not only are they the leading retailer in Hong Kong, now they have Lane Crawford stores in China and more than fifty Joyce Boutiques across the region. Chi-Tze says they're the perfect bridge between East and West when it comes to fashion."

"Evidently a woman who works there knows me."

"A *woman*? Carrie Song is vice-president of merchandising, which is like being God. Chi-Tze and Gillian tried and failed for more than a month to get an appointment to see her or one of her staff. Finally May used a board of directors connection to get in, but even that didn't go very well until your name was mentioned. All of a sudden there was interest, and then out of the blue one of Ms. Song's assistants advised us that they're coming to the launch."

Ava shrugged. "I have no idea who she is."

"Maybe you'll recognize her when you see her face."

"I hope so."

"Now why don't you and May go inside and get a drink and mingle. Gillian and I are on door duty."

"Let me know when Carrie Song arrives."

"Count on it."

"And my friend Xu, if he makes it," Ava added. "I was told earlier that he might be tied up in a meeting."

"*Momentai.*"

Ava walked over to May and Gillian, who were deep in conversation. "We should go in," she said, touching May's arm.

Ava glanced around the spacious suite and saw about twenty people standing around a grand piano that had a bar set up beside it. Just beyond, a sliding door opened onto a white-tiled terrace, where most of the guests had chosen to congregate around another bar and a table laden with hors d'oeuvres. The sight of it made her stomach rumble, and she realized it had been a while since she'd eaten. She walked out to the terrace and was examining the food when Gillian appeared by her side.

"Carrie Song is here," she said.

"Where is she?"

"At the door, chatting with Amanda."

Ava walked back through the suite and looked towards the door. Carrie Song was several inches taller than Amanda and much broader, solidly built, with thick legs and torso. She was what her mother would call "sturdy." Ava felt embarrassed for using one of Jennie Lee's code words and banished the thought from her mind.

Song's hair was pulled back tightly and secured by what looked like a platinum pin set with a row of small red stones. She wore a red silk dress with a high, straight neckline, sleeves that came to the elbow, and a mid-calf hemline. Like the pin, the dress looked to be worth a small fortune. Her eyes were heavily made up and a swath of bright red lipstick gleamed on her lips. Ava searched her memory but didn't recall ever meeting her before.

Amanda turned towards Ava and smiled. Carrie Song also looked in her direction, and then her eyes blinked in confusion. *I don't think she knows me either*, Ava thought as she walked towards the door.

"You can't be Ava Lee," Song said when Ava reached her.

"I am," Ava said, extending a hand.

"But you're far too young."

"I most certainly am Ava Lee, and I'm not quite as young as you might think."

"You did work with Uncle Chow?"

"He was my partner, my mentor, and the most important man in my life for more than ten years," Ava said. Those days of collecting debts now seemed so far away, even though Uncle had been dead for less than a year.

Song shook her head. "It was eight years ago that my family hired you and Uncle. I just assumed then that you were older."

"I was in my mid-twenties when we became partners. I felt old enough at the time. And the job had a way of accelerating experience."

"Knowing what you went through with my family, I can understand that."

"Carrie, you have me at a disadvantage," Ava said. "Until you tell me your family's name, I can't know what we're speaking about. The name Song means absolutely nothing to me."

"It's my married name. My brother is Austin Ma, and my father was Ma Lai."

"Was?" Ava said, as the faces of the two men appeared in her mind.

"My father died three years ago."

"I'm so sorry."

"At least he died with his business, his money, and his pride intact, thanks to you and Uncle," she said. "And I can't tell you how many times my brother has said he owes his life to you."

Ava felt words of protest form in her mouth and then swallowed them. Uncle had always said that false modesty was a ploy used by egotists to gather more praise. "Yes, we did retrieve the money and rescue your brother from his kidnappers. We did as well by them as was possible."

Carrie became quiet. Amanda, who had been listening to their conversation, edged closer to them. "Perhaps we should move away from the door," she said. "And neither of you has a drink. We have excellent champagne."

"Champagne sounds terrific," Ava said.

"Yes, for me too," Song said.

"There's a seating area in the corner of the suite that would give the two of you some privacy if you want to continue this discussion. Why don't we go there, and I'll have some drinks brought to you," Amanda said.

Ava nodded, pleased with the subtle manner in which Amanda had taken control.

Carrie and Ava settled into chairs separated by a small round table. Amanda waved at a server carrying a tray of champagne flutes. Each of the women took a glass.

"To health," Ava said.

"Health," Carrie and Amanda said as one.

"Now I'll leave you two," Amanda said.

Carrie Song perched on the edge of her chair and turned sideways so she could face Ava. "When I told my brother I thought I would be meeting you in Shanghai, he became quite excited," she said. "He said he saw you at Uncle's funeral but doubts you'd remember him being there."

"It was an emotional day. The names and faces were a blur."

"I understand. I was the same at my father's funeral."

"But I do remember your brother and father from the case. It was a tough one."

"I was in my last year of university in the U.K. I didn't know anything about the problem until it was over. I was really angry when I found out they hadn't told me about something that important. But father explained, very patiently, that there was nothing I could have done from the U.K., and that my knowing about it would only have caused him and my mother extra stress. He was right, I think."

"Your father was very calm and thoughtful in the face of considerable adversity. After all, the thieves had most of his money and his son. He showed a lot of bravery. So did your brother."

"My brother doesn't feel that way. He says he was so scared when they grabbed him off the street that he wet his pants."

"That happens to a lot of people, and after the initial shock he carried himself well. I remember speaking to him on the phone when we were negotiating the ransom, and he was in complete control of his emotions."

"Our family owes you a tremendous debt."

"We were paid well for what we did."

Carrie shook her head. "My father went to several organizations for help before he found Uncle and you. None of them would touch us once they found out who'd made off with most of our money, and was holding my brother ransom for the rest of it."

"Most debt collectors want only the low-hanging fruit. Uncle built our business by taking on jobs that they wouldn't handle. He liked to think of us as a last resort. It was a bit romantic of him, I always thought, but in some cases it was the truth. And we did have some expertise and contacts that other companies lacked."

"*Expertise*. You make it sound so academic. My brother said you risked your life to save his."

"That's a bit dramatic. The guys guarding him were amateurs."

"There were three of them, no?"

"I think so."

"And they had knives, and one had a gun."

"True, but I had Carlo and Andy — two of Uncle's men — and Carlo had his own gun."

"Austin said you were wounded by a knife."

"It was a small cut on my arm. It looked worse than it was."

Carrie lifted the glass to her lips and sipped. "No matter how much you want to downplay it, both my brother and I think the Ma family owes you more than the money you were paid."

"That's very kind. But I hope you're not here just because of that."

"I am."

"That makes me quite uncomfortable," Ava said softly. "This new business has to stand on its own merits or it won't be sustainable."

"Thank you for saying that," Carrie said. "I can't tell you how many invitations we turn down every month. If we accepted even a quarter of them, I'd never be in my office. So my coming here is a bit unusual. But the bottom line is still that we'll do business only if the clothes meet our standards — and those standards are high."

"That makes me feel a bit better."

Carrie smiled. "Good. Now let's hope the clothes are exceptional."

"They're wonderful."

"Is that dress you're wearing a PÖ?"

"It is."

"Then we're off to a good start."

Ava saw that Carrie's glass was empty and looked for a server. Before she could find one, Amanda reappeared.

"Excuse me, but May Ling wants Ava to know that Mr. Xu is here."

"That's perfect timing," Carrie said. "Please go and see your guest. I'm going to mingle for a while and then leave early. I'll see you at the launch tomorrow."

"Will we have a chance to talk before you leave?"

"Do you mean after the show?"

"Yes."

"That's not something I normally do, but then, coming to Shanghai isn't either," Carrie said. "So yes, we can chat."

"Thanks."

"It's still too soon to say that."

Ava smiled and walked away, feeling satisfied with the way things had gone. She had no doubt that Carrie Song would be fair, and that's all they could expect.

She saw Xu standing just inside the doorway, talking to May. He was dressed, as was his habit — which Ava was sure he'd picked up from Uncle — in a black suit and white shirt. But instead of his normal black tie, he was sporting one in light blue silk patterned with red and white dragons. About six feet tall, he was slim and elegant. His fine features were accented by strong eyebrows and a thick head of hair that he wore swept back. He looked every inch the successful professional. And so he was, except that his profession was running the Triad organization in Shanghai and functioning as chairman of the Triad societies across Asia.

May was standing close to Xu, looking up at him with her hand resting on his arm. It unexpectedly occurred to Ava that May was flirting with him. If she was, Xu didn't seem to be discouraging it.

"Hey, what's going on with you two?" Ava asked as she drew near.

May moved back, looking a bit flustered. *You were flirting*, Ava thought.

"I was just telling our silent partner how well the money he put into our business is doing," May said quickly.

Ava was slightly taken aback by the comment, and she glanced around to see if anyone else might have heard it. Xu had put $150 million into Three Sisters. He had carefully assembled the money from his many enterprises, including factories that made knockoff electronic devices and designer bags and clothes. Then he had separated the money as far as possible from its Triad roots before transferring it to them.

"I'm quite sure that come as a surprise to him," Ava said, relieved to see that no one was in earshot.

Xu smiled at Ava, but she thought it looked a bit tentative. She immediately noticed that there were dark circles under his eyes and that his face looked gaunt. She wondered if he was having lingering health issues from the knife wounds he'd received in Shenzhen five months before, when his main competitor for chairmanship of the Triad societies had tried to take him out of the running.

"*Mei mei*, it is good to see you," he said.

Ava stepped into his arms. "And you."

"May said you were meeting with a very influential woman from Lane Crawford. I hope I did not drag you away from her."

"Our business was done."

"How did it go?" May asked.

"Well enough, I think."

"How do you know her?" Xu asked.

"Uncle and I did a job for her family."

"It was successful?"

"Yes."

"And she feels indebted?"

"Enough that she came here. For the rest of it, she has to see and like Clark's clothes. I told her that's the way it should be."

"Getting her here was a feat in itself," May said. "Ava is always teasing me about my *guanxi*, but now she's demonstrating her own."

"Don't exaggerate," Ava said, and then turned back to Xu. "There's champagne and other drinks and food on the terrace if you want some."

"I am sorry, but I cannot stay."

"Suen told me you have visitors from Nanjing."

"I do, and I have to take them to dinner."

"You're coming to the launch tomorrow?" May asked.

"That is still the plan, and I will be bringing the manager of our main clothing factory with me. His name is Wu."

Ava couldn't help but notice how intently May was staring at him. For his part, Xu seemed detached, and his face, as well as being gaunt, looked weary. "May, I do not mean to be rude, but I have to leave soon and I would like a word alone with Ava, if you do not mind." Xu spoke so softly that Ava wasn't sure she had heard him correctly.

"No, of course not," May said. Nearby, Amanda and Gillian were still greeting people as they arrived. May went to join them.

Xu looped his arm through Ava's and gently led her away from the door.

"What's this about?" she asked.

"When the reception is over, could you possibly join me at the restaurant where I am taking my guests?" he said.

His question surprised her, and it showed.

"I am sorry for dropping this on you so suddenly."

"Is it a business dinner? I wouldn't want to get in the way."

"It is not supposed to be about business, and even if it is, you are never in the way."

"They won't find it strange that you invited a woman?"

"That is one of the reasons I would like you to come. I was told a few minutes ago that Pang Fai is going to be there."

"The actress?"

"Yes."

"I love her work," Ava said. "I must have seen ten of her films, and I don't think there's anyone better at drama. But she's so famous. What's she doing at your dinner in Shanghai?" She saw his brow crease ever so slightly. "Oh, Xu, I hope that didn't sound rude. You must know what I mean. It is Pang Fai, after all."

He smiled. "She is the girlfriend — or at least a friend — of the main guy in Nanjing."

"He must be wealthy."

"He is, and powerful."

"Would I know him?"

"His name is Tsai Men. His father is the governor of Jiangsu."

"I've never heard of him."

"There is no reason why you should have."

Ava hesitated. The idea of arriving late at a dinner party held little appeal, but she was intrigued by the prospect of meeting one of China's biggest movie stars. "Xu, I have no idea when this reception will be over, and I can't leave early."

"Come whenever you can. I have made a reservation at Capo. It is next door, on the fifth floor of the Yifeng Galleria. You can walk."

"Capo? That doesn't sound Chinese."

"It is Italian. That is where he always wants to go, even though he never orders anything Italian. He says they have the best fresh oysters and steak in Shanghai."

Ava shook her head. "Xu, I'm not sure —"

He squeezed her arm gently. "I do not care when you come. Knowing Tsai, it will be a long night anyway."

"And look at the way I'm dressed."

"You look stunning. I have been with Pang Fai before, and believe me, she does not dress down. You will fit right in."

"Okay, I'll be there," she said, giving in to his persistence.

"Thank you."

"But arriving in the middle of dinner is going to look odd. How will you explain it?"

"I will tell them you were at a reception."

"And how are you going to introduce me?"

"As my girlfriend."

## ACKNOWLEDGEMENTS

*The King of Shanghai* is the seventh book (not counting the novella *The Dragon Head of Hong Kong*) in the Ava Lee series, and it seems that with each book there are more and more people to thank for their assistance and encouragement.

Sarah MacLachlan and her team at House of Anansi Press continue to provide tremendous support. So my thanks to her and to Barbara Howson and her sales team, Laura Meyer on the publicity side, and Carolyn McNeillie, a digital whiz.

As always, this book owes much to my editor, the great Janie Yoon. She doesn't particularly like the word *collaboration*, and she may be correct that our working relationship falls a bit short of being exactly that. But it's close nonetheless, and it's amazing how often we're on the same wavelength when it comes to identifying gaps and weaknesses in manuscripts.

My agents, Bruce Westwood and Carolyn Forde, are two of my earliest manuscript readers, and their support and input have been unfailing. Many a miserable writing day has been brightened by talking to them. It's much appreciated.

My rather large family continues to beat the drum for the books, and I know we wouldn't have had success without them. I love them all.

Last, there are some individuals who made direct contributions to *The King of Shanghai*. I want to thank Robin Spano and Farah Mohamed for their editorial input. Vincent Yin very generously reviewed my Chinese references and word usage and made sure they were accurate. And Carrie Kirkman, whose day job is CEO of Jones New York in Canada, took the time to educate me about the business of fashion.

# NOW AVAILABLE
## From House of Anansi Press

The first six books in the Ava Lee series.

**Prequel and Book 1**  **Book 2**  **Book 3**

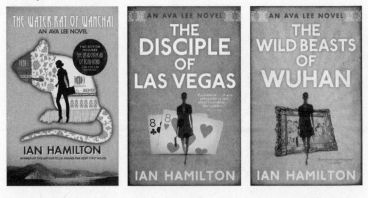

**Book 4**  **Book 5**  **Book 6**